ON THE MELDON PLAIN

ALSO BY PAM BRONDOS

Gateway to Fourline

ON THE MELDON PLAIN

BOOK TWO OF THE FOURLINE TRILOGY

PAM BRONDOS

SKYSCAPE

SKYSCAPE

Published by Skyscape, New York

www.apub.com

Amazon, the Amazon logo, and Skyscape are trademarks of Amazon.com, Inc., or its affiliates.

ISBN-13: 9781503953208
ISBN-10: 1503953203

Cover design by Chelsea Wirtz and David Drummond

Printed in the United States of America

To Mom

CHAPTER ONE

The sky reminded Nat of stone.

She turned onto a side street, running in the middle of the road to avoid the ice patches and clumps of snow covering the sidewalks. She passed a row of dilapidated Victorian houses. Smoke curled from their boxy chimneys and blended into the gray sky.

Late afternoon traffic poured onto the street. A dirty yellow truck missed hitting her by a few inches, and the driver slammed on his horn. She jumped over a sheet of ice, skipped onto the sidewalk, and continued her steady pace without giving the driver so much as a glance. Her feet fell rhythmically as she ran block after block. Each breath brought an icy ache of air into her lungs.

At the red metal bridge spanning the Cannon River, she turned onto the limestone riverwalk. She tore down the walkway, scattering pigeons and winter crows. Restaurants, shop fronts, and offices flashed by. Her lungs and legs burned, distracting her from the pulsing pain of her shoulder wound.

A second bridge came into view. Intricate circles reminding her of the vine pattern twisting up her forearm swirled around the railing. She glanced at the tip of the vibrant vine and spear peeking from underneath her sleeve. The pattern had yet to fade as Sister Barba had promised. Instead, since her return from Fourline, its hue had only deepened, just like her guilt over Soris. She sprinted to the bridge, rapidly moving her legs and arms and pushing away thoughts of her Sister markings and her friend.

When Nat reached the bridge, she quit running. She pressed her hips against the cold metal railing and watched the river flow toward her. Water rushed around ice sheets, creating little clusters of dull bubbles. She gently massaged her shoulder, avoiding the center of the wound as she followed the course of the water with her eyes.

The river snaked past the bridge, auto repair shops, industrial buildings, and a warehouse fronted by a stucco building. A sign reading "Gate's Costumes" hung from the front of the stucco structure. Nat pushed her green knit cap off her forehead and wiped the sweaty strands of brown hair from her brow. She watched the costume shop sign flicker on and off in the gray afternoon light.

Two months had passed since she'd pushed through the membrane tucked deep within the cliff wall behind the costume shop, leaving the world of Fourline and the Nala behind, but bringing her wounded friend Soris through. Her skin crawled as she remembered the humanoid Nala, with its lancing forelimbs and spiderlike fangs, slashing her shoulder and biting Soris. She placed her hands on the railing, the numbing cold surging through her fingers as memories of her quest into Fourline tumbled through her mind.

She'd ventured through the portal to Fourline to help Estos, the realm's young king, leave the safety of his exile in her world and return to his own. Estos' loyal rebel band needed him to lead the fight against Lord Mudug, the corrupt usurper who'd ordered the murder of Estos' sister, Queen Emilia. Nat had donned the garb of a Warrior Sister so she and Soris could destroy the Chemist's tracking device and create a safe passage for Estos' return to Fourline. But Soris had paid a price for accompanying her. She could blame only herself for not having protected him from the predatory Nala. Her journey with Soris had taught her that the Nala could turn humans into halflings called duozi with one bite from their venomous fangs. Unaware she wasn't a real Warrior Sister, Soris had trusted in her ability to keep them both safe.

Nat shook her hands and cupped them around her lips, blowing warmth back into her fingers as she thought of all the things she'd done wrong in Fourline. Failing to take Soris straight to the membrane after the Nala bit him was her biggest mistake. The skin around his wound had already turned blue like the Nala's by the time Annin helped pull his body through the resistant membrane. Nat hadn't brought Soris to Ethet, the Healing Sister who lived in her world, fast enough to curb his transformation into a duozi.

What exists in only one of the worlds cannot exist in the other. Her guilt deepened as she thought of Estos' words to her. He'd said Soris wouldn't survive in her world, that the Nala venom had progressed too deeply through his body for him to remain on this side of the membrane. Sister Ethet told her he'd have to return to Fourline, where Nat knew he'd be condemned to live the life of a duozi, targeted by both the Nala and the humans prejudiced against halflings.

Nat's legs, stiff from the sudden rest, cramped when she turned toward campus and ran away from the blinking "Gate's Costumes" sign. Hot tears, turning cold in the frigid temperature, streamed down her face. *I know you're gone, Soris,* she thought, feeling the familiar emptiness eating away at her. She brushed her arm across her eyes, and a sting of pain ripped down her shoulder to her arm. *You're gone, except in my nightmares.*

"How many is that today?" Viv, Nat's roommate, glanced up from her sketchbook. She scratched her face, and a black smudge appeared above her nose.

"How many what?" Nat carefully pulled her thin fleece sweatshirt over her head. An oozy gray stain from her weeping shoulder wound marred the fabric. She turned her body, keeping her shoulder away from Viv's line of sight, and tossed the garment into the laundry basket. She gingerly touched the loose bandage taped to her shoulder.

"Miles, kilometers, leagues, rods, *li*, minimarathons." Viv dropped the sketchbook on the floor and lifted herself out of the striped chair. Her blue hair was arranged in tiny topknots.

"Your hair looks cute," Nat said halfheartedly.

"You're evading my question, and I know for a fact you don't think my hair looks cute. The last time I wore it like this, you said I looked like a pincushion with zits."

"Your hair was red then." Nat shoved her head through the neck hole of a clean shirt, wincing when she brought her arm above her shoulder. *I'll rebandage the wound later,* she thought as Viv babbled in the background. Nat grabbed her new computer and slid it into her backpack.

Viv watched Nat change socks and slip on a pair of leather boots, her tangled brown ponytail skimming the floor when she tied the laces. Nat looked up and knew she wasn't going to escape the room easily, not without a roommate interrogation. Viv crossed her arms and leaned against the door, barring her escape.

"Three miles this morning and three this afternoon. That's how far I ran today," Nat responded.

"Are you kidding me?" Viv's brow creased. "Have you looked at yourself? I don't know how much weight you've lost since you got back from January term, but your clothes are hanging off of you and your face is all . . . sunken looking. If you'd J-termed in the tropics and picked up a tapeworm, I'd get it, but you were in Canada, so what's the deal?"

Nat stared at her roommate. If she had really been in Canada, everything would be different. She felt the tears well in her eyes and looked at the floor, pretending to struggle with her laces.

"You're right. I need to eat more. I've just been busy." She wiped her eyes, stood, and grabbed an apple from a dark-blue bowl on top of their minifridge. She took a bite. "I've got to get to my lab. I promise to eat dinner after."

Viv stepped away from the door. "You won't grab dinner after lab, because you're coming to Butler's. It's his birthday, remember?"

"A night with a bunch of inebriated artists. Looking forward to it." Nat took another bite to placate her roommate and lifted her jacket off the coat hook with her good arm, thankful Viv had yet to notice how left-handed she had become.

Viv plopped back into the chair. "It's the best company you'll get smelling like that." She scrunched up her nose. "You're turning me into a nagging roommate, Nat! Take a shower and eat, and you'd better be at Butler's by ten or I'm coming to find you," she threatened.

Nat slammed the door behind her. The late March wind stung her face as she plowed through the dorm's heavy doors. The half-eaten apple pinged against the side of the metal garbage can next to the entrance and landed in a clump of dirty snow. She buttoned her coat and walked with her head down, passing through the parking lot toward the Student Center. Safety lights shone brightly on the cars. She looked up, searching for a distraction from her thoughts and the pain in her shoulder.

Yellow light illuminated the wide first-floor windows of the Speech and Theater Building set behind the Student Center. A figure moved into the light of one window, and Nat halted. Sister Barba, the Wisdom Sister from Fourline who had drawn Nat's markings on her arm before sending her through the membrane, passed in front of the window. Nat veered away from the path between the two buildings. Her guilt over Soris was already ever present in her mind. With her shoulder wound and markings, she needed no more reminders of her quest. *It'll get better,* she told herself. *I'll forget all of them. I'll forget Soris. My wound will heal.*

The Science Center loomed in front of her. She pushed open the glass doors and slowly climbed the stairs. A rush of students brushed past her. Someone's backpack slammed into Nat's injured shoulder, and she bit down on her tongue to keep from crying out in pain. She climbed the remaining stairs and leaned against a window, pressing her hot forehead against the cool glass. When the pain subsided, she walked into the lab. A graying sunset filtered through the lab's floor-to-ceiling windows. The fading light left her with an unsettled feeling. Night brought no rest, only more nightmares.

Signe, her lab partner, looked up from their assigned table. Nat dropped her bag and jacket next to a metal stool, grabbed a pair of goggles, and pulled out her lab book.

"Testing for micronutrients, right?" she asked her partner.

"Yeah," Signe said. Standing a foot taller than Nat, she pulled her white-blonde hair back into a clip and pointed at a small container of seeds. Nat reached for the container.

"What's your rush? The teaching assistant isn't even here."

"We should check for copper, too, along with the other micronutrients," Nat replied, thinking the copper test would take an extra half an hour—time she could use to focus on something else other than Soris, her shoulder, and her nightmares.

CHAPTER TWO

The glowing red numbers cast a tiny halo around her alarm clock. One thirty. Nat turned onto her back and sucked in a sharp breath when she pressed her shoulder into the mattress. Viv snored loudly from the bunk below. Nat listened to the sound of running water coursing through the pipes in the ceiling above her. After the noise faded, she scanned the room trying to stay awake, but sleep pulled her in. Her eyes fluttered closed, and she fell into a fitful dream.

Blades of grass tickled the back of her neck. She shifted onto her side and looked past Soris, who lay sleeping in the grass next to her, peaceful and healthy. From the top of the hill, Greffen's stone cottage in Fourline looked tiny. Ris, Greffen's dog, barked wildly and strained against a rope tethering him to the gate of a sheep pen. Soris' eyes—green with brown flecks—flickered open.

"Where do you think Greffen is?" Soris tucked a strand of dirty-blond hair behind his ear.

"I don't know, but something has Ris riled up." Nat brought her hand to her forehead, shielding her eyes against the sun.

"Natalie, look." Soris pointed to a figure near the sheep pen. A Nala crept on its angular arms and legs past Ris, hissing as the dog lunged toward it. It scurried up the base of the hill and lifted its bulbous head. Even in the distance, Nat could feel its concave silver eyes settle on them with a predatory gaze.

Soris leapt up from the grass and grasped Nat's hand, pulling her to her feet. They plunged into the forest behind the hill. As they ran, the sun disappeared. Dense clusters of trees shut out all but the dimmest light. A cold darkness descended on the fleeing pair. Nat tried to hold tight to Soris to keep from losing him in the choking woods, but their hands slipped apart. Pine boughs pricked her bare arms as she ran farther into the woods, calling out his name over the sound of a nearby river. A glimmer of movement drew her eyes to the boughs of an enormous pine tree, and she stopped running.

A Nala, clinging to a bough, opened its black mouth, and a stream of venom dripped down and crackled on the dry leaves near her feet. Nat slowly eased away from the blue creature before turning on her heels and sprinting past the trees toward the river.

"Soris!" she screamed as she burst onto the riverbank. The slate-colored water roared, drowning out her cries.

Gasping, Soris emerged from the woods farther upriver and stumbled onto the gravel bank. The Nala jumped from a branch and slammed into Nat, sending her crashing into the icy water. The current pulled her feet toward the violent water racing down the center of the river. She coughed up water and called out to Soris just as the creature turned and sprang onto his back.

"Natalie, help me!" Soris shouted from the riverbank, thrashing his arm at the slick blue-skinned creature.

Leave him alone! Water poured into her mouth, preventing her from answering Soris' cry for help. Nat swam against the current, trying to reach the bank, but the water pulled her farther and farther downstream. She grabbed on to an overhanging tree branch and twisted around in time to see the Nala bite into Soris' shoulder.

Soris' cry reverberated through the river valley. Nat's hand slipped. She clutched the branch with her other hand and watched, helplessly, as Soris' skin turned dark blue, an exact match to the Nala looming over his body. The creature stood upright, exposing its arachnid-like abdomen.

"He's mine, Sister," it hissed. Nat choked, unable to breathe from the shock of hearing the familiar voice and recognizing the slanted gash in its gut.

"I killed you!" she shouted. She stared in disbelief at the creature; it was the same Nala that had bitten Soris on the riverbank in Fourline months ago. "This is a dream! It has to be!" she yelled. "I killed you!" Her hand slipped from the branch, and she fell into the water.

Nat swam blindly into the inky depths of the river, frantic to leave this nightmare for the safety of her dream space. Her fingers fumbled over the rocky river bottom, searching for the rough ledge to her haven. Her knuckles slammed into its jagged surface, and she pulled herself over. Coughing violently, she flopped onto the floor of the dark, empty space where no one—no images, no nightmares—could reach her unless she invited them in.

"Lights," she said weakly. The protective bars of light shot up along the ledge. She closed her eyes and let her tight muscles relax as the nightmare played out beyond the barrier of her dream space without her. "The Nala is dead," she said over and over, reassuring herself that the creature from the nightmare no longer existed.

The clock read 4:45 a.m. when Nat opened her eyes. The room felt stuffy. She threw her blanket off and stared at the ceiling before climbing down from the loft bed. The frame creaked under her shifting weight, and

Viv mumbled in her sleep. Nat grabbed a towel and headed toward the shower they shared with the adjoining dorm room.

The hot water kicked in after a few seconds. She stuck her face under the spray and shivered despite the heat. She thought back to the nightmare. It was so similar to what had actually happened, when the Nala had attacked both of them on their return from the Chemist's quarters. But unlike in her dream, she'd killed the Nala after it bit Soris, and its lifeless body had floated down the river. *Why do I keep having this nightmare?* she wondered.

She pressed her head against the tiled wall, letting the water slide down her back. The hot stream stung her shoulder, and she stepped to the side to avoid the pain. She glanced at the wound. The ugly bluish-purple spot the length of her thumb was the same. Two months with no ebb to the ache. "The wound that never heals," she said to herself, thinking of Soris. She switched off the shower and dressed for a run.

Viv was still curled into a ball on her bed when Nat returned from her run around campus and into town. She kicked the leg of the bunk, and Viv groaned.

"I'm going to breakfast, want to join me?" Nat pulled on a pair of rumpled jeans and ducked, avoiding Viv's pillow.

"I have a headache, leave me alone."

"I told you to steer clear of Butler's punch. It lit on fire when I dropped a match in it."

"Stop making noise and go away," Viv said, her muffled voice rising from under the comforter. "Wait," she called out just as Nat put her hand on the doorknob. She emerged from under the covers, her hair sticking up in every direction. "Did Dermot ask you out last night?" She yawned.

"Why do you ask?" Nat crossed her arms.

"No reason. He just . . ."

"You put him up to it, didn't you?" Nat glared at her roommate. Viv slunk a little deeper under her covers.

"You need a life," she said indignantly. "Besides, he's wanted to ask you out for ages."

"The last thing I need right now is a boyfriend, especially one that needs encouragement from both my roommate and a drink." Nat glanced at the worn carpet. "He's not really my type, anyway."

"Type? You don't have a type." Viv tossed the comforter to the side and clambered out of bed.

"I do, too, and it's definitely not Dermot," she said, thinking of Soris' green eyes.

"Then who? The foreign guy from your theater class last semester, Estos? What about him?" Viv clutched the loft post and rubbed her forehead.

"Estos? No, he's just a friend, and I think he took the semester off, anyway." She grabbed her backpack, wanting to end the conversation. "I'll see you this evening, I've got class all morning and lab in the afternoon. I want to squeeze in—"

"Another run. I know." Viv waved her arm at Nat. "If I didn't know better, I'd think you were trying to avoid me."

"You could always run with me," Nat offered.

Viv hefted a book from her bedside table and threw it just as Nat ducked out the door. The book landed with a thud.

Nat dropped her backpack by the empty cafeteria table. The ache in her shoulder was worse. *Maybe it's time to see campus health again,* she thought as she slid her tray onto the circular top with her left hand and sat down.

A few students wandered along the buffet, filling bowls with cereal and grabbing fruit. She stared out the dining-room windows, past the dormitories to the bleak snow-encrusted fields. Clouds hung heavy in the morning sky. She played with her oatmeal, her thoughts straying to Soris and his broad smile. She tossed her spoon into her bowl and pushed the tray away. *I miss you, Soris. Maybe it would be better if I could just forget you, forget Fourline.*

But she couldn't, and Annin wasn't around to wipe her memories. Annin would be back in Fourline with the rest of the former rebels-in-exile by now, anyway. Nat had seen Sister Barba and Professor Gate from a distance a few times since her return, but no one else. *Besides,* she told herself, *I don't really want to see any of them except Soris.*

She cleared her tray and wandered out of the cafeteria. Students threaded their way past her, and she stepped cautiously to the side to avoid bumping her shoulder. From a distance, she saw Signe's tall figure pass through the Science Center doors. Nat hurried down the path. If she caught up with her, they could work through their lab notes before class. Her phone vibrated as she jumped over a pile of slushy snow. She pulled the phone from her back pocket and checked the number.

"Hey, Mom." She grimaced from the sharp ache in her shoulder and shifted the phone to her left hand.

"Nat." Her mom sounded surprised. "I wasn't expecting you to answer."

"It's your lucky morning," she said through the pain.

"Really? Doesn't sound like it. What's going on?"

"Nothing, just a busy week, that's all."

"Hmm. You've been pretty busy since January, as far as I can tell. Which brings me to the point of my call. I am officially giving you three weeks' notice so you can free up some time."

"For what?" Nat passed the library and skipped onto the path leading to the Science Center.

"Cal's decided. She'll be attending school with you next year." Her mom's voice rang with pleasure. "She has an appointment with the dance department the third week of April to meet with more faculty."

"What? Cal's not coming here." A flock of pigeons scattered at the sound of Nat's voice. "You can't afford the tuition to send her here." She regretted the words as soon as they came out of her mouth.

"Your new scholarships freed us up to help her, and the dance department gave her the Shiffer Scholarship. She would be a fool to turn it down," her mother said stiffly.

"I didn't go through everything I did to get those scholarships so Cal could leech off you." Nat's voice seethed with anger. The money for her tuition wasn't from a scholarship. Estos had originally agreed to cover her tuition in exchange for her traveling to Fourline to help him. The fact that she no longer had to worry about her tuition only served as a reminder that she'd ruined Soris' life.

"Leeching off us!" her mom yelled through the phone. "I can't believe you said that. Natalie, I stayed silent when you chose not to come home during your breaks, I even bit my tongue when I saw that absurd tattoo on your arm over Christmas, but I won't keep quiet while you insult your sister. Cal is not perfect, but neither are you. She is as deserving of the chances and opportunities you've been given. If you opened your eyes and saw how talented she is instead of cutting her down, you'd know what I'm talking about. I thought with time you two would grow close again like when you were younger. But after that comment . . ." Her mom's voice broke off. Nat's ears rang with the echo of her anger. She listened as her mom took several deep breaths. "Your sister will be there in three weeks, and you will treat her with respect, do you understand me?"

"Yes, Mom," Nat said, feeling lower than a worm. Her mom disconnected the call. Nat shoved her phone into her pocket and dropped her chin. She stormed down the path to the Science Center and brushed against someone in her haste.

"Natalie!"

Nat looked up to see Sister Barba tripping off the path. She reached for the Sister's elbow to steady her.

"You're in a rush," Barba said as she stepped back onto the path. Nat dropped her hand. The breeze lifted Barba's red hair in every direction.

"I'm sorry, Sister," Nat mumbled as she shifted from one foot to another.

"Not a problem. I was hoping to run into you. Maybe not so literally, but I did want to see you. How are you, Natalie?"

"Fine, I'm fine, Sister. Just a little distracted today."

"Hmm. I suppose you are wondering about Soris?" Nat's head shot up when Barba said his name. The lines around Barba's eyes deepened. "Ethet took him back to Fourline shortly after you returned. He is in good hands, Natalie," she said reassuringly. But Nat felt anything but reassured. She wanted to run as far from the Sister as she could.

"I need to get to class." A knot formed in Nat's throat. "It's . . . it's good to see you," she lied and pressed past Barba.

"You, too, Natalie," Barba said. Her eyes lingered on Nat's wrist when she opened the Science Center door. Nat glanced down at the edge of the vine-and-spear pattern, then at Barba. "There is a reason your markings never faded, Natalie. Please find me if you'd ever like to learn why." The Sister gave her a sad smile and walked away, leaving Nat so rattled her hand shook as she let go of the door.

CHAPTER THREE

Nat stared at the campus health clinic posters lining the exam-room walls.

"I don't see the necrosis normally associated with a serious spider bite. But there is an open sore," the doctor said. Nat looked over her shoulder and clenched her fists as the doctor gently pressed her long brown fingers around the wound.

"Like I said, I'm not sure what caused it. I was just guessing maybe a bite," Nat lied, knowing she'd been wounded by the Nala's hand cutting into her skin. She swallowed sharply, feeling her gut twist.

"When did you notice the discoloration of the skin?" The doctor sat down in a swivel chair and pulled a rolling tray holding a laptop closer to her. She peered at the screen before looking over her glasses at Nat.

She looks like Sister Ethet, Nat thought, instinctively glancing at the woman's arm for the sun markings that covered the forearm of every Healing Sister. Ethet would have an idea why Nat's shoulder hadn't healed after her fight with the Nala. But Ethet was gone. Barba had said as much during their brief encounter three weeks ago.

"When did you notice the discoloration?" the doctor repeated.

"Sorry, um, end of January. Something happened to it during J-term. I can't pinpoint anything specific, that's why I wondered if it was a bite," Nat said. The doctor would send her off to a behavioral-health clinic if she told her the truth.

"I have the write-up from your visit at the end of January." The doctor read the chart notes on her laptop. "The pain is constant?"

"Yes," Nat answered.

The doctor typed as Nat responded to each question.

"Same amount of pain as in January, or different?"

"A little different." Nat wasn't sure how to respond. Each morning when she awoke after her nightmares, the ache was sharp and deep, then it receded as the day wore on.

"How?"

"It's intense in the morning. I must be sleeping in the wrong position." She rubbed her forehead, feeling the creeping fingers of a headache.

The doctor nodded. "The PA's notes from January indicate you were suffering from exhaustion and dehydration as well as the wound to your shoulder." She pushed the laptop away and crossed her arms. "How much sleep would you estimate you get each night?"

"Enough," Nat didn't like where this was heading. "Enough for a college student."

"Hmm. You've lost several pounds since January, so I won't bother to ask how much you eat, because it is clearly not *enough*." She grabbed a notepad and began scribbling. Nat clutched her paper gown and cursed herself for coming here. The doctor ripped two pages from the tablet and handed them to Nat.

"I want to run a blood test and do a biopsy of the skin."

Nat looked out the window to avoid making eye contact. The April day was coming to an end, and a warm orange light shone through the windowpane. She bit her fingernail and looked away from the glow.

"You can come back tomorrow for the tests."

"I can't tomorrow," Nat protested, finally meeting the doctor's insistent eyes. She'd promised the biology department head she'd help him with a research project, and Cal was due to arrive soon for her three-day campus visit.

"Monday, then," the doctor said definitively. "This is the contact information for the counseling center." She pointed to a phone number on the second page. "I've seen enough students to know where you're heading, Natalie. Please call the center, they really can help you."

Nat's eyes wandered from the scribbled handwriting on the tablet paper to the dingy linoleum floor.

"Call them," the doctor said and left the room.

Nat sat on the exam table and stared at a poster listing the side effects of overprescribing antibiotics. After a few minutes, she crumpled the papers in her hand and slid off the table. *None of these people can help me,* she thought as she gingerly pulled on her long-sleeve shirt. She was a fool to think they could.

She signed out at the reception desk in the empty waiting room and exited the clinic. What would counseling do? She didn't need to talk to anyone except Soris and maybe Ethet, and that would never happen.

A bus pulled in front of her and parked by the Student Center. *I'll get through this on my own,* she thought. She didn't have a choice. Her shoulder would eventually heal. It had to.

Nat groaned inwardly when she recognized Cal's long figure alighting from the bus. Her shoulder hurt worse than ever, her head felt like it was about to explode, and her stomach churned with the nausea she'd had all afternoon. She needed at least a few minutes to herself before she had to deal with her sister.

Cal set a duffel bag on the sidewalk. She glanced around, a look of uncertainty on her face. *No such luck,* Nat thought when Cal caught sight of her and strode down the sidewalk, bag in hand.

"Hey." Cal fidgeted with the handle of her duffel.

"Hi," Nat replied. Cal's eyes darted from Nat to the sidewalk. *Is she nervous?* Nat wondered. She studied her sister for a second before her thoughts strayed to the conversation with the doctor.

"Are you waiting for someone?" Cal looked around.

"Huh? No, I'm just preoccupied. Let's drop your bag in my room. I've got class in forty-five minutes and won't be home until late, but Viv's around." Nat walked in the direction of her dorm.

"Suits me," Cal said, matching Nat's quick stride. "I don't need a babysitter."

"Good, because I wasn't offering." The familiar sense of irritation with her sister flared up inside her.

"Are you mad at me because I'm coming to school here?"

"Does it matter what I think? It's your life, as you so often remind everyone," Nat grumbled. She felt like she was going to throw up.

Cal dropped her bag and caught hold of Nat's sleeve, pulling her to a stop in the middle of the sidewalk. "I know I gave you a hard time when you came here, about Mom and Dad having to pay a stupid amount of money for your tuition." She dropped her head, looking almost contrite.

"They aren't paying any part of my tuition now, Cal," Nat interjected. She took a deep breath to try to control the negativity brewing inside her.

"I know. So I get that you're worked up about me coming. But Nat, I got this huge scholarship, and the dance department really—"

"Would you stop?" Nat held up her hands. "I am not worked up about you. Good for you for whatever scholarship you received, but I have bigger concerns than where my little sister is going to college."

"Fine." Cal grasped her bag and shrugged.

Nat felt a pang of regret for biting at her, but she had no energy to deal with her sister's center-of-the-world attitude. They walked the rest of the way to Nat's dorm in silence.

Nat punched in the key code. The resident advisor looked up from the check-in desk, and Nat pointed to the register. Cal signed in and followed her up a flight of stairs. They passed a group of sophomores who turned and watched Cal as she ascended. She winked at one of the boys.

"Cal, these aren't high school boys," she said, remembering her sister's poor choices when it came to boyfriends. Soris' face suddenly flashed in her mind.

"You care that I wink at a guy, but you don't care where I'm going to school. Interesting." Cal pursed her lips.

"Forget I said anything." Nat took the rest of the stairs by twos even though she felt like puking. When she opened the door to her room, Viv had one arm in the sleeve of a purple tweed coat.

"Hey, Cal," Viv said.

"Finally, a friendly greeting." Cal tossed her bag on the floor. Nat took a few short breaths. Bile filled her mouth.

"Nat, you don't look so hot," Viv said as she set her coat on the striped chair and then took a step toward her roommate.

"I'm fine," Nat said, holding up her hand, wanting everyone and everything around her to disappear. "I'll be home late. Cal, find your own way around." She slammed the door behind her and rushed to the bathroom at the end of the hall to lock herself in a stall. She heaved into the toilet. *When is this going to end?* Tears slid down her face, and she made no effort to wipe them away.

CHAPTER FOUR

Nat yawned and gazed at the protective beams of light Annin had taught her to visualize along the barrier of her dream space. They emitted a bright light, illuminating the empty darkness surrounding her. She brought the beams up each night out of habit now, even though nothing but the wisps of her nightmares tried to invade the safety of this refuge.

She yawned again and relaxed her body. She knew staying in her dream space night after night was keeping her from getting the rest she needed, but it was better than facing her recurring nightmare about Soris and the Nala. She settled back into the chair, worrying about her wound, and wondered if her recent nausea was somehow related to the injury.

She looked past the ledge to her dream landscape. A bank of thick clouds swollen with rain rolled across the horizon. Lightning crackled and raindrops hit the edge of the barrier. The sound of the storm reminded her of the crunching gravel on the banks of the river where the Nala had attacked Soris. A wave of guilt washed over her, and she quit worrying about her wound. *My problems are nothing compared to his.*

"I am so sorry, Soris." She dropped her head into her hands, feeling completely alone.

"For what?"

Nat tensed at the sound of the voice. She scanned the dream space.

"Over here." Soris hovered on the other side of the ledge. His blond hair was plastered to his forehead. Rain dripped off the tip of his broad nose. His eyes were green, and his skin was a golden color, as if he'd spent too much time in the sun. She stared at him a moment, unable to see any of the markings of a duozi. No blue skin, no disc eye.

"Soris? How can you reach me here?" She looked at him in wonderment. She knew Annin could access someone's dream space from a great distance, but she never heard her mention it was possible to reach someone across the membrane.

"I figured out a way to find you. Let me in." His voice sounded faint. He floated a few feet away from the bars of light. Nat cautiously crept closer to the ledge.

"This isn't going to hold me much longer." He gestured to the cloud hiding his feet. He sank midcalf into its swirling gray wisps. "Let me in."

"Lights down," Nat said. The bars of light disappeared, and the room was thrown into darkness. A triangular pendant light appeared above her and cast a warm glow.

"You need to invite me in," he reminded her. He sank lower into the cloud.

"Come in," she said quickly before he fell out of sight. Soris jumped over the ledge. "You look completely healed." Nat gazed at the exposed skin around the neck of his loose brown shirt, unable to find any hint of blue skin or bite marks. "She did it. Ethet healed you," she said, amazed. Hope surged within her.

"No," he said and turned away from her when she stepped closer.

She felt her heart ache at the coldness in his voice. She wrung her hands and was about to apologize when his voice cut through the silence.

"No one healed me," he hissed. He spun in place and stood directly under the pendant light. Smooth blue skin rippled over his face, neck, and torso. His fingers fused together into the pointed ends of long spiderlike limbs. The brown shirt fell to the floor, exposing a gaping wound running down a rigid abdomen. Nat stumbled back as Soris transformed into the Nala she'd killed by the river.

The creature's meaty back legs twitched, and then it sprang into the air. Nat's instincts kicked in even though her mind was tied up with the horror of the metamorphosis in front of her. She sprinted into the darkness of her dream space. A thin, high-pitched hiss filled the air, its horrible sound wrapping around her. The Nala's feet jabbed the ground behind her. She instinctively veered left and felt a slight breeze cooling her brow. Her brain started thinking clearly, and she remembered this was her dream space. She could visualize anything she wanted.

She imagined a protective space, and instantly a smooth cylinder thrust out of the ground, lifting her into the air. She closed her eyes and thought of Barba's orb. She felt blazing warmth around her and opened her eyes to a hundred orbs hovering next to her. She focused on the balls of light to make them rain down on the Nala, pelting its skin.

The creature dodged the orbs and probed the slippery surface of the cylinder for some purchase to cling to. Nat felt the weight of Barba's old cloak around her shoulders. A dagger hung from her belt. A sense of strength surged through her, and the Warrior Sister markings of a vine and spear on her arm pulsed.

"You're dead!" she screamed at the Nala, enraged. The creature scurried around the base of the cylinder. "I killed you," she growled.

As she watched it open its black mouth and bite at the orbs hovering around it, she felt her anger bubble over. The cylinder disappeared. Nat landed softly behind the Nala. She stepped to the side and punched the old wound in its abdomen. The Nala doubled over with a gurgling sound.

"What did you do with Soris?" she demanded. It stabbed the ground and vaulted toward her. Nat ducked and spun into the protective light of the orbs. The spheres brightened and locked together to create a blinding wall between Nat and the creature. The Nala dropped to all fours and shifted its weight back and forth as if it were winding up, ready to strike. Nat closed her eyes and let images roll through her mind.

A spiral of wind rose from the ground and lifted the creature into the air. Nat focused on the spiral, making it spin faster and faster. The orbs dispersed, and the wind whipped Nat's cape violently around her legs.

"What did you do with Soris?" Her voice rose above the roar of the wind. The Nala responded with a long hiss from its narrow lips.

Nat screamed in rage and the funnel twisted toward the ledge. A human figure shot out of the tornado's eye. Instead of the Nala, Soris floated over the ledge and spun head over heels into the storm clouds of her dream.

"No!" Nat screamed.

"Nat! Wake up!" Nat's eyes flew open. Cal and Viv stood at the foot of the loft bed, shaking her.

"Are you okay?" Cal asked. Her eyes were wide, and her blonde hair stuck out at odd angles.

"I'm okay, I'm okay." Nat pulled away from them, her heart pounding.

"You were screaming some weird name." A deep line formed between Viv's eyebrows. "It sounded like you were yelling 'Soris.'"

At the mention of his name, Nat leaned over the side of the loft and threw up.

Viv brought Nat a cup of tea and tucked the edge of a blanket under her legs, swaddling her in the striped chair. Nat's hands quivered when she took the mug. She sipped the hot liquid, burning her lip. Cal wiped the bottom rail of the loft bed a final time.

"I am so sorry, Viv," Nat said. The room smelled of vomit and herbal tea. Cal tossed the paper towel into the garbage and disappeared into the bathroom.

"Could have been worse. You missed my bed, at least." Viv shrugged. She pulled up a small square ottoman. Nat took another sip, then Viv removed the mug from her shaking hands. Cal emerged from the bathroom and sat on the edge of Viv's bed, away from the freshly scrubbed floor.

"What's wrong with you?" Cal ran her hand over her hair. "I mean, it's not like I see you that much since you never come home. But even I can tell you're a serious mess."

Nat pulled the blanket tighter across her shoulders.

"I'm fine."

"You're not *fine*." Cal stood and paced the room. "Viv agrees with me and she lives with you."

Nat turned to Viv. Her roommate gave her an apologetic look and said, "Ever since you got back from J-term, you haven't slept well, you're constantly distracted, you've dropped weight. Every time I try to talk to you about what's stressing you out, you blow me off or avoid me."

"I was busy like this before, Viv. I'm just not feeling . . ." Nat's voice trailed off. The sharp pain burned deep in her shoulder. She grimaced and looked down, hoping neither Viv nor Cal would notice.

"And then there's the money that magically appeared in Mom and Dad's account," Cal continued ranting. "I know that money came from you. I don't know what you did to get it." She tilted her chin so Nat had to look up to meet her sister's gaze. "My bet is it has something to do with why you're a wreck. Mom and Dad can figure out their own problems. They don't need you trying to fix everything and suffering a nervous breakdown in the process."

"Velvet touch, Cal, velvet touch," Viv said. She pulled Nat's hand into hers. "Look, can you agree with us that you need help?"

Nat swallowed and nodded.

"Good. Will you promise you'll see someone?"

"And not next week or next month—tomorrow," Cal interjected. Viv held up her hand.

"It's okay, she's right," Nat admitted. "Tomorrow, I promise. I know who I need to see, and I'll go tomorrow." A strange sense of relief filled her as she spoke.

"Good." Cal flopped onto the air mattress shoved against the desks and pulled the green comforter over her head. Her feet dangled over the edge.

"Do you need help getting back into the loft?" Viv asked, a look of concern on her face.

"I think I'll just stay in the chair, Viv." Nat pulled her hand away.

"Okay." Viv switched on a dim light. "You're probably not going to sleep, are you?" she asked as she got into her bed.

"Probably not." Nat took a long breath to steady her nerves. "Viv?"

"Yeah?"

"Thanks."

Viv nodded and laid her head on her pillow, falling quickly asleep. After watching her roommate's sleeping form and hearing her sister's peaceful breathing, Nat pulled her arm out from beneath the blanket. She touched the vines and tiny spear, feeling a sense of calm even though Viv and Cal had just convinced her to do something she'd promised herself she'd never do.

CHAPTER FIVE

"You're kidding me," Nat said to herself and banged her head against the doorframe. A "Closed" sign hung above a handwritten note on the glass-paned door of the costume shop. "Closed for the season, please contact Barba Gate for inquiries at . . ." An illegible phone number followed.

Desiccated leaves clustered around the door. She peered through the dirty windows. The shop was dark. A zombie dummy she'd dressed in the window when she'd worked in the costume shop in October lay in pieces on the floor. Her eyes lingered on the broken bits of the mannequin, wishing she'd known then what she knew now. *If I'd been honest with Soris, he would've known I couldn't protect him from the Nala.*

She walked past the building's stucco front, determined to find Barba. She turned the corner of the adjoining warehouse to find the secure door Estos had brought her through so many months ago. Andris' beat-up truck was parked next to it. Muddy snow covered the broken tailgate.

She brushed a leaf off the intercom panel next to the metal entrance and pressed a button. "Sister Barba? Professor Gate?" She paused and glanced at the cab of the truck, half expecting to see Andris glaring back at her. "Um, it's Nat, I need to—" The lock clicked open. She hesitated, then grabbed the handle and opened the door.

Her boots clanked against the metal stairs. She leaned against the railing when she reached the walkway overlooking the interior forest, greenhouse, and practice arena that took up most of the warehouse. The blue training dummies still hung from the ceiling, interspersed among the trees. She picked up a small rock jammed into a walkway grate and tossed it at one of the suspended figures. The rock missed its mark and tumbled through the thick pine branches.

Other than the familiar, continuous hum from the greenhouse fans, the warehouse was eerily quiet. She passed through an open door at the end of the walkway. Her steps down the stairs into the kitchen rang out. A single cup sat on the wooden kitchen table. She breathed in, smelling the dried herbs hanging from the ceiling racks, and tried to settle her nerves.

Silence greeted her when she poked her head into the hallway leading to Ethet's laboratory. It was dim, but a ray of light shone underneath the doors of the lab. She stumbled on the worn carpet and cursed under her breath before pushing open one of the doors.

"Hello, Natalie." Barba lifted a beaker of boiling water from a Bunsen burner and smiled. Nat took a seat on a familiar bench and watched Barba pour the water into two coffee cups. The table where Soris had lain after she'd brought him through the membrane was directly across from her. She looked away and found herself staring into the dark mouth of the tunnel leading to Fourline. She removed her jacket and cleared her throat.

"Here," Barba said. She handed Nat one of the cups. Steam curled around her face.

"Smells familiar," Nat said, glancing at the array of vials and bottles lining the shelves behind Barba. *Did Ethet leave anything that will heal my wound or help me sleep through the night?* she wondered.

"Meldon tea, common beverage for Sisters," Barba said, interrupting her thoughts. "You had several cups before you returned to Fourline."

Common for Sisters, but not me, Nat thought and placed her cup on the bench, in the void between her and the Sister.

"I can't tell you how happy I am that you've finally come back here. I understand why you left us so quickly after you returned with Soris." Barba's intelligent eyes softened into a sympathetic look. "I suppose you're now wondering why your markings never faded?"

"Barba," Nat interrupted. Being in the room with the tunnel to Fourline had only increased her anxiety, and Barba's preoccupation with her markings put her on edge. "I didn't come to discuss my markings. I'm having some problems." Her eyes flickered toward the tunnel entrance.

"What kind of problems?" Barba adjusted her glasses.

"Sleeping, for one. I can't sleep without dreaming of Soris and the Nala that bit him, the one I killed."

"You killed a Nala?" Barba sat upright.

"Didn't Soris tell you?"

"Natalie, Soris had very little memory of what happened after the Nala attacked him." Barba placed her cup next to the Bunsen burner and turned down the flame. "I think it's best you share what occurred with me."

Barba's serious tone caused a flutter of nerves in Nat's stomach. Her chest tightened and she swallowed. She didn't want to relive the memory of that day.

"Well?" Barba crossed her arms and waited. The thrum reverberating from the tunnel entrance filled the silent space between them.

"I fell asleep instead of watching out for him." Nat's voice broke. She traced the lip of her cup with her finger. "When I woke up, I knew something was wrong. The forest was quiet, no birdsong. Soris was by the river, filling our water flask." Nat closed her eyes, remembering him turning and yelling before the Nala pounced. "A Nala leapt over me, slammed into my shoulder, and landed on Soris. I froze, Sister. I couldn't move." Her chin slumped against her chest. "It bit Soris and told me it would make him a duozi." She wiped a tear away with the back of her sleeve.

"Natalie, what happened to the Nala?"

Nat sniffed and glanced at the Sister. She'd never seen Barba look so concerned.

"It threatened me. I used your dagger and stabbed it, but it was too late for Soris. It was my fault, Barba. If I'd been honest with Soris and told him I wasn't a real Sister, then maybe he wouldn't have trusted me so much to protect him. Instead of protecting him, I froze," she said, her lips turning down.

"What did you do with the Nala's body?"

"What does it matter?" she asked, irritated with Barba's interest in the creature. "It's dead."

"It matters a great deal."

"I pushed the body into the river and went to find help for Soris."

Barba entwined her fingers and walked toward the tunnel entrance. "Natalie, these dreams you've been having . . . Are Soris and the dead Nala in them?"

"Yes, and last night the creature got into my dream space."

"You invited it in?" Barba spun around so fast her glasses lifted off her nose.

"No . . . Well, yes. I thought the Nala was Soris. Maybe it was. I don't know." She pressed the heel of her hand against her forehead. "Look, Sister, like I said, I need help. The Nala wounded me, and the wound hasn't healed. And these dreams—"

"It bit you?" Barba rushed to Nat.

"No, it just grazed my shoulder."

Barba pulled the neck of her shirt down, exposing the discolored skin. She poked around the wound.

"Did Ethet leave anything here that can heal this and stop my nightmares?" Nat stared at the wall of bottles and vials. "Ouch!" She flinched away from Barba's probing fingers. Barba readjusted the neck of her shirt. She twisted her lips and regarded Nat for a moment before she spoke.

"You'll have to ask Ethet, Natalie."

"She's coming back?" Maybe there was an end to her pain.

"No, my dear, she's not coming back. But you're going to Fourline."

"What?" Nat's mouth hung open. "I'm not going back! I never should have gone in the first place." She thrust a finger at her chest. "If it wasn't for me, Soris would be . . . Well, he'd be what he was instead of a duozi."

"Listen to me, Natalie." Barba grasped her forearm. "You made it possible for Estos and everyone else to return to Fourline. Since then, we've learned how closely linked Mudug and the Nala are. He and the Chemist . . ." A distasteful expression crossed her face. Her grip tightened. "I don't know how much you saw of Mudug's dealings, but know this: The people of Fourline are nothing more than disposable pawns to him. People who disagree with him disappear or die like Emilia. He will continue to destroy anyone who counters him, and he's letting the Nala run rampant. More people will end up like Soris if Mudug isn't stopped."

She took a deep breath. "Estos is the one person who can expose Mudug for what he is and what he's done." She dropped her hand. "Without Estos, the rebels have no rallying cause. Don't for a second think what you did was a waste. I am certain Soris feels the same way, regardless of his transformation."

"None of that changes the fact that Soris believed I would—that I could—protect him. He believed in me and I lied to him." Nat clutched the front of her shirt and blinked away her tears. Expressing her guilt openly wasn't cathartic; it was a knife to her heart.

"When we sent you in, none of us believed a Nala would attack a Warrior Sister. What happened to Soris wasn't your fault. It was ours. The Nala were bound by an accord that should have kept both of you safe. We were wrong. The accord is broken."

"The Rim Accord." Nat wiped her nose with her sleeve. She felt exhausted from the rawness of her emotions.

"Yes, the Rim Accord," Barba responded. Her expression shifted and she gave Nat a compassionate look. "Wrong or right, I understand you feel responsible for what happened to Soris. If you return to Fourline, you can help not only yourself but Soris as well."

"What do you mean?" she asked, feeling numb and dizzy at the same time.

"You need to end the Nala that attacked Soris."

"Didn't you hear me?" Nat snapped. "I stuck a dagger through its abdomen. It's dead."

"No, Natalie, it's not. Part of it still lives on in both you and Soris."

Nat stood up but swayed slightly, shocked by Barba's words.

"Sit," Barba ordered. She ushered Nat to a stool across from the stainless-steel counter. "The Nala have something similar to a gland located in their lower abdomen that's connected to their brain through a neural pathway. The gland secretes a substance that we Sisters call 'remnant.' It is transmitted through Nala venom, and we think it passes indirectly through their blood, sweat, and saliva as well. The Nala use remnant for many purposes: directions, communication, and"—Barba placed her hands on the counter—"as a way to connect with their victims even after they die."

Nat looked up, her mouth parting slightly before she spoke. "How can a dead Nala connect with anything?"

"The Sisters never discovered how it works. But we know that unless the Nala's neural pathway is severed, ending the link between the brain and the gland, the connection remains between the Nala and its victim. Every Sister, no matter what House she comes from, learns the importance of beheading a Nala and severing the neural pathway if she ever comes into significant physical contact with the creature."

"Dead is dead," Nat protested.

"A Nala may be dead as we understand death, but its remnant and the connection remain unless the neural pathway between the brain and gland are cut," Barba repeated and frowned. "I'm offering a poor explanation, Natalie. Ethet would provide a better one. It was an area of study for Healing House, not Wisdom House, Sisters."

"How does this remnant affect me? How could a dead Nala have a connection with me? I'm not even in Fourline!" She pressed her hands against her temples, feeling like she was about to completely lose control.

"A secretion must have entered the cut in your shoulder during combat. Based on what you've told me of your dreams, the contact was significant enough that you have the Nala's remnant in you, and so does Soris. The remnant creates a connection that will never go away. I'll be blunt with you, Natalie: your physical and mental suffering will only increase the longer the remnant stays in you."

"And will it get worse for Soris, too?" she asked, suddenly not caring about her own wound.

"Much worse. We believe active remnant nourishes the venom in a duozi's body. A duozi with active remnant loses all ability to be . . . well, like Annin. She has some physical attributes of the Nala, but she's more human than Nala, and she's free of any connection." Barba pressed her lips into a thin line. "Soris' body will constantly fight the venom, until it wears him down and takes over completely."

Nat closed her eyes, remembering how Soris transformed into the Nala in her dream space. She pressed her forearms against the sharp metal edge of the counter, tuning out Barba's voice.

". . . regardless of what Ethet does. You must seek her advice. She may have an idea other than—"

"Other than what, Sister?" Nat forced herself to listen to Barba, feeling sick to her stomach.

"I think you have to find the Nala you killed and sever the neural tie," Barba said, confirming Nat's nightmarish realization.

"How am I supposed to find its body? I pushed it into a river months ago. It's probably decaying at the bottom of an ocean right now." The sick feeling in her stomach was growing stronger.

"No, the Nala always find their dead." Barba glanced at the smooth floor with a haunted look on her face.

"And if I don't find the body and sever the tie, Soris and I . . . ?"

Barba took a deep breath. "I'm sorry, Natalie, I really am. If we'd known the Nala had grown so brazen and were breaking the terms of the Rim Accord, we would have trained you as all Warrior Sisters are trained."

"Sister, this is so far beyond an apology." Nat pushed the stool away. She stared at the tunnel entrance. Before, when she'd returned to Fourline, the choice had been hers. Now, there was no choice. The vibrations from the tunnel shook under the soles of her shoes.

"Perhaps, if you give me time, I can think of another solution," Barba said. But Nat heard the doubt in her voice.

"And what happens to Soris while you're doing that?"

Barba said nothing. She didn't need to.

Nat let out a long breath. Minutes passed. She stared at the tunnel entrance, processing Barba's words, when a strange feeling of relief struck her. *At least I finally know what's wrong with me.* She dropped her head and stared at the markings on her arm. *And I know what I have to do, even if it is impossible. I owe it to Soris.*

It took her a few moments to muster the courage to say what her mind had already accepted.

"I don't have a choice. I'll go back in, Sister." She turned and leveled a look at Barba. "But before I go, you're going to do the one thing you should have done in the first place."

Barba tilted her chin to her chest, and her glasses slipped slightly down her nose.

"You're going to turn me into a real Warrior Sister."

CHAPTER SIX

"Done?" Barba asked as she stirred a metal spoon in a cast-iron pot. A delicious smell filled the air.

Nat flipped the page of the musty-smelling book in front of her. She paused, then set her pencil down next to a sheaf of papers covered with her handwriting. Tapping the edges of the papers together, she flicked her gaze toward Barba's orb bobbing back and forth on either side of her head. Barba shot an irritated glance in the orb's direction, and the sphere settled into a slow spin.

"Done," Nat said, feeling nervous despite her certainty that she'd answered Barba's random questions correctly. She'd never written an essay like this before. The correct tactical maneuvers when fighting in the Keyen Mountains, native Fourline plants with poisonous properties, and indicators of the presence of Nala and key elements from the Sisters' first encounter with the Nala were only some of the topics covered in the thick handwritten stack. She relaxed her cramped hand, still rankled that Barba hadn't let her use a computer to type the responses.

She flexed her back, feeling the soreness of her muscles from yesterday's sparring session. Barba had her training daily with a local tae kwon do instructor Andris had sparred with before his return to Fourline.

Each morning, she ran to the trainer's dojo for two hours of grappling, sparring, and drills before her classes, then squeezed in an hour of rapier and broadsword training with the college fencing instructor Cairn used to train his theater students. Her afternoons were allotted to classes with Barba in the basement of the theater department and her regular classes. Evenings were spent in the laboratory of the costume shop for more lessons and training with Barba.

The schedule of the past five weeks had been grueling, but her mind and body were strong and healthy. Barba regimented every second of Nat's day, and Nat was thriving. She glanced at Barba, feeling grateful for the sense of purpose and relief that had settled over her under Barba's care and instruction. She felt like a fog had lifted from her mind.

Barba slid onto the bench across from Nat. She placed a china cup and bowl of stew in front of her and motioned for Nat to eat. Nat's mouth watered.

"How come you know so much about the Warrior House?" Nat asked, thinking about the lectures and training sessions she'd undergone with Barba. The Sister had even corrected the local martial arts instructor on a mistake in Nat's defensive techniques. "I thought a Sister's training was limited to one House." She blew on a spoonful of the stew.

"Wisdom House holds my oath, but I was a selector for each House. My assignment required I know the skills necessary for a girl or woman to excel in each House. That, and I trained with the Warrior Sisters when I had a falling out with my Head Sister over my area of study."

Nat's eyes widened and her lips parted in a slight smile. "That sounds intriguing. What were you studying?"

"Predictions," Barba said, keeping her eyes fixed on Nat.

"Predictions? Predicting what, the weather?" Nat joked. Her smile faded when she saw the pensive look on Barba's face. A moment of silence passed. Nat felt suddenly self-conscious. She set her spoon against the rim of her bowl and wondered if the conversation was leading to another strange test.

"No, not the weather." Barba shuffled the pile of papers in front of Nat and shook her head as if changing her mind about something. *That was less than subtle,* Nat thought as she watched the intense expression on Barba's face fade away.

"How do you feel about having chosen the Warrior House over the others?" Barba asked, switching subjects. "With your education, you're a natural fit for the Healing House." She brushed a red strand of hair away from her face.

Nat looked thoughtfully at Barba as she chewed another bite. They'd had this conversation at the beginning of her training, when Barba had explained the path to becoming a Sister. At first Nat had been concerned that training would take months, even years, but Barba had assured her she already possessed many of the necessary skills. What she needed more than anything was knowledge and understanding of the Warrior House and how a Warrior Sister's actions and decisions were guided by a desire for peace in the face of the ever-present threat of the Nala. Since the formation of the first Houses, the Warrior Sisters' role had transformed from one of hunting down and killing the Nala to that of ensuring the creatures remained in their territory near the coast as mandated by the Rim Accord. *Peace through protection, and more than a share of violence,* Nat thought.

"Well?" Barba prodded. Nat took another bite and considered how to verbalize her reasons for selecting the Warrior House. Every time she pondered the Houses and how each uniquely supported peace in Fourline, she thought of Soris and the impossible task that lay ahead of her.

"Did it ever seem that the House chose the Sister instead of the Sister choosing the House?" Nat asked. She knew with certainty that she needed to be a Sister from a House whose purpose was to suppress and destroy the Nala.

"Yes." Barba cupped her chin in her hand.

"Well, I guess that's how I feel about the Warrior House, or being a Warrior Sister, since this isn't a regular House." She glanced around the kitchen and thought of the ruins of two Houses she'd seen in Fourline.

"Not a regular House?" Barba dropped her hand from her chin and a defensive look crept across her face. "Did the original Sisters have some marble monstrosity in which to contemplate the best course for dealing with the Nala, for creating a path to peace?"

"Of course not," Nat replied quickly, knowing she'd struck a nerve.

"Houses became physical places over time, but the core of a House has always been its philosophy and purpose, not some silly physical structure. The best opportunity for training and learning is not dependent on a location, Natalie." Nat said nothing but felt doubtful. "You disagree?" Barba's eyes narrowed.

"I encountered a mix of opinions when I was in Fourline. Soris said it didn't matter where I trained, but Benedict implied I was less of a Sister because I was from the fringe, not an established House," she added with a rueful expression.

"Benedict?" Barba's brows scrunched together. "Natalie, Benedict's a snoot. Would it help you to know that he considered my House a fringe House?"

Nat looked up, surprised. The few people she'd encountered in Fourline who knew Barba held her in the highest regard. Nat had assumed she'd trained and lived in one of the grand Houses destroyed by Mudug.

"Do you recall the mental map I gave you of the western coast, near the swamps?" Nat nodded, remembering the bleak landscape. "My House was not far from there. It was built high up in a canopy of massive trees and made of wood, grass, and mud, not stone and stained glass. Release your doubt about the location of your training." Barba's mouth was set in a firm line.

Nat glanced around the kitchen and thought of everything she'd learned and mastered under Barba's instruction. She nodded in agreement.

"Don't doubt." Barba wagged her finger at Nat, then collected the papers. Nat ate the remaining stew as quietly as she could while Barba read her responses.

"What are the tenets of the Warrior House?" Barba asked suddenly.

"Strength in mind and body, knowledge of the world around you, and peace through protection. Like the creation of the Houses themselves, all tied to the existence of the Nala."

"Exactly." Barba lifted her chin. "You've progressed in your training to achieve each tenet. It's time for a surprise." She scooted her bench away from the table and swiftly stood. Nat followed her out of the kitchen to Ethet's laboratory with a growing sense of anticipation, wondering what new training lay ahead. She felt the usual vibration under the soles of her shoes when she entered the laboratory and looked around. Barba walked over to the stainless-steel counter and gestured to an orb suspended between two discs connected to circular stands.

"Is that mine?" Nat felt her heart skip a beat.

"Not yet. Come look."

Nat didn't have to be asked twice. She sprinted toward the counter. Barba turned on the flame of a burner next to the orb. Bubbles rose to the top of the clear liquid suspended in a flask above the burner.

"How'd you make this?" Nat asked, greedily eyeing the orb.

Barba looked at her over her glasses. "It's complicated, Natalie."

"I like complicated." She touched the smooth surface of the sphere and noticed a hole at the top leading to its center.

"It took me ten years to master the art."

"Oh." Nat's shoulders dropped.

"You have a core of understanding, skill, and knowledge that will mature and develop like any Sister's. If you choose to learn the art of orb construction, it's highly satisfying, but there are few who have the required patience. All Head Sisters know the skill."

"Do I get to do anything to help create it?" she asked with a hint of disappointment. Barba's orb, which Nat had carried with her through Fourline, continued to amaze her. She'd been looking forward to making one.

"Of course."

"What do I do?" A tingle of excitement shot through Nat.

Barba retrieved a small pair of clippers from a drawer under the counter. "You need to physically imbue the orb first, then mentally imbue it to seal the connection. Turn your head." Barba held up the clippers and Nat shrank back. "If you are frightened of a pair of clippers, maybe we need to rethink this entire endeavor."

"No," Nat said quickly and leaned in. She felt a painful pinch in the upper curve of her ear. Barba pressed a piece of gauze against the cut and dropped the cartilage, no bigger than the tip of Nat's pinky finger, onto a clean cloth. Nat eyed the bit of her ear while Barba taped a small bandage over the gouge. Her hands came away covered with streaks of blood.

"Ear cuts always bleed, but not as much as scalps," Barba said and washed her hands under the sink. Nat shuddered, wondering what other body parts Sisters had used to physically imbue orbs.

"It's ready when you are. Flesh and breath." Barba gestured to the opening in the top of Nat's orb. Nat gingerly picked up the piece of her skin and dropped it into the hole. It landed in the center and marred the bottom with a pink stain.

"Now breath." Barba pointed to the opening again and lifted the hot flask with a pair of tongs. Feeling foolish and excited at the same time, Nat leaned over and breathed into the opening. Barba immediately poured the hot liquid into the hole, filling it to the curve. Nat focused on the ball as the liquid cooled and hardened.

"Don't strain yourself." Barba laughed seeing Nat's red face. "It's a lifeless ball right now. The connection will come tonight when you mentally imbue it. Find it in your dreams. Then it's up to you to figure out how to open yourself to it and create the connection. Drink this before bed, it will help." She handed Nat a vial of clear liquid, then carefully removed the suspended sphere from the vise to place it into Nat's hands. The orb felt cold in her palms.

"And if it doesn't work?" Nat asked with a tremor in her voice.

"Then you were never meant to be a Sister," Barba said without hesitation. She turned off the burner. "The ability to know the world around you requires, at its core, an understanding of the self. Share that understanding with your orb." She paused and took in Nat's worried expression. "Stop doubting, Natalie. It will happen. Come, I'll drive you home after I set the protections for the entrance."

"Protections?" Nat asked as she retrieved her backpack from the bench and placed the sphere into a zippered slot, tucking her fears away with it. She watched Barba approach a panel next to the solid wooden doors.

"Cairn's away, and we never leave the entrance unsupervised unless the protections are in place. The Nala may not be able to get through the membrane, but humans can," she explained and punched a series of keys. Nat nodded, remembering everyone's lack of concern when she'd told them she'd spied a Nala on the cliff near the membrane.

"Barba, I've never really understood how Annin and Soris passed through if nothing can cross the membrane unless it exists on both sides. Duozi don't exist in this world."

"In their cases it was a matter of balance. Annin's more human than Nala." She pressed a few more keys, and Nat felt the vibrations grow stronger. "But even she has to fight to push through. Soris, I'm afraid, is more Nala. When you brought him, he was still human enough to pass through, but crossing over was already difficult. With what Ethet said about the level of venom in him, he'd never be able to cross over if he tried again. The membrane would not give way for him now."

The guilt Nat had been trying to suppress about Soris surged forward. She opened her mouth to ask another question about Soris, but stopped as a wall slowly descended over the opening. Barba pressed in another code, and a rocky-looking surface rose up from a slit in the cavern floor and curved around the interior of the tunnel as the wall ground into place. She looked at what was once the mouth of the tunnel in wonder. If she didn't know better, she'd have no idea what lay on the other side.

"Cairn's father's creation. An impenetrable metal designed to look like rock encases the entire tunnel, sealing it off from this world," she explained with a serious look in her eyes. "If someone managed to pass through the membrane, all they'd find is a long cavern ending at a wall that looks like stone. The system also activates if an intruder were to try and access this room."

Nat ran her hand across the surface of what used to be the opening. The stone seamlessly blended into the surrounding rock wall. "That's amazing."

"Necessary precaution years in the making. Even this room is carved out of the cliff and can be cut off from the rest of the building. My orb watches the entrance when I'm sleeping. If I'm gone, we have enough sensors to let Cairn or whoever else is around know immediately if someone passes in or out. But enough of that. Your focus should be your orb and the long night ahead," she said with a knowing look.

"Thanks," Nat responded faintly, tearing her eyes away from the blocked entrance.

The orb nestled in the crook of Nat's arm as she lay in bed. She yawned and pressed it closer to her body. The fear of failing to connect with the orb lingered in the back of her mind as she tried to relax. Feeling thirsty from the syrupy liquid she'd downed before bed, she pulled off her blanket and climbed carefully down the loft to get a drink, carrying the orb with her.

She held the ball tight in one hand and grasped the handle to the adjoining bathroom. The hairs on the back of her neck stood on end when she heard a sound like air escaping a tire behind her. Slowly, she turned. Her room was gone. An enormous black pit like the one in Gennes' camp swallowed the space in front of her. A Nala, monstrous in size, crept out of the hole. Nat spun back around, opened the door, and slammed it shut behind her.

She clutched the orb to her chest and looked around. Her breathing slowed when she realized she was in her family's barn. Lambs bleated in their wide pen in the corner. Her father looked up from his lathe. He smiled at her and brushed the sawdust from the thick leather apron covering his chest and legs. Nat ran to him. He enfolded her in his arms with the orb pressed between them. The moment she touched him, a rush of memories of her family flowed through her mind. Visions of her sisters when they were just babies—Cal, then Marie Claire born eight years later. Nat riding on the rocking horse her father had made for her one Christmas. Snuggling next to Cal in bed when thunderstorms shook the hills around their house. Letting MC struggle with a horse before stepping in and boosting her onto the saddle. Her parents singing, fighting, crying, hugging, laughing.

It was overwhelming. She lost all ability to pause or control her thoughts as memories she had forgotten surfaced, only to be replaced by streams of emotions and questions. When had she and Cal grown apart? How had her parents found a love so strong? What would MC be like when she was older, carrying so much concern for others at such a young age? Did any of them know how much she truly loved them?

She opened her eyes and found herself in a room with walls so white she immediately brought her hand to her brow to shield against the light. A square block rose from the center of the floor. Curious, Nat approached a screen centered in the middle of the block. A simple equation flashed across the screen. Nat tucked the orb into her pocket, knowing she had to provide an answer. The moment she typed the solution on a keyboard at the base of the screen, a chemical equation appeared. She glanced at it and realized something was wrong, then moved the cursor to fix the mistake. Another problem followed by a question popped up. Her hands flew over the keyboard with lightning speed, answering every question that materialized. After what seemed like an endless series of questions, the screen went suddenly blank.

She stepped back, and an image appeared above the screen. The hazy forms sharpened into Estos sitting on a metal bleacher next to her. Nat recognized the encounter immediately. It was from the morning he'd explained how Mudug had ordered the death of his sister, Emilia, the morning Nat had agreed to help him return to Fourline. The image swirled and she saw herself talking on the phone while walking through campus. Voices filled the room, and she listened to herself explaining to MC how to send their mom and dad's account information so she could pay their mortgage.

The vision reshaped itself again. Nat was talking to a boy from her high school as he leaned against the gray lockers. Her skin crawled at the memory. She did not need to hear the voices to remember the conversation. The boy had posted explicit pictures of ex-girlfriends online and had set his eyes on Cal. His defiant look disappeared when Nat's track team suddenly appeared in the hallway and stood behind her. He'd never said another word to Cal.

More images materialized. She watched scene after scene of problems that had popped up in her life or in the lives of those around her and how she'd dealt with them. Nat dropped her eyes, confused. She pulled her orb from her pocket and felt the comforting smoothness of its surface.

When she looked up, she gasped. She saw herself cradling Soris' head in her lap as a river coursed behind them. The fabric around his shoulder hung in shreds. Blood and venom stained the skin encircling the deep bite wounds. The body of the dead Nala lay curled up near the water. Nat felt a fury inside her and brought her fist slamming down on the screen. The glass splintered and the walls of the room fell, then disappeared like the image.

She was alone in a field that spread forever in every direction. She stood in the long grass and turned, wondering which way to go. Curling her fingers around the orb, she set off running down a dirt path that appeared at her feet. She felt the ground beneath her rise slightly as the path cut over a hill. The grass disappeared. Slabs of split granite shot up from the top of the hill. Nat held on to her orb tightly and climbed up and over each ancient rock until her fingers brushed the familiar ledge of her dream space.

Nat paused before pulling herself over the ledge, remembering Barba's words. *You can come in,* she said to her orb, then threw her leg over the boundary and tumbled onto the floor. The bars of light along the ledge lit up like a series of fireworks, but she hardly noticed. She held the orb in her hand. It felt solid, real. *Is it really with me, or is it just a figment?*

She glanced around the empty space, remembering how she'd touched people and objects in her dream space in the past. She clutched the orb, convinced of its physicality, and sat with her legs crossed on the floor. She stared at it, knowing everything her dreams had revealed. *Did you see all of it, too?* she silently asked the orb as she thought of the images, intentions, feelings, and beliefs she hardly remembered and those painfully new. She stared intently, willing it to accept her emotions.

After what seemed like hours, Nat fell onto her back, exhausted. The ball rolled onto the floor, lifeless. She closed her eyes, knowing she'd failed. *It's okay, I can still go back to Fourline, find the Nala, and finish it off so Soris and I can be free of the remnant. I know so much more now. It doesn't matter that I'm not a Sister. It doesn't matter. It doesn't matter.*

She sighed, feeling the heavy weight of her doubt return. She glanced at the floor, looking for the useless orb. It was gone. *Figures,* she thought as she stood up and walked glumly toward the barrier lights. *I can't even conjure a working orb in my dream space.* Nat rubbed her forehead and wondered how Barba would take the news.

She stretched her arms above her head, trying to loosen the knot forming in her neck. She knocked into something hard and glanced over her shoulder. Her orb spun away from the impact with her hand. A faint light pulsed from deep within its core.

"No way!" Nat cried. The orb burst with light, filled with the joy spilling from Nat. A nervous thought fluttered through her. Hesitating a moment, she dropped her light barrier. The orb zipped across the ledge into her dreams as if it'd read her mind.

Okay, now for the real test. She turned her back on the orb and forced her mind to think of nothing but a blank sheet of paper. Warmth tickled the back of her neck. She opened her eyes and spun around. The orb had crossed her barrier without an invitation. *You are part of me!*

"Yes!" she cried, feeling as free as a child. The sphere whizzed around her head and Nat raced toward it, exuberant. The ball settled into her hand and warmth spread through her cold fingers. A smile broke across her face, and she released the orb. An undulating meadow flowed in front of her. Nat ran through the blanket of yellow flowers, laughing uncontrollably while her orb bobbed and spun around her.

CHAPTER SEVEN

Nat thought back to the dreams of the night before as she stood at the edge of the warehouse near Andris' training arena. She glanced at the glowing ball of light hovering next to her head. She closed her eyes and silently ordered the orb to search for Barba, who had hidden herself somewhere in the warehouse. Barba had said this was the last test to see if the connection between Nat and her orb was strong enough.

The sphere bobbed and whizzed toward the pine trees growing at the far end of the massive room. Nat felt a sense of elation as she watched the orb—*her* orb—weave between the tree trunks until it hovered above a sickly-looking pine tucked near the back of the indoor forest. Barba emerged from behind the tree, applauding. Nat closed her eyes again; the orb zoomed toward her and landed in her hand. When she opened her eyes, Barba stood before her with her chin tilted up and her shoulders perfectly straight.

"A Warrior Sister honors the memory of the Four Sisters. Her loyalty rests with the Four Houses and a just regency. She offers aid to any Sister and fights for peace and stability regardless of personal cost or sacrifice. But above all else, she seeks to diminish and destroy the Nala through strength and wit. Are you such a person, Natalie Barns?"

"Yes."

"Do you, on your oath, accept these obligations and duties willingly?"

"Yes."

Barba wrapped her arms around Nat and gave her hug. "Congratulations, Sister," she said.

Nat's cheeks ached so much from smiling that she simply nodded in response. *Sister,* she thought. The title meant something deeply personal to her now.

The women turned away from the trees. Nat's heart beat faster and her mind spun as the meaning behind her oath sank in. She cupped her hands around her orb and rolled it between her palms, feeling its warmth seep into her.

They passed Ethet's neglected greenhouse. "You've told your family and friends of your plans for the summer?" Barba asked as they walked out of the warehouse into the hallway. The question caught Nat by surprise and she frowned.

"Viv knows I'm working on another show with you." She trailed Barba into the kitchen and settled onto a bench next to the long table. Her orb spun in circles around a dark-blue bowl, and Nat had a fleeting thought that its movements looked almost agitated, the same way she felt. "She thinks I've been going to counseling, and since I've put on some weight and haven't woken up in the middle of the night screaming, she's happy enough for me whatever I do." She shrugged the lopsided shrug she'd adopted since her shoulder wound.

"And your family?" Barba asked as she placed a thick slice of pie in front of her. Nat sent her orb to eye level and grabbed a fork.

"I haven't told them yet."

Barba looked at her over her glasses.

"I'll call them," she said, not relishing the idea of informing her family she was leaving to work on another "show" for the costume shop in Canada instead of returning home for summer break.

"Don't delay telling them. I expect you here ready to leave in two days' time. We received word from Riler last night." The mention of Riler, one of Estos' private guards, got Nat's attention. "Gennes and the rebels will start a string of minor assaults on Mudug's garrisons in the North soon. They want to clear the way for any Sisters living in the fringe who wish to return once Estos' presence is revealed."

"Mudug still doesn't know he's back?" Nat asked, surprised.

"Fortunately, no. Mudug has no clue Estos has returned. Whatever you and Soris did to the Chemist's tracking device worked beyond our best expectations, thank goodness. Although he's claiming to be only temporary regent, you know as well as I that Mudug would expend every resource available to kill Estos if he appeared before his birthday next winter. Mudug will want formal recognition as regent, and that can only happen if Estos fails to claim the regency once he reaches the age of majority. His death would cement Mudug's rule. My point is Mudug will be occupied in the North. Now that your training is done, it's a good time for you to slip back into Fourline."

Nat stared at the plate. "Did Riler's message say anything about Soris?"

"No, we still have to assume he's with Ethet. It would be difficult for a duozi anywhere in Fourline without friends to hide him," Barba explained gently.

Nat clutched the mug Barba set in front of her and silently sipped the hot tea.

"Your grades this semester are excellent. I'm sure your parents will be as proud as I am," Barba said, changing the subject.

Nat felt a tinge of pride when she glanced at the small red-haired woman in front of her. She'd grown to deeply respect Barba despite the grueling schedule and the panicky fear that overshadowed every part of her training. "Thank you," she said.

"I've said it before, Natalie. Your intelligence is your best asset. Rely on it and it will see you through anything. Now finish up, Sister. I need to show you your new cloak."

"You sure MC doesn't want my turtle for the summer?" Viv asked as they looked around their nearly empty dorm room. She wore a black T-shirt with "Vengeance Is Mine" emblazoned on the front, and her hair was spiked up like a hedgehog.

"She'd love it," Nat said, knowing her little sister would flip at the chance to take care of a turtle. "But like I said, I'm not heading home."

Viv shrugged and lifted her final box off the floor. "Call me from the hinterlands of Canada this summer," she demanded. "I go into withdrawal when I don't hear your melodious voice."

"I'll make sure to call you every morning at the crack of dawn before I go for a run." She held the door open for Viv.

"Don't you dare," her roommate huffed and shoved the box into the already cramped backseat of her car.

"It's a.m. calls or nothing."

"Nothing it is, then. I'll speak to you in August." Viv gave Nat a quick hug. "I'm glad you got your ducks in a row, honey," she whispered into her ear. Her eyes were misty when she pulled away. Nat's throat tightened.

"Thanks, Viv. I'll be even better in August." She gave her roommate another quick hug, hoping that there was truth to what she'd said. She watched Viv drive away before grasping the handle of her bag. Cars and trucks were parked on the sidewalks and lawns as students loaded their belongings. Nat wove her way in and out of the traffic and climbed into the back of the small maroon bus idling in front of the Student Center. She placed her bag on the seat next to her and retrieved her phone as the bus lurched down the road. Her dad picked up on the second ring.

"Hey, Nat. You making it home tonight?" She heard a little buzzing sound in the background and knew her dad must be in his shop.

"About that, Dad . . . I tried to call yesterday and the day before and only got your voice mail. I'm not coming home right away. I got another job this summer in Canada." The driver steered the bus around the students and parents clogging the road. He honked, but Nat didn't notice. She was listening to the silence on the other end of the phone. "Dad, did you hear me? I got another job this summer in Canada. I leave this weekend," she said softly.

"How long this time?" His tone was terse.

"I don't know. Could be a month, but they may run two shows, so it might be longer." Telling her father the string of lies felt horribly wrong.

"Your mother will not be happy. And what about MC? Do you have any idea how crazy she's been waiting for you to come home? Even Cal's been asking about you."

"I'll make it up to MC," she said, unsure how she would make anything up to MC. She doubted Cal cared whether or not she came home, but she was still grateful to her sister for not sharing her breakdown with her parents. She thought back to the dream images she'd shared with her orb. Maybe she and Cal could find a way to be close again.

"Nat, there is more to life than money and working all the time." Her dad continued his lecture. "I'm starting to think that when you left for school, you decided to leave your family behind as well."

"It's not just about money." *It never really was,* she thought. "It's an opportunity I can't pass up." She shifted in her seat to avoid pressing against her wounded shoulder.

"How is working on sets in some theater in Canada going to help you? You're a biology major." The bus bumped over the bridge and turned onto Grand Street.

She swallowed. She couldn't explain Soris or any of her problems to him, but she had to say something so he'd understand. "Dad, you know how you're always telling the three of us to live our lives the right way? It's hard to explain, but that's what I'm trying to do now. Trust me on this." She sighed. "I'm sorry I can't come home. I really am."

"I trust you, Nat. I . . . We just miss you. I guess we'll see you when you get back. I suppose it's the same bad cell coverage as before?"

"Yeah, it is. Same bad cell coverage." She watched the town slip past as she said good-bye to her dad and the bus brought her closer to the entrance of Fourline. Thinking about home, she walked to the costume shop, where she met Barba at the back entrance.

Barba left her alone as she dressed. She stood in front of the mirror, looking at her reflection. She took in her tightly braided brown hair, the drape of her new cloak, and the flash of the dagger sheath hanging from her belt. Her orb spun next to her wounded shoulder. She turned away from the mirror, letting her thoughts of home disappear with her vanishing reflection.

"How are you feeling?" Barba asked as Nat walked into Ethet's laboratory.

"I'm petrified." She looked at the shadowy entrance to the tunnel and swallowed.

"Good." Barba adjusted the clasp on her cloak. Nat glanced at her right arm and wiggled her fingers as Barba fussed over her. Her exposed Warrior markings twitched with the movement. She'd hidden them under long sleeves for months, afraid of her parents' disapproval and hating their constant reminder of Soris' fate. Now they held an entirely different meaning for her.

"Barba, I was wondering about my Sister markings. You told me they'd fade away and they haven't."

"I lied." Barba met her eyes and smiled. "Your markings were always permanent, Natalie."

"I don't understand."

"I knew you were destined to be a Sister, a very special Sister. I just didn't know when, or the path that would lead you to make the decision for yourself." She paused and her smile faded. "The markings I gave you last year are a symbol of my faith in you and your ability to do what needs to be done, Natalie." She took a deep breath. "They will never fade or disappear. You are and always will be of a very unique House."

Nat choked back her tears and flung her arms around Barba.

"Now go," she urged Nat as she released her. "You're ready." Her green eyes were moist with tears. Nat clung to her hand a moment, then let her fingers slip free. Her orb spun past the rocky entrance, casting a curve of light on the uneven surface of the tunnel floor. Nat kept her gaze forward, afraid that if she looked back, she might change her mind.

The tunnel curved, and Nat felt the familiar vibrations increase until they tickled the soles of her feet. The orb circled back to her every few seconds as if making sure she was okay. She took a couple of deep breaths and quickened her pace. The sphere was hovering above the membrane when she rounded the final curve. She stopped in front of the opaque surface and took another deep breath before reaching for her orb. After tucking it safely into her cloak pocket, Nat pressed both hands on the membrane. "Here we go, Sister," she said and pushed through, leaving all doubt behind.

CHAPTER EIGHT

Droplets of rain pelted the crumbling roof of the abandoned trapper's hut where Nat had sheltered for the night. She sheathed her dagger and eyed the rusted-out traps clustered in the corner, wondering what had happened to the hut's former occupant. She flexed her hand, working out a cramp from clutching the dagger hilt while she'd slept. A tingling sensation spread through her fingers.

She pulled her hood over her head and bent down to remove a wire trap near the opening of the hut. She'd placed the trap the night before as a precaution against the Nala. The smooth wire wound into a tight circle in her palm. She slipped it into her pack and glanced around the ramshackle hut before edging through the broken door.

A few paces from the hut, Nat released her orb into the air. It spun as if on an axis and warmed her face with its glow. *At least I have you for company,* she thought, feeling lonely after the long cold night in the hut. The orb dipped and bobbed, exposing a faint game trail with its light. She stepped onto the trail, recognizing it from Barba's map, and ran into the woods.

After a few hours of steady jogging, the game trail grew more difficult to follow. Nat paused near a stream, trying to remember any helpful details from Barba's mental map of the forest. *Why would Ethet be here? Maybe Barba's information was wrong,* she thought as she jumped across the thin, muddy stream swollen with rainwater. The eastern forest led to the upper coastline, the Nala's main territory. This was the last place she imagined Ethet would come.

Thinking of Ethet brought Soris to her mind. As much as she wanted to see him, she hoped he wasn't with Ethet. Unless Annin had erased his memory, he knew now how Nat had lied to him and pretended to be a Warrior Sister when all she'd really been was a college kid from another world fumbling her way through Fourline. He had to hate her for it. She'd rather find and behead the Nala on her own and help Soris without him ever knowing. Maybe then she could feel a little less guilty.

Thunder rattled across the sky. Nat paused. Between her hood and the storm, she'd never be able to hear approaching Nala. Dropping to a crouch, she unhooked her cloak, shoved it into her bag, and applied a thick layer of mud to the exterior of the bag. *A little camouflage won't hurt.* She dug her hand into the bed of decaying leaves and smeared mud across her face, neck, and hands, covering any exposed skin.

The game trail disappeared entirely not far from the stream. She glanced at the daylight above the tips of the pines. *I guess I'll go with my gut,* she thought and jogged around a fallen tree. Cold rain trickled down her mud-encrusted face as she ran.

Hours passed. The only thing she heard was the beating of her heart and the rain pattering against the pine trees. She stopped to sip from her water flask. Light filtered in front of her where the trees thinned slightly. Nat capped her flask and edged toward the light, trying to focus on the distant rumbling and not the ache in her shoulder.

Nat stepped out of the tree line and found herself on a slab of rock jutting over a river. Raging water rushed through a small canyon. She crouched next to a cluster of boulders set above the river and watched the water flow, looking for a place to ford. Barba had mentioned the river to her, but she'd described it as lazy and placid, not the death trap that coursed below.

A huge tree trunk lay in the water about a hundred yards downriver. White froth formed around its dead branches. She crept toward it. Just as she emerged from behind an outcropping of rock above the trunk, a cry, like that of a small child, echoed across the river. She stumbled back, surprised.

She heard another cry, followed by a sound she knew too well: the commanding hiss of the Nala. She pressed her chest against the rock. *Move,* she ordered her body. Taking a deep breath, she settled her nerves and crawled toward a low thicket of brambles. The branches of the bushes were sparse, offering a good view of the other side of the river and the source of the crying and the hissing Nala.

Dozens of children lined the opposite bank of the river, dipping their water gourds into the fast-flowing water. She edged toward the spiky tips of the bush for a better view. A small boy with dark curly hair slipped on one of the river rocks. He righted himself and brushed mud from his tattered tunic. The way he held his head at an angle and his soft, rounded chin drew Nat to look more closely at his face. She blinked to clear her eyes. When the boy tilted his head in her direction, she saw his Nala eye and the bluish tint of his cheeks. She recognized him immediately as Neas, the duozi boy Benedict had tried to capture back in Yarsburg.

The branches of the slender tree behind Neas quivered. Two blue arms emerged from behind the leaves. The arms disappeared, then reappeared at the tip of the tree. A Nala flung itself from the top of the tree onto the bank next to Neas and landed in a crouch as if ready to spring on the boy. Nat stifled a scream as five more Nala joined the first, scurrying around the bank on all four limbs and forming a half circle around the children.

The Nala rushed forward, some still on all four limbs while others stood and slapped the children with their angular arms, pushing them into the forest. Nat looked closer and her horror turned to puzzlement as none of the children cried out. Most walked in a docile manner as the Nala herded them into the woods. A few resisted and received a sharp slap or hissing bark from the creatures. One child's head snapped to the side when slapped and the sun shone on his neck, exposing blue skin. A girl dipped beneath a low branch and cast a glance back toward the river. Her silver eye glimmered. Nat sat back in the mud, stunned, realizing she was watching dozens of duozi children disappear into the forest.

"Let go of me!" Neas' voice brought her attention back to the riverbank. A Nala curled its hand around his skinny arm and lifted him off the ground. Nat eased her crossbow out of her bag, thinking not only of her oath but also how much she'd enjoy sending an arrow into the creature's head. Neas landed a kick to its abdomen, and the Nala dropped the boy. He hit the pebble-strewn bank and scrambled toward the remaining children. The Nala bowed its back and issued a string of barking hisses from its black mouth. Before Nat could find a decent angle, the remaining Nala scurried up the bank into the woods, kicking pebbles with the quick movements of their limbs.

The cold mud seeped through her clothes as she watched them fade into the forest. How had the Nala gotten ahold of Neas? The Hermit's face came quickly to her mind. *Benedict.* He hated the duozi enough to entrap Annin. Nat wouldn't put it past him to have made a side trip to Yarsburg just to snitch on the boy. She untangled her pack from the branches and crawled from underneath the bush, angry with the Hermit. Did he have any idea what happened to the duozi when they were cast out into the forest?

"What is one like you doing so deep in the woods?"

Nat stopped short and looked directly into the face of a Nala. It hung upside down from a branch above her. It swiveled its head and sniffed the air. "You're not a duozi."

"You took my brother," she said, thinking quickly as her heart beat faster. She stepped onto a low boulder, distancing herself from the creature. She tucked her right arm behind her, hiding her markings. With the Nala no longer adhering to the terms of the Rim Accord, the creature might attack if it discovered she was a Sister. She didn't have time to engage in a fight or risk its following her and discovering her destination.

The Nala curled an arm around a branch and lowered itself to the ground. "Your brother?" the creature said in a breathy hiss. Its tapered limbs disappeared into the mud as it crawled toward her, close to the soft ground. Nat glanced behind her, edging her feet over the boulder.

"My brother Neas from Yarsburg. Where are you taking him?" It took little effort for her to make her voice quiver in fright. She scrambled to the next boulder and again glanced over her shoulder. The river ran directly beneath her.

"He's not your brother anymore." The Nala scurried onto the first boulder and crouched low, tensing against the rock. "But if you want to join him . . ." The creature shot into the air just as Nat jumped from the boulder and tumbled toward the river. The Nala's hissing scream followed her down as she crashed into the cold black water. She pushed against the current with her arms and kicked violently to break through the surface just in time to see the dead tree trunk looming in front of her. The water thrust her toward a sharp limb. She ducked and covered her head with both arms. When she emerged, the tree trunk was far behind her. Blood seeped from a gash in her arm.

She sputtered, clearing water from her mouth before the current pulled her under again. Her leg smashed into a rock and she shot back to the surface. Disoriented, she tried to swim to the bank. A log floated within an inch of her head, and she grasped for its sodden surface. The log flipped. Water filled her nose. Her hands frantically searched for the floating limb. She pulled her head out of the water and clutched the log as close to her head as she could. Water poured out of her mouth as she coughed, struggling for breath.

The river spun the log around, giving Nat a clear view of the approaching rapids. She frantically looked toward the bank. A crystalline patch of water caught her eye, and she kicked toward the eddy. The log caught on a tangle of river grass and spun around, slamming Nat against a narrow spit of land. She flung her arms over it and crawled onto its muddy surface, taking deep, heaving gulps of air.

She sat upright and realized she was on the opposite shore. *At least that problem is solved,* she thought, then noticed the blood flowing from the gash in her arm. Nat tried to stand, but her leg buckled and she fell hard against the bank. She clenched her teeth and moved on hands and knees toward the forest edge. She propped herself against a tree and let her breathing slow while she scanned the treetops. Spotting a broken limb a few feet away, she hopped toward it and twisted it free. Her leg held when she leaned against the tree limb and took a few steps forward. She knew she needed to keep moving.

Her pack felt like a boulder bouncing against her back with each hobbled step she took. The sound of the raging river grew faint as she walked as quickly as she could away from the riverbank. The water could have taken her a mile or more downriver. She'd had an idea what direction to travel before she'd jumped in. Now, she was clueless. If Barba's map was right, the river flowed east toward the ocean. If she kept moving in her current direction, she should be in the right area. Then it was just a matter of finding the clearing in the forest where Ethet was supposed to be.

The trees creaked and groaned as she walked on. Her clothes stuck to her body and sweat trickled down her back. Her shoulder, arm, and leg throbbed with each step. She unhooked her water flask and took a drink. Light shone through the canopy. She considered climbing one of the trees to get a better look around, but thought better of it when she tried to step forward without the support of the tree limb. Pain shot up her thigh. Clutching the makeshift cane, she readjusted her backpack and started walking again at a slow, steady pace. Her boots made crooked indentations in the muddy forest floor, and her mind wandered to the children she'd seen along the riverbank. *Where were the Nala taking all those children?* she wondered, knowing whatever the destination, it wouldn't be good.

Out of the corner of her eye, she saw a treetop sway in the distance. She broke into a limping run. Branches dug into her clothes and skin as she ran. Her vision blurred slightly, and she imagined a gap in the thinning trees. She wiped her eyes and stumbled out of the forest into an expansive meadow of bright-yellow flowers. The meadow dipped, and she tripped on a rock, tumbling down a flower-laden hill. Her head smacked against a rock and her vision clouded to black. A distant hissing scream filled the air.

CHAPTER NINE

"Are you sure she's sound in her head?" The voice trembled slightly with age. "Only an utter fool would travel through that forest alone."

"What does the presence of her orb and markings tell you? She's a Warrior Sister." The familiar voice held a hint of respect. Nat's eyes fluttered open.

"Warrior Sister," the other voice grumbled. "Whatever she is, she risked exposing this House."

"Hello, Sister Natalie." Ethet loomed over her. Her glasses magnified her large brown eyes, and she gave Nat a curious smile. Her long fingers curled around Nat's orb, and she placed it on a table covered with bandage clippings and ointments.

"Sister Ethet, am I glad to see you." Nat lifted her head. She noticed a tiny wisp of a woman, hardly taller than Marie Claire, standing at the footboard of the wooden bed.

"You'd better be," said the woman. A puff of white hair surrounded her wrinkled face. She pursed her thin lips. "She saved your life."

"Sister Natalie, this is my predecessor, Sister Ethes Fairbog. She is the Head Sister of this Healing House."

"Healing House?" Nat scanned the narrow room. The walls made of smooth chinked logs gave it a warm glow.

"Not just any Healing House," Head Sister Ethes Fairbog said with a huff. She skirted a spindly chair and peered into Nat's eyes. "It is the First House. We rebuilt it. Now stick out your tongue," the tiny woman demanded. Nat immediately complied. Ethes grasped it between thumb and index finger and pulled it up and down. Nat gave Sister Ethet, who stood a good foot and a half taller than Sister Ethes, a questioning look. Ethet pursed her lips but said nothing. When Nat's tongue was safely back in her mouth, she sat up. A sharp pain shot through her head. She gingerly touched the edge of a bandage taped to her forehead.

"She'll survive," Ethes said dismissively. The little woman wrenched open a door set in the wall opposite Nat's bed and hustled out of the room.

"Don't mind her, Natalie." Ethet pulled the chair close. "She's always had a rough bedside manner. Would you try standing for me?" Nat nodded and slowly swung her legs over the side of the bed. She glanced down and noticed she was wearing a loose green tunic. A bandage covered her lower leg. She grasped Ethet's strong hand and stood slowly.

"You've been unconscious for about two days. Expect dizziness with that bump on your head."

Nat clutched Ethet's other hand and fell back abruptly on the bed. "Dizziness, definitely dizziness," she said, lowering her head. Ethet slid her arm behind Nat's neck and guided her head to the pillow.

"Barba never said anything about a House when she told me where I might find you. I thought Mudug destroyed all the Houses." Her head spun.

"So Barba sent you," Ethet replied. She lifted Nat's hand and pressed her fingers to her wrist. "No, no," she said when Nat opened her mouth to speak. "You will have plenty of time to explain your presence. Rest for now." She gently placed Nat's hand on the woolen blanket.

"But what about this House?" Nat persisted.

Ethet's silvery eyebrows arched above her glasses as she gave into Nat's questioning. "Head Sister Ethes disappeared a few years before Mudug orchestrated his plot to murder Emilia and destroy the Houses. I believe she sensed the precarious nature of those times better than others, including myself. But her disappearance didn't surprise any of the Sisters given her area of practice."

"Area of practice?" Nat's brow furrowed and a stinging pain rippled down her face.

"Sister Ethes is the foremost expert on treatment of those bitten by the Nala," Ethet said. "She's devoted her life to helping the duozi. When she vanished, I assumed she'd ventured too far into Nala territory in hopes of finding them. Turns out I was right, but the end I imagined for her was thankfully not what happened." Ethet gave Nat a smile.

"Before we fled to your world, a duozi, beaten within an inch of her life, arrived at my Healing House. Neighboring villagers had attacked her when she'd passed too close to the boundaries of their town." A somber look passed over her face. Nat's muscles tightened and her thoughts strayed to Soris. "Duozi have never been accepted by our culture, and Mudug's added fuel to the fire by spreading lies about their connections with the Nala," Ethet explained.

"I didn't know it was that bad for the duozi," Nat whispered.

Ethet continued her story. "Before the girl died, she told me of an enormous wooden house in the middle of a field of yellow flowers with an old Sister who took duozi in and cared for them. I knew immediately that she meant Sister Ethes. Unfortunately, the circumstances of the times prevented me from finding Ethes. After we passed into your world, I relied on Annin to search for her during her infrequent excursions into Fourline. She found the House last winter. Once you broke the tracking spell, it made sense for me to come here and help my old colleague."

A knock sounded and the door opened. Annin walked into the room with a steaming bowl in her hand. A strip of blue-tinted leather held back her curly hair, exposing both her human and Nala eyes.

"The Head Sister said she was finally awake." Annin handed the bowl to Ethet. "Took you long enough," she said to Nat.

"Good to see you, too, Annin," Nat said weakly. She swallowed the spoonful of broth Ethet offered her.

"You'd better have a phenomenal explanation." Annin crossed her arms and scowled.

"For what?" A throbbing pressure pulsated in Nat's head. She wasn't sure if it was the bump or the realization that Soris' problems as a duozi extended far beyond fighting off the Nala's venom.

"Why you led a Nala to our boundary."

"Annin, she just woke up," Ethet scolded and held another spoonful in front of Nat.

Nat pushed it away and broth dribbled onto her tunic. "I didn't lead a Nala anywhere. The creature was chasing me, and I jumped into a river to shake it off." She took a few quick breaths, trying to settle her racing heart. "And what boundary are you talking about?"

"Is that what I think it is?" Annin asked, ignoring Nat's response. Her eyes locked on Nat's orb.

"It's mine," Nat said, reaching protectively for her orb. Ethet placed another spoonful of broth in her mouth.

Annin let out a low whistle. "If you went to the trouble of making that, you must have a good reason for coming back to Fourline."

"Annin, leave Sister Natalie to rest." Ethet rose from the bedside. "We'll have plenty of time to ask questions later."

"No, let her stay." Nat slumped back in her bed. Annin could pepper her with as many questions as she wanted as long as she told her what had happened to Soris.

Annin shrugged and plopped into the chair. She reached for the spoon and shoved broth into Nat's mouth.

Ethet looked skeptically at her. "Make certain she rests, Annin," she said, her eyes narrowing.

"Of course," Annin replied innocently.

"Hmm . . ." Ethet paused once more at the door, looking at the two young women so vastly different from one another, then closed the door behind her.

CHAPTER TEN

"Is he here?" Nat asked.

Annin pursed her lips. "He's here." She fidgeted with the spoon in the bowl.

"Is he . . . ?"

"Is he what? Fine? Normal? No, at least not what you'd consider normal. He's a bit more on the Nala side than I am." Annin gestured to her face. "He's much better at communicating with our little friends, and his reflexes are, well, amazing. But enough about him, why are you here?"

"I'm here because of him," Nat said, wondering who the "little friends" were.

"You came back for Soris?" she asked with a note of surprise in her voice.

"I messed up." Nat stared at the rough-hewn planks of the ceiling. She filled Annin in on her wound, her dreams, and her training with Barba. Her voice caught when she told her about killing the Nala.

"And you're sure you didn't behead it?"

"Yes, I'm sure," she said. "Do you really think I'd forget doing something like that?"

"That's a problem. For both of you." Annin pushed the chair away, and it scraped the worn wooden floor. "I need to tell Ethet about this. Why don't you get some . . . Well, some rest," she said and awkwardly patted Nat's head.

Nat's vision began to blur slightly. "Annin, what about Estos and Andris? Where are they?" she asked, wanting to distract herself with more information before Annin left her alone.

"North. They went north to meet with Gennes and his camp of rebels." Annin turned toward the door and paused. "Andris doesn't hate you, by the way. You did the right thing when you brought Soris through."

"That's hard to believe after what happened," Nat said, feeling the familiar crush of guilt.

"You saved his brother, Nat. How could he be angry with you?"

Nat stared at the ceiling. Her lids grew heavy. "He'll find a way to be angry with me. He always does."

"It's not what Andris thinks that matters, though, is it?"

Nat's eyes fluttered closed, and Annin's words echoed in her mind.

When Nat awoke, an orange glow filled the small window across from her bed. She eased the cover off and sat up. The room stayed in place instead of swirling in a dizzy spin. *That's an improvement,* she thought. She clutched the back of the chair and stood.

She limped to the window and gasped. In front of her spread a massive garden. Trellises covered in vines provided cover and shade for row upon row of herbs, flowers, and vegetables. People worked the rows, pulling and moving the rich soil with small hand tools. The three-storied Healing House encircled the garden like a massive log fortress. How had Head Sister Ethes rebuild this House?

Clean mended clothes hung from a hook on the back of the door. She removed the loose tunic and dressed. Her fingers fumbled with the buckle on her belt. She eased open the door to her room and found a common washroom halfway down the hall lit by high, narrow windows. She splashed cold water on her face, avoiding the bandage on her forehead. The remaining grit from her ride down the river fell to the bottom of the washbasin. Her hair was full of tangles, which she tried to smooth out with her fingers as she peered at her reflection in the dull mirror.

When she opened the door, she scanned the hall and froze. Soris stood under one of the windows. His sinewy arm was pressed against a rough-hewn log wall. He stared at a beam stretching across the ceiling. With his chin tilted up, his blond hair brushed his shoulders. A whirlwind of emotion passed through her as she unabashedly stared at him. She wanted to call out to him and run away at the same time. She pressed her trembling hands to her sides and stepped into the hallway. Soris dropped his gaze and his eyes met hers.

"Hello, Natalie." He wore a shirt of brown fabric with a notch at the neck exposing blue skin. Her heart lurched at the sight of a Nala eye marring his face. "So it's true." He walked toward her with long strides.

"What's true?" she asked, struggling to find her voice. His beautiful green eye and the Nala eye blinked. *This is my fault,* she thought as she stared at his face. She glanced at the floor, feeling wretched.

"You're a Sister now." He regarded Nat's orb hovering over her head.

She looked up at it and let out a bitter laugh. "Yes, but a little late to do either of us any good." She reached for his hand, readying an apology. Two of his fingers were fused together into a point. Shocked by the sight of his transformed hand, she dropped hers as if it were made of lead. Soris' expression soured and he looked away.

"It's in the past." He crossed his arms, tucking his deformed hand under his other elbow, hiding it from her view. "If you hadn't brought me through to Ethet, I wouldn't be alive. Thank you for that, Sister." His voice held a formal tone.

"Soris, I didn't know how much danger we were in from the Nala." Her heart felt sick when she saw the cold expression on his face.

"It doesn't matter, Natalie." He turned away and moved down the hall. Nat fell in step next to him, not knowing what else to do. She wished she could rewind the last few moments. He must think she was horrible, the way she pulled her hand back.

They passed under an arched doorway. "Ethet sent me to get you," he said curtly. He gave her a sideways glance. "Why are you here?"

Nat's throat tightened. She couldn't meet his eyes and pretended to examine a frieze of the sun, the Healing House emblem, carved into the wall. The last thing she wanted to do at this moment was tell Soris what a huge mess she'd made.

"I think Ethet can explain it better than I can. It's complicated," she said, hating that she was evading his question but not knowing how to explain the problem without fouling things up even more with him.

He pinched his full lips together. "Complicated? It must be to bring you back to Fourline."

The comment stung Nat. She bit her lower lip, knowing she deserved much worse. They walked in awkward silence down more hallways and up flights of stairs. Soris paused frequently, letting her catch up or politely helping her manage the stairs with her wounded leg. But his hand would drop away as soon as she'd balanced herself. She tried to focus on the changes in him instead of his coldness toward her. She had no recollection that he was so fast. She was always the one who'd waited for him when they were running through the forest.

They reached an enormous meeting room. Massive log beams criss-crossed the ceiling, and thick wooden posts rose high from the floor to the curved supports. Portraits hung on the walls, and Nat scanned their faces as she walked past.

"Who are these women?" she asked, examining a few of the por-traits. Maybe talking about something ordinary would help ease the tension.

"Different Sisters, apprentices, and temporary students of the Houses. The portraits were salvaged from the ruins of other Houses, and Sister Ethes had them smuggled here. Cassandra's here somewhere," Soris said as he drew closer to a small portrait. "Here she is." Cassandra's image, free of the flaming scar, stared back at Nat.

"I would never have guessed this was her." She looked at the Warrior Sister's confident expression. A wave of sadness swept over Nat as she thought about the contrast between the portrait and the insane woman living in the mining pit at Gennes' camp. Wanting to move on, she studied the next portrait in a large gilt frame. She stopped short.

"Soris, who is this?" Nat asked in wonder as she stared at the portrait of a raven-haired girl with startling blue-gray eyes. Her heart beat a little fast.

Soris' voice broke. "That's Estos' sister, Emilia. She apprenticed with each—"

"Soris, that's the woman!" Nat said excitedly. She reached for his arm.

"What woman?" He glanced at her hand tightly clutching his sleeve.

"The one in the Chemist's lab, the one who helped me. That's the woman who helped me destroy the tracking device."

"Are you certain?" he asked, his voice growing as excited as hers.

"Absolutely."

"We need to tell Ethet—now." He wrapped his hand around hers and pulled her, limping as fast as she could, out of the room.

CHAPTER ELEVEN

"Are you certain it's Emilia?" Ethet eyed Nat. Nat and Soris sat in Ethet's private quarters around a square wooden table inlaid with a golden sun.

Nat nodded, and Ethet settled back in her chair. "If true, this is the most amazing news," she said. She tapped her fingers against one of the sun's rays.

Soris stood and gripped the back of his chair. "We need to get word to Estos. He needs to know."

Ethet's expression held a hint of irritation as she replied, "Annin will be here momentarily. She is the most successful in dream-speaking with Estos. I'm sure she'll do everything she can to inform him. But right now, I have a more pressing concern."

"What?" Soris released the chair, and it tipped slightly from the force.

"The Nala that bit you," Ethet said. Nat felt her cheeks flush.

The door, carved with two identical suns, opened, and Annin stepped into the room. She wore a sleeveless green tunic over a tight shirt that covered her neck. Soris spilled the information about Emilia before Annin could even sit down. She stared at him in disbelief and asked him to repeat what he'd said.

"Emilia? In the Chemist's quarters?" She looked dumbfounded when she turned to Nat after Soris finished speaking.

"Yes," Nat confirmed. "I saw her."

"I'll try to reach Estos tonight." Annin walked toward a window and gazed out the sectioned panes. "After all these years . . ." Her voice trailed off. "What about Nat and Soris' problem?" Annin asked, now facing Ethet.

"I was getting to it," Ethet said, looking pointedly at Soris. "As I was saying, Soris, the Nala that bit you was not finished."

"What do you mean 'not finished'? Natalie killed it."

"She didn't behead it." Annin broke in. "It left remnant in her through a small wound that won't heal, and it's getting into her dream space. That's why she's here."

"Wait, let's back up a second," Nat said, wanting to explain that there was more to her coming back than saving her own skin.

"You didn't behead it?" Soris turned to her before she could say anything else. His eyes were wide with disbelief.

"No, I didn't behead it. I didn't know I was supposed to. Now I do," she said, keeping her voice level. She met his eyes. *He thinks I'm an imbecile.* She felt as if they were a million miles apart when she saw his confused expression. For a moment, the only sound was the ticking of the glass-encased clock on Ethet's mantel. Soris shifted away from Nat and stepped toward the window.

"It explains some things, doesn't it, Sister Ethet?" he said after a moment. "Why the venom keeps progressing through my body despite your efforts. Why I have the dreams about the creature."

Ethet nodded.

"You have the dreams, too?" Nat asked, wanting desperately to engage with him.

"Nat let the Nala into her dream space." Annin leaned against the window casing. Her face held a knowing look. Nat longed for a strip of duct tape to bind over her mouth.

"Why would you do something so stupid?" Soris stormed over to Nat. "Don't you know what could happen to you?"

"I didn't mean to. It looked like you," she explained, feeling more and more defensive.

"How did it look like me?" He gestured to his body. "Am I that repulsive in your eyes?"

"Children!" Ethet yelled, and the volley came to a halt. "And yes, I do use that word in the pejorative sense." She pressed her hands against the table. "Stop acting like fools bickering amongst yourselves. We have a problem. Work toward a solution."

"What do I need to do?" Soris turned his back on Nat and addressed the question to Ethet.

"Not you, me. It's my problem, not yours." Nat touched his shoulder. He flinched, and she dropped her hand.

"Wrong. It is my problem." He brought his hand to his chest. "Do you understand what remnant does to a duozi?" His single green eye bored into her.

"Yes," she replied. "Why do you think I came back?"

Ethet cleared her throat. "Sister Natalie has less of a connection with the Nala than you, Soris. Her tie will allow her to find it, and as a Warrior Sister, she is unquestionably the better choice to sever the neural path. We know remnant and proximity to the Nala can impact a duozi's behavior."

"Don't even think about telling me not to go, Sister." Soris' voice was cold. "Natalie may have become a Warrior Sister and walked through the eastern forest on her own, but she's not attempting any of this without me."

"You're free to make your own decisions when they don't pose a risk to others. But your tie may create significant problems." Ethet looked over her glasses at Nat. "Sister Natalie, do you want Soris to accompany you?"

Nat felt as if a heavy weight had descended upon her. What did she want? The thought of searching for the Nala on her own was beyond daunting, but what if something happened to Soris? She would never forgive herself.

"What if I go?" Annin plucked at the edges of her sleeves. "In case Soris gets overwhelmed," she added.

Ethet considered her apprentice. "You would be in a unique position to assist him, Annin, but the choice is yours."

"They are better off with me than without. I'll go."

"Sister?" Ethet addressed Nat.

"That works for me," Nat said, feeling relieved Annin had volunteered to come.

"It's settled then. Nat's wounds will have healed sufficiently by tomorrow. There is no time to waste with this task."

"We leave tomorrow, first thing." Soris stood.

"One question." Nat held up a hand. "How do I find the body?"

"Your dream space, Sister. Your dream space." Ethet tapped her forehead. "You will grant Soris and Annin access so they can assist you and then"—she paused and placed her chin on her folded hands—"you will let in the Nala."

Nat propped herself up on her elbow on the lumpy bed. Her muscles felt rigid and tight. She held the vial of sleeping syrup in one hand.

"This will put me in a dream state?" she asked Annin, who perched on the edge of a chair shoved next to the bed.

"Your head will hit the pillow before the last drop slides down your throat." Annin gave her a mischievous smile. Nat flicked her gaze to the end of the bed, where Soris sat, waiting to create a physical link with Annin before they approached Nat's dream space.

"Are you ready?" he asked. Deep lines were etched into his face. Nat stifled an urge to reach out and brush her hand against his skin to ease the lines.

"Yes." She took a deep breath. He set one hand on Annin's arm and slipped his other hand around Nat's bare ankle. His touch sent a shiver through her body, and she felt a flush spreading across her cheeks. She lifted the vial to her lips and swallowed the sweet liquid in one gulp, hoping neither Annin nor Soris had seen her blush. Her eyelids grew heavy and her arms relaxed beneath her. The last thing she heard before slipping into her dreams was Annin saying, "Why, Soris, I believe you've made her blush."

Yellow flowers hung from vines, cascaded over boulders, and covered each inch of ground under and around Nat's body. She opened her eyes and inhaled deeply, smelling the crisp scent of the meadow. She gazed past the field of flowers toward the forest, reached for a vine dangling near her face, and started to climb.

Nala after Nala jumped from the treetops at the edge of the meadow. Hissing filled the air as she climbed, hand over hand, into the sky. When she looked down, the flowers evaporated and the Nala raced into the center of the field toward the vine.

Her hands and arms burned from exertion. She pulled herself higher and higher into the sky, away from the dream. The vine shook violently, but Nat refused to look down. Pressing upward, she saw the distant outline of the border to her dream space. A hissing sounded beneath her, and she brought her heel down onto the face of the Nala before propelling herself over the ledge.

"Let us in—now!" Annin called. She and Soris hung from separate vines on the opposite side of Nat's dream barrier. Soris kicked at the Nala springing up the vine.

"Come in!" Nat shouted and grabbed each of their hands. Soris and Annin leapt over the stone partition. Nat imagined the protective beams of light. The beams shot to the sky, and the three jumped away from the ledge to avoid having the hot lights sear their skin.

Nat relaxed her hold on Soris' hand. He let go immediately and averted his eyes from hers. The light from the ledge cast odd shadows on his face. *I've got to get through this, and then I'll fix everything with him,* she thought as she watched him scan her dream landscape.

Annin dusted off her tunic. "I hate climbing," she grumbled.

"Sorry my subconscious wasn't more accommodating." Nat gave her a withering glare.

Annin shrugged. "I suppose it could have been worse. At least it wasn't difficult getting Soris here. I thought it would be more of a challenge." She focused on Soris. "Have you been here before?"

"Not here, no," Soris said too quickly. "I saw a piece of one of her dreams after I was bitten, that's it." Now it was his turn to blush, and Nat gave Annin a confused look, wondering what had made Soris look so uncomfortable.

"Must just be that friendly connection between you two that made bringing him along so easy. Am I right?" Annin lifted her beautifully arched brows.

"How am I supposed find the Nala again, Annin?" Nat asked, wondering why she was teasing them. She had to know how angry Soris was with her. *Just look at him,* she thought. His once open face was set in a scowl, and dark circles shaded the skin under his eyes.

"Just like we discussed. Start with protection." The humor faded from Annin's expression.

A transparent column formed around the three of them. Nat stood on tiptoe and touched the smooth ceiling, checking its structure. She released her orb from the confines of her pocket.

"I still can't believe you actually made one of those," Annin said with a hint of envy.

"Barba made it," Nat corrected. "I made it my own." She held up her hand and the ball spun around her fingers.

"Can we get on with this?" Soris asked.

"Look who's in a rush," Annin quipped. "You of all people should enjoy what time you have here." His cheeks flamed again.

Annin's Nala eye contracted and she focused intently on Nat. "Can you feel the Nala out there?" she asked her as she gestured to the dream landscape.

"I feel something. Like something's pulling on my shoulder." She gently rubbed her wound and peered through the column, past the beams of light shining along the ledge.

"I can feel it, too." Soris joined her and looked as if he saw something in the distance. "Be careful, Natalie," he whispered. She pressed her fingertips against the column and focused her eyes in the direction Soris was looking. Her other hand brushed his, and she felt his fingers twitch.

"Allow it in and use your dream space abilities to force yourself into its thoughts immediately. You have to visualize what you want and keep control, or you risk letting it into your own thoughts," Annin said, grabbing Nat's hand.

A single Nala materialized on the opposite side of the ledge. Nat took a sharp breath when she saw the gaping wound in its abdomen. Steeling herself, she let her barrier lights dip.

"Come in." Her voice was a hoarse whisper.

The Nala flew over the ledge and slammed into their invisible protective cage with enough force that it shook with the impact. Nat gasped and fell against Soris as a fiery sensation spread through her shoulder.

"Soris, take her hand! Help her keep control!" Annin ordered above Nat's frantic breaths. The Nala paced around the exterior of the column, poking and probing for a weak spot. Soris, eyes full of pain, clutched his arms across his chest.

"Soris!" Annin yanked at his arm. "Take her hand now!"

Soris shook his head as if trying to wake himself. He pried Nat's hand from her side and squeezed her fingers. Nat slowed her breathing.

"Control it, Nat." Annin's voice was barely a whisper. "Remember what you can do in this space. Make it reveal itself to you."

Nat glanced at Soris. His face was contorted, but he managed a nod, encouraging her. She held tightly to both Soris' and Annin's hands and looked directly at the Nala and imagined peering into its thoughts. The creature ceased pacing and opened its wide glistening mouth.

Darkness descended over the dream space. Nat felt Soris and Annin slip away. Huge waves tossed her about, lifting her up into their violent foamy crests before dragging her down again. Black rock loomed in front of her, and a wave spit her onto a narrow, rocky ledge high above the ocean. Below her, the waves swirled and beat against the jagged rock cliff. Rock formations, erupting through the surface of the ocean, rose higher and higher into the dark-blue sky. She placed her hand against the stone to steady herself. The eruptions stopped, and sharp pinnacles now formed a barrier around the cliff.

Nat turned away from the ocean and faced a dark opening in the cliff face. Water droplets fell from the ceiling, trickling down the back of her neck when she entered the dim cave. She stepped carefully to avoid falling onto the craggy, razorlike rocks bordering a worn path. A blue light deep in the cave pulled her farther and farther in, until she reached an expansive cavern with a peculiar pool set in the center. She stared at the pool, riveted by a white flash under the smooth surface of the water. The sound of dripping water echoed around her.

She turned in a circle, scanning the high cavern walls. Little pockets of blue light emanated from them. A single light, halfway up one wall, shone with a bright, beckoning hue. She found the base of a narrow trail chiseled into the rock and set out for the light. The trail wound around the cavern, leading her upward, past narrow openings. She peered into a few of the dark gaps, but a sensation pulled her onward toward the special light.

When she reached the source of the light, she found an entrance similar to the dozens she'd passed. A wave of cold air washed over her when she ducked into a passage leading to a small chamber. Someone or something had chiseled a bench into the wall on the opposite side of the chamber. The body of the Nala Nat had killed on the riverbank was lying on the bench.

She approached cautiously from the side, pulling her dagger free from her belt. Her heart pounded as she held her dagger above the inert Nala. Sweat trickled from her forehead down her cheek and landed on the Nala's smooth head. Its eyes flew open. One silver eye and one with familiar green and brown flecks stared at her. The Nala's face transformed, taking on Soris' features. Her dagger clattered to the floor.

"Break from its thoughts, Natalie! Remove it from your dream space!" Annin's urgent command echoed in the chamber. The chamber grew blurry and Nat found herself in total darkness. She clenched her jaw and thought of the crashing waves barreling against the cliff. A wave bursting with blue light formed in front of her. The Nala tumbled from the crest of the wave onto another wave Nat imagined in her mind. Water poured over Nat as she ran next to the wave, propelling it along until it crashed into the ledge of her dream space. The Nala disappeared the moment it passed over the barrier on the crest of the wave. Her protective lights shot up. Silence replaced the roar of the water. She stumbled from the ledge into the emptiness of her dream space, realizing she was completely alone.

CHAPTER TWELVE

Sun burst through the window of her room. Nat opened her eyes. The cheerful light did nothing to erase the dark images from her mind. Annin barged in and set a steaming mug on the table.

"Compliments of Ethet. Drink up, we're leaving shortly."

Nat sat up, rubbing her eyes. The tea tasted like algae mixed with soy sauce. She forced a few gulps before standing and stumbling toward her clothes hanging from a hook behind the door.

"How much of the Nala's thoughts and my thoughts did you see in my dream space?" Nat asked warily as she pulled on her boots.

"Enough." Dark circles hung under Annin's eyes, and Nat wondered how much sleep she'd had after she'd left Nat's dream space.

"What about Soris?" Her fingers caught in the leather laces, and she silently hoped Soris hadn't seen the Nala when it had opened its eyes.

"You'll need to ask him. He wasn't too communicative when we broke the connection to your dream space."

Nat's heart sank. Annin tossed her a leather bag. She caught it with one hand and swung the straps over her good shoulder. She grabbed her orb and tucked it into the inner pocket of her cloak.

Annin led Nat down the hall to a set of thick wooden doors emblazoned with the emblem of the sun. When she pushed them open, the hallway flooded with light. Even at this early hour, dozens of people, young and old, tended the gardens that grew just beyond the door. The looming fortlike walls cast geometric-shaped shadows over the gardens. Nat followed Annin down a twisting stone path that bisected the rows of plants. A woman with brown plaited hair looked up from a mound of slender-leaved stalks and watched them pass. Annin gave her a curt nod. The woman's hand holding the harvested stalks formed a perfect tapered tip. Nat quickened her pace.

"Does she make you nervous?" Annin asked, hopping over a stray rake.

"No, just mad."

"Good, you'll need that anger where we're going."

"Have you ever seen the cavern from my dream before?"

"No. But based on the pinnacles in the sea, we know where it is. Two days' journey from here will get us to the coast . . . That is, if you don't slow us down." She nodded respectfully to a pair of Sisters conversing with a duozi boy whose only Nala feature was the bluish tint of his skin.

"You don't need to worry about me," Nat said. "My leg is good. Whatever Ethet and Ethes did worked. Soris is kind of slow, though, he couldn't keep up with me when I was here before."

Annin laughed.

"What's so funny?" They passed under an open-air walkway. Stone replaced the wood, and worn carvings covered a section of half walls. Nat ran her fingers over a frieze of flowers. She recognized the flower with the small petals. They were the same ones in the meadow near Benedict's house and the field where she'd hit her head days before.

"Soris!" Annin beckoned him as he and Ethet emerged from behind a stone pillar. Soris and Ethet joined them. "Nat's worried you might not be able to keep pace with us."

"I'll do my best not to slow you down, Sister," he said as he adjusted the strap of a satchel over his shoulder. Nat mouthed a sarcastic "thanks" to Annin.

"All of you must travel swiftly." Ethet gave each of them a stern look. "Once you emerge from the safety of the meadow, you'll be in Nala territory. You have the map in your head, Soris, correct?"

"Head Sister Ethes gave it to me this morning," Soris answered.

"Good." Ethet nodded. "Traveling through the Meldon Plain is the most secure route. The Nala won't venture anywhere near the flowers. You must rest before you leave the plain and enter into the southern tip of the forest for the coast." She looked at each of them in turn, letting the admonition settle in. "You'll have no safe place to stop once you enter the forest. If the Nala are bringing duozi into the woods like Natalie said, they will have sentinels looking for escapees. You'll travel north once you reach the coast. I know the route adds more time to the journey, but I believe you'll sense the Nala better in the open area near the sea."

"Sense them, Sister?" Nat asked.

"Soris and Annin can tell if Nala are near," Ethet explained. "Stay close to them, Natalie. Once you arrive at the cliff opening, it will be you who must lead them. Based on what Annin told me, you controlled your dream space and the Nala despite the remnant in you. Soris, like so many other duozi infused with remnant, would never be able to control a Nala without assistance if it entered his dream space." Nat looked past Ethet toward Soris. His jaw tightened. "Your success in your dream space suggests that you will be able to maintain control of your thoughts when you do encounter the Nala."

"I won't let the Nala control me, either, Sister." Soris interrupted Ethet before she could continue.

She folded her hands together and shook her head. "With more time, training, and treatment, possibly, Soris. But right now, I can't be certain you will be able to maintain yourself once in the cavern. Rely on Sister Natalie and Annin if you feel yourself fading." Ethet handed Annin three vials of yellow liquid. "Pure meldon-flower extract. Drink it before entering the cavern. It offers some, though not complete, protection against the effects of the Nala venom." Without comment, Annin tucked them into a pocket in her tunic and buttoned the pocket closed.

Ethet placed a sheathed sword in Nat's hands. "Natalie, this sword is very old, designed by the first Warrior Sisters. They used it for the efficient beheading of the Nala. It was among a collection of items Ethes saved from one of the Warrior Houses." Nat removed the sword from its sheath. Sunlight glinted off the sharp blade. A delicate vine-and-spear pattern was engraved above the fine edge. "If the Nala see it, their response will be . . . aggressive."

"They're always aggressive, Sister." Nat gently touched her thumb to the blade. A drop of blood welled into her fingernail.

Ethet watched Nat sheath the sword. She gestured toward two Sisters guarding a stone stairway extending up the exterior wall of the House. The Sisters stepped away from the stairs, and Soris flew up the steps before Nat had her foot on the first step. His Nala eye glimmered in the sunlight when he looked down at her.

"What are you waiting for, Sister?" he called from above, a smirk on his face.

"That was fast," she admitted. *What else has changed about him?* she wondered and proceeded up the steps. She glanced down. Annin tucked an orange vial into her cloak and nodded at Sister Ethet as if in agreement. She then pulled the hood of her cloak over her thick hair and ran up the stairs.

"Annin!" Ethet called from below. "Did you reach Estos?"

"No, the trip to Nat's dream space took too much time. I'll try before we enter the forest."

"Don't. It's too dangerous from this distance. You may end up in someone else's dream space."

"I don't think that will be a problem, Sister. He's an easy mark for me," Annin said confidently.

They reached the narrow ledge of the stone wall and made their way down a series of steps and walkways that spanned the exterior of the House. At the base of the steps, a single Sister guarded a wooden door that rose high above her head. She unlatched a series of locks and opened the door onto a blazing yellow meadow, and Annin, Soris, and Nat left the safety of the Healing House behind them.

CHAPTER THIRTEEN

After running at a slow jog for several minutes, Nat glanced over her shoulder and took in the sprawling Healing House. From a distance, it looked like an old Western fort. She wondered why the Nala left the House alone, and why Mudug's men hadn't yet learned of its location.

She stooped to pick one of the tiny yellow meldon flowers that made up the pale carpet covering the undulating meadow. The bowl shape of the small flower consisted of five delicate petals. Multiple stamens made up a fuzzy, circular interior. The flower looked familiar to Nat, as if she'd seen it in her world.

"Nat!" Annin waved to her. She and Soris were already well in front, standing on a low rise. Nat pocketed the flower and hurried to catch up. Despite the bump to her head, gash on her leg, and shoulder wound, she felt good. Ethet's rancid teas and poultices had served their purpose.

"She's slower than a turtle," Annin said when Nat reached the pair and matched their pace.

"No, she's slower than that. Plenty of time to turn back and go home, Sister. Annin and I don't need you," Soris said with his face turned aside. He continued to jog. She glanced at his profile, then skipped ahead and got a glimpse of his face. His green eye flashed and his Nala eye looked foreign and cold.

Her heart ached. She missed the open way he used to speak to her, the smile that never seemed far from his lips, his optimism even during the darkest moments when he'd been in excruciating pain from the porc needles Benedict had stabbed into his hand. Now, the negative emotions rolling off him left her feeling like she'd never known him.

"You never complained about me being slow before," she said quietly, thinking about all the times she'd purposely slowed her pace to let Soris catch up.

He stopped. "I don't make a habit of criticizing Sisters, so I didn't want to make you feel bad." His eyes flickered over her as if she weren't worth more than a glance.

"Really?" She tossed her satchel on the ground. "Let's race and see who feels bad." If she had to prove to him that she was up to the task, so be it.

"You're injured. I'm not racing you," he said dismissively, but the arrogant look on his face that reminded her of his brother Andris disappeared.

"I'm just fine. To that ring of boulders." She gestured to a curve of rock in the distance and took off through the field. She hit her stride and glanced back. Seeing his pinched lips and narrowed eyes a few paces behind, she picked up the pace. Her fear and uncertainty served as fuel, and she sprinted ahead.

"Stop, Natalie! Your leg's bleeding." He raced up from behind. His voice rang with impatience, as if he were speaking to a misbehaving child.

She ignored him and pressed on toward the boulders. A warm, wet sensation spread down her calf. Within arm's reach of the boulder, she caught her foot on a ragged stone and sprawled to the side, barely missing cracking her head against the rock.

"What are you trying to prove?" he yelled as he crouched next to her.

"Why are you so mad at me?" she yelled back, letting out her pent-up emotions. "I know I messed up! I know you must hate me for what happened to you. But I'm here to fix my mistake."

"So you do think I'm a mistake."

"No, I—"

"Don't, Natalie. Your dream space vision said enough. Deep down, you think I'm just like the Nala."

"No," she said adamantly. "Last night, I opened up my mind to the Nala's thoughts to find out where it was. It projected your face onto its body. I had no part in creating that image. It's using you to get to me since we both carry its remnant."

Annin jogged up behind them and tossed Nat's and Soris' satchels at his feet. "Get a mule next time." She eyed Nat's bloody leg. "That's the dumbest stunt I've seen in a while. Use your head, Sister. Do you really want to enter the Nala cavern with blood dripping down your leg?" She dropped to the ground and pulled a clean roll of linen from her bag.

"You shouldn't have come back." Soris watched Annin wrap the bandage around Nat's calf. A look of angry desperation flashed behind his eyes. "You should have stayed home, stayed where it was safe. You don't belong here. You never did."

The words stung. Nat squinted and glanced at the ground to keep him from seeing her wounded expression. "Maybe, but it's not your decision to make, it's mine," she said, fighting to keep tears from welling in her eyes.

Soris clenched his fists and jumped effortlessly on top of the boulders behind her. He disappeared from view without another word.

Annin secured the wrapping around Nat's calf. "If—"

"Don't say anything." Nat held up a hand, then wiped her eyes.

Annin grew silent. She packed up the extra linen and extended her hand to Nat. "We have a lot more ground to cover before dusk." Nat stood, and they walked in silence, watching Soris' figure in the distance.

"You want to know why we're safe in this meadow? Why the Healing House remains undisturbed?" Annin asked.

Nat nodded, not really caring at the moment but thankful for an opportunity to move her mind away from Soris.

"It's the meldon flowers. Nala never venture into the meadow. There's something in the flower that repels them." She extracted one of the vials filled with yellow liquid from her pocket. "The Sisters use the flowers as an herbal remedy to protect them from the venom. The extract lessens the effects of the venom. If administered immediately after a bite, it can even prevent transformation into a duozi."

"Would the extract have helped Soris if I'd gotten him to Ethet right away?"

"Maybe." Annin shrugged. "But it doesn't prevent a transformation in every instance." Nat mulled over the information.

"Why didn't the Sisters plant meldon everywhere?" Nat asked, looking at the sweeping field of flowers in front of them. "They could have kept the Nala away from everyone."

"They tried, but the meldon flower only grows in two places. Here"—she gestured to the field around them—"and on another small plain near Benedict's." She spat his name. "You are walking on one of only two Meldon Plains in Fourline."

Nat stooped and plucked another flower while Annin walked ahead. She twirled it between her fingers, wondering how the little flower and its extract worked to counteract Nala venom. *Would it weaken a remnant tie as well?* she wondered. *Maybe Ethet will let me see how they prepare medicine from the flower when—if—we return to the Healing House.*

Nat stood up and tucked the flower into her pocket. Favoring her good leg, she jogged over the carpet of flowers to catch up to Annin. The spring grass bent under their boots as they walked. She kept glancing at Annin, wondering how she'd ended up a duozi but avoided being infused with remnant.

"Stop looking at me, Natalie, it's wearing on my nerves."

"You don't have active remnant, do you?" Nat shifted the strap of her bag to keep it from digging into her shoulder.

Annin lifted her chin and her curls brushed her shoulders. "No."

"Did someone behead the Nala that bit you?" Nat knew the answer was obvious, but maybe there was another layer she was missing, something that would help her better understand how remnant and Nala venom affected people.

"Yes." Annin looked at Nat as if she were an idiot.

"I'm just trying to understand how someone can be a duozi without remnant."

"The venom, if not counteracted with the right medicine made from the meldon flower, will make anyone a duozi regardless of remnant. But, like I said, you need the medicine immediately after you're bitten. My guardians had a small complication to deal with before they were able to get me to the Sisters for treatment. A few hours' delay and there I was, a duozi for life." She increased her pace.

"What complication? So many Houses were open before Mudug destroyed them," Nat pressed, wondering what had delayed Annin's guardians.

"I was with Benedict when the Nala bit me." Annin's hateful expression sent a chill through Nat. "Enough questions," she said curtly and pulled away, leaving Nat standing by herself in the bed of yellow flowers.

Why didn't I keep my questions to myself? Nat wondered as she scanned the woods, looking for any movement in the treetops. Nat had volunteered to watch the woods the moment the three had reached the edge of the Meldon Plain, knowing neither Annin nor Soris wanted to talk to her. The trees that lined the edge of the meadow stood motionless. She glanced at Annin and Soris, who were on the other end of the rock outcropping that bordered the Meldon Plain and the forest. Their eyes were closed and their hands were clasped. *Are they picking up any sign of the creatures?* Her eyes lingered on their hands, and she felt a twinge of jealousy.

Her thoughts strayed to the evening she'd spent with Soris above the merchant wagon train during her last foray into Fourline. She'd felt so close to him then, after their successful but harrowing venture into Rustbrook. She remembered how his eyes had settled on hers before he'd kissed her. All the fear and stress she'd been carrying had melted away in that one moment. Now, it seemed her only link to him was the Nala's remnant.

A cracking sound brought her attention back to the forest. She watched the motionless woods. *Must have been a branch,* she thought and lowered her crossbow. Her eyes again strayed to Soris. The setting sun glowed against his forehead, leaving the rest of his smooth face in shadow. His now open eyes widened, and he leaned in toward Annin, exposing the blue skin of his neck. He whispered in her ear. She opened her eyes, and they exchanged words that came across as low murmurs to Nat's ears.

Nat cleared her throat. Annin glanced in her direction, then returned to their conversation. Nat looked away, toward the forest, feeling her jealousy grow.

"See anything?" Annin asked when she joined Nat by the tree line.

"Not in the woods, no," she said with a hint of sarcasm.

"We didn't sense any Nala," Annin responded, oblivious to Nat's mood. "But I want to wait before we move into the woods. The Nala could be anywhere. We both feel them better at night, when they're moving freely." Soris walked past Nat and stood near Annin.

"When do you and Soris think it'll be safe to enter?" Nat kept her eyes locked on the forest and kicked a loose stone by her foot.

"Later tonight." Annin brushed an unruly lock of hair away from her eyes. Soris fiddled with a leather quiver of arrows. "I'm taking first watch so I can reach Estos once night falls. We leave after I've made contact with him. Soris, you take second watch."

"I'll take second," Nat said, knowing she wouldn't sleep.

"No," Soris said firmly. "I'll take second watch."

"Frosty," Annin said in an exaggerated tone and shivered. "Both of you can take second watch for all I care." She shrugged and clambered up to the crest of the boulder.

"Soris . . ." Nat turned toward him, but he walked away as if he'd heard nothing.

CHAPTER FOURTEEN

Waves smashed against the black cliff. Nat and Annin stood on a precipice overlooking the churning sea. In front of them, surrounded by swirling water, stood the jagged pinnacles from Nat's dream. She shivered in the wind, thinking how they looked in real life like the teeth of an ancient leviathan. Overcome by vertigo, she took a clumsy step away from the edge of the cliff. Strands of her brown hair lashed her face and stuck to her lips. The ache in her shoulder throbbed with the rhythmic crash of each wave. Annin twisted her fingers around the thick fabric of Nat's cloak, pulling her farther away from the edge.

"Can you feel that?" Nat asked, the vibrations running through the ground to the soles of her leather boots. Annin, wild-eyed, said nothing. They retreated into the forest and found Soris leaning against a decaying tree trunk. His face was ashen when he looked up. Nat felt uneasy as his gaze flickered past her as if she weren't even there. Both he and Annin had grown increasingly tense and distant as they'd approached the coast.

Nat picked up a thin branch and pressed it into the dirt. She drew the pinnacles and the cliff face. "There, that's where the entrance is," she said, pointing near the upper part of the drawing. She glanced up. Soris had a vacant look in his eyes.

"Soris . . . Soris, focus on what Natalie's saying," Annin whispered, waving her hands in front of his face.

"There are so many of them." His voice sounded far away.

"I know." Annin placed her hand on his shoulder.

"So many what?" Nat asked, growing more concerned.

"Nala, I think. They feel different, more like duozi." She glanced past the trees toward the cliff. "Whatever they are, I think we want to avoid them." Annin frowned.

Nat sat back on her heels. The only things she felt were the slight vibration in the ground, the ache in her shoulder, and a twisting in her stomach. Sun filtered through the tree limbs, casting moving shadows on their faces. Soris and Annin both seemed lost in their own worlds with their eyes wide open.

"We'll try to enter from that narrow ledge then?" Nat suggested, her voice demanding they focus on her.

"Hmm?" Both Annin and Soris gazed toward the cliff.

"From the narrow ledge along the rim," she repeated, her voice tinged with concern.

"Along the ledge, yes." Annin blinked frantically. Soris said nothing.

"Are you two okay?"

"Yes," Annin said and blinked a few more times as if clearing away a vision. She reached into her pack and extracted three vials of yellow liquid. "Drink the meldon extract now, I'm not sure we'll have a chance later." She passed vials to Soris and Nat. His fingers shook when he broke the wax seal. Nat tucked her chin and sniffed the vial's contents before drinking. A bitter taste filled her mouth.

"I'll take the lead," Nat said. Soris stared at the ground. "Maybe you should bring up the rear, Annin."

Wordlessly, Soris and Annin followed Nat. She ran at a slow pace past the wind-shaped trees, keeping a narrow buffer of the woods between them and the coastline. Nat heard a muffled cry and glanced over her shoulder. Soris was on his hands and knees. Annin grasped his elbow and helped him rise. He clutched her arm, and a look of desperation flickered across his face. Nat skipped over a jagged trunk toward him, but Annin waved her away.

"We'll catch up. Go on." Annin brushed a streak of dirt from Soris' hip. "Go on!" she barked. Startled, Nat stepped backward, eyes locked on Annin's. Her expression changed from demanding to pleading. Nat bowed her head and retreated.

The soft sound of their voices chased her as she ran. She looked back. Annin pressed an orange-colored vial into Soris' hand. Palm open, he stared at the container. Nat whipped her head around so they wouldn't catch her watching, and a sharp branch dug into her shoulder. She pressed her fingers against the new wound and cursed under her breath.

A few heartbeats later, Annin and Soris were by her side, emerging from the forest edge with her. A rock in the shape of an eroded *L* marked the start of the narrow ledge leading down the black face of the cliff. Nat paused and faced them.

"I think I should go in alone." The roar of the waves tossed her voice into the air. "All I feel right now is the ache in my shoulder, nothing else. But you two, I can tell something has a grasp on both of you."

Soris took a jerky step forward. "We are all going together." His tone let Nat know arguing with him would be pointless. She sighed.

"Fine, but I go first," she said and took off down the cliff path.

The path was little more than a foot wide and covered with loose rock. Nat put one foot in front of the other, wedging her hands into crevices to keep from toppling into the sea. An abrupt set of stairs chiseled into the cliff led them onto a wider switchback. Nat grabbed Soris' hand, and he jumped from the upper stair. He stared at her for a moment, taking in a deep breath. He tightened his fused fingers around hers and then dropped his hand. Annin landed behind Soris, and all three crept toward the shadowy entrance. Annin pulled on Nat's arm and mouthed, "Two Nala" as she pointed toward the dark opening in the cliff face.

Nat nodded and unsheathed her old dagger. She released her orb and poured her thoughts into the sphere, preparing it for a fight. It bobbed unevenly as the wind beat against the cliff, then floated toward the entrance. Nat turned and followed the glowing ball toward the mouth of the cavern. It paused at the entrance and dropped until it hovered a few inches above the rocky ledge. Nat pressed against the rock with her head turned toward the dark opening. She inched forward.

A Nala emerged from the entrance. The orb shot up, driving itself into the creature's chin and sending it crashing against Nat. She buried her dagger deep in its abdomen as it thrashed against her, slamming her into the rock. Soris and Annin swept past. Flickers of violent movement flashed in the entrance. She pushed the Nala away, unsheathed the ancient sword, and cut its head clean off.

Another Nala flew out of the entrance. Soris landed on it, smashing its head against the rocks. Its eyes widened when Nat's ancient sword sliced through the air above it. She struck its neck and the Nala's headless body shuddered, then slumped lifeless against the ground.

"Thanks," Soris gasped. A thump sounded behind them. Annin kicked the headless corpse of a Nala off the cliff. She brought her boot back and the head sailed over the rocks, trailing down the cliff face after the body. Anger flooded her eyes.

"Two, maybe three more farther down the opening," Annin said in a rough voice.

"Where are the rest of them?" Nat asked. "There have to be more than that." She wiped away a smear of blue blood dripping from her cheek and flicked it to the ground. Her orb landed in her trembling hand.

"They're all around, but quieter," Soris said ominously.

CHAPTER FIFTEEN

The raging wind and the bright daylight disappeared the moment Nat, Soris, and Annin passed through the entrance of the cavern. A drop of water landed on Nat's cheek, dripping from a rivulet in the black rocks above her head. Her eyes adjusted to the dim light and the shadows sharpened, revealing a worn footpath.

Their boots sounded softly against the slippery rock. Farther and farther down they wandered into the blackness. Nat felt an odd sense that she'd walked this path before and realized it was the same one she'd seen in her dream space. She peeked over the rigid curve of a fallen stalactite. Soris and Annin knelt next to her. Rhythmic vibrations traveled through the rock floor up their legs. A dim blue light filled the cavern passage.

A boy wearing ragged clothes carried a basin of water down the path in front of them. Droplets splashed onto the ground when he stepped over the rocks. He disappeared around a bend.

Nat lowered her head. "Duozi?" she whispered.

Annin and Soris nodded, a look of confusion crossing Annin's face. A thin sheen of sweat covered Soris' brow and his body trembled. Nat placed a firm hand on his arm, trying to steady him. He took a deep breath and rubbed his hand against his chest. His eyes flickered to Nat, giving her a nervous look.

"You can stay here and keep guard," she offered, knowing he'd refuse to leave the cavern.

"No, we go together," he said, shaking his head.

Nat looked over the edge again, then leapt, landing with a soft thump on the other side. Soris jumped next, followed by Annin. Narrow slits peppered the walls on either side of the path. Cold blue light spilled out from each slit. With her dagger held at an angle, Nat rounded the corner. Her hip bumped into something soft, and she brought her dagger down an inch away from Neas' face.

The boy sucked in a breath. He pressed his back against the wall, away from the tip of the dagger.

"Neas, what are you doing here?" Nat helped the boy to his feet. Annin and Soris shuffled nervously behind her.

"How do you know my name?" His face showed no recognition.

"We met months ago in Yarsburg. Don't you remember?" Nat brushed her fingers against his sunken blue cheek. A puffy welt marred the skin around one of his eyes.

"You were with that man." Neas looked at her suspiciously and edged away. "He came back and told Yester what I was. Mam had to send me away with the soldiers."

"Benedict," Nat fumed. Her anger toward the Hermit burned inside her.

"What soldiers?" Soris bent closer to Neas.

"The ones with the white circles on their sleeves. They took me and two girls that weren't like us." He waved in the direction of Soris' Nala eye. "And they left us at the edge of the forest for them." He jerked his thumb toward the gloomy darkness.

"They took you to the Nala, Neas?" Nat held tightly to his sleeve. Neas pulled his arm away from her.

"It's okay to answer her question. She's not like that man she was with before. She's a friend." Soris placed his hand on the boy's shoulder. Nat gave Soris a grateful look.

"They took me and a whole bunch of others to the Nala."

"Neas." Soris crouched down so he was looking into the boy's eyes. "You said the soldiers took two girls that weren't like us. What do you mean?"

"No bites. They were like her." He tapped Nat's forearm. "But they got bitten later, and now they're like the rest of us down here." Annin and Nat exchanged glances. Nat felt a surge of revulsion.

"Mudug's men are bringing the Nala unbitten children," Nat whispered, horrified by the thought.

"Something feels off here," Soris suddenly said and leaned over the rock, eyeing the path.

Nat tried to stay focused on what lay ahead and not her rage at Mudug and his guards. *How can Mudug do such a thing?* She glanced at the boy with dirt streaks covering most of his exposed skin, and she knew she couldn't leave him behind. "Can you wait here for us? We'll get you out."

Neas shook his head. "I can't leave my friends." His long tangled hair brushed his shoulders.

"Friends?"

"There are lots of us here taking care of them."

"Taking care of who?" Annin's brow creased.

"The Nala," the boy replied.

"Nat." Soris' voice sounded strained.

"Hold on, Soris." She kept her attention focused on the boy. "Neas, what do you mean you're taking care of them?" This whole situation was worse than she could ever have imagined.

"We wash them, clean their wounds . . ."

"Nat." Soris tapped her shoulder. She looked away from Neas to see a Nala emerging from one of the slits in the rock directly in front of her. The creature rolled its head as if it were an infant unable to control its neck muscles. A puckered cut ran down its sternum, but no blood spilled from the wound. Nat grasped her sword and lunged toward it. The Nala didn't flinch when the blade struck its leg. It wobbled across the onyx-colored rock as if it didn't notice the stream of pale-blue blood pouring from its upper thigh. She swung her blade again and severed the creature's head from its body. The Nala stumbled back and landed with its feet sticking out of the slit in the wall. Its head rolled to a stop by Annin's feet. Neas held tightly to Soris' arm as he stared at the headless Nala.

"Why didn't it attack?" Nat lowered her blade and took a cautious step toward the creature.

"They're all like that." Neas picked up his bowl and held it in front of him like a shield. "It takes them a few days to wake up and get nasty when they come out of those caves." He gestured to the slit in the rock.

"Help me pull it back inside." Annin grabbed the Nala's feet. Nat stepped over the body and through the narrow slit. An electric shock of pain stabbed her shoulder, and she clutched her old wound. In the darkness, she fumbled with the Nala's arms, then pulled it inside the small cavern using her good arm. Annin came next, lifting the legs, followed by Neas, then Soris, holding the Nala's head in an outstretched hand.

Nat backed into a rock wall and released her grip on the Nala's slippery skin.

"Nat?" Annin whispered in the darkness.

"I'm okay, hold on." Her orb appeared and light filled the room.

"Oh no . . . no," Annin moaned and dropped to the ground.

The body of a duozi girl was sprawled across a crudely carved alcove. Her thin blue arms stuck out at an awkward angle from her shredded sleeves. Her eyes were open and empty of life.

Nat reached for her hand, her fingers brushing against the girl's cool skin. "She's dead." She gently folded the girl's arms near her chest. The tip of a deep cut was visible above the collar of her tunic. Nat brought her hand over the girl's eyes, closing the lids. Her foot knocked against a basin similar to the one Neas had held tight to his chest. Water sloshed to the ground, pooling around the Nala.

"It must have killed the girl . . ." Soris trailed off. His hands shook, and he threw the Nala's head to the stone floor.

"Neas, look at me." Nat grabbed the boy's shoulder, pulling him out from where he was hiding behind Soris. His eyes were locked on the girl. Nat gently slapped his cheek and he snapped to attention. "How many more duozi are here?"

"Bunches, bunches, and bunches," he whispered. Annin glanced at Nat as she knelt in front of the boy.

"Neas, can you get word to as many of them as you can that we'll help you escape? They need to be prepared to run hard and fast out of this cavern." Nat could never leave a child behind in this nightmare.

He nodded. "Most of them are by the pool." He glanced toward the opening of the tomblike cave.

"We have to find a Nala first, and then we'll help all of you get out. Understand?" The boy nodded again. Nat glanced up. Soris' eyes were closed, and his jaw muscles twitched. Annin bounced on the balls of her feet, her gaze flitting around the room. Both looked unhinged.

"Hey," Nat said sharply. Soris' eyes flew open and Annin settled on her feet. "Stay with me." She turned to Neas. "Are there more Nala here?" she asked, satisfied that she had everyone's attention.

"Mostly sleeping ones." He looked at the body of the Nala at his feet. "Only a few awake ones. The big one left this morning. She took most of the awake ones with her." He trembled when Nat released her grip and immediately grabbed Soris' sleeve. He pressed his face into Soris' stomach. Soris' hand shook as he smoothed Neas' tangled hair.

She? Is there a single female Nala? Nat wondered. She glanced around the small tomb and thought of the other slits they'd passed. *Is this den like a hive?*

"I think we should go now," Annin said and ducked her head through the slit in the rock. She checked the passage for more Nala, then motioned for the others to follow. Nat gently touched the dead girl's cheek, then exited the tomb.

Nat's feeling of déjà vu grew stronger as they followed the path deeper into the cavern. Neas ran in front and gestured when the way was clear. They all stopped when they heard the sound of shuffling and hissing. Soris moved close to Nat, and Annin pressed in behind him with her dagger drawn. Nat peered around the corner of a craggy rock and brought her hand to her mouth in horror.

Dozens of duozi children, some younger and smaller than Neas, circled the base of a naturally formed amphitheater. Their bleeding bare feet shuffled over the ground. Some of them were naked and bruised; others wore nothing but burlap sacks with openings cut for the necks and arms. The mass of hollow eyes and emaciated bodies moved together as if each child's feet were propelled forward by some unseen force. An eerie blue light reflected off the basins clutched in their hands. A few children glanced nervously toward the two Nala guards positioned near a pool ringed by rocks in the center of the amphitheater. Most walked around in circles dead-eyed until it was their turn to approach the pool and fill their basins.

Nat choked on the smell rising from the open cavern. It reeked of the sickly-sweet smell of decay. She watched, unable to move, as the children filled their basins. A few climbed a rough path cut into the rock, while others disappeared into shadowy openings dotting the curved rockface. She dropped her hand away from her mouth and clutched her sword's hilt. *Whatever I have to do, I am not leaving any child in this hellhole.* Nat turned around. Annin's and Soris' expressions told her they were of a single mind.

"The Nala first, then the children," Nat said. Soris lowered his chin in agreement, but he had a gray pallor, and Nat noticed the tremor in his hand had become a serious shake. She swallowed her concern and turned her attention back to the cavern. "There." She pointed in the direction of an opening in the rocky wall above the amphitheater, recognizing the gap from her dream. She felt an odd pulling sensation, but brushed it off and looked squarely at Annin. "We need to take out the two Nala guards."

Annin slid in beside Nat. "Soris and I will take the guard on the left, you take the one on the right."

"I'll take mine out first," Nat added. "I think I can work my way around the children without the Nala noticing." Her shoulder burned as if a thousand tiny pins were stabbing the muscle over and over. *If only we had Andris or Oberfisk as backup,* she thought. She glanced at Soris. Sweat trickled down the side of his face. "Do you think he can do this?" she whispered to Annin.

Annin frowned. "I can feel him struggling against something . . ."

"What about the other Nala? Can they feel you?" Nat glanced nervously at the guards.

"I doubt it, since there are so many duozi in here. I can feel Soris because he's close and I know him. The rest of the Nala, the other duozi . . . They're all mixed-up senses in my head. There is something, though. Something above the duozi and Nala." Annin dug her fingers into her palms. "But I can't tell what it is." She looked up, lifting her head slowly as if it were heavy.

Nat motioned for Soris to join them. Neas crept closer, too. "Stay put," she ordered. Neas nodded and wedged himself behind a rock. Keeping low to the ground, the three of them rounded the chunk of rock separating the path from the amphitheater. Nat joined the flow of the duozi and almost broke down when she saw the gashes and cuts on their bare arms and legs. A few of the children looked curiously at her, but most pretended not to notice. They clutched their basins with rigid hands and shuffled forward.

Nat wove through the ring of children, breathing through her mouth to avoid the overpowering smell of rotting flesh that hung heavy in the air. She paused and peered over a child's head to check the guard's location. A boy stepped too close to her and tripped on her cloak. His basin fell to the ground and rolled end on end, making a tinny sound. A barklike hiss echoed through the cavern. The children froze.

Crouching low, Nat watched the Nala pivot, then rise on tiptoe. The sharp ends of its limbs made no noise as the creature drew silently closer to her hiding spot. A warm puddle appeared next to Nat as the child next to her urinated down his leg. *What have they done to them?* Her anger erupting, she released her orb and rose amid the quivering children.

"Looking for me?" The sphere of white light slammed into the Nala's head, then shot into the air and descended with furious speed, crashing into the creature's face. Hissing echoed across the chamber. The children scattered like leaves in the wind, screaming and clearing the floor. Nat lifted the hilt of her sword chest high and swung the blade. Her shoulder screamed in pain, but she brought her sword across the Nala's neck. Its head toppled to the ground and rolled toward the pool.

Nat sprinted through the fleeing children toward Soris and Annin. Cries bounced off the walls. The body of the other Nala crumpled to the ground, revealing Annin clutching her bloodied dagger behind it.

"Up the path!" Nat cried, gesturing to the narrow walkway cut into the cavern wall.

Annin severed the creature's head and followed Nat, pulling Soris up the walkway with her. The children's confused cries echoed up the wall. Nat glanced over the edge of the path. The children milled about the edge of the amphitheater, still clutching their basins.

"Neas!" she called out. The boy popped out from his hiding place. "Get them moving. Now!" Nat gestured to the children. Neas nodded, then waved his arms wildly in the air and yelled at the other children. They dropped the basins and ran toward him. A few stood frozen in place, looking at the pool. The water churned with flashes of blue light.

Nat turned her attention back to the narrow walkway, hoping Neas would convince the rest of the children to follow him out.

"In here," Nat directed. Her orb disappeared into a slit in the rock a few paces in front of them. She took a deep breath and stepped through the opening.

The orb emitted a dim light, and it took a moment for Nat to see the dead Nala. The rigid corpse was draped over a rocky bed cut into a wall of the tomb. The pulling sensation in her shoulder intensified until it felt like sharp claws were digging into her flesh, tugging her toward the creature she thought she'd killed months ago.

Nat heard coughing behind her. Annin bent over and vomited from the stench. Soris lurched past Nat toward the Nala, his eyes completely glazed over. She reached out to stop him, but he wrestled free of her grip, dropping to his knee before the dead creature. His movements were stilted, as if he were a puppet. He dipped his fingers into a basin lying on the floor and brought them to the rubbery lips of the corpse. Drops of water fell from his fingers and trickled down its chin. He bent to repeat the movement, but Nat wrapped her arms around his torso and pulled him to the side. Her orb spun frantically above them, sending pieces of stone showering onto her head when it struck the ceiling.

"Finish it, Natalie!" Annin called out, struggling to hold herself up against the wall. Nat's arms felt like lead, and Soris broke free. The room grew dim and her orb flickered. Water spilled again from Soris' hands, falling haphazardly over the seeping tissue of the Nala's wound. "Natalie, sever it!" Annin cried.

Her sword felt so heavy. Its tip scraped across the floor as she lifted it in what felt like slow motion before dropping the blade across the creature's neck. The pain in her shoulder exploded when the blade sliced through the Nala's neck. She fell to her knees next to the beheaded corpse and sucked in a deep breath.

The pain subsided, and she sighed in relief. She swallowed and leaned against the damp wall to steady herself. Soris' eyes flickered toward her. His glazed look faded into a look of confusion when he glanced at his damp hands.

A tremor ran through the wall. The ground quaked and a dark crack opened near the Nala's head.

"Annin, Soris, out—now!" Nat yelled in fright as the rock split apart. She grabbed her sword and pushed them to the opening. When Nat exited the tomb, the shaking intensified. Tremors shook the cavern, sending showers of dust and rock into the pool in the center of the amphitheater.

"Help me! I can't carry him," Annin called out. She knelt next to Soris at the edge of the path. Nat lifted his arm and draped it over Annin's shoulder while Soris muttered a string of incoherent words. The women carried him to the base of the walkway.

"I'll find Neas and the other children. You get Soris out," Nat ordered.

Annin hesitated, clinging to Soris' arm.

"Go!" Nat yelled.

Soris lifted his head and pushed his feet erratically against the stone floor. Annin dragged him to the path leading to the entrance. They disappeared behind the rocks, and Nat turned her attention to the quaking amphitheater. She scanned the deserted space as rocks tumbled from the ceiling high above her head. A few small faces peered over the rocks that encircled the open room.

Nat sprinted toward the children hiding among the rocks. The floor shook and water splashed out of the pool. She yelled and motioned wildly for the children to come toward her. Half a dozen ragged duozi jumped from their hiding spots. They ran in her direction, giving the pool a wide berth. Nat jogged behind them and noticed Neas standing near the edge of the amphitheater.

"Annin told me to wait for you!" he yelled over the rumbling. A stalactite crashed to the ground behind him, shattering into hundreds of pieces.

"Lead them out," Nat ordered. Neas grabbed a child's hand and pulled her up the path. The others ran behind like lemmings. Nat sent her orb out into the cavern. It flashed around the space, looking for any more children. The ball narrowly missed a falling spray of rock and returned to her hands.

She was swaying on the quaking ground and had rotated toward the path when a flash caught her attention. The water in the pool bubbled. A white curve breached the surface, and the room filled with a deafening hiss. Two blue Nala shot out of the pool and scrambled toward her on all fours. Their mouths hung open and venom trailed behind them. Nat steadied her sword.

A Nala landed with a thud in front of her. She twisted her hips and kicked the creature, sending it sprawling into the center of the amphitheater, where it hit its head on the floor. Nat edged away as the second Nala approached. The quaking dislodged a huge rock from the ceiling that crashed onto it, knocking it out. Nat exhaled in relief and turned to follow the children, but a sudden gushing noise caused her to whip around.

A stream of water spurted from the pool, and a long white arm slammed against the rocky rim. An enormous gleaming white head with silvery-black eyes broke the surface and locked its hateful glare on Nat. She slashed her sword in the air in warning. Her sleeve rolled down, revealing her markings.

The monstrous creature froze. Its eyes locked onto Nat's markings. Nat watched in horrified fascination as a look of disbelief seemed to cross the creature's face. "Noooo Sisssssssster," it hissed then slithered out of the pool to reveal a huge white body.

Fear gripped Nat and she fled up the path. The creature's hissing echoed around her as she sprinted up the passage, dodging falling rocks. She spotted the light coming in through the cavern entrance and ran even faster. She burst out of the darkness into the blinding daylight and nearly toppled off the ledge into the sea.

Cries sounded above her. Children scrambled up the stairs onto the narrow ledge. Nat jumped onto the steps and lifted the remaining children to the rocky shelf above, yelling for them to move quickly. The cliff face trembled. Nat grabbed the blue arm of a girl stumbling toward the edge. She glanced over her shoulder and watched rocks pour down below them, filling the entrance of the cavern.

"Run!" she cried, knowing rocks would not stop the nightmarish monster she'd seen inside. The dozens of children scurried up the path toward the forest, little hands helping each other. Nat glimpsed Annin's wild hair at the front of the group and looked frantically for Soris.

"Nat!" Soris stood at the tree line, beckoning to her. Relief pushed away her fear and she ran toward him. He grabbed her hand, and they crashed through the woods behind the children.

CHAPTER SIXTEEN

Nat shivered against the chill of the night. She surveyed the field covered with meldon flowers and the little bodies curled against each other for warmth. She wrapped her cloak around the girl standing in front of her. Hair as black as a starless night hung in dirty clumps around her soft face. Nat took her to be older than the other children. The girl had been in the cavern so long, she barely remembered that her name was Tally and had forgotten her age.

"The children disappeared when the sleeping ones woke?" Nat asked. She hated to ask, but she needed to understand what the Nala were doing to the duozi.

Tally nodded and clutched the cloak to her chest. "It happened to my brother," she said. "After his sleeping Nala woke, I didn't see him again."

"What do you mean by his Nala?" she asked gently.

"The one he washed, the one he took care of." Her voice trembled. "My brother was my only family after the guards killed our parents. Now they're all gone."

Nat wrapped her arms around the girl's reedlike body and pressed her close until she could feel the child's heart thudding against hers.

"We're taking you someplace safe now." It was all she could think to say, all she had to offer the child who'd been through so much. She settled Tally on the meadow next to Neas and a flaxen-haired girl with a malformed arm. She arranged her cloak over them and choked back her fury as she took in their blue skin and misshapen eyes. "Sleep." She leaned down and brushed a lock of black hair from Tally's face. The memory of the other child, motionless in the Nala's cavern, flooded her mind. She closed her eyes, feeling only the warmth of Tally's face under her fingertips, a reminder of all the beating hearts sleeping safely in the field.

Clouds passed across the moon. Nat looked over the slumbering children. *Normal children would never have survived that run through the forest,* she thought. But these were not normal children. Someone, something, had taken everything normal in their lives away.

"How are you holding up?" The moon reappeared and its light reflected off Annin's pale skin and faceted eye.

Nat laughed, unable to help herself. "That's the first time you've ever asked me that," she said, thinking of all their encounters. "Maybe I need to raid a Nala den more often."

Annin's stony expression vanished and she smiled.

"Annin." Nat's eyes settled again on the children. "Do you have any idea how all these children ended up in the cavern?"

She nodded and looked out over the field, too. "I spoke with a few of them. Some the Nala took after their transformation, and some were taken to the Nala by Mudug's guards even before they were bitten. Just like Neas said."

The deep, burning sense of outrage flared within Nat. "Why would Mudug do that?"

"I have ideas, and none of them are pleasant."

"What do you think happened to the dead girl we found in the tomb?" Nat asked, wanting to hear Annin's thoughts before she expressed her own.

Annin's eyes narrowed. "Based on what we saw, the Nala are using them somehow to regenerate, I think."

Nat nodded in agreement, shuddering at the thought. The two women continued to look out over the sleeping children with somber expressions. Nat's orb swooped into her hands as Annin touched Nat's shoulder.

"You're different, Natalie Barns. I never met anyone from your world who would've, or could've, done what you did today, even if your motivation was to save your own skin." She stooped to pick a meldon flower. The petals twirled as she rolled the stem between her fingers. "You risked your life to save duozi, not to mention Soris. I guess you really are a Warrior Sister."

Nat fiddled with her orb, uncertain how to respond to the compliment. The sphere circled her hand and then shot into the middle of the field. Nat followed its path and saw Soris pacing back and forth on the other side of the circle of children. She watched with interest when he knelt down to speak to a sleepy child.

"What happened to him in the cavern?" she asked. Soris moved from child to child reassuringly, touching and talking to each one.

Annin frowned. She fixed her eyes on Soris. "There was a presence in that cavern. It's hard to describe, but it felt like hundreds of Nala bundled into one source, pushing into my brain. I had difficulty focusing, and I don't even have remnant. Soris didn't stand a chance."

"But I had remnant, and I didn't lose control like he did." A thought tickled the back of her mind.

"Your senses are different when you're a duozi, Natalie."

"It's good he has you to understand him." Nat picked at her fingernail. "I'll take watch. I'm not tired," she said abruptly. Her orb returned, skimmed up her leg, and hovered near her old wound. She rolled her shoulder, feeling only the memory of an ache now.

"You're exhausted—and a lousy liar." Annin's empathy vanished, and her familiar caustic tone emerged. "But I do need to reach Estos again to let him know what's happened and what we found. He planned to send someone to meet us at the Healing House. Probably wouldn't hurt to let them know there may be some angry Nala in the vicinity. We can rouse the children once I've gotten through to him and whatever lackey he's sent for us." Her voice softened as she glanced down at the children near them. "They need the Sisters."

"They do," Nat agreed. The flowers bent under her soft boots as she stepped back.

"Natalie," Annin called softly, "Soris needs something, too. And it's not me." She turned away, leaving Nat to wonder what she meant.

Nat knelt with one knee up and the other pressed into the ground. Her legs trembled with exhaustion, but the discomfort kept her awake.

Telling Annin she wasn't tired had been a lie. She was completely drained. The dark field blurred in front of her eyes. "Stay awake," she mumbled to herself. Her head drooped again. Images of Soris' hands flashed through her mind. His hands cupped over the Nala, his hand reaching for hers when they fled into the forest, his hand pulling her through the crowd on execution day in Rustbrook.

She stood abruptly, needing to move to stay awake. She could sleep when she returned home. *Home.* The idea that she could return home didn't provide the comfort she expected. Her mind flipped through images of the cavern and the children shuffling around like drones. She stifled a yawn and adjusted a sleeping girl's torn sleeve so it covered her bare blue arm. When she looked at her profile, she saw the face of the dead girl.

Pull yourself together, she thought. She took a deep breath. The cool night air flooded her lungs. But the dead girl's face and her deathly wound stuck in her mind. She thought of Tally's description of how her brother had vanished after his sleeping Nala woke and Annin's belief the Nala were using the duozi to regenerate. *Could the Nala be transferring their wounds, their deaths, to the children?* Nat wondered. Her skin crawled at the thought. *And Mudug's men are bringing duozi and unbitten children to the Nala.*

"I owe you an apology."

Nat swung her crossbow around. The tip of the arrow was inches from Soris' face. His hands shot into the air and he jumped back.

"Don't sneak up on me like that. I could have . . ." She dropped her bow abruptly and it smacked against her thigh.

"I wasn't sneaking," he said defensively. Her orb arced over his head, casting a ray of light onto his blond hair. He dropped his chin.

"I . . . ," they both said at the same time.

"You first." Soris lifted his head and his eyes met hers. She couldn't read his expression but sensed his weariness.

"You, um . . . You kind of lost it in the tomb. Are you okay?" she asked.

"I don't know what happened. My mind went all foggy. I don't remember what I did, what you did." He met her gaze. "But I know you finished the Nala. My head's clearer now than it's been since . . ."

"Since it bit you." She completed his thought. "I feel different, too. My shoulder doesn't hurt. What about your bite?"

"It never ached much, but I always had a feeling, like something pulling on me. That's gone." He tilted his head to the side, and the light of her orb fell over his face. "I guess Sister Ethet was right about me being a liability. I couldn't have done what you did. Thank you." Soris awkwardly extended his hand. The fused pointed fingers trembled slightly. She grasped his hand immediately.

"You were not a liability. You got Neas to trust us. He wasn't about to listen to me until you told him to." She gestured to the field of children. "Do you think any of them would've followed us without Neas urging them on?"

"And what about you?" Soris squeezed her hand. "I wasn't the one rounding up the ones too frightened to leave. You risked your life to get them out of there."

"Bastle herders and invaders of Nala dens. We make a decent team," she said. He laughed, and her heart warmed at the sound. "That's the first time I've heard you laugh since I've been back."

"Not much to laugh about these days, Natalie." He let go of her hand and held up his fused fingers, reminding her of her earlier gaffe.

"Soris, when I saw you for the first time at the Healing House, the way I acted wasn't because of the way you looked. Well, I guess it was." She sighed and averted her eyes. "Seeing you for the first time again made me realize how much you were paying for my mistakes and dishonesty. You had no idea I wasn't a Sister on our quest together, and I should have trusted you enough to tell you. I didn't, and you got bitten. I can't make any of that go away for you." She focused on the flowers clustered near her feet, afraid to look at him but relieved she finally had a chance to say what she'd needed to say to him for months. "I am so sorry."

"Apology accepted, Natalie, but I never needed an apology. What's done is done, and you've risked yourself more than you should have for me and others. Now it's time for you to go home and be safe."

"I guess," she said, feeling unsettled that he'd forgiven her and told her to go home in the same breath.

Something poked her in the back. She looked over her shoulder to find Neas with her cloak draped over his arm. "Annin says it's time to go," he said. He yawned and scratched his head. Around them, small bodies rose, stretched, and stood in the field. Annin ran through the circle, tapping children on the shoulder and rousing them into motion.

Nat accepted her cloak from Neas. When she turned, Soris was walking around the circle, too, gently shaking the remaining sleeping children. He lifted a little boy no older than four onto his back and held the hand of another child. He murmured comforting words. She fastened the clasp on her cloak, wondering why, after finally apologizing to Soris, she felt so empty.

The last of the children clambered down the stairs of the inner stone ring surrounding the Healing House. Sister Ethes briefly examined each child before shrilly triaging them and sending them off with a Sister or older duozi into one of the many infirmary rooms. Nat steered Neas toward Ethes, her hand firmly on his shoulder.

"Open your mouth," Ethes ordered. Her white hair was drawn tightly back from her face, giving her little black eyes a menacing appearance.

"It's okay," Nat whispered to Neas when she felt him flinch away from Ethes.

"Don't be ridiculous, of course it's okay. Strapping boy like you afraid of a little mouse like me, ha!" As she said those words, Ethes checked his pulse and reflexes and removed a ball of wax from his ear.

"Sister Tamara!" Ethes called out. A stout woman with bluish-black hair limped toward them. The limp reminded Nat of Benedict, and she placed a protective hand on Neas' shoulder. But Sister Tamara beamed at him. He gave her a goofy smile in return.

"Aren't you a dear?" Tamara placed a gentle hand on his other shoulder, and Nat relaxed.

"Focus on facilitating healing, not friendliness." Ethes directed her sharp stare at Sister Tamara.

"But Head Sister, he is—what's your name, dear?" She leaned toward him as if expecting the answer to be a great secret.

"Neas." His smile grew wider, exposing an upper row of crooked teeth.

"Neas," she said with a lightness in her voice. "You remind me of my younger brother when he was your age." She clasped her hand over his.

"Your brother is not a duozi, if I recall correctly, Sister Tamara. Neas is. Dispense the meldon tincture, suture the leg wound, and examine him for any bites or injuries." Ethes' clipped voice rose above Sister Tamara's cooing. Nat watched her hobble away with a protective arm over Neas. She wondered if anything was in the meldon tincture besides the plant extract. Did Ethes and Ethet have a way to treat any of these children beyond providing them with the flower tincture and healing their superficial wounds?

"Well, Sister?" Ethes asked.

Nat yawned and looked around to see who Ethes was addressing. Ethet, robed in a long gray overcoat, was speaking with Annin and Soris near the stairs to the outer wall.

"Sister, is there something else? I have places to be." Ethes' sharp eyes narrowed at Nat.

"Me?" She stifled another yawn.

"Do you see another Sister?" Ethes gestured to the open air around them. "Ethet said you were bright, but I have my doubts." She crossed her thin arms in front of her petite body.

"Sorry, Head Sister, I'm not used to being called a Sister," Nat said, feeling flustered and exhausted.

"When you go to the trouble of getting that"—she pointed to the markings on Nat's arm—"and imbuing an orb, I'd think you'd be a bit boiled if someone *didn't* call you Sister." Ethes pivoted swiftly on her heel.

"I do have something else to ask you!" Nat called out after her. "Do you know exactly how Nala use remnant after they've bitten someone?"

Ethes took a few steps toward her and stuck her hands in the loose sleeves of her overcoat. She pursed her lips, and the wrinkles around her pale mouth grew deeper. "Yes. It creates a dangerous mental connection between the Nala and its victim." Her eyes narrowed. "You are certainly aware of that link."

"Yes." Nat struggled to formulate her next question, and the sharp edges in Ethes' face grew sharper with impatience. "Beyond the connection, how else can the Nala use remnant? Is it possible that they can take something from a person who carries their remnant . . . to heal themselves?" she asked, her voice faltering as she thought of the dead girl and her wound.

"Spit out the specifics, Sister."

"In the cavern, we came across a Nala who was not quite right. It was disoriented and didn't even notice us. We were only a few feet away. It had an odd wound in its chest that appeared to be healed, but it wasn't the kind of wound that should heal. We found a girl with a similar wound on her chest, except hers was fresh and deep. Both Annin and I think the Nala are using the children to regenerate." There. She'd said it, crazy as it sounded.

"That is a most disquieting thought, Sister. I will interview the children and see if your theory has any weight. I hope for all the duozi it does not, but it would explain certain happenings." Ethes pressed her fingers to her lips. "Any other morbid theories you wish to add?"

"No." Nat felt a little dizzy from fatigue and took a deep breath. "What can you do for the duozi? I mean, is this all there is for them?" She gestured to the Healing House grounds. When she saw Ethes rapidly blink her dark eyes, she dropped her hand.

"Is this all there is!" Ethes drew back her shoulders and glared at Nat. "We provide them with a diet and medicines rich in meldon flowers, and we teach them a life beyond the forest, beyond the prejudice of the villages, beyond the losses they've endured. Who else will do that? Hmm?" Her tone was high and clipped. "Because of Mudug, we are one of the few safe places for the duozi. Maybe you should concern yourself with your own duties. Because as it stands, it's this House or the forest for most of them," she huffed. Nat's cheeks reddened as Ethes' tongue-lashing continued. "If the remaining Warrior Sisters think they have no obligations because they've been pushed out of their little castles, all of us, not just the duozi, are in for a sorry future."

"I'm not from a castle, and I want the Nala and Mudug gone just as much as you do," Nat replied with a vehemence that surprised her.

"Then do something other than asking me if this is all there is." She pinched her lips together. "Anything else?"

Nat cringed and nodded, knowing she needed to ask one more question.

"Something more!" Ethes threw her hands in the air, and Nat instinctively jerked back from the little woman, who seemed to have grown in size in her agitation.

"Have you ever seen a white Nala?" she asked before the enraged Sister could take her head off. Nat noticed a small twitch near her left eye.

"Why do you ask?"

"I saw a monstrous white Nala emerging from a pool in the cavern."

"What did you see?" Annin asked. She, Soris, and Ethet stepped next to Nat.

"A white Nala bigger than any I've ever seen, bursting out of the pool."

Ethes glanced at Sister Ethet and tapped her finger against her lips.

"Is it possible she saw the Nalaide?" Ethet asked her predecessor.

"Unless she was hallucinating, I would say yes," Ethes responded and turned to Nat. "Congratulations, Sister. You are one of very few who have seen the Nalaide, queen of the Nala, and lived." Ethes cocked her head to the side.

"Queen of the Nala?" Nat asked, feeling uneasy.

"Yes. She hasn't been seen in ages. Many believe she is more lore than flesh. I will certainly ask our new guests what they observed of her activities. Sister Ethet, join me." The invitation was given as a command, and Ethet followed the Head Sister and her clacking boots as they echoed down the stone walkway.

"You'd think she'd thank you for freeing the duozi," Annin said to Nat as she tilted her head like Sister Ethes. "Instead she congratulates you that your intestines aren't decorating the inside of the Nala den."

"Annin, stop," Soris said.

"I'm only joking. The Sister here is a hero. She cut your remnant tie, saved the duozi, and faced the Nalaide."

"*We* saved the duozi," Nat corrected.

"True, but I didn't have a personal confrontation with the Nalaide."

"I didn't confront her, I ran from her," Nat said, thinking of the creature's venomous glare when she'd spotted her markings.

Annin shrugged and grabbed both their elbows. She steered them toward the inner gardens. "I've some news from Estos."

"Estos? Is he here?" Nat pulled her elbow away and nearly stepped onto a pile of drying valerian root.

"No, what a puerile thought." Annin scrunched her brows. "Do you think I'd let him risk his hide by coming through the eastern forest?" She twisted a small weed around her finger, pulled it from the loose soil, and dangled it in front of Nat's face. Nat stared at the bits of soil clinging to the roots. In her exhaustion, the dark clumps blurred in and out of focus. Annin dropped the weed at Nat's feet and ducked under a low-hanging branch of a fruit tree. Nat felt a gentle tap on her shoulder.

"You're falling asleep standing up. Go get some rest," Soris whispered as Annin twittered on.

"He did want to come after he heard your news about Emilia, but I dissuaded him," Annin said as Soris held Nat's arm, steadying her. "He sent a messenger who arrived last night. He's to accompany us north to meet with Estos."

"What?" Soris barked, and Nat was suddenly alert.

"Estos is working on some type of plan and wants our assistance." Annin wrapped an arm around the slender trunk of a plum tree.

"That is, assuming you're not ready to bolt back into your mousehole, Natalie?" Her lips curved slightly.

"He wants *my* help?" Nat pointed to her chest.

"She's not going anywhere but home." Soris stepped between them.

Annin twirled around the tree so she could look directly at Nat. "Yes, he does want your help." She ignored Soris to answer Nat's question. Soris' face turned an odd shade of crimson. "Estos' messenger is anxious to speak with you."

"Whoever Estos sent can wait a few more hours." Nat stepped around Annin, feeling irritated and spent. Ethes' words still burned in her ears. She was not in the right frame of mind to consider any request from Estos' messenger. "Right now, I need to sleep, and then I need food," she said, walking in the direction she hoped led to her room.

"I'll be sure to let him know you wanted a nap first before meeting with him," Annin called out behind her. A wicked look crossed her human eye.

"You do that," Nat said without looking back. All she wanted to meet right now was her bed.

CHAPTER SEVENTEEN

"Kept me waiting half a day! Half a day! Like I was on some piddling errand." Andris thrust his finger at Nat. She glared at Annin, who had a huge smirk on her face. It would have been so easy for Annin to have told them that Estos' messenger was Andris. Annin slid into a chair by the fireplace. The embers popped and flickered, offering little heat for the damp room. The rain had returned with its chill.

Soris held his hands up. "Brother, we didn't know it was you, and to be fair, we'd just returned from raiding a Nala den with dozens of duozi in tow." He took a step forward and placed a hand on Andris' shoulder. "It's good to see you, temper and all."

Andris stroked his blond beard and eyed his brother. He touched the skin under Soris' Nala eye. "It's good to see you, too, brother, even with that awful thing gawking at me." He embraced him.

"How are you possibly related?" Nat asked the two men. Not waiting for an answer, she joined Annin by the fire. Andris released Soris and raised his foot onto a long bench opposite the hearth. Soris strode to the rain-spattered window and leaned against the wall. He glanced from Andris to Nat with an uneasy look on his face.

Andris picked a clump of mud from the sole of his boot. "You're certain it's Emilia?" he asked.

"Yes." Nat crossed her arms. The question was starting to irritate her.

"How can you be sure?" The bench creaked when he leaned toward the hearth with a skeptical look.

"Her face isn't one I'd forget. The woman I saw in the Chemist's quarters is the same woman in the portrait," she said, remembering her crazed behavior. *Even if she wasn't acting very queenlike.* She kept the thought to herself.

Andris cracked his knuckles and planted his boot on the rosewood floor. "You'd better be right, Natalie Barns . . ."

"Sister," Nat corrected. She couldn't care less if anyone else called her "Sister," but with Andris, Ethes was right—it boiled her.

"Sister?" His eyebrows shot up. Nat stretched out her forearm, exposing her markings in the firelight.

He waved his hand dismissively. "Markings on you don't mean—"

Her orb shot toward his face, veered to the left, and grazed his dirty-blond hair. His eyes widened.

"I stand corrected, Sister. Barba's doing?" She nodded. "She always made odd choices," he mumbled, then cleared his throat and gave her a mock bow. "Now that we've dealt with your ego, on to more important matters. If, and I'm still not convinced, what you say about Emilia is true, we have a problem." Andris pulled a crumpled bit of parchment from his pocket and sketched a map. "Estos is set to attack a dam in the Keyen Mountains, north of Rustbrook. The dam controls the flow of the Rust River into the city. Meanwhile, Gennes will lead a second attack on Mudug's mining colonies east of the mountains."

"You're cutting him off from his supply of riven." Annin nodded appreciatively. "That fool still thinks riven will protect him from a Nala bite?"

"Our spies in Rustbrook say the Chemist is sending Mudug's private guard to the mines to ensure a constant chain of supply to the city.

Once Gennes has control of the mines, he'll halt the flow of metals Mudug uses for weapons, and it will send him into a tailspin over the riven. We know riven is useless, but if Mudug's been clinging to the belief that he can control the Nala if he has it, he'll be quaking in his boots when Gennes succeeds."

"I'm actually impressed," Annin said.

"It gets better," Andris said enthusiastically. "The nearest city large enough to supply Mudug's garrison with fresh water is Ballew." He pointed to a dot far south of Rustbrook. The dot marking the location of the city sat at the base of a crude rendering of a semicircle-shaped bluff.

"Closer to the Nala." Soris traced a finger down a line of trees representing the eastern forest.

"Gennes' spies report increased Nala attacks on merchants traveling up from the coastline. Whatever agreement Mudug has with the Nala doesn't appear to be working out well." Andris smirked. "With Mudug's garrison away from Rustbrook and more than likely occupied with fending off the Nala, Estos can slip back into the capital. Once the people learn the true regent has returned, Mudug's grip on Fourline will start to slip away."

"But the Nala's won't. And I wouldn't be so sure about Mudug and the Nala not working together still. Mudug's been delivering children to them, bitten and unbitten," Nat interjected, thinking of both the horror of the den and Ethes' challenge.

"What?" Andris crinkled his nose in disgust.

"It's true," Soris said and stepped closer to Nat. "Whatever Estos and Gennes have planned, they need to stop Mudug from kidnapping children and delivering them to the Nala."

"Estos has been in the fringe for the last month with Sister Rory searching out any remaining Sisters. He's found many willing to offer their support and help the rebels. I suppose they can address this kidnapping problem as well. We'll need to discuss it with Estos," Andris said dismissively.

"What's to discuss? The kidnappings have to end now." Nat slapped her hand against the table. If Andris thought he'd push this problem aside, he was wrong.

"It's not as if we can station Sisters and Gennes' men in every town in Fourline to prevent kidnappings. We will discuss it with Estos and figure out the best options." Andris glanced at his brother, who stood with his arms crossed tightly over his chest. "What?" he asked him.

"Make it a priority," Soris said.

"Fine, we'll call it a priority, we'll call it whatever you want. But let's get back to the plan in place, which is complicated enough, and now fouled up because of you." He pointed at Nat.

"How did I foul it up?"

"Mudug doesn't know Estos is alive. If he finds out, and he will since Estos is leading the mountain operation, he'd be a fool not to use Emilia as a pawn."

"Why can't Estos just sit this one out? He can sneak back into Rustbrook after Mudug's garrison's left." The solution seemed obvious to Nat.

"Our force is strong enough to take the mining operations, but not the mountain outpost at the same time. We know the mountain outposts are still loyal to the regency and would turn easily in favor of Estos. We believe that Estos will only need a small band of fighters. But he can't sit this out. We need control of both the dam and the mining colonies to push Mudug's garrison south, out of Rustbrook."

"There must be an alternative," Nat said.

"That's where you come in, and trust me, this plan was not my invention."

"Estos wants her to find Emilia, doesn't he?" Annin leaned forward, her chin resting on her hands.

Andris nodded. "Since the Sister did it once, Estos figures she can do it again." He looked grudgingly at Nat. "With help," he added quickly. "He wants you, too." He gave Annin a cursory nod.

"Why not me?" Soris broke in. "Natalie doesn't need to go. I was in the Chemist's quarters when she saw Emilia."

Andris glanced at the fire. "I thought it best you remain here with the Sisters."

"Remain here while she risks her life?" Soris' eyes widened and he leaned toward his brother. "You can't be serious."

"You can provide the Healing Sisters with much-needed support." Andris averted his gaze.

"Get this into your head, brother. I am not staying here. Especially not if Estos expects her to head back into that wasp's nest." He placed his hand on Nat's arm and stared defiantly at Andris.

"I knew you'd give me grief," Andris muttered. "Fine, fine, you can come. You're certainly worth more in a fight than the others." He looked pointedly at Nat. "But you are to come back here after this mission is over, brother."

"Do you seriously think I'd skip back here while you and Gennes fight on?" Soris asked.

Andris scowled and grumbled something under his breath. "Fine," he said again and gestured with an open palm toward Nat. "Well?"

"Well what?" she shot back, upset that Soris had dismissed the idea of coming back to the Healing House, the one safe place for him.

"Will you agree to help Estos? Without pay this time," he added. The comment rankled Nat. She glared at the soldier.

"You don't owe Estos anything, Natalie. You should go home where it's safe," Soris said before she could answer Andris.

"You just yelled at him for telling you to stay here," Nat countered.

"There's a difference. I'm from here, you're not."

"Annin, does blood run cold and unfeeling in my world?" Nat kept her eyes locked on Soris.

"Not to my knowledge, Sister, not to my knowledge," Annin quipped and smiled, knowing where Nat was headed.

"Exactly. If I were cold-blooded and unfeeling, home would be an easy choice. But I'm not, and after being in that death-hole with those children, there is no way I'd pass up a chance to mess with Mudug."

"You're a fool." Soris' eyes bored into hers.

"You feel the same way I do about those children. I'm making the same choice as you, Soris."

He brushed past her and thrust open Ethet's door. The room vibrated when he slammed it behind him.

Andris tugged at his beard and gave Nat a questioning look. "Sister," he said and lifted his chin, "to quote an expression from your world, I do believe you've grown some . . ."

"Andris, behave," Annin growled. He shrugged. Nat stared at the door, wondering how long Soris would stay mad at her.

"Maybe you're not a selfish scrounger after all," Andris said as he collected the parchment from the table. "We leave in the morning. And don't keep me waiting."

The day following their departure from the Healing House was cold and gray. It was drizzling lightly, coating the tall grasses, their cloaks, and each horse with a fine mist. Nat gently wiped her gloved hand down her horse's neck and flicked droplets of water onto the ground. She whispered into his ear, trying to settle his nerves.

Annin, Andris, Soris, and Nat were strung out in an elongated diamond formation with Annin in the lead and Nat bringing up the rear. Nat turned her horse for the seventh time in the last hour, surveying the gray sky and open plain behind them. They'd made it through the eastern forest without a Nala attack, but Nat felt wary and unsettled as she scanned the top of the tall grass. She turned her horse again and urged him forward, wanting to decrease the distance between herself and the others.

Andris' and Soris' fan-shaped cloaks spread out over their horses' backs. The heavy drape of their hoods folded when they spoke to each other. Andris' hands flew into the air every so often, and their occasional laughter punctuated the quiet, damp day.

Watching Soris and Andris riding together made her think of riding with her sisters. Until Marie Claire was big enough for her own horse, she'd ridden in front of Nat, brushing her ponytail against Nat's face every time she turned her head to point out a butterfly or bird. Even Cal used to ride by her side when they rode into the hills surrounding their farm.

She pushed away the thoughts of home, tired of fighting the overwhelming doubt of her choice to stay. She'd felt certain in her decision when she'd told Andris she'd help, and she knew it was the right thing to do, but thoughts of home were messing with her emotions.

She shifted in the saddle and felt a sharp object press into her hip. She pulled out the small leather-bound book Ethet had given her before their departure. Nat hunched over the book, protecting it from the rain. The pages were filled with ancient illustrations from the First House. Ethet had suggested she might find answers to her questions about the Nala's remnant within the volume. Nat tried to decrypt the foreign script under the image of a meldon flower, but eventually shut the book and tucked it safely into her satchel.

She looked up to find Soris approaching from a safe distance. Her horse jerked his head to the side when he neared. Soris pulled on the braided reins, bringing his horse to a halt a few paces away.

"Do you think your horse can stand my presence for a bit?" he asked.

Nat tightened her grip. "I'll keep a tight hold," she said, pulling hard to the right with her reins to keep her mount under control. Her horse was jumpy around both Annin and Soris, but if Soris wanted to ride with her, she'd keep the animal under control. The bit cut into the flesh of the horse's mouth, and the animal snorted. Soris kicked his horse into step, and they rode together with a healthy amount of space between them.

"What were you and Andris laughing about?" she asked, wanting to control the direction of the conversation.

"Just a memory."

"Care to share?"

"No." He leaned back in his saddle. "Not yet. Since you've decided to stay, I think you owe me a few memories or something I don't know about you first. I recall spilling my guts to you in the ruins of a Warrior House. It's your turn."

"What do you want to know?"

"Since you're not from Fourline"—he paused and looked directly into her eyes—"tell me what your real home's like."

Nat let out a sharp laugh. Her horse cantered to the side, already nervous from Soris' presence.

"What?" he asked.

"Of all the questions to ask. I've been trying not to think about home all morning," she explained. She caught a glimmer of understanding in his eye.

"Well then, I insist," he said.

She sighed. "I live on a farm, or I do when I'm not at college." She readjusted her reins and set a comforting hand on her horse's neck.

"What kind of farm?" His voice was soft and encouraging.

"Small but beautiful. We raise a few sheep but mainly grow corn and barley. My dad runs the farm. He's a woodworker, too. He can make the most beautiful furniture and carvings, Soris. He's amazing with his hands. He can fix anything, which is good because we always have stuff breaking down. My mom's a librarian at an elementary school. She's smart and patient. And my sisters . . ." She sniffed and wiped her nose. "Cal will be eighteen this month. She's attending the same college I do next year. MC, or Marie Claire, is my little sister, but she has the biggest heart." A lump formed in her throat. She stopped talking and turned in her saddle. "You knew what talking about my family and home would do to me, didn't you?"

"Not too late to change your mind. Sounds as if your home is a blessed place. Where we're headed is not." He shifted easily in his saddle and his beautiful green eye looked entirely sincere.

"You are sneaky." She gave him a perturbed look and pulled on the reins to keep her horse from rearing.

"No, just motivated to see you home and out of Fourline," he replied. "Move up with Andris before that beast bucks you off because of me. It's my turn to take rear watch." He spurred his animal away, leaving Nat to wonder why he so clearly wanted her to return home. She sighed and kicked her horse, leading him toward Andris.

Nat's horse fell into step with Andris', and they rode in silence for a few moments. They watched Annin disappear around the base of a hill covered in long lush grass. Nat glanced over her shoulder, looking back at Soris.

"I wouldn't, if I were you," Andris said, keeping his eyes fixed on the spot where Annin disappeared.

"Wouldn't what?" Nat straightened her back and tightened her grip on the reins.

"Grow any more attached to my brother. His fate as a duozi is settled. No need to complicate his path with unnecessary emotion." Andris flicked his gloved hand in the air.

"What are you talking about? No one's fate is settled." She clenched her jaw and tugged her cloak tighter around her body to keep out the chill.

"The duozi haven in the Healing House is not how it works in the rest of Fourline, Natalie. Outside the Healing House, duozi are feared and hated." He let his warning hang in the air.

Haughty, arrogant, intolerant eyes, Nat thought as she stared at him. "Duozi or not, Soris can choose his own path."

He yanked his reins, bringing his horse to a full stop. His face was swathed in fury as he leaned sharply toward Nat. "You know nothing. You may have the markings and the orb of a Sister, but you have no understanding of the ruin his life became when that Nala bit him."

"Why do you think I came back? For a summer vacation? I'm here to help him."

"He's a duozi. No one can help him or change that, especially not you."

Nat opened her mouth in reply, but the sound of hoofbeats hurtled toward them. Annin's hood flopped off as she pulled her horse to a stop near them.

"There's someone up ahead, in the draw." She gestured toward the bend. Soris' horse danced behind them.

"Just one?" Soris asked.

"I'm not sure, but it's not a Nala."

Nat's shoulders relaxed.

"Natalie, you and Annin take the west ridge." Andris pointed to the hill opposite the bend. "Soris and I will come from the east." He kicked his horse and sped away.

"West ridge it is. Keep up, Sister. You never know what's around the bend." Annin winked her Nala eye.

"I don't see anyone," Nat whispered to Annin. They lay in the wet grass, scanning the valley below. Clusters of rocks covered the hillside, rooted in place by tiny bowl-shaped bushes and wild grasses. Boulders, some big enough to hide a car, littered the floor of the valley.

"Someone's behind that boulder." Annin pointed toward one of the massive rocks. The tip of a brown boot disappeared behind it.

"Andris should be close to whoever's down there," Nat whispered.

She caught a flicker of movement out of the corner of her eye when she looked at Annin. A cloaked figure rushed from behind one of the boulders at their backs. Nat rolled to the side, barely missing being cut by the blade of a sword. Nat hopped to her feet and faced their attacker. Dirt-encrusted dreadlocks spun in the air when the attacker lunged again.

"Cassandra?" Nat blocked the crazed Sister's sword with her own. Vibrations shimmied up her arm from the impact. At the sound of her name, Cassandra lowered her sword and lifted her chin. The flaming scar marring the left side of her face contorted when she smiled. Her smile grew wide, revealing mossy-gray teeth.

"I know you." She wagged her finger. "You've improved since last we met."

Nat studied the other Sister. She'd met her at Gennes' rebel camp when Benedict had sent her down into the mining pit to collect riven. "What are you doing out here?" she asked.

Cassandra ignored Nat's question. She regarded Annin. "Who's the duozi?" she asked and pushed past Nat, heading straight for Annin.

Annin brought the stock of her crossbow to her chin. Cassandra froze. "Nice eye," she said and spat. The glob landed on Annin's boot.

"Do that again and you'll be missing an eye," Annin said with the bow pointed at the wild Warrior Sister.

Nat inched closer to Annin's side, watching Cassandra as if she were a prairie snake. Her feet crunched against the rock with each step.

"Put your weapon down." A woman's voice came from above.

Cassandra laughed triumphantly and glared at Annin. "Sister Rory will split you like a pea, halfling," she said and spun toward the woman crouched on top of the boulder. Her bow was pointed at Annin.

"Sister Rory! Hold up!" Andris shouted. He and Soris ran down the ridge. Rory lowered her bow and slid off the boulder. She shook her hood off, revealing short brown hair and piercing brown eyes.

"I should have known," she said with a scowl as Andris and Soris joined them. "You never make it easy, do you, Andris?"

"What?" Andris frowned. "How was I supposed to know it was you?"

Rory brushed past him and grabbed Cassandra's elbow, guiding her away. "Would you put that crossbow down?" She looked steadily at Annin, who still had her weapon pointed at Cassandra.

"Say please," Annin said through clenched teeth.

"Annin, put it down," Nat and Soris said in unison.

"We know these Sisters," Nat added.

"Good friends?" Annin lowered the weapon.

"She saved our lives." Soris nodded toward Rory.

"And the one with the impeccable manners?" Annin glared at Cassandra.

Rory tightened her grip on the Sister's elbow. "Enough with the reunion. You have horses?" She gestured to the thin tree line behind them.

"Of course we have horses. I told Estos I didn't need an escort to the base." Andris looked perturbed. Nat enjoyed watching Rory disregard his irritation with a wave of her hand.

"There's been a change in location. Get your horses—now," she said.

Cassandra broke away from Rory and sauntered up to Nat. A faint smell of decay still clung to her. Soris appeared at Nat's side, inserting his shoulder protectively between the two women.

"You picked up a bit of a blue rash." Cassandra traced the edge of Soris' neckline. He shot his hand out and pushed her away.

"Cassandra, leave them alone." Rory's threat projected clearly, and Cassandra backed away.

"Soris! Let's go," Andris barked. Soris glanced at Nat, giving her a reassuring look, then walked back to his brother.

"Who was the crazy?" Annin asked while untying her horse.

"A Sister I met in Gennes' camp." Nat tugged her horse's tether free and pulled him away so Annin could get to her horse without having to dodge flying hooves.

"Different kind of Sister. If she looks at me again like that, I'm going to punch her."

"I wouldn't, Annin. She has a lethal bite," Nat replied.

CHAPTER EIGHTEEN

Striped gray stone lined either side of the dry riverbed. Nat's horse careened behind Andris over the choked, dry ground. Dust billowed violently behind his horse and mingled with the clouds formed by Rory, who rode lead.

Nat strained to see through the haze and the fading daylight. She heard hoofbeats and dared a quick glance. Cassandra was a length behind her, slapping the haunch of her horse. She grazed Nat's ride, forcing the animal to jump over a tangle of dead trees. The crazy Sister disappeared into the cloud of dust. Infuriated, Nat leaned in tight to her horse, urging him to keep pace and push through the dust.

The riverbed curved left into a wider expanse of dried dirt. Nat spotted Rory waving her arm near a fissure in the cliff flanking the riverbed. She pulled the reins slightly, easing her horse's gait. A confrontation with Cassandra would have to wait.

"Ten lengths forward and then take the sharp curve to the right," Rory ordered. A layer of dust covered her face.

Nat passed into the shadow of the fissure. Her legs brushed against scraggly branches protruding from crevices in the rock. The horse snorted when she yanked her reins to the right, barely making the turn.

The path opened. The remaining daylight poured into a triangular-shaped rock enclosure. Oberfisk, one of the private guards who'd traveled with Estos through the membrane, stood on a rocky path above her. Sunlight gleamed off his bald head as he passed the reins of Cassandra's horse to a slender young boy wearing a dusty brown tunic. Nat slid off her horse. As soon as she hit the ground, her legs buckled. Thick fingers grabbed her elbow, pushing up her sleeve.

"Well, Ms. Natalie!" The startled words boomed around her as two massive arms embraced her, then thrust her backward into the light. "Look at you!" Oberfisk's smile spread across his broad face as he held Nat by her shoulders. "I can't believe my eyes. Hey, Riler!" he yelled and spun Nat like a rag doll toward an incline at the base of the triangle. "Look who's here!"

Riler's head popped out from behind two horses.

"It's Natalie!" Oberfisk yelled right next to her. Riler waved.

"Oberfisk, my ear." She brought a hand to her head. "And my shoulders," she added. Oberfisk dropped his hands. She planted her feet firmly to keep from collapsing to the rocky ground.

"Sorry, Ms. Natalie." His white teeth shone in the disappearing light. "I never expected to see you again, let alone here." His smile disappeared and deep lines formed on his forehead. "What are you doing here?"

"It's a long story, Ober." She patted his trunklike arm. He handed her horse's reins to the boy as Annin, Soris, and Rory turned onto the path.

"Take this one," he ordered the boy. "Be quick about it." The boy didn't move. He stared at Annin and Soris as they dismounted. Nat's horse jerked his head, pulling away.

"Do you want your head mashed in by hooves?" Oberfisk roared, snapping the boy to attention. "Get the horse out of here!"

"Sorry, but th-they're . . . ," the boy stammered as he pointed at Annin and Soris. His other arm flailed wildly as the gelding thrashed against his reins.

"I know what they are, now move!" Oberfisk bent his bulky frame over the boy, who stumbled up the path toward Riler, casting nervous looks toward Annin and Soris every few steps.

"Thanks for arranging the warm welcome, Ober." Annin clutched her reins.

"Not my doing, Annin." He stuck his arm out for Rory. The Sister grasped it and dismounted. "He's Benedict's apprentice."

Annin whipped her head around. "Benedict's here?" Her eyes widened.

"Estos wanted him," Rory said as she brushed past Oberfisk, her horse in tow.

"Estos? Estos would never . . ." Annin pressed her full lips together and stormed after Rory. Nat, Soris, and Oberfisk gathered the remaining horses in silence and followed Annin's curses up the hill.

"You're looking a bit better than last time I saw you." Oberfisk broke the silence as he punched Soris lightly on the arm.

"Yeah, I feel amazing. Fabulous stuff, this Nala venom," Soris responded. Oberfisk paled. "I'm kidding, Oberfisk. Sister Ethet did what she could," he said.

"If you don't mind my saying, maybe Ethet needs to do more. You're a bit snarky." Oberfisk's laughter died when he saw Soris' expression.

"I mind." Soris pushed past them.

"What's gotten into him?" Oberfisk asked Nat.

She watched Soris disappear over the hill under the watchful eyes of two cloaked Sisters guarding the path. "We had a rough encounter with some Nala a few days ago, Oberfisk. Don't take it seriously."

"We've all had rough encounters with the Nala."

"Not like this." Nat pressed her lips together as they reached the top of the hill. As much as she liked Oberfisk, the last thing she wanted to do was recount their experience in the Nala den.

The two Sisters guarding the entrance to the camp nodded respectfully as Nat passed by. She tilted her chin in response. Oberfisk watched the exchange and gave her a questioning look. Nat let her orb float out of the folds of her cloak. She smiled to herself as a look of shock passed over his face.

The other side of the hill rolled into a flat plateau dotted with a handful of tents. Torches flickered as they passed two more guards.

"This way. He'll want to see you now, I expect," Oberfisk said, finding his voice. He gestured to a large canvas tent set off from the others. Light spilled out of the open flap and flickered off the tip of the spear held by the Sister blocking the entrance. She stepped aside, allowing Nat and Oberfisk to pass through.

Lanterns hung from wooden support beams crisscrossing the tent's ceiling. Two compact tables occupied the center of the open room. Andris and Soris leaned over another table set in the corner. Maps and sketches were strewn over its surface. He shuffled through the papers while Estos and Annin argued.

"How could you?" Annin yelled at Estos. Bits of debris fell from her curly hair as she shook her head. Estos reached for her shoulder, but she jerked away. He dropped his hand to his side. Bandages covered the last three fingers of his left hand.

"If the woman is Emilia, and the Chemist has her, I need Benedict. To leave him out of this would be a mistake. You know that as well as I do." Estos rubbed his forehead and closed his pale eyes. His brown hair had grown since Nat had last seen him. He wore a thick woolen vest over a gray tunic that hit his long figure midthigh. The sleeves and bottom of the tunic were edged with tiny embroidered vines. "You have to put aside your feelings." His voice was calm but adamant.

"Put aside my feelings? Did you really say that?" She held her finger under his chin. A look of impatience flickered across his face but disappeared quickly. "He betrayed your sister, he betrayed Gennes, he left me—"

"I know what he did, you don't need to remind me. I don't have many options here. If it means getting her out, then I'm going to take the chance and use him. This is my sister we're talking about."

"You don't know that for sure. Just because Natalie thought she saw someone . . ."

Nat balked at the door. She expected Andris to question her credibility, but not Annin.

Andris shuffled through more maps. "Why don't you ask her?"

Estos looked past Annin, noticing Nat for the first time. A smile broke through his worn expression, and he strode toward Nat. He wrapped his long arms around her, and she breathed in the smell of sweat and campfire.

"Annin told me why you came back. It's good to see you," he whispered in her ear before letting her go. Dark circles shaded the skin under his eyes. The scar running from his ear to his neck was more pronounced against his pale skin. He looked like he needed a week's worth of sleep.

She gave him an awkward smile. "It's good to see you, too, Estos." Seeing him felt like a reunion with an old friend.

Andris cleared his throat. "Your Highness, now that we're all here, shall we start?" He dumped a pile of maps on the long table. Estos nodded and took a seat at the head. "Get over here, we're not on holiday," Andris barked at Nat and Soris.

Nat slid into a chair next to Soris and stole a quick glance his way. He rested his chin in the palm of his hand, his fused fingers curled around his cheek. She wondered if he was scowling because of the encounters with Benedict's apprentice and Oberfisk.

"Natalie." She looked up to find Estos staring intently at her. "Please tell me everything you can remember about the woman in the Chemist's quarters. Take your time and don't gloss over any details."

All eyes turned toward Nat. "Well, after I made the deal with Mudug—that is, traded the riven in exchange for the Chemist's help—a guard led us from the hearing chamber to the Chemist's quarters in an interior courtyard."

"Here." Andris slid a crude sketch out from under the pile and pointed to a picture of a long building surrounded by the castle walls. Estos reached for the paper and pulled it close.

"That's it, but there are three doors, not two. One's set right in the middle." Nat pointed to the center of the drawing.

"I've never seen this building before." Estos slid the page back to Andris. "Mudug must've built it after we left in search of Gordon," he said, referring to Soris and Andris' oldest brother, who went missing after Emilia was killed.

"He did," Andris confirmed. "Mervin and Matilda smuggled these and other drawings to Gennes, two, maybe three years after we passed through the membrane."

"Keep going, Natalie." Estos nodded in encouragement. Annin paced the room like a pent-up animal.

"The Chemist came out the middle door when we first arrived." Nat paused, remembering her shock upon seeing Benedict's twin emerge. "We both had a chance to look into the room before he shut the door." She turned to Soris, who nodded in agreement but kept his eyes fixed on the drawing.

"I didn't see much, but I remember a lot of books and clutter." Soris' voice was gruff.

"I snuck into the room while the Chemist worked on Soris' fake pory bite." She grabbed a piece of blank parchment and sketched out the room. "There was a long map with little orbs hovering along the edges." She whisked her hand over the paper, and little circles appeared above a map on a low table. "Like Soris said, the place was a mess, books strewn on the floor—"

"Are those little orbs?" Rory stepped forward from the corner of the tent. Nat hadn't noticed the Sister slip in behind them.

Nat pulled her orb from her pocket and it hovered in the air. A soft light pulsed from the sphere. "Maybe a tenth of the size of mine, Sister. They weren't transparent, either. One was blue, another was yellow, and I remember another was red."

A look of concern settled on Rory's face.

"What's wrong?" Nat asked, but Rory waved her hand at the table. "Finish your story," she said. She examined Nat's sketch.

"I sprinkled the suix stone around the map. The orbs started to drop. Then I heard a voice, and there she was, standing in the Chemist's quarters with me." She looked up.

Estos had a hopeful look in his pale eyes. "Emilia?" he asked. When she nodded, he slumped forward, resting his head in his hands. Andris glared at her.

"It was her," she said, answering the challenge in Andris' expression. She placed her hand on the sketch. "She was in that room. Same person as the one in the portrait."

"What? Did she provide a formal introduction?" Andris demanded.

"No, but she had Estos' eyes. I remember thinking there was something familiar about her when I saw her, but everything went haywire. I didn't consider the resemblance until I saw her portrait a few days ago."

"Where'd she come from, then?" Andris set his boot on a stool. "Did you see another door or window? Did she slip in behind you? How did she get into the room?"

"I have no idea, and I don't remember another door besides the entrance. There was a window at the back of the room, but I don't think it was open or big enough for her to crawl through. I don't know how she got in. All I know is one minute I was alone in the room, the next she was right across from me, telling me where to put more suix stone to disable the tracking device. Then she yelled at me to get out of the room and went berserk, tossing glass against the wall, throwing books, knocking down shelves."

"Sounds exactly like Emilia," Andris said sarcastically. He ran a hand over his dirty hair and faced Estos. "She has no real proof. This is just a waste of time. Emilia's dead," he said with authority. "Someone would've seen her before if she were still alive."

"It was her!" Anger coursed through Nat when she saw the disbelief in Andris' face. *Not again,* she thought. She'd had to fight with him so many times to prove herself or justify her actions to him.

"Natalie has to be mistaken." Andris softened his tone, continuing to address only Estos. "You heard her yourself, the woman went berserk, there was a lot going on . . . Anyone would have a difficult time remembering what someone looked like under those circumstances."

Nat bristled. "I'm not an idiot, Andris. I know what I saw."

"I believe her." Soris lifted his head, exposing the blue skin around his collarbone. He shifted in his seat. The lantern cast a crooked shadow over his face, hiding his Nala eye. "I've seen Natalie under pressure. She's always had her head about her. I can't verify the encounter, but if she says it's Emilia, then it is."

Nat's throat tightened and she glanced at Soris. *I didn't have my head about me when that Nala attacked you,* she thought.

Andris didn't give up. "How could Mudug have kept her under his thumb all this time? Emilia was a force to be reckoned with. No one—nothing—could have kept her hidden away for so long. She's dead."

"The same could be said about you and Estos, and yet here you are." Soris' voice had an edge to it.

Andris smacked his fists on the table and leaned toward his brother. "Hiding away was not my choice, it was my duty to protect him—"

"It was our duty to protect Emilia as well. We both failed." Soris looked at his brother coldly. "If there's even the faintest chance that she's alive, you and I are the ones that need to find her." He faced Estos and added, "Andris and I, not Natalie."

"Sister Natalie can make her own decisions, Soris," Estos said, giving her a respectful nod.

Nat felt as if the room were about to explode. She took a deep breath. "There's another thing you should know," she said, breaking the angry silence between Soris and Estos. She pressed her thumbnail into her index finger. "She was emaciated, and I saw lots of bruises and puncture marks on her skin."

Nat heard a sharp intake of breath from the corner of the room. Rory stepped into the light, her face ashen.

Estos stood slowly and walked to the canvas flap of the tent. He stared into the night. "Andris, I respect your opinion, but my mind is made up," he finally said. "You will lead a band into Rustbrook. Our other plans will have to wait."

Andris gave a quick nod of assent, all argument gone from his expression. "I'll assemble a team and leave in the morning."

"I have in mind who will accompany you." Estos held his hands behind his back. "Annin, you know the Sisters' tunnels in and around the castle better than anyone except Sister Barba. They'll be of use sneaking around the castle. But if you can't tolerate Benedict, I won't send you."

"Don't worry, Your Royalness, I'm going. Someone has to keep an eye on the pig."

Estos' jaw tensed. "Annin."

"I'm going." Her eyes flashed in the lamplight.

"Fine." He looked at Nat, his expression weary. "Andris, Annin, Oberfisk, Benedict, Soris, and you, Natalie. We've all asked too much of you, but . . ."

Andris let out a low groan.

"I know where the Chemist's quarters are as well as she does. Like you said, we've asked too much of her." Soris kept up his argument as he stood behind Nat. His fingers tightened protectively around her shoulder.

"Yes, we have," Estos agreed. "But she is a Warrior Sister, and if Andris needs someone to anonymously move around the castle, she's the one to do it."

"No one recognized me when we were there months ago," Soris protested.

"Yes, but now——"

"Now you're like me." Annin linked her arm through Soris' and shot Estos a contemptuous look.

Nat eased out of her chair. "I've already decided. I'm going," she said.

"Thank you, Natalie." Estos tipped his chin toward his chest, then stared thoughtfully at the map in front of him.

"Estos." Nat approached the young king. "Soris, Annin, and I have something else we need to discuss with you." He looked up. Nat nervously cleared her throat. "We need to talk about what's happening to the duozi."

Soris gave her an encouraging nod, the look of irritation gone from his face. She continued, "Mudug's guards are kidnapping children and taking them to the Nala to be slaves. Annin and I think they may be using them to regenerate somehow."

"How do you know this, Natalie?" Estos asked, focusing on her as if she were the only other person in the tent.

Annin spoke up. "A few of the children we rescued from the den gave us information that suggests the dead Nala use remnant to regenerate. We found the body of a young duozi girl as well."

Estos glanced at Annin. "Thank you for that information. Rory, join me for a moment, please." He walked to a shadowy corner. Rory eased herself next to him, and the two spoke in hushed tones. *That's not the end of the conversation, Estos,* Nat thought as she glanced at

Annin. Her eyes were like little slits as she followed Estos' movements. *Definitely not the end.*

Andris brought another map to the table. Oberfisk joined him, and a loud discussion about the route to Rustbrook filled the room. Soris strode away from the group with a downcast expression. Nat followed him.

"Can I talk to you outside?" she asked. His mouth seemed stuck in a permanent frown when he looked at her, but he joined her as she stepped into the cool night past the Sister guarding the tent.

"Why did you argue with Estos about my joining the mission? I'm not changing my mind," she said the moment they were out of earshot of the Sister.

His cocked his head and leaned toward her. "This isn't your fight."

"What about all those duozi children we saved from the Nala den? You know as well as I do that Mudug's guards turned them over to the Nala. If finding Emilia means Estos and the rebellion have a better chance of ending Mudug's rule, then I'm in. And I . . ." Nat stopped, holding back. If going meant she could keep Soris safe from another Nala attack or Mudug's guards, then there was no chance she'd go home now.

"You're going to do what Estos asks regardless of what I say." He pressed his lips together.

"If Andris asked me to go, I would. It doesn't make a difference who's asking," she argued.

"Why do you have to be so stubborn? You could be safe at home right now." He crossed his arms, but the corner of his mouth twitched upward.

"Am I really that bad to be around?" She offered a weak smile.

"Yes, definitely," he said, but the hard look in his eyes momentarily softened. He stepped back into the light spilling out from the tent. "Andris is going to make your life miserable, you know that, don't you?"

"When has he not?" she replied, annoyed that he was again trying to convince her to change her mind. "I'd start to worry if he treated me like something other than a doormat."

His brow creased.

"Look, how would you feel if Estos ordered you to stay here?" Nat asked him.

"Wouldn't happen."

"That's not an answer. How would you feel?"

He examined her face for a moment and then looked up at the stars. "Useless. I'd feel useless."

"Useless is only a fraction of what I'd feel if I returned home now."

"Is feeling useless truly worse than getting hurt for a cause that isn't your own?" He stood so close she could see his neck muscles tighten.

"I don't plan on getting hurt." *And after what happened to you, helping you will always be my cause,* she thought.

"And I never planned on turning into a duozi." He took a step away from her. Nat's body tensed and a flush rushed into her cheeks. An awkward silence settled between them. She stared at the ground, feeling cold guilt wrap around her. Soris touched her chin and lifted her face to meet his gaze.

"I only meant that what we hope will happen rarely does." He gave her a sad smile, dropped his hand, and disappeared into the night.

CHAPTER NINETEEN

Nat closed the leather-bound book Ethet had given her and flopped down on the woven mat on the hard floor of the Sisters' tent. She was tired but couldn't seem to fall asleep like the slumbering Sisters around her. The tiny images in the book didn't help settle her mind. She'd found illustrations of the Nala and Nalaide, but the script was small and made no sense. She gave up and tucked the book into her satchel.

She glanced nervously at Cassandra, who sat across the tattered tent from her. Her dreadlocks hung down to her legs and her head rested against the canvas at a crooked angle. She looked at Nat contemptu ously with her one open eye, her chest rising and falling rhythmically. *How does she sleep with one eye open?* Nat wondered. Overcome by weariness, she closed her eyes and fell into a fitful sleep.

The bars of light bordering her dream space flickered. Nat lifted her head from a woven hammock and focused on them. Burnt pine trees creaked and groaned on the horizon beyond the now solidified beams. She shuddered, thankful she had chosen to avoid her dreams for the night even if it meant she'd be exhausted in the morning.

"Hey!" Annin's face appeared on the other side of the ledge. She clung to the tip of a charred tree. "Are you going to let me in?"

The lights dipped, and Annin hopped over. A chair appeared at her side. "Nice upholstery," she said, fingering the polka-dotted cushion.

"My sister has that chair in her room. I go with what I know." Nat flopped back into the hammock. Her braid caught on the steel loop holding the woven bed to the metal frame. She twisted around, untangling herself. Annin collapsed into the round puffy chair and frowned.

"Well, you're pleasant company," Nat said, yanking her hair free.

"Why aren't you dreaming?" Annin asked, folding her legs under her.

"I had a feeling someone or something would encourage me to go to my dream space tonight, so I got a head start. I didn't think it would be you."

"Who did you think it would be? Soris?" Annin cocked her head to the side.

Nat nestled into the hammock. "I don't know," she mumbled.

"I just left Soris' space. He's not coming here tonight."

"Thanks for the update."

"He doesn't need a babysitter, you know."

"Neither do I." Nat's retort was sharp.

A satisfied look spread over Annin's face as if she knew she'd hit on what was occupying Nat's thoughts. "He's a duozi. Accept it. I believe what you say about wanting to end Mudug's deal with the Nala and helping the duozi, but you're also hanging around to make sure nothing else bad happens to Soris, am I right?"

"So what if I am? It's my choice," she said.

"Guess what, Natalie—you can't undo a duozi. Sticking around doesn't help him."

"It can't hurt. Besides, I can't go back home now." She looked beyond the beams of light to the blackened forest. "I'd go crazy," she admitted.

"Too late for that." Annin smiled. "Just do me a favor. As one duozi speaking on behalf of another, the sooner you start treating Soris like he's Soris instead of someone who needs to be saved, the better off he'll be."

Nat fumed. "What are you doing here, anyway? You've got other people you could harass besides me."

"If you really must know, I'm avoiding Estos. He's waiting in my dream space, and I have no intention of conversing with him." Annin kicked the floor.

"Because of Benedict?"

Annin glared at Nat.

"Estos must have a good reason for wanting Benedict to come along," Nat said, remembering Annin and Estos' argument in the tent.

"He thinks Benedict can help save his sister because he's the Chemist's twin. But Estos has no idea what a rat that old man is."

"Then I'd think you'd want him where you can keep an eye on him." She thought of Neas and how Benedict had exposed what he was to the villagers. "As long as he's with us, he's not sneaking around causing problems, right?"

Annin twisted her lips to the side. "Maybe. But I doubt his loyalty to Estos or Emilia—if she's alive—is stronger than his hatred of the duozi. He's got to have an inkling of Estos' plan for them. This mission will be like traveling with a viper."

"What plan?" Annin had Nat's full attention, but her leg involuntarily jerked forward, and she tumbled to the ground.

"Someone's trying to wake you, and not gently." Annin hopped out of the chair.

Nat dropped the lights and grasped the ledge, pulling herself up. Her leg buckled again. "You can stay here if you want," she offered and climbed onto the ledge. Her leg involuntarily shot out again.

"No, never let someone stay in your dream space when you're not there. They can get into your private thoughts." Annin lightly touched the ledge and jumped up, straddling the rough stone.

"I thought you said Estos was in your dream space?" Nat raised an eyebrow.

"That's different."

"How?"

"We have a certain mutual trust," Annin said right before she slid off the ledge down into the burnt forest.

Trust? Nat tumbled after her, diving into the ruined woods of her dreams.

"Wake up, Sister." Rory kicked Nat's thigh. "Guard duty." An orb hung irritatingly in front of Nat's face. She sat up, knocking into the hard sphere with her nose. Rory dangled Nat's belt above her and then released the leather strap. It fell into Nat's lap with a clank. She rubbed her thigh and climbed out of the bedroll.

"Does she always sleep like that?" Nat suppressed a yawn and gestured toward Cassandra. Her open eye seemed to follow Nat when she stepped over the sleeping Sisters.

"No." Rory splashed cold water on her face from a rough wooden basin next to the tent flap. "Sometimes she sleeps with the other eye open."

Nat dipped her hands into the icy water. A subtle grassy smell enveloped her. She felt suddenly refreshed and alert. She peered into the bowl, examining the clear water.

"Coming?" Rory asked from the other side of the tent flap.

The night air stung Nat's wet cheeks, instantly sapping away any remaining sleepiness. She looked around the camp. Other than a dim orange light seeping out from the base of a small tent, the camp was dark.

Moonlight reflected off the light-colored stones scattered over the ground. She followed Rory, keeping pace with her long strides as she crested the top of the ridge overlooking the camp. The blue of the night was thick and inky, but Nat could make out the dry riverbed and tributaries spreading below them like gnarled fingers.

A hooded Sister approached Rory. Cracked lips and the tip of a rounded nose were all Nat could see of her. Rory motioned to the side, and she and the guard spoke in low voices. The hooded Sister nodded. She climbed a small outcropping and flattened her body against the rock.

"You'll take Sister Mertan's post after I'm done asking questions." Rory placed a firm hand on Nat's arm and gestured to a flat-topped rock. Nat sat on the edge overlooking the riverbed. Rory pulled a leg tight to her chest, letting the other one dangle from the boulder.

"When you made your orb—the one you have now, not the one some fool of a Sister let you borrow," she clarified. Nat thought back to her first encounter with Rory along the riverbank outside Rustbrook when she had Barba's orb. "How did you imbue it?"

Rory's question brought her back to the present. "I used a combination of breath and cartilage, then completed the connection by bringing it into my dreams." She touched the notched curve of her ear.

Rory nodded. "Common combination. Not so intrusive, but enough . . ."

"Enough to make it feel and understand me." Nat finished her thought.

"Did your Sisters teach you about imbuing orbs with only memory?"

"No." Nat drew her cloak tighter against the chill. The process of making an orb was still puzzling to her, even after completing her own. Rory looked out over the canyons surrounding the riverbed. A sliver of gray light broke on the eastern horizon.

"Many Houses ago, Sisters attempted to create orbs using only memory as the link. They hoped to eliminate some of the physical pain involved in the process and provide each orb with a deeper understanding of its maker."

"Did it work?"

"Not well. The orbs rarely connected with the maker. They continued to absorb more and more memories if the maker persisted in attempting to establish a connection."

"I don't understand, Sister."

"They latched onto the subject of the memory, not the Sister. If a Sister's memory concerned a person, the orb would only respond when she visualized other memories of that person. They were worthless from what I understand. Odd colors, small in size, terrible at following commands . . . Sound familiar?"

Nat thought of the colored orbs surrounding the Chemist's map. "You think the Chemist's orbs were some kind of memory orb?"

"I do, but modified to track the person who was the focus of the memory."

"Wouldn't he need the help of a Sister who knows how to make such orbs?" The idea that any Sister would help Mudug and the Chemist was anathema to what the Sisters stood for. Mudug had killed or driven away so many of them.

"Emilia trained with each House before becoming regent," Rory cut in. "She apprenticed in my Warrior House and the other Houses as well. Because of her position as future regent, her training in each House was deep and extensive. It's unlikely she learned how to create the core of an orb like a Head Sister, but it is possible. The Chemist may have used her to figure out how to make the orbs and then forced Emilia's memories from her to imbue them."

Nat thread her fingers through the loop attaching her dagger to her belt. Her stomach twisted and the muscles in her back tightened. "You think Emilia is helping the Chemist?"

"Not voluntarily, no." An owl with a mouse dangling from its beak glided past and landed gracefully on a rocky ledge below their feet. It turned its moonlike eyes toward Nat, then efficiently swallowed the small rodent.

Rory looked in the direction of the sunrise. "If the Chemist used Emilia's memories to imbue orbs, she won't be the same person she was before. When the Sisters experimented with imbuing orbs that way, they discovered unpleasant side effects. It created memory holes. In some extreme cases, the Sisters became irrational and even delusional. Finding Emilia may be the easy part of your mission, Sister." Rory's expression was guarded as she watched Nat for some reaction. "Emilia may have no memory of the others traveling with you. She may act . . . violently. Do you understand how that may impact others who knew her personally?"

Nat nodded, imagining what it would be like if her parents, Marie Claire, or even Cal took her for a stranger. A few moments passed. The sounds below them ceased, and the owl flew away from the narrow ledge.

"Should I go to my post now?" Nat asked. Morning was burning away the night sky. She wanted time alone to think about what Rory had told her.

"Yes, but one more thing. When I met you, the only thing that kept me from killing you were the markings on your arm."

Nat's heartbeat quickened.

"It was clear you weren't a Sister, despite your fringe claim and the borrowed orb." She unfolded her legs and stood up. "Generations have come and gone since those markings covered a Sister's forearm. Yours are the markings of the first Warrior Sisters, the first Sisters to purposely seek out and kill the Nala." A smile crept over her lips. "Whoever drew those on you intended to send the Nala quite a message."

"What message is that?" Nat's voice quivered.

"That the Predictions of the First Sisters are true. The time for the annihilation of the Nala has finally arrived."

CHAPTER TWENTY

Questions played over and over in Nat's mind. *Why did Barba give me those markings? And what predictions? Barba had only said that my markings were from the first Warrior House.* Nat remembered the Nalaide's disbelief and enraged reaction when the creature had seen her markings. *Why . . . ?*

"Any closer and I'll run you through," Benedict threatened while waving one arm wildly at Annin and clasping his saddle horn with the other. His cape hung askew, revealing his thin leg, useless in controlling the skittish horse. Annin guided her horse in a zigzag pattern behind him, agitating Benedict's horse with her presence.

"I'd like to see you try," she mocked.

Benedict shifted from side to side in the saddle. He strained to pull himself upright. Annin urged her horse forward again. Benedict's horse reared, kicking his hooves in the air, then slamming them into the ground. Benedict rolled from the saddle and landed in the knee-high grass. The horse reared again and streaked away. Annin's horse pawed the ground a few inches from Benedict's face.

"Annin! Stop it!" Nat cried out and slid off her saddle, afraid Annin's horse would trample the Hermit. Dirt streaks covered Benedict's red face. His fingers dug into the mud as he scrambled away from Annin's horse.

"Don't ever threaten me." Annin pointed at him and her Nala eye seemed to grow in size. He pressed a hand into the mud and pushed himself into a sitting position. Nat ran in front of Benedict and grabbed the reins of Annin's horse.

"If it wasn't for Estos"—Benedict lifted his small frame as straight as he could—"I'd have your hide."

"You missed your chance," Annin spat back. Nat held firm to the reins, fighting Annin for control of the horse.

"I should have let that Nala rip you to shreds," Benedict growled.

Nat dropped the reins and spun around to face him. "Don't ever . . ."

A shadow passed above Nat. Annin landed on top of Benedict and the two rolled onto the ground.

"Get off him!" Andris spurred his horse toward the trio, holding Benedict's runaway mount by the reins. His legs clamped hard against his horse, controlling the animal in Annin's presence. Nat grasped Annin's shoulder and wrenched her away from Benedict.

"I swear on the Rim, if you do that again, Annin, I'll send you packing." Andris cursed and tossed the reins to Nat.

"Send her now." Benedict brushed dirt from his arms. "Vermin duozi will bring the Nala down on all of us. Mark my words, she'll use her dream manipulation on us like she's done to Estos. She'll twist her way into our minds, make us weak, and then lead us to the monsters." Spittle flew from his mouth as he ranted.

"Are you crazy?" Nat couldn't believe what she was hearing.

"That foul half-breed has no place among humans, no place among any of us." Benedict made a wide arc with his arm and his hand froze in the air.

Soris was staring at him from atop his horse. A glimmer of anger passed over his face. When he blinked his faceted Nala eye and hazel-green eye, the emotion disappeared.

Oberfisk rode up behind Soris. His thick hands held tightly to the leather reins, easing the gelding's nerves. "Everything all right here?" He glanced at Andris, whose face was so red he looked like a raspberry.

"Let me make one thing perfectly clear," Andris said, ignoring Oberfisk. "Each of you will follow my orders." He pressed his fist to his chest, his knuckles white. "You do what I say, nothing else. Your personal vendettas and prejudices mean nothing to me. But if they disrupt this mission, I promise to tie you to a tree in the middle of the eastern forest and call the Nala in myself. Any questions?" He whipped around, glaring at everyone. The horses stamped their hooves. No one said a word. "No?" His lips tightened as he stared down Annin and then Benedict. Annin tossed her head in the opposite direction and blew a bit of curly hair out of her face.

"Help him up," Andris ordered Nat.

She clasped her hands to give Benedict a foothold to remount. He dug his heel into her hands as he clambered on top of his horse.

"Sends me with a bunch of misfits," Andris muttered loud enough for everyone to hear.

"Andris." Oberfisk interrupted his cursing. "We found a spot about a half a mile from here. Abandoned farmhouse and barn. It's on an open plain in the foothills, no chance of anyone sneaking up."

"Soris, take Annin and the good Sister, scout out the farmhouse, and set up defenses. Oberfisk, Benedict, and I will check the foothills for any sign of Mudug's guard. We're too far from Nala territory to have any encounters with them. Focus your defenses on guards. That is, unless you have anything to share?" Andris directed his question at Annin.

"Ask your brother, he's as good at sensing the Nala as I am." Annin kicked her horse and rode away through the low scrub brush. Soris pulled his reins low and to the side. He ignored his brother and followed Annin's trail. Nat shoved her boot into the stirrup and grasped the saddle horn. Andris reached out and grabbed her arm as she passed him. His fingers dug into her skin.

"We are here because of you, Natalie. I shouldn't have to explain the enormity of the risk involved. These squabbles must cease."

"I know. Do you mind?" She looked at her arm.

Andris loosened his grip and let out a long breath. "Do what you can to keep Annin in line."

"What about Benedict? He's not making it easy for either of them." Nat looked over her shoulder and watched as Oberfisk helped balance Benedict in the saddle with his meaty arms. The Hermit's lips moved continuously. She could only guess the poison coming from him now that Andris was out of earshot.

"He has too much at stake to sabotage this mission, Natalie." She raised an eyebrow and Andris gave her an irritated look. "History and oaths serve as mighty constraints." He turned his horse, leaving her to wonder what oath could constrain Benedict's hatred.

Jagged holes marred the curved roof of the barn. Weak light from the setting sun created a patchwork of light and dark on the floor. Nat kicked a clump of gray mortar where the bumpy rock wall met the earth. The place smelled of stale manure and moldy hay.

"The house isn't much better." Soris stepped through the broken doorframe. "The floor's rotted and covered with glass."

Nat walked through the rays of light toward Soris. An owl flew from the wooden rafters, sweeping past his head into the fading day. He looked up at the thick beams covered with owl droppings.

"Birds don't like me much, but at least it means no bird droppings on us tonight." He gave her a wry smile. "Think Benedict will thank me?"

"What do you think happened here?" she asked, diverting the subject away from Benedict.

Soris shrugged. "Dreams of impossible things."

Nat joined him by the door, and the two of them took in the ruined expanse of the barn. Partitions leaned against each other in fragile support. The rungs of the ladder leading to the hayloft were broken in half.

"What do you mean by that?"

Soris stepped into the barn through a beam of light. Dust floated and swirled around him. "Someone believed in a future here." His voice was caustic. "Why is it some people fail to see the futility of their actions?"

"Maybe they saw an opportunity, a chance to make something better," Nat said, feeling defensive.

"Natalie." He drew out her name when he spoke and stepped into the shadows. "Thin soil, scarce water. Why would anyone try to grow anything here?" he challenged.

"Because sometimes you have to take the risk."

He moved to her side so quickly she let out a little gasp. "But you don't. You don't." His breath fell upon her ear. "You don't have to take the risk. You don't have to be here."

"It's a risk worth taking." She turned, steeling her voice.

Soris let out an exasperated breath. "No, it's not, Natalie. It's not." He kicked a pile of rotted leather tack. "Even if we manage to pull off Estos' plan, make it into Rustbrook, and find Emilia, do you really think the Chemist is going to let us walk out with her? This endeavor is night and day to what you and I had to accomplish."

"If you think it's so impossible, why'd you agree to come?"

"I have absolutely nothing to lose." The shadows turned the blue tint of his skin gray.

"Really? Nothing?"

"You heard Benedict." He held up his hands, silencing her. "Half-breeds have no place among humans. Trust me, Natalie, the utopian life of the duozi at the Healing House ends the moment you pass through its walls and away from the Meldon Plain. Estos can't dictate tolerance, even if he regains the regency. I have no chance of a normal life."

"Yes, you do," she argued.

"Tell me how? To be a duozi in Fourline is like living with a curse." He crossed his arms and leaned against a broken post.

"The Sisters may come up with something that purges the venom or cures whatever causes the transformation. There has to be some way to heal you." She sounded unconvincing even to herself.

"There've been duozi since before the Rim Accord. Do you really think they're going to find a magical cure? You're dreaming of things that can never happen, Natalie." He gestured to the decaying barn and looked at her sadly. "Here's the result."

She instantly brought her hand to his cheek to soothe the deep lines on his face. He clenched his jaw.

She drew her hand away. "Fine, be a fatalist," she said, feeling the flush in her cheeks. "But know this: I left you in a lurch once, and it didn't work out well for either of us. I try to learn from my mistakes. I'm not going back home until this is over and you're back with the Sisters at the Healing House. There has to be more they can do to help you."

"I'm not going to live a life behind walls, waiting for an impossible cure."

"Then get used to me, because I am not going anywhere. Ever hear the expression 'like flies on—'"

"You're a stubborn fool, Natalie." He dropped his arms, his pointed hand dangling at his side.

"Maybe, but a fool with something to lose."

"What could you possibly have to lose by leaving Fourline?"

"Being your friend," she said, knowing that might be the only thing he'd ever let her be.

His expression softened. "My friend?" He regarded her a moment, and she met his gaze, refusing to look away. The corner of his human eye turned up. He stepped close to her and tucked a stray lock of hair behind her ear with his fused fingers. She tilted her head toward his hand as he brushed her jawline. "Did you know being my friend comes with some conditions?" His Nala eye contracted.

"Defenses set?" Oberfisk's voice boomed through the barn. Nat and Soris jumped apart. Oberfisk appeared, his great bald brow scrunched into half a dozen lines. "Haven't done a thing, have you?" He tsk-tsked.

"We were just discussing our options." Nat glanced at Soris. He rolled his human eye, but a small smile appeared on his lips. Her heart skipped a beat.

"Stop discussing and get the defenses up, unless you want to discuss it with Andris," Oberfisk threatened.

Nat and Soris hastened toward the door. "If we're going to be friends, then you have to drop the idea of me returning to the Healing House," he whispered out of Oberfisk's earshot.

"No, I don't. Friends can always disagree," she shot back. He groaned in response. Nat took two steps for every one of his as she followed him up the hill from the barn. "Just like I disagree with you about me leaving Fourline," she added when she caught up with him. He handed her the blunt end of a spool of thin wire and stretched a length between the thick stems of two spiny bushes.

"You're making me regret my decision to be your friend, Natalie," he said as he clipped the wire. He glanced up and handed her a small stake. She shoved the stake into the soil, feeling a little triumphant that he was agreeing to be her friend.

"I never promised being my friend would be easy."

"Understatement of the year, Natalie," he muttered and busied himself with setting the snare. She watched him nimbly wind the wire with his good hand. Even though he faced the ground, she could see his smile broaden and matched it with one of her own.

CHAPTER TWENTY-ONE

Water fell from the holes in the roof of the barn, expanding the size of the puddles spreading across the floor. Nat shifted her position. She lifted her head from her satchel and listened to Benedict's snores intermingle with the incessant dripping of the rain. How he could sleep was beyond her. Oberfisk rolled over and his arm flopped against her side like a baseball bat. Grimacing, she carefully scooted from underneath his thick arm, setting it gently against his sleeping form.

She sat up and searched the folds of her cloak for her orb. It emitted a gentle glow at her touch, casting soft shadows around the end of the barn. She pulled her knees to her chest and breathed in a long, deep breath. The smell of fresh horse manure overpowered the smell of the rain. She watched the sleeping horses' breath puff out of their nostrils like little smoke signals.

The ground felt spongy under her feet as she stepped through the crooked opening of the barn. Water poured off the broken end of a narrow overhang, splashing against the side of a splintered barrel. Her eyes strained in the dark to find the outline of the dilapidated house where Annin slept. Soris and Andris were on second watch somewhere in this soggy weather.

She tucked the orb away and let her eyes adjust to the darkness. The broken house came into focus against the foothills. She shifted carefully, settling onto the worn wooden top of the barrel. It creaked under her weight.

Even his brother is segregating them, she thought. Andris had given in to Benedict's grousing and separated the group earlier in the evening. No one believed his pretext that the horses would sleep more soundly away from duozi or that it offered a defensive advantage. Soris had grabbed his satchel and strode off toward the house with Andris' excuses trailing after him. *At least Andris has the decency to join them in the house.*

She closed her eyes for a moment and listened to the rain. As much as she hated to admit it, Soris was right about his options. Even if Estos removed Mudug from power, she wasn't sure Soris' life would be much better. Mudug had orchestrated such a successful campaign demonizing the duozi and the Sisters that it would take at least a generation to bring people around to accepting duozi into daily life. Nat remembered the story the old shepherd Greffen had shared with her about the villagers sending a young girl out into the woods after she was turned into a duozi. What would it take to erase such deep-seated prejudice?

Soris had said the duozi had been around since before the Rim Accord. If Benedict's treatment of Annin as a child was any indication, it wasn't like people had ever embraced the duozi. Unless a Sister found a cure or a way to reverse the transformation caused by the venom, maybe the Healing Houses were their only places of refuge.

She pushed her fingers against her temples, wishing for the hundredth time that she'd taken Soris straight to the membrane after he'd been bitten instead of waiting at Greffen's. *Ethet could have stopped the venom quickly, preventing the transformation or at least rendering him more like Annin so he could stay in my world.* She thought of what Barba had said about Soris never being able to push through the membrane now. She wondered if Barba had any idea how deeply her words plagued Nat.

"You're stuck here because of me," she whispered to the rain. She straightened her back. She had to convince Soris to return to the Healing House. *If the Nala ever catch up with you* . . . She shivered, remembering his dronelike behavior in the horror of the Nala den.

"You make a lousy guard," Annin said, stepping from the wet shadows to a narrow strip of dry ground next to Nat.

"You make an excellent sneak." Nat's heartbeat settled to its normal pace.

"I'd rather be me. Soris and Andris are back. It's our watch."

Nat slid from the barrel and followed Annin into the night. Water dripped from the rim of her hood and landed cold against her chin. They made a wide arc away from the house to the rise above the ruined farm. The wet ground was covered in scraggly clumps of brush.

As they trudged up the rise, a thin ray of moonlight shone over the landscape, revealing miles of foothills leading to the mountains. Annin nodded to Nat and the pair broke apart. Annin snaked up the low branches of a lone twisted tree, her figure hugging the curved limbs. Nat waded through the mucky open space between the tree and an outcropping of eroded granite slabs. She jumped over an almost invisible wire, thankful she remembered the location of the trip wire they'd set earlier. Andris' wrath would be unmatched if she accidently triggered one of their defenses.

The crossbow bumped against her leg when she placed her foot into a low cleft in the ancient rock. She pulled herself up and propped her back against one side of the rock. Like the slabs of Stonehenge, the formation was out of place in these foothills of low shrub brush and scraggly trees.

She scanned the foothills from the front and back of the rocky opening. The rain slowed and gradually tapered off until the only droplets falling near Nat were from the pools of water shining in the moonlight on top of the slabs. She blinked, keeping her eyes clear of sleep, and listened to the night. Moonlight now flooded the land. In its silver glow, she barely noticed the small white beam cutting across the foothills. A sound mimicking a screech owl, Annin's warning call, filled the air. Nat tensed. The white light bounced up and down erratically and grew in size.

She dropped to the base of the slab and crept past the edge of the rocks, keeping the beam in sight. A shadowy shape began to form behind the beam, and Nat recognized the brilliant white circle emblazoned on the arm of the person running toward them. *Mudug's guard,* she thought, remembering the first time she'd seen that emblem. Her gaze swept over the foothills beyond the guard. The moonlight exposed nothing but low hills. *What is he doing out here in the middle of the night on his own?*

Just as the guard was about to pass between the boulder and the tree, he tripped over the wire. His small lantern flew into the air and landed with a thud right at Nat's feet.

"Stay down." She kicked the lantern to the side. The guard lifted his head to find a crossbow pointed directly at him. His eyes grew wide as he took in Nat and her Sister cloak hanging heavily around her shoulders. Sweat and drops of rain trickled from his matted brown hair down his cheek and into the bristles of his two-pronged beard. He slid his hand toward his side. Nat swiftly planted her heel against his nose. The guard's head snapped back, and he crumpled with his face to the ground.

"Nice kick," Annin said from behind her. "I'll get Andris, if he's not on his way. You have him?"

"I don't think he's going anywhere," Nat responded. The guard moaned. Annin took two quick steps toward him and pulled his sword from his sheath and a dagger from his boot. With his forehead pressed to the ground, the guard didn't see her.

"I'll keep these just in case he's feeling stupid." The weapons clanked together in Annin's hands. She sped off toward the farmhouse, jumping over the snares and traps.

Nat pulled out her orb and steadied the crossbow. Her neck muscles were knotted and a tense ache settled over her shoulders. The guard crawled to his knees, keeping one hand clamped over his nose. Blood covered his chin. She stepped to the side and noticed a black leather bag hanging between the slits of his thick wool tunic.

"You're a Sidder, doughd they were all gone," the guard said. His eyes followed the orb as it darted around his face.

Nat tightened her hands around the stock of the crossbow. The guard held out a hand. "Don shood, don shood."

"Put both hands back over your nose and don't move." The ache coursed down her neck into her arms. Where was Andris? The guard obeyed. Dark eyes peered out above his fingers as he examined Nat in the flickering light of the orb.

"Any others with you?" Nat asked, watching him. He shook his head. "What are you doing running through nowhere in the middle of the night?"

His eyes darted down to the leather pouch. "God lod," he said, too quickly.

"Lost? Isn't it your lucky day, then, running into us?" Oberfisk strode past Nat and clamped one hand around the guard's biceps. He lifted him easily into the air. The guard's knees buckled slightly when Oberfisk dropped him on the ground.

"Take him to the house," Andris ordered. He stepped into the light of the orb.

"Rebels," the guard muttered as he passed Andris.

"And a genius to boot! Stop the gawking and move." Oberfisk pushed the guard, directing him toward the house. "Step to yer right." His voice trailed behind them. "Don't want you to lose a foot before we can show you some hospitality." His low laughter faded away as he led the guard down the muddy hill.

"I sent Soris and Annin to search for any more. Did you see anything?" Andris asked as he scanned the foothills.

"No." Nat searched the dark hills, then joined Andris as he followed Oberfisk's tracks in the mud. "What would he be doing out here alone at this time of night?"

"No idea, but I intend to find out."

CHAPTER TWENTY-TWO

A circle of broken glass surrounded the guard. He sank to his knees on the rotted floorboards. Oberfisk's boots crunched against the glass as he took a wide step back from the kneeling guard.

"Deserting, you say?" Andris stroked his beard. A look of sympathy passed over his face. "I can understand that. We all know Mudug's a phony usurper," he said encouragingly to the man.

"I wad lookin for rebels, to join dem." He glanced at Andris expectantly.

"Of course you were." Oberfisk nodded in agreement.

Andris leaned in, inches from the guard's face. "What I don't get is if you were looking for rebels, why were you traveling toward Rustbrook instead of away? That's what's got me a little tripped up." He fluttered his fingers in front of the guard's swollen nose.

Nat watched as the guard's eyes shifted away from Andris toward her. He remained mute.

"I wouldn't look at the Sister," Andris advised. His voice held no hint of friendliness. The guard's eyes darted back toward him. Nat's orb hung directly above his head, casting an eerie glow over his sweat- and blood-drenched face. "You didn't see her markings, did you?"

The man's head twitched.

"She's a Warrior Sister. Your like eviscerated her House, killed her Sisters. I wouldn't expect much in the way of friendship from her." Andris smiled. Nat narrowed her eyes and glared. "Let's try a little truth, shall we? Or I might have to step away for a moment, and I can't promise that she won't take that blade of hers and finish you like you were some scum of a Nala." Andris knelt next to the man and clamped his hand over the now-quaking guard's shoulder. Glass crunched under his high leather boots.

"See, I'm not buying any of your story, friend," Andris said, his tone light. The man said nothing. "He's all yours, Sister." Andris stood and lowered his head as if in sorrow. Nat stepped into the light and reached for her blade. She caught Ober winking and smiling at her from behind the sniveling man. She kept her expression stony.

"I'm delling the drood," the guard whined. "Mudug's mines are a nydmare. They have us working dwendy-hour shifd. No breaks above ground, no fresh air, jusd the dark pid day afder day. And de duozi and de scum from de Rewall working . . ."

"What duozi? Mudug has duozi children working in his mines?" Nat interrupted. What else was Mudug doing to the duozi, and what was the Rewall? Andris shot her a scathing look. He wanted her to act like a vengeful thug and keep quiet.

The guard babbled on, oblivious to Nat's blunder. "No children, he has de older duozi working in the pids. I even saw a Nala creeping around when a load of workers from de Rewall came in. Duozi and Nala probably plodding do join dogeder." He twisted his face upward and searched for some agreement from Andris. Andris nodded understandingly and handed the guard a soiled cloth. The guard gingerly cleared his nose.

"You ran away because of the duozi? I thought Mudug had the duozi under control," Andris said, sounding uninterested.

"No, no, he sends the adult duozi to the mines with the Rewall filth, but some escape," the guard said, his enunciation much clearer now that a good deal of the blood was gone from his nose. Nat wondered if he knew about the other place Mudug was sending duozi.

The man waited for some response from Andris. Nat's eyes landed on the leather pouch and she cleared her throat. "What's in the pouch?" she asked, ignoring Andris' repeated glare.

"Nothing," he said quickly. Fresh beads of sweat sprouted on his forehead. Andris smashed his fist against the guard's broken nose. The guard let out a gurgling scream and Andris snatched the pouch free, jerking the guard forward so his hands landed on the shards of glass.

Andris opened the pouch. "Recognize this?" he said, ignoring the guard's agonized wail, and passed it to Nat.

Purple-tinted crystals lined the inside of the bag. Nat didn't bother looking deeper into its contents. She recognized the crystals. "Riven."

Oberfisk let out a low whistle. Andris lifted his hand victoriously into the air. "Mudug's guard with a bag of riven on his way to Rustbrook." He clapped. "It's so clear now, my friend." The guard shrunk back, whimpering. "We have ourselves one of Mudug's own, his inner guard. Sent you on a little mission to bring back riven, didn't he?"

The guard said nothing, clutching his nose with his bloody palms.

"Sister, come with me." Andris turned and gestured toward the door. "Shoot him if he moves," he said over his shoulder to Oberfisk. He and Nat ducked under the crooked doorframe.

"With pleasure," Oberfisk responded and bumped the tip of his crossbow against the guard's head. The guard made a pitiful blubbering noise.

Andris veered away from the barn, taking her past the ruined buildings and skirting the snares. A weak morning light covered the eastern foothills. He rubbed his face. The lines around his eyes deepened as he squinted against the daybreak. For a moment, he had the same focused expression Soris had when contemplating a problem. Nat felt an odd pang of sympathy.

"It would be easier to kill him, but Oberfisk will have to take him back to base. He may have some helpful information for them that Gennes can use when they attack the mines."

Nat thought about losing Oberfisk. He was the one neutral person in this mixed-up group. She wondered how they would function without his easygoing manner buffering Benedict's animosity toward Soris and Annin, and Andris' obvious dislike for her.

"We can't risk his seeing Benedict, and that old man couldn't handle the trek on his own, anyway, let alone guarding one of Mudug's men," Andris said as if reading her thoughts.

"What about Annin?" Nat suggested.

Andris shook his head. "We can't risk that, either. If Mudug found out we were working with duozi, he would just use it as another weapon to poison the minds of the people against the rebellion."

"What?" She shook her head in confusion.

"Don't be so naive, Natalie. No one trusts the duozi. Everyone believes they are tied to the Nala." He said it as if he held a similar sentiment.

"Your brother is not tied to the Nala. Annin is not tied to the Nala."

"Don't lecture me about my brother," Andris cautioned.

"You could take the guard back," she said, trying to keep the bitterness out of her voice.

"No," he responded, "I'm not turning over command." He gave her a curious look. "I'm almost tempted to send you, it'd be one less headache to deal with. But I hate to admit it, I need you to keep the peace between Benedict and the others."

She clamped her mouth shut, wanting nothing more than to curse Andris up and down. But fear of him ordering her to leave Soris kept her quiet.

"Soris and Annin should be back from searching for more guards. Tell them and Benedict to stay out of sight. And get Ober's and Benedict's horses ready. The guard can ride on Benedict's horse. One of us can double up with Benedict until we reach the river."

Nat nodded and hastened down the hill.

"Natalie!" he called after her. "Out of sight," he repeated.

Nat sighed. *Even his own brother wants him out of sight.*

Nat yawned, tired from the previous night's interrogation of Mudug's guard. She pulled the thick leather tongue of the saddle's cinch. Her horse waited, holding his breath as she fed the tongue through the buckle.

"Come on now, let it out," she coaxed. The horse snorted. She yanked on the tongue, pulling it tighter before the animal took another deep breath. She touched the straps of the bridle, felt the edges of the saddle blanket, and gave the stirrup a rough tug. Now that they were a horse short, the last thing she wanted was a loose saddle or buckle if Annin or Soris were riding with her.

She slopped through the mud surrounding the barn. Strong morning light warmed her face. She closed her eyes. The smell of the mud and horses and the peaceful quiet of the morning reminded her of home.

"I'm not riding any of those creatures. They've been fouled by carrying duozi." Benedict's voice sliced through the serenity of the moment.

"Don't test me, Hermit, or I'll set you in front of a duozi for the rest of the day. Pick a horse to ride," Andris replied, gesturing to the animals. Nat opened her eyes. Benedict hesitated in front of Annin's and Soris' horses.

Not wanting to listen to Benedict's invective, Nat slipped behind the barn and away from their bickering. She unhooked the vine-shaped clasp of her cloak, rolled up her sleeves, and walked up the hill. She wandered up to the spot where she'd captured the guard, thinking about Mudug's mines. *The Nala enslave duozi children while Mudug enslaves the adults and people from the Rewall, wherever that is. No one is safe, especially not Annin or Soris.*

A blur of movement caught her attention, and she dropped to the damp ground, fumbling for her dagger. She peered through the branches and climbed back to her feet. Annin's wild curls sprang around her head like Medusa's snakes as she and Soris ran up to Nat.

Nat sheathed her dagger and brushed the clumps of mud off her knees. "I didn't know Andris sent the two of you out again," she said, feeling rattled that she'd mistaken them for someone or something else.

"He wants us out of the way until Oberfisk and that guard are long gone." Annin's flushed face matched Soris'. Nat caught herself staring at him, remembering how his hand had felt on her face when they'd talked alone in the barn. He came to a stop next to Annin. Sweat covered his forehead.

"We figured we may as well do something useful," Annin added. "Scouting is a long sight better than hiding away in the barn with Benedict and a bunch of jumpy horses. Feels good to get out and run, doesn't it?" She placed her hand on Soris' shoulder. A look of contentment passed over her face. Nat averted her eyes and rubbed the remnants of dried mud from her hands.

"It does." He paused and scanned the foothills. "Do you sense anything?"

"No. Do you?" Annin tied her hair away from her face with a worn leather cord.

"Something." He hesitated. "Must have been another predator." He shook his head.

"A gunnel?" Annin's hands slipped from her hair. Nat wondered what a gunnel was.

"No. It was probably nothing." Soris settled his gaze on Nat. His breathing slowed but damp curls now framed his face. Nat let her eyes wander from the curls to his full lips. "Natalie?"

"What?" she asked quickly, feeling utterly foolish for staring at him like a smitten schoolgirl.

"Is Andris ready to leave yet?" He gave her a curious look.

"Um, I think so. He and Benedict were loading the horses when I came up here," she said, keeping the details to herself. No need to let them know about their argument.

"Stop straightening your legs." Benedict sat in the saddle with Nat and whipped his head around.

"Then stop fidgeting. Every time you move, it pushes my feet out of the stirrups." She thought of the almost gleeful look Andris had given her when he told her Benedict would ride with her to the river.

Benedict hunched over the saddle horn and grumbled, ignoring her complaint. Soris' and Annin's horses wove around Andris' horse far ahead of them. They'd spent the morning working their way deeper into the foothills of the mountains, then turned west. Tall grass replaced the scrub, and the tips of the blades brushed against the bellies of the mounts. The sun warmed the air. The heat and change in scenery should have helped her mood, but with Benedict sitting in front of her grousing about the duozi, nothing helped. The breeze flipped loose strands of hair into her eyes, and she frowned.

"Hold these." She handed Benedict the reins and twisted her hair into a tight knot at the nape of her neck, catching all the strands. The sun highlighted the markings on her arm.

"Still haven't learned to keep those covered." He pointed at her bare forearm. "You never know when we could run into someone."

"We haven't yet." She grabbed the reins and purposely straightened her legs, sending him into the saddle horn. "Besides, being recognized as a Sister is low on my list of concerns."

Benedict let out a wheezy laugh. "We're approaching Rust River, the main trading route leading to Rustbrook, and you're flashing your markings like a squirrel scampering in front of a bear den in April." He gestured toward Soris and Annin, now riding astride Andris. "You're no better than those two."

"And what are they supposed to do? It's not like they can cover up their eyes and skin all the time."

"They will be the downfall of this mission, mark my words," he said, all mirth gone from his voice.

Nat kicked her horse and slapped the reins against his neck.

Benedict swayed, then righted himself. "Slow down!" he bellowed as they raced through the grass.

"You can ride with Andris," she said but slowed the horse. If he fell off and hurt himself, Andris would probably make her carry him to Rustbrook. "Why do you hate them so much?"

"They're half Nala. Even a fringer like yourself knows that," he sniffed.

"But they're half human, too."

"Makes no difference when the other half is foul. They have no place among the rest of us."

"Really? So if a Nala bit you today, off you'd go into the forest?" She gestured toward the distant woods.

"If a Nala turned me into a duozi?" Raspy laughter spilled from his mouth. It turned to coughing, and Benedict's face became a splotchy crimson. Nat slapped his back. Her horse tossed his head to the side in agitation. Benedict wiped his eyes and spit into the grass.

"What's so funny?" She loosened the reins, letting the horse pause. He lowered his head to the ground and bit into the blades of grass.

"What did they teach you?" Benedict twisted in the saddle to make eye contact with Nat. "Nala only make the young, strong ones duozi. The rest they kill. I have about as much chance of being made a duozi as you do of becoming a Head Sister." His eyes traveled to the markings on her arm. "Waste," he muttered.

"You didn't answer my question." She pulled sharply on the reins and urged her horse toward the others. The animal snorted in protest. "Hypothetically, if you were a duozi, would you voluntarily leave humans and go into the forest?"

"Yes," he responded with irritation. "I'd go into the forest and accept my fate. A duozi that remains around humans invites trouble and creates chaos."

"Annin doesn't invite trouble. She's solved more problems than I can think of."

"Given your apparent lack of aptitude for thought, I'm not surprised."

Nat eyed the grass, thinking maybe the thick foliage would break his fall.

"They make you think what they want you to think, twist your thoughts by weaving falsity into your dreams." He drew circles above his head, nearly knocking into Nat's nose.

"I don't believe you," she said, sick of listening to the generalizations and insults.

"You want an example? Fine. One of them drove my mother mad. I watched it happen myself. My father waited too long before he sent her away."

"Sent who away?"

"My sister." He straightened his back and looked toward the horizon. "My sister was a duozi. After she was bitten, my mother tried everything to cure her. Mind you, my mother was a rational woman, a scientist. She'd studied with the Sisters and knew more about herbs and plants than anyone else we knew. But after my sister was bitten, my mother lost all logic. She became frantic, impulsive, and completely inconsolable. My brother Berndle and I thought it was grief, but we were wrong."

In the distance, Annin and Soris dismounted near a cluster of wide-canopied trees. Andris looped his reins through a ring on Soris' saddle and did the same with Annin's horse, making an equine train.

"You think it was something else?" she asked, prodding him to continue with the story before they reached the others. She wondered if Berndle was the Chemist or if Benedict had another brother.

"Unquestionably. The Nala lurked in the forest near our farm. My sister would spend hours sitting near the tree line, staring into the woods with her nasty Nala eye. She used her half-breed way on all of us. She called hundreds of spiders on Berndle once when he cornered her in the barn."

"Called spiders?"

"You haven't seen them do it?" He nodded toward Soris and Annin. "I've seen her call creatures more than once. I don't know about the other one."

"His name's Soris." Nat took a deep breath, trying to suppress her growing anger.

"He's no longer Soris, just like my sister was no longer my sister."

"I'm not sure what's clouding your mind, but other than the physical changes, Soris is the same."

"You think so? Has he tried to get into your dreams yet?"

Nat tensed, remembering how Soris had seen her dream the night after he'd been bitten.

Benedict took her silence for affirmation and continued in his nasal voice. He eyed her. "My sister was my triplet. She used that connection to wheedle her way into my dreams, but I learned to shut her out. My mother did not." He paused. A sparrow flew in front of them, chasing a blue-winged bird away from a copse of trees.

"My mother woke up every night for months screaming. She'd scramble to find Brenia, like the girl was in danger. But we were the ones in danger. Finally, my father did what all the neighbors had been telling him to do for months and sent her away into the woods where she belonged. I never saw her again. But she wasn't done with us, or with my mother. Night after night my mother would wake up screaming for Brenia. She'd scream and cry for hours. My sister was still twisting her dreams, you see. She wanted her and invaded my mother's mind, poisoning her against my dad, Berndle, and me." He stared at his hands.

"What happened to your mom?" Nat asked in a hushed voice.

"I fell sick." He gestured to his leg. "Mother couldn't travel, wouldn't even try to heal me, so Father took me to the Healing House. When he returned, Berndle told him our mother had deserted us and gone into the woods in search of my sister. I never saw my mother again. Two years later I saw my father and brother. By then my father was so gone to drink that the Sisters wouldn't let me stay home. They brought me right back to the Healing House. I lived there until my sixteenth birthday, when I learned Father had passed away. I went into the service of Emilia and Estos' parents immediately after. Never even returned home. There was nothing to return to."

"What about your brother?"

"The Chemist? You know what happened to him, Sister. He devoured my mother's books and journals, but without my mother to guide him, his path took a dark turn. My sister destroyed my family, you see, each of us in a different way. That's what they do, destroy the ones around them, the ones who love them."

Nat halted her horse several paces from Andris. She watched Annin uncap a water flask and pass it to Soris. Water ran down his chin, soaking the edge of his shirt where the skin was blue.

"I'll take him from here." Andris grasped the reins. "They'll just make the horse jumpy." He nodded toward Annin and Soris. Nat slid

CHAPTER TWENTY-THREE

Nat watched a pair of sparrows chase each other down the lush green folds of the valley toward the port town. The tiny black specks disappeared in the sparkling reflection of the sun on the Rust River. She squinted in the bright light and turned her attention from the sparrows to the town, looking for any sign of Andris. He should have been back by now, whether he'd found a boat in town or not.

Seeing nothing, Nat settled back onto the tree limb, rubbed her tired eyes, and listened to the warble of the birds darting around the trees above them. Snoring disrupted the birdsong. Below her, Benedict was propped up against the base of the tree, his chin tucked against his chest. A field mouse sat brazenly beneath his clasped hands and nibbled on crumbs hidden in the folds of his worn tunic.

Annin sat some distance away from Benedict. Her moss-colored hood hung low, camouflaging her black hair as she scanned the valley. Soris lay next to her with his elbows digging into the ground, staring in the same direction. Every few minutes Annin would tilt her head or nod, and Soris would follow the path of her gaze. Low murmurs floated from the pair toward Nat, who was perched above them all.

off the saddle quickly, wanting to get away from Benedict. He moved stiffly, bringing his leg around and dismounting with a thud.

"Take my word, Sister, it's what they do," he said to her back as she walked toward Soris.

Andris wanted her to be the neutral party, which meant not spending too much time with Soris or Annin in Benedict's presence. She wondered if Andris had more than Benedict on his mind when he'd admonished her to keep some distance from Soris. She'd caught Andris watching Soris' relaxed interaction with her before they'd left the barn. He'd looked like he'd swallowed a lemon wedge.

Nat pulled her knee toward her chest and rubbed the cramp in her calf muscle. Soris looked her way. The sun played against his concave eye. She focused on his curly hair and human eye, and he was the same person she'd met months ago. He wasn't a dream-twisting monster bent on luring them to the Nala like Benedict claimed. Soris beckoned her, and his entire face came into focus. Nat glanced at Benedict's sleeping form. His snoring continued, interrupted by a grunt. *He'll never know,* she thought and slipped to the ground. She crawled toward Soris, staying low in the grass.

"Nice of you to finally join us," Annin said while keeping her eyes locked on the distant town with the silvery river running past it.

"She was just doing what Andris told her to do." Soris inched closer to Annin, giving Nat a better view of the valley and the river between the blades of grass.

"You heard him?" Nat looked at Soris with surprise. She'd been certain Andris' directive had been well out of earshot.

"'Keep your distance from them. It'll be easier for me to manage the Hermit if you three aren't constantly banding together.'" Soris mimicked his brother's clipped tone.

"Since when do you listen to Andris?" Annin plucked a blade of grass and twisted it around her finger. "Especially when it comes to Soris," she added. A confused look crossed Soris' face.

"He had a point," Nat said and swallowed her retort. Annin had grown surlier with each day in Benedict's presence. Nat had spent the last few hours wondering how they were going to make it to the outskirts of Rustbrook with the constant bitter back-and-forth between

Benedict and Annin. A verbal spar with Annin now wouldn't help the mood. "With Oberfisk gone, Benedict might feel outnumbered."

Annin turned her head away and pulled blade after blade of grass from the ground. Nat pressed on, hoping to convince her Benedict was worth tolerating. "We really may need him. I'd rather have someone who knows the Chemist as well as he does helping us. Wouldn't you?"

"No." She dropped a fistful of grass onto the ground. "Leave him tied to the tree for the crows."

"I don't know how much help he's going to be, Natalie," Soris said, ignoring her silent plea for help. "You saw the Chemist. Their faces are the same, but their bodies are nothing alike. No one is going to believe Benedict is the Chemist."

"We can pad him up, make him look bulkier. Annin, you lived in a costume shop for years, you know what we can do to alter his appearance."

"Why are you taking his side?" Annin glowered at her.

"I'm not taking his side." Nat glanced at Benedict to make sure he was still asleep. "What he did to you and Neas was wrong. But I think I have a better understanding of why his thinking is so twisted."

"Better understanding? Are you serious? He wants all the duozi gone, annihilated. I sometimes think he considers us more of an enemy than the Nala." A flush flooded Annin's pale cheeks.

"Then let's show him who the duozi really are and what they can do, and change his mind."

Annin yanked her hood from her head and leaned over inches from Nat's face. "You're not one of us, so stop trying to tell us what we should do."

Her words pierced the air. Nat opened her mouth to speak but felt a strong hand grasp her leg. Soris' eyes were full of warning. Nat shrugged him off. She thought of the full-blown lingering prejudices rife in her world. "Trying to create understanding will lead to a better result than despising those that fear you. All hatred does is create more conflict, more war."

"You sound like an Emissary Sister, not a Warrior Sister," Annin said. "Maybe that should have been your House, given what happened to Soris."

Nat sat back as if slapped.

"Annin," Soris said sharply.

"Two duozi, including my brother, arguing, a sleeping Hermit, and a noisy Sister. I could have killed all of you three times over." Andris emerged from behind the trees. The dark material of Mudug's guard's uniform stretched taut over his shoulders, and the white sun on the sleeve appeared ready to rip.

Nat stood and swiftly walked away from them. Her cheeks burned from the sting of Annin's verbal attack.

"You're speechless, Sister! That's a first. Rouse the sleeper," he called after her and waved at Benedict.

Nat shook Benedict's thin shoulder and he jumped.

"Andris is back," she said in a strained voice. Leaf-shaped shadows played over his face as Nat helped him to his feet. She stepped away after he steadied himself, wanting distance from all of them, but Andris, Annin, and Soris walked up to the tree.

"I've secured a boat for Mudug's personal guard, me." Andris paused, oblivious to Nat's discomfort. He looked at each of them in turn as if assessing their value before continuing. "I'm leaving in an hour. There's a sharp bend in the river three miles south of here. You four ride to the bend and wait for me in the trees. I want Soris in the front leading and Annin bringing up the rear. Stash the saddles. Let the horses go once you see me. Any questions?" He crossed his arms. "Good, don't muddle this up." He unbuckled his saddlebag and retrieved the guard's black leather pouch full of riven. He gestured to Benedict, who limped through the grass. Andris lifted him onto his horse as if he weighed no more than a child.

"My horse is too much for Benedict. If he falls off, you need to help him back up. Am I clear?" he said as he gave Nat a slight boost. She swung her leg over her saddle, still reeling from Annin's words.

"Yes," she mumbled.

Soris lingered nearby, glancing from Annin to Nat. "Natalie, are you all right?" he asked.

"I'm fine," she said and kept her head low.

"Get moving, Soris." Andris gestured to the hills. Nat kept her eyes fixed on her horse's mane and away from everyone else. Soris kicked his horse. The animal responded instantly with a lunge forward, passing Nat and Benedict.

"Remember what I said before, keep Annin in line." Andris nodded toward Annin, who flew on top of her horse and circled behind Benedict. The Hermit clutched the reins as he cursed at her.

"I'm not sure I can keep anyone in line," Nat replied.

"Well, use those brains of yours, Sister, to figure out how." He stepped back a few paces and smacked the back of her horse to send him racing after the others.

Nat sat on the ground near the bend, peering through the spindly bushes. She set her sword in the sandy soil and rolled her orb in her hands, looking across the sandbar to where the river abruptly turned and merged with a rust-colored tributary. Water lapped over the red mud of the riverbank. Benedict huddled near a rotted root ball. Blood trickled from beneath the bandage pressed against his forehead.

"Hold still." Annin peeled the blood-soaked wad of cloth off his forehead. She held his face steady with her palm as she spread an opaque ointment over the cut. Blood mixed with the ointment, leaving a pink smear. Annin quickly covered the wound with a fresh bandage.

"Keep your hand here." She brought his palm to his temple. "Do you have another bandage? I'm out," she asked Nat without looking at her.

Nat tossed her satchel to Annin and kept her gaze focused on the river, watching for Andris and wondering how much longer Annin would keep up her cold demeanor. She'd agreed to patch up Benedict after his fall from Andris' horse because Soris had insisted. She'd flat-out refused Nat's request.

Annin ferreted through the contents of the satchel and extracted a thin piece of cloth. She tied the strip around the bandage and secured it behind Benedict's head. Benedict closed his eyes. "You're lucky." Annin gathered the old bloody bandage and remaining strips of cloth. "The rock missed the blood vessel by a hair's breadth."

"I feel anything but lucky." He opened his eyes and watched Annin as she collected the remaining debris. He shifted as if sitting on a cactus.

"Don't thank me or anything. I could have left you in that gully to bleed your brains out." She spun away with her hands full of bloody garbage.

Nat glanced at Benedict. His chin pressed into his chest, he gently probed the area around the wound with his fingers. "She's lying, you know," she said to the Hermit.

"Hmm?" He lifted his head. Puffy purple bags hung below his eyes in contrast to the pale pallor of his skin.

"She would have helped you even if Soris hadn't insisted," Nat said. She knew Annin's initial refusal to help Benedict was because Annin was still mad at her. "She's too much Ethet's apprentice not to," she added, swallowing her earlier hurt. Even if Annin had castigated her and was now ignoring her, she had to try to create the unity they needed to get through this mission.

Benedict didn't respond. The corners of his mouth turned down. She looked away toward the river and sighed. *What am I supposed to say when he won't even acknowledge that she helped him?* Andris wanted her to keep the peace, to keep Annin in line, but Benedict was the real problem. She let go of the branch, and the leaves sprang back into place, obscuring her view of the river.

"Why can't you put your feelings about them aside?" she asked.

He looked up, startled by her question.

"You locked her in a cabinet when she was a child, but she just willingly helped you. The least you can do is say thank you after she bandaged your head."

"How did you know . . . ?"

"About the cabinet? She's been in my head twisting my dreams." The sarcasm was heavier than she'd intended, but she let her tongue fly when she saw his eyes narrow. "And Soris asked that she help you despite knowing that you ratted out Neas."

"Who?"

"You don't even remember his name." She crossed her arms and shook her head at the old man. "The boy we met in Yarsburg, the boy you forced from his family, from his home. Mudug's guards turned him over to the Nala. The Nala enslaved him along with a hundred other duozi children just like him." She stepped closer to the Hermit. "You talk like you're the savior of humanity, but your anger and hatred serve the needs of the Nala. You're no better than Mudug."

"Don't you dare." His voice cut through the quiet whoosh of the rushing river. He pushed his hands into the ground as he tried to straighten his thin leg into position to stand. "I've devoted my life to the regency. What have you done, Sister? What have you done?"

The anger that had flared in her subsided as she watched him take ragged breath after ragged breath. She was supposed to keep the peace, and what had she done? *Alienated and made everyone mad, that's what I've done,* she thought in silent response to his question.

He looked past the bushes to the river, refusing to meet her eyes. She turned away. What both of them needed at this moment was some time apart. She hurriedly ducked under the bushes and trees into a clearing. She dropped into the long grass and hugged her knees, feeling like a hypocrite. *Nice job, Nat. You preach to Annin about patience and understanding, then you get so riled that now Benedict won't even look at you.*

Horses whinnied, and Nat looked down the clearing to see Soris struggling with her horse. Soris slipped his hand over the bridle of Nat's unsaddled mount. The horse reared, knocking him to the ground before taking off to join the others running free. Nat jumped up and ran down the sloped tree line. She reached for Soris' hand and helped him to his feet.

"Good riddance." Soris slapped the dust from his clothes as he watched the horses pause at the top of a hill. "They're jumpier around me now than when we first got them." He brushed off his sleeves, and Nat plucked a leaf out of his blond hair. His eyes settled on hers. "How are you? You haven't been too talkative since we left Andris."

She met his gaze, and his open expression reminded her of the first time she saw him in the tent in Gennes' camp. "Not great," she admitted. Soris didn't say anything. He grasped two other satchels from the grass and waited for her to continue. "Annin and Benedict probably hate each other more because of me. Now they're both angry with me as well. So much for keeping the peace."

She let out a breath and watched the horses whirl and rear on top of the hill. Their nervous whinnies carried through the air. *What's with the horses?* she wondered. They were already far from Annin and Soris, but maybe they still sensed them.

"Annin doesn't hate you, Natalie. She lashed out because Benedict's got her—well, both of us—wound so tight, it's hard to think straight about him sometimes."

She accepted a satchel from Soris and their hands met. She let her touch linger on his fused fingers.

"You're the one who should be upset. After what you managed in the Nala den, Annin never should have questioned your place with the Warrior Sisters."

She let her hand fall away, realizing he'd hit the core of what was eating her. "Thanks, but if all I'm doing is making them dislike each other more, I'm not helping anyone." The Warrior Sister tenet of understanding the world around her was taking on a new meaning. She knew awareness of how humans would and could interact with one another was as important as understanding the unique natural world of Fourline.

"Some rifts never mend, Natalie, regardless of what you do or how you try to fix them." He placed his hand on her shoulder and looked her in the eye. She felt the sharp edge of her doubt ebb when she met his gaze. A quiet moment settled over them, and Nat realized how comforting his hand felt resting on her shoulder.

"Haruu!" A voice rose from the direction of the river. Soris dropped his hand and turned toward the trees and bushes. He squinted as if he were trying to see something in the thick foliage choking the bank.

"Sounds like Andris." Nat's hand brushed her empty belt, and she realized she was missing her sword. "Will you find Annin? I'll make sure Benedict gets in the boat." He nodded, and she barely registered the odd expression passing over his face. She was already retracing her steps to the thicket where she'd left the Hermit and her weapon.

By the time she pushed the thorny branches aside, Benedict was already in the long boat resting on the bank. She could hear Andris muttering about Benedict's injury and knew she was in for a tongue-lashing. She searched under the low branches. *I know I put it here.* She heard a splash. Soris had walked into the river and tossed the satchels into the skiff.

"Where are the other two?" Andris barked. "We don't have all day."

Nat glanced through the branches. Soris stood ankle-deep in water, looking down the bank. He didn't answer.

"I'm here, Andris!" Nat called out. "I'll be there in a second." *Why does Soris look so dazed?* she wondered. She caught sight of her sword leaning against a rotted stump and grasped the hilt.

"Hurry up, Sister. I *will* leave you behind," Andris warned. He extended a hand toward his brother to help him into the boat. Water lapped around Soris' ankles. He ignored Andris' hand and turned around to focus on the bushes obscuring Nat.

"I'm coming!" she called and pushed the branches aside. A thick white thorn scraped across her right arm.

"Natalie!" Soris cried in warning. He crashed through the water toward her.

The thorn curved and wrapped around Nat's wrist like a snake. A sickly white Nala head with reflective eyes lowered itself between the branches. Twigs snapped under the pale Nala's weight as it dropped to the ground while holding on to Nat with a crushing grip.

Nat felt cold fear. She'd never seen a Nala like the one in front of her. Its mouth opened before her like a black pit. A circular ridge bulged from its heaving chest. The smell of brackish water rolled over her as it dug into her arm.

"Sister," it hissed. More branches broke as Nat jerked her arm in the direction of the ground, pulling frantically to free herself. The creature only tightened its hold.

Nat balled her fist around her dagger hilt and swung her free arm against the creature's cheek. It stumbled to the side, its mouth hanging open from the force of the impact. Venom streamed from its pointed teeth. Nat heard the branches rustle and braced herself for another attack, but the sound was from Soris storming through the bushes.

He landed on the Nala's back, driving his dagger into its spine. The creature's hand uncurled from Nat's wrist the moment Soris stabbed it. Annin ran into the thicket behind Nat in time to see the Nala crumple to the ground. Soris pulled the creature's head back and sliced through its neck. He scooped the slack-faced head into his hands and yanked it away from Nat.

"What's going on?" Benedict called out, peering nervously over the side of the boat. Andris hurdled the wooden edge of the skiff just as Soris lobbed the Nala head into the river. It sailed over Benedict and splashed into the water. Benedict shrank back and disappeared from sight.

Andris ran through the bushes and stopped short. "Where in the Rim did that come from?" He rubbed his temple as he stared at the headless Nala's body.

"Does it matter?" Annin said, a little breathless. She wrapped her arms around its legs and dragged it toward the sandbar. "Nat, empty your satchel and fill it with rocks," she ordered, taking control of the situation. Andris grasped the headless creature under one arm and carried it with Annin toward the water. "Get rid of our trail!" she yelled to Soris, and they threw the body into the boat. Soris scrubbed the mud with his boots, covering their prints and the Nala blood.

"You're not putting that thing in here?" Benedict crawled to the stern, away from the corpse. Shaking, Nat tossed her rock-laden satchel into the boat, then leaned against the stern. Soris joined her. The mud made a sucking sound as they eased the boat into the water. She grasped the side and flung a leg over the worn wood. Soris kicked mud into the trough made by the boat, then plunged into the water. He grabbed the stern and hauled himself inside just as the current caught the boat and sent it coursing downstream.

"Hand me that rope." Annin ripped it from Benedict's hand when he lifted it with a trembling arm. Andris dropped Nat's satchel on the Nala's abdomen and grabbed the rope from Annin. He wrapped it tightly around the creature, binding the satchel in place. Annin grabbed the legs, and Nat scurried out of the way as Annin and Andris tossed the body overboard. Bubbles erupted on the surface of the water, then disappeared just as quickly in the fast-moving current.

CHAPTER TWENTY-FOUR

A pungent odor, like old tennis shoes and spoiled milk, filled the air. Nat breathed quickly through her mouth, trying to calm her nerves. She scanned the boat for the source of the unpleasant smell as Annin worked her fingers up and down her forearm.

"I'm fine, no bites. It scraped me but Soris beheaded it," she said, brushing Annin's hands away.

Annin glanced up, rolled her deep-blue eye, then settled her gaze back on Nat's arm. "I'd rather be certain." She raised Nat's arm and ran her fingers over the scrape and the tips of the Warrior House markings.

"Ouch!" Nat yanked her arm away. "I told you I'm fine," she lied. Her heart still slammed against her chest, and she felt like she was sitting on a million needles. She thought of how strange the Nala had looked when it'd grabbed her arm. A chill settled over Nat. She started to shiver.

Soris saw her quaking and stepped over a burlap bag sitting in the center of the boat. He clasped the edge of the boat by Nat's head, and the boat rocked slightly as he slid down next to her. He eased his arm around her shoulder and pressed her close to him. Dampness seeped into her tunic from his wet clothing. She nestled closer to him, wanting nothing more than to press her face into his chest and cry.

"I didn't sense it fully until right before the attack." Soris' arm tightened around her as he spoke softly to Annin.

"I only felt a flicker of a presence right as I stepped onto the sand-bar." A puzzled look crossed Annin's face.

"Did you get a look at the body?" Nat lifted her head. "It looked emaciated, like it hadn't eaten for weeks, and it wasn't blue," she said, remembering its sickly pallor. She stared out over the rim of the boat. Scraggly bushes and slender trees lined the bank. "It had a ridge sticking out of its chest, too."

Annin slid onto a small bench built low into the side of the boat. She stared at Nat and Soris a moment, then nodded. "Even for a Nala, it didn't look normal," she agreed.

"I've never heard of Nala this far north. There's too much open space and not enough trees until you reach the mountains." Soris shifted, creating a pocket of cold air between them.

"Maybe it was lost?" Nat suggested.

"Nala don't get lost, Natalie. It was here for a reason." Soris pulled her cloak closer around her.

"Is she . . . undamaged?" Benedict crouched on the bench in front of Andris, who stood at the tiller.

"Don't worry, Hermit, you're not outnumbered yet. No bites, no wounds, just a small scrape. Nothing to worry about. Soris cut off its head." Annin shot Nat a poignant look. "Since you almost got your head ripped off back there, I suppose I should apologize for what I said earlier."

Soris gently squeezed Nat's shoulder, urging her to respond.

"Um, it's okay." Nat hugged her knees, thinking that only Annin would pick a time like this to apologize.

Annin stood and turned around on the boat with her hands on her hips. "What is that smell?" She scrunched her nose.

"Rounds of rudit cheese. Stroke of luck." A wicked smile crossed Andris' face. "The bags were already in the boat when I arrived at the dock. The owner of this leaky tub was put out that Mudug's man was taking his boat all the way to Rustbrook, so he threw in this delivery." Andris gestured to the burlap bags with his free hand. "I cursed him up and down the dock. Made him think I was angrier than a cornered cat. It stinks, but it'll work to our advantage."

"How? It's like being in a refuse pit in the middle of the summer. I can't breathe this stench all the way to Rustbrook," Benedict whined and clutched his nose. His face was the same pale color as the bandage wrapped around his head.

"You don't have to. We'll abandon the boat at dusk. Make the owner think I sabotaged it and dumped the delivery out of spite."

"What good does that do us?" Annin pushed one of the coarse bags away with her foot.

"Hopefully he'll report that I requisitioned the boat in Mudug's name. If you remember, I was wearing the guard's uniform. I flashed the leather pouch of riven in front of the owner and claimed I had an important delivery for Mudug. When he reports his boat and cargo are missing, he'll claim one of Mudug's guards took his boat for a delivery. Mudug will think his riven courier made it this far. It may make our entry into the castle a little easier if some of his guards are off searching for this leather pouch." He tossed the black bag into the air, then snatched it with his other hand.

The plan sounded sketchy to Nat. Why would Mudug send his inner guard and not regular soldiers to search for the missing courier? She breathed in and the smell curled into her nostrils, making her gag.

"What is rudit cheese?" She coughed, trying to clear the smell from the back of her throat.

Soris leaned over Nat, pressing his chest into her side, and extracted a fat disc from the top of a burlap bag. Thin braided twigs bound the outside of the disc. Soris pried his finger between the twigs and poked a hole in the thin casing. A horrid smell wafted up from the cheese.

"Cheese created in containers made from goats' stomachs. My mother used to make it." He held a curdled blob on the end of his finger and inhaled. "Reminds me of home. Andris, catch!" He flung the round toward his brother, who snatched it out of the air with one hand and lifted it to his nose.

"Remember when you sabotaged Gordon's room with rudit?" A light shone in Soris' face. Andris lifted his chin and smiled. "Andris was put out that Gordon was leaving for Rustbrook to train with the soldiers after harvest," Soris explained to her. Andris smirked and leaned against the tiller. "He smeared a round of rudit under Gordon's bed before we left for the fields. When we returned, everything in Gordon's room smelled like a rotten barrel of fish. Our mother moved Andris straight into that room the morning Gordon left as punishment."

Nat laughed, wishing she'd had the opportunity to meet the woman who'd raised such different boys.

"Did you know I stuck a round in his kit before Emilia's coronation as regent?" Andris asked his brother.

"Now that you mention it, I do remember his smelling like a dead fish." Soris laughed. "He had to hate you."

"He was riled, but Emilia was furious. If she hadn't been so preoccupied with outmaneuvering Mudug, I would've been relegated to stable duty for life."

"If she'd sent you to fling manure, we wouldn't be on our way back to Rustbrook looking for her now." Benedict's high voice broke through the brothers' laughter. A grim look descended over Andris' face. Soris' laughter died. Annin let out a low whistle.

"Hermit, you'd do well to remember your own failures that day," Andris said, his voice cold. He stared downriver. Benedict muttered to himself. Soris released Nat and leaned over the side of the skiff. His fingers trailed through the water.

Nat looked at Annin, hoping for some explanation. She shrugged and plopped down between two smelly bags near the bow.

The boat cut quietly through the water. The thorny silver-tipped trees along the riverbank grew denser. Their slender branches dipped into the river. Swirls of water spun around their submerged ends. A log spun past the boat only to disappear under the shadowy curtain of the graceful branches.

Nat's eyes grew heavy. She turned and pressed her knees against the side of the boat. Her elbows rested on the rim next to Soris. They looked beyond the trees and foliage lining the bank to the green meadows spreading outward from the river like velvet blankets.

"It's beautiful," she said quietly. Black-throated birds with iridescent wings settled gracefully in the tops of the arched trees.

"Kimis." He pointed to the birds. One stretched its wings in the setting sun, the light playing off its colors.

"They're amazing." Nat marveled at the flashes of green.

"They only live along this stretch of the river," he said, turning to her and watching her face.

"They don't migrate?"

"They can't, or I guess they could, but they'd die. They eat the green scum that grows along the riverbank. It turns their feathers that emerald color." One of the birds flew off a branch and gracefully curved over the trees with a few beats of its wings. "In the fall, they build mud nests in the hollows of the trees and disappear during the winter. When they emerge in the spring, their feathers are dull and gray. The color slowly changes, growing more and more beautiful." He paused. "Sometimes I forget how little you know about Fourline."

"I learn more and more each day." She paused and looked over her shoulder. Andris stood straight with the tiller clasped in his hand. He gave her a hard look. She shook him off and focused on Benedict, who gazed out over the water with a troubled look on his face. "What was that exchange back there between Andris and Benedict?"

Soris glanced at his brother, then turned his attention to the water swirling around the boat. "Do you remember when you and I spent the night in the ruins of the Warrior House?" His voice was low.

She nodded, thinking how long ago that seemed.

"I told you about how I was supposed to watch Emilia for Andris so he could go look for Gordon."

"I remember," she said.

Soris gestured to Benedict. "Benedict was charged with watching Rusrel. But he fell asleep in the Sister tunnel where he was spying on Rusrel and—"

"Rusrel murdered Emilia. At least that's what we thought," Andris said. He dumped a heavy tarp near them. "How deep was your guilt then, Hermit? You'd been Emilia's childhood guide before she even started her schooling with the Sisters." He gave Benedict a withering look. The Hermit's chin quivered and he said nothing. Andris sighed, looking suddenly remorseful for what he'd said. He clapped Benedict on the shoulder. "Maybe the Sister is right about the queen, and all our failures can be forgotten." He turned back to Soris and Nat. "Tie the tarp over the front. The four of you need to be out of sight before we reach the next town." He retreated to the tiller. The boat rocked back and forth.

Nat flexed her ankles, wanting desperately to stretch her legs. Four bags of rudit crammed near the lip of the tarp penned her in on one side. Benedict leaned against her on the other side. Annin and Soris sat across from them with their knees drawn close to their chests. Between the stench of the cheese and the motion of the boat, Nat fought to keep the contents of her stomach down. The last thing she wanted to do was throw up.

Benedict's thin hand clutched her shoulder. His face was the color of chalk.

"No, no, no, don't . . . ," she whispered as his vomit hit her feet and mixed in with the dirty river water coating the bottom of the boat.

"Ugh." Annin turned away, pressing her nose into Soris' shoulder.

Something scraped sharply against the side of the boat. Nat heard a splash as she wiped her boots against the wooden planks, trying to remove the vomit covering the worn leather. The boat shuddered to a stop, sending Nat plowing into Benedict. He groaned, holding his head and stomach. The rope securing the tarp in place zipped through the fabric rings. A shadowy light fell upon the four occupants.

"What—" Andris shied away. "It smells like someone died in here."

Soris and Annin vaulted over the side and splashed into the water near the bank. Benedict swayed uneasily on the bench.

"Put your arm around me." Nat sighed as the other three pulled the boat farther up the bank underneath the cover of twisting branches.

Soris splashed around to the opposite side of the boat and grasped Benedict's arms as Nat guided him over the edge. She jumped into the water, and her boots sank into the soft mud. She gulped in the fresh sweet smell of the air.

"Grab the side, Sister!" Andris called out.

They pulled the boat up the bank through the mud. Her arms strained against the wood as they pushed it farther into the thicket of trees lining the bank until finally the boat was out of the water. Soris led Benedict to a nearby tree. He clutched Soris' arm as he slid against the trunk. The rasping sound of a blade against wood filled the air. Andris cut branch after branch from the surrounding trees and tossed them into a pile near the bank.

"Retrieve two of the bags of cheese," he ordered.

Annin returned to the boat. She skirted around the curdled puddle and tossed a bag to Nat. Another bag landed on the ground, followed by their satchels. Andris wove the cut limbs across the boat. After a few minutes, the vessel disappeared, camouflaged by the leafy branches. Soris raked a twisted branch across the mud, obscuring their footprints.

"We have a ways to walk," Andris said as he sheathed his dagger and draped the frayed strap of his satchel over his shoulder. "I'm not leaving you here, Hermit. Can you walk or do I need to get one of them to carry you?"

"I can care for myself." Benedict waved him off.

A look of impatience flickered across Andris' face. "Suit yourself, but if you slow us down, I'm strapping you to someone's back and it won't be mine."

Benedict stood with a sour look on his face and limped after him.

"Grab the bags, they're coming with us." Andris cut through the thin line of trees toward the meadow growing dim in the setting sun.

"Is he kidding?" Nat looked at the lumpy rudit bag near her feet.

"Have you known him to kid about anything, ever?" Soris flung one burlap bag over his shoulder.

"That one's yours." Annin smiled as she pointed to the other bag. She turned to follow Benedict out of the tree line. Andris was already well into the long grass of the meadow.

Nat lifted the bag. It settled against her back, and the aroma curled around her. Soris laughed at her scrunched-up face.

"Come on, Natalie. After today, a little rudit stench is nothing." He smiled, but his human eye held a hint of concern.

"Soris, this cheese is the worst thing I've ever smelled," she said, seeing only his smile and not the apprehensive look in his eye.

"We'll carry them together." He reached for her hand and pulled her up the embankment, holding on to her a moment longer than necessary.

"Thanks." Another waft of the rancid aroma went up her nose. She walked a few paces, wondering how anyone could eat anything that smelled this bad. "Coming?" she asked after glancing over her shoulder to find Soris still holding the branch and staring across the river.

"Yes. I'll be there in a moment." He scanned the banks of the river one more time and hurried after Nat.

CHAPTER TWENTY-FIVE

Nat chewed an oily nut and stared at the night sky. The stars shone with a shocking brightness. She wadded up her cloak and rested her head against the wool fabric. The smell of rudit permeated the air around her. She sniffed the cloak, turning her face away in disgust. Grass swished behind her. She bolted upright and drew her sword.

"Relax." Soris eyed the point of the blade.

"You startled me." She sheathed the sword. The Nala attack had left her agitated and jumpy.

He lowered himself into the grass next to her. "Here, compliments of Andris." He handed her a dry piece of bread slathered with rudit. "Give it a try," he said with a smile.

"I can't tell what smells worse, me or this cheese." She held her breath and nibbled the crust.

Soris leaned toward her and breathed in. "Definitely you."

"Thanks," she said, knowing she'd opened the door to the light insult. She turned toward him and studied his face. The anger and pain she'd seen so often when he looked at her was gone. She felt a sense of relief wash over her. He held her gaze with his own steady expression.

"You're welcome." His lips were inches from hers. She felt suddenly warm despite the cool evening air. His fingers came to rest over her trembling hand. "You're shaking."

"I must still be rattled from the attack," she lied. She let out a little laugh. "I haven't even thanked you for saving me."

"You would've killed the Nala in another second." He leaned back on one elbow and took a bite of his bread. In the darkness she couldn't see the blue shade of his skin. His head was tilted in a way that obscured his Nala eye. She watched him chew his food and stare at the stars as if everything in his life were normal. Melancholy settled over her like a heavy blanket when she thought how far from normal his life and his future were.

"Have you thought about what you'll do once Estos returns to Rustbrook?" she asked.

He turned on his side so he was facing her. "You think we'll beat Mudug and I'll survive the effort. I like that optimism even if it is a stretch."

"You're not answering my question."

"I don't know, Natalie. I haven't given it much thought." His expression changed as he pondered her question. Lines formed across his forehead. "It's not like I can go back to our farm like this." He gestured to his face.

"Why not? I'm sure people that worked with your family would work with you."

"With the old me, yes. But with a duozi, doubtful." He shrugged.

"What about the Healing House? You could help the Sisters and the other duozi," she said, refusing to give up on the idea of him returning to the safety of the House.

He groaned. "You don't give up with the life behind walls. Look, it's not that I don't appreciate what Ethet and the other Sisters did for me there, but the idea of returning to the Healing House for good is not appealing."

"Why not?" she pressed. "You could work with the duozi children. I saw how they respond to you."

"Or I could kill Mudug so he stops trading kids to the Nala. What's the point of fixating on the future when he's still in power?" He rolled onto his back and clasped his hands behind his head. She glanced up at the stars and wished for the thousandth time that she could turn back time and change everything that had happened to him that day at the river.

"What about you?" he asked, breaking into her thoughts. "What are your plans?" He looked at the stars, not her.

"My plan at the moment is to stick by you to make sure you don't go off half-cocked and do something stupid, like try to kill Mudug by yourself when we rescue Emilia. I want him gone like you, but a brute attack won't end him. The man's too tricky."

"True, but now you're the one evading questions. You have a life somewhere else. A family. How will you live it after you leave Fourline?"

Her mind went blank. Her home and her family were so far away. "I have no idea," she said with such intense honesty that Soris sat up and reached for her hand.

"Natalie—"

"Blasted duozi!" Benedict's voice cut across the meadow. "You almost poked my eye out!" His string of loud curses dislodged nesting doves from a nearby tree. Soris' gaze flickered over Nat's shoulder and he dropped her hand.

"Annin must be stitching up Benedict's wound." He sat back, pressing his hands into the grass behind him. "His head wound hasn't stopped bleeding. Andris told Annin to take care of it."

Nat frowned, wishing for just a few more moments of unbroken peace with Soris. "Andris should stitch Benedict up himself," she said sharply.

"My brother isn't your favorite person, is he?" He tilted his chin toward the end of the meadow where Andris stood.

"It's hard to like someone who loathes you."

"Annin's point to you just this afternoon."

"Ouch," she replied, realizing the truth in his statement.

Soris gave her a crooked smile. "Besides, he doesn't really hate you." He glanced in his brother's direction, then turned to her. "I've been thinking lately about how trapped he must have felt in your world. Maybe it's like how I feel trapped being a duozi. I think you remind him of being stuck and unable to do anything to stop Mudug or really help Estos. I wouldn't want to be holed up someplace unable to live the way I want to live or do what I know needs to be done." His expression was calm, but Nat heard the challenge in his voice.

"I'll give Andris credit for something. He stayed where it was safe until he could return home." *Something you should do, too,* she thought.

"I knew you were going to turn that around on me." He shrugged. "No more talk about our lives after this mission. Eat your bread." He gestured to the crust that Nat had dropped. "Take a big bite."

Her nose wrinkled.

"Go on, it's not going to kill you. You got attacked by a Nala today and you're balking at eating a piece of cheese?"

She bit into the bread. A smooth flavor filled her mouth.

"What do you think?"

"A creamy rancidness."

Soris took a bite of his bread. Crumbs fell onto the front of his tunic. She flicked the crumbs to the ground. A spider the size of her thumb climbed out of the folds of his tunic and onto her finger. She stiffened. The corner of Soris' Nala eye crinkled. The spider crept off her hand and disappeared into the grass. Nat shuddered.

"Don't tell me you're frightened of spiders?"

"No." She examined the folds of his tunic and the blades of grass. Finding no more spiders, she lay on the grass next to him and looked at the sky. "As long as they keep their distance." Soris lay next to her and they gazed at the blinking stars. Nat felt a tinge of homesickness as she searched the sky. "They're so different."

"Hmm?"

"The stars, the constellations." She closed her eyes. "The surge of the unknown," she said quietly.

"What do you mean?" He turned toward her and brushed a stray strand of hair from her face.

"Sometimes when it's quiet, I'll notice something. Like the birds we saw today or these stars. They're not my stars or my constellations. And then all these questions come to mind . . ." Her voice trailed off.

"How do you know they're not your stars? You may be looking at them from a different angle, that's all."

"A different angle?"

"Why not?"

"I guess it's possible."

"It's more than possible," he said in a determined voice. "Name a summer constellation."

"Ursa Major. It has this pan shape inside it."

"Does it have a brighter star, like that one?" He pointed to a star low on the horizon.

"It has two really bright galaxies near the top of the bear's head." Her eyes darted from star to star, looking for the bright pair. "And this fuzzy nebula, I think it's called the owl nebula."

"What's a nebula?"

"A big cloud of space dust and gas." She yawned and glanced at Soris. His head was a few inches from hers.

"Space dust . . . ?"

"You need a telescope, like what Ethet had in her room in the Healing House, except bigger. Sometimes you can see them without a telescope. Look for something that's bright, but with a weird shape. Like that one." She pointed directly overhead. "To the right of that faint star. See it?"

Soris moved closer. His hand touched hers and followed the path of her finger into the sky. "That's the nose of the long-eared hare constellation." He traced a figure in the air. "See, its ears are hanging behind it as it smells the spring air. The nose is a nebula then? A bunch of dust?"

"I think so. That almost looks like Orion's nebula." Nat searched for the three familiar stars of Orion's belt. She yawned again and her eyes grew heavy. The sound of Soris' comforting voice grew faint and she drifted off to sleep.

The night sky darkened into an inky blackness. The nebula widened. Swirls of glowing gas and dust spread in every direction, filling up the darkness. A tendril curled toward her, enveloping her and pulling her up to the sky in a swirl of radiant light. The tendril thrust Nat's body into space, far away from Soris and the verdant field. Tiny bursts of light played on her fingers, obscuring the shrinking planets and sun.

Streaks of red and purple danced before her eyes. She floated weightlessly past galaxies and ancient stars on the verge of collapse. The tendril condensed, and a thick blanket of dust settled around her. Then like a parting curtain, it separated. Nat was face-to-face with the long-eared hare.

The eyes of the hare were like giant pools. A galaxy swirled in the middle of each eye. She felt the velvety softness of the hare's nose under her. Silver light spun in spirals, shaping the hare's long, slender ears. The hare lifted its nose higher, taking Nat with it. It breathed in the luminescent dust.

Nat placed a pointed toe on the hare's nose and pushed. Soft fur brushed her feet. She sailed between its enormous eyes and landed on the wide expanse between its ears. The hare sniffed the nonexistent air, pulling in bright dust and exhaling long puffs of the same. It cocked its gigantic head to the side. Its ears stood on end, and Nat felt its furry skin tighten beneath her. A cold white light flashed in front of them and compressed into the long shape of the Nalaide. The creature's cruel black eyes fixed upon Nat.

The hare sprang to the side, away from the floating figure. Nat grasped the hare's dark fur tightly, holding on as it bounced across space. Vibrations trembled through the hare's body into hers. Its fear matched her own.

The curtain of luminescent dust parted again, and the hare shot out into the blackness of space. Nat turned her head. The Nalaide transformed into a streak of white light and cut through the dust storm, chasing after them. A deafening hiss filled the silence.

The hare streaked away and burst through a meteor cloud. It plunged into a red sun, trying to escape the light. Radiant flames dripped from the hare's powerful legs. Nat felt a flash of heat followed by bitter cold. She let go of the thick fur and floated above the celestial creature. The hare's enormous eyes blinked once, then it bounded away as Nat fell into a suffocating blackness. She pried her arm from her side and brushed the rough ledge of her dream space. Scraping her legs against the edge, she pulled herself over.

"Lights up," she whispered. The beams pulsed at the ledge of her dream space. A white light swept past the beams, then disappeared.

Nat awoke and sat up, groaning at an ache in her hip. A quiet pink light spread along the horizon, pushing away the night. Soris lay on the ground next to her. His eyes were closed, but his face was contorted in pain.

"Soris, wake up." She shook his shoulder and his eyes shot open.

"Natalie! Run, it's after you!"

"Soris, nothing's after me." She gestured to the meadow, then let her hand fall into her lap. "What were you dreaming?" she asked, feeling uneasy.

His chest rose and fell quickly. He gripped her hand, squeezing it tightly. "The Nalaide tracked you through the sky." He touched her face as if to assure himself she was really in front of him. "You were up there, balancing on the hare's nose, and jumped between its ears. Then the Nalaide came for you." He paused and a look of confusion came over his face. "How did I see that?"

"You've seen my dreams before, Soris, in Greffen's cottage, remember?" she said, trying to calm him.

He loosened his hold on her hand. "This was different—sharper, fuller. I don't even remember falling asleep. It was like I was instantly in your mind, watching you." He paused and then suddenly flushed as if thinking of something embarrassing.

"What?" Nat asked.

"Nothing." He stood and helped her to her feet. "Probably some residual connection with you because of the remnant," he said, sounding unconvinced. "I mean, since I saw your dreams before."

"No, that doesn't make sense. The tie's severed, and you just said this was different, sharper. Maybe we should ask Annin."

"I'll ask Annin," he said too quickly, then paused in front of her. A worried look crossed his face. "But the Nalaide chasing you in your dream felt real to me, Natalie. I could feel it searching for you, focusing in on you." His eyes met hers. "It felt real," he repeated.

She shuddered at the thought and the vision of the Nalaide pursuing her. It reminded her of the Nala that had attacked her in the brush by the river.

"Haruu!" The shout sounded faint. Nat looked away from the worry etched in Soris' face and saw Andris waving his arm over his head impatiently. He stood in waist-high grass near the crest of a hill. Soris placed his hand on her lower back as if to guide her forward. The touch was soft and comforting after his discomforting words.

"You'd know if a Nala was around here, right?" She shrugged off the idea that the Nalaide was searching for her. It was only a dream. She walked slowly toward Andris, enjoying the feeling of Soris' hand on her back. Grass swayed in the morning breeze as far as they could see.

"I should know, but I'm not so sure after the Nala attack yesterday."

"If you didn't sense it yesterday, it's probably because that Nala wasn't even normal," she said, trying to make up some rationale in her head. "It looked sick and its color was almost . . ."

"White," Soris said. "Like the Nalaide in your dream. I'll talk to Annin."

"It was just a bad dream." Her cloak swished against the grass.

"I'm not so sure about that." Soris scratched his head.

Benedict emerged from behind a little copse of trees. He scowled at Soris and walked stiffly toward Andris.

"Eat up and get your fill of fresh air." Andris tossed a broken loaf of bread toward them. Soris' hand shot out and caught the bread. He tore the crusty loaf in half, handing Nat a chunk. She took a small bite, feeling little appetite.

"He's got the wheel off." Annin brushed past Andris and stood in front of Benedict. She touched the small bandage now covering his forehead. He flinched. "Hold still." She peeled the bandage away and examined the neat stitches in the middle of his forehead. She retrieved a small jar from her satchel and dabbed the ointment lightly over the sutured wound. Benedict looked away with a deep-set frown.

"Don't like a duozi touching you, do you?" Annin smirked as she placed a neat square of bandage on the wound.

Benedict grunted and crossed his arms.

"I didn't do this for you. The Chemist doesn't walk around with a flap of skin hanging from his forehead. At least now you might pass for him if you wear a hat or wig." She screwed the lid back on the jar and dropped it into her satchel. Soris walked through the grass toward Annin, and Benedict limped away from the pair like they had the plague.

Curious what Annin had seen, Nat joined Andris at the crest of the hill. A wagon sat idle on a rutted road. One wheel balanced against a rock near a set of draft horses busily munching on grass. A tall figure bent over the wheel, pounding at the rim with a hammer.

"You're riding in style to Rustbrook, Sister." Andris gestured to the wagon and handed her a bag of rudit. The cheesy stench filled her nose.

"Who is that?" She dropped the bag quickly to her side and watched the man strike his hammer against the wheel. A tiny echo sounded from the road as his hammer struck the metal rim.

"An old friend who's willing to transport a load of rudit and misfits to Rustbrook."

"Is that . . . ?" Benedict stepped between them. He shaded his eyes from the morning light.

"Indeed it is, Hermit." A look of delight spread across Andris' face.

"Are you happy?" Nat asked, incredulous.

His smile grew wider. "I believe I am, Sister. Things are looking up." Andris rubbed his hands together and gave her a slap on the shoulder. "Now unless you want me to toss you down the hill, collect your things. It's time to head for Rustbrook."

CHAPTER TWENTY-SIX

Sweat trickled past Mervin's long black bangs and down his cheek. His shadow loomed over Nat and the bulky bag of rudit at her feet.

"Mervin!" she greeted the bookshop owner.

He placed the hammer on the rim of the wheel and stuck his thumbs in the armholes of his wool vest. "Don't think we've met, Sister," he said, his eyes locked on her markings and her orb hovering near her ear.

"Do you remember a pair of bastle herders, one with a nasty pory bite?" She tightened her hood across her forehead like her disguise months before. Mervin crossed his long arms and leaned back.

The grass parted behind Nat, and Soris and Annin stepped onto the overgrown road. The draft horses stomped and shook their long manes as Annin approached. The blinders covering their eyes flapped with each violent shake of their heads.

"Whoa." Mervin eased his hand over one horse's neck. The horse snorted but settled under his reassuring strokes. Wiping his forehead and holding up the tip of his worn gray cap, Mervin stepped away from the animals. He paused a moment and regarded Soris. Nat tensed, waiting for some harsh remark about Soris' eye. Instead, Mervin slapped his large hand on his shoulder.

"Looking a bit better than last time I saw you, Soris," he said gruffly. "Not so pale and feverish this time round. Is your hand healed up from that pory bite?" His eyes glittered and his lips curved into a wry smile. He reached for Soris' hand and examined the calloused skin where Benedict had stuck porc-tree needles.

"It's healed up fine, Mervin. We never got to thank you and Matilda for helping us in Rustbrook." Soris turned his hand to grasp Mervin's. "We couldn't have made it into the castle without you."

"Anything to help Gennes' brother and cause Mudug and that Chemist a bit of trouble." He let go of Soris' hand. "And I hope you put an end to the Nala that did that to you?"

"We did." Soris glanced at Nat. "But there are always more out there . . ." He looked straight into her eyes.

"Well." Mervin coughed. "That is an unfortunate given. And you, Annin Afferfly, it's been a long time," he said with delight. Nat stared in amazement as the lanky man enveloped Annin. When he pulled away, a smile stretched across Annin's face. He stared down at her. "You've grown mightily, and your hair." He tucked a wild curly lock behind her ear. "Matilda will want to do something about it."

"I never let her before, and I don't intend to now." Annin laughed.

"I've wondered about you and the others," he said. "Every day since you left Rustbrook, I've wondered." His voice was steady, but his hands trembled slightly.

"All of us made it, even Estos." Annin touched the sleeve of his thick cotton shirt. Her face lit up as Mervin looked at her in wonder.

"Estos is alive?"

"Good day, Mervin." Andris emerged from the tall grass with Benedict trailing behind him.

"Another surprise. Are there any more of you tucked away in that field? It is a good day, Andris, a good day indeed."

"I was worried Gennes' message might not reach you." He clasped Mervin's hand.

"If you mean the message about being on this nowhere road pretending to fix a wagon wheel, yes, I received that message. The one about the dead returning to life must have missed me, though. If you weren't here in person, I wouldn't believe any of it." Mervin scratched his head. "Maybe you can explain a few things while you help me get this wheel back on. Annin, roll out the tarp that's in the box."

Soris and Andris grasped the wooden wheel, lifting it easily. A splintered wooden box stuck out from the back of the wagon. Annin flipped the brass clasp up and opened the lid.

"Good friends?" Nat asked, pulling out the thick tarp. Moths flew into the air, freed from the folds of the fabric.

"My guardians," Annin responded curtly. "Mervin and Matilda knew me and my parents, before I was bitten. What?" She dropped her edge of the tarp. "Why are you looking at me like that?"

"Nothing," Nat responded quickly, ducking under her side of the tarp. She'd never seen Annin respond with such warmth to anyone or anything. She bit her lip to keep herself from prying. Annin would go ballistic if she asked more questions.

Keeping her eyes on the tarp and away from Annin, she unrolled the cloth over the wagon bed. The smell of mildew grew stronger with each inch of exposed material. Nat cleared her throat and turned her head to the side, away from the dank odor. "Smells better than that bag of rudit, but not much." She wrinkled her nose and hopped off the rim of the wagon. She landed right at Mervin's feet.

"I do remember you, Sister. I never would've guessed you were a Sister when you walked into our bookshop with Soris draped over your shoulder. You did a fine job playing the bastle herder. I'm happy to see you both made it out of Rustbrook. Matilda and I assumed the worst when you didn't return for your horses."

"After Sister Camden escaped from Mudug's guards, the crowd went crazy. We took advantage of the confusion and slipped out of the city," she said, replaying the chaotic scene of the execution day in her mind. "We didn't have a chance to make it back to your shop."

"We left Rustbrook by boat. Too much happened afterward for us to send word." Soris gestured to his face by way of apology. "But the Sister accomplished what we set out to accomplish."

Soris' compliment didn't sit well with Nat. She'd destroyed the Chemist's tracking device through plain luck.

"And now you want to go back? I'm wondering if all of you are right in the head. Hermit, you really plan on returning to Rustbrook?" Mervin raised his eyebrow as he addressed Benedict for the first time.

"The risk will be worth it." Benedict lifted his chin in a haughty manner.

"I hope so." Mervin's eyes narrowed. "Catching any of you would send Mudug into a fit of ecstasy," he said as he tightened the fasteners around the hub. "You know what he'd do to each of you?"

"The same thing he'd do to you if he learned you were aiding Gennes and the rebellion. Benedict is right on this one, Mervin: the reward is worth the risk," Andris said.

"And you're not going to tell me what that reward might be, are you?" Mervin slipped heavy clips sewn into the side of the tarp under the lip of the wagon's rim. He pulled the tarp taut across the top of the wagon as each clip slid into place.

"You'll know if we're successful," Andris responded.

"I figured you'd say something like that. I'll plan for the worst, then, since you're involved." Mervin slapped Andris on the shoulder.

"Everyone in the wagon under the tarp. I want your weapons out and ready," Andris ordered, his manner morphing into that of a soldier. "And tuck the bags of rudit near the front."

Soris vaulted over the side of the wagon. Mervin pulled his cap off and spoke in a low voice to Andris as the others climbed aboard.

Annin peered under the tarp. "You get to snuggle with the Hermit. He likes throwing up on you," she said to Nat.

"Thanks." She grasped Benedict's thin hand and helped him up the narrow step. She lifted the edge of the heavy tarp out of his way. He stooped low, took a deep breath, then disappeared under the cloth behind Soris.

"Annin?" Nat kicked a bag of rudit closer to the edge of the tarp.

"Hmm?" Annin gazed down the overgrown road.

"I had this dream, and Soris . . ."

"He told me."

"What do you think it means?" she asked, rankled that Soris had already confided in her. He must think the dream meant more than he'd let on.

"The dream, or the fact that Soris saw it so clearly?" Her blue eye held a hint of impatience. "If you're asking about the dream, I don't know." She continued, not giving Nat a chance to respond, "As for Soris seeing your dream . . . Well, the remnant's severed, so it's something else." Her answer sounded purposely vague.

"It's not just a weird dream, or a weird coincidence?" Nat tugged on the tarp.

"Is that what your gut's telling you?" Annin slipped another clip into place.

"No."

"I'm happy to hear your internal senses are still sharp." Annin unhooked her cloak and stuffed it under the worn fabric covering. Nat knew Annin was holding something back.

"Natalie, you and Soris get up here near the front by the rudit bags." Andris stepped on the rusted metal step by the wagon bench. Mervin placed his boot on the step, and the wagon tilted slightly under his weight. "Two taps at a sign of trouble, Mervin," Andris said over his shoulder.

Mervin held the worn crop and rapped it lightly against the wagon board. The bags of rudit landed with a thud in front of the tarp. Andris dipped under the fabric and flattened his body near the back. Annin followed.

"Sister." Mervin pointed to the opening. Nat took a deep breath, then crawled under the tarp next to Soris, thankful she was next to him and not the Hermit. He gave her a wink and pulled her closer to him, away from the opening. She suddenly didn't care that they were packed in like sardines.

"No talking, and keep your movements to a minimum. We've got a long ride to Rustbrook, but guards could stop us at any time." The daylight disappeared as Mervin slipped the last clip into place. A bulky object pressed against Nat from the other side of the tarp. The sharp, tangy smell of rudit filled the small compartment. She swallowed and rolled against Soris as the wagon lurched forward.

CHAPTER TWENTY-SEVEN

"What I'm telling you is I don't need to join your convoy. I've got a wagon full of rudit. The fool that attacks me will get what he deserves. I could buy a new set of horses with what you're asking me to pay."

Mervin's voice vibrated through the thick tarp. The wagon stood motionless. Every muscle in Nat's body tensed as she listened to Mervin argue with the soldier. Soris tilted his hip upward, freeing his crossbow. A dull gleam shone from the back of the wagon, where Andris lay pressed against Benedict.

"Doesn't matter what you want. Every wagon coming into Rustbrook is accompanied by a guard and pays the tax. They're Mudug's orders," the gravelly voice responded. "It's not thieves he's protecting you from, it's the Nala. They're climbing out of every nook, invading terrain they've never been in before. Something's got them riled, and Mudug's not willing to risk injury to his people."

"Bah! He just wants his tax. There are no Nala around here."

"I'd watch what you say about the acting regent," the voice warned.

"Acting regent is right," Mervin grumbled.

"What do you mean by that?"

The wagon creaked. "You know exactly what I mean."

"I'm this close to taking you in," the gravelly voice threatened.

Nat's eyes grew wide in panic. She turned slowly toward Soris, a look of worry spreading across her face. She had no idea what Mervin was doing. He was going to expose all of them, arguing with a transport guard. Soris' eyes met hers and he brought a finger to his lips.

"Be my guest, you'd be doing me a favor." The wagon creaked again. "You can drive this stinking load of rudit to the castle kitchens. Take a good whiff, it's spoiling fast in this heat." Mervin's voice sounded from the side of the wagon now.

"Soldier!" the guard barked. Nat drew her dagger close to her chest. Bodies shifted in miniscule movements under the tarp as hands tightened around weapons.

"Take this man and his wagon to the road where Nala were spotted yesterday. Make sure you see him off. I want no guard or convoy to accompany him."

"Yes, sir."

"Change of plans, merchant. You may proceed on your own without a guard. If luck is with you, you may make it to Rustbrook without encountering Nala. If luck's with me, you'll keep the Nala occupied while I bring our transport through. Now get out of my sight before I change my mind and leave you trussed up on the road."

The sound of heavy footsteps followed by more creaking cut through the thick barrier of the tarp. Nat relaxed her muscles.

"*Heyah!*" A short whip cracked and the wagon lurched forward. Soris held on to Nat's shoulder and glanced at her, looking as relieved as she felt.

The wagon lumbered on. Inaudible voices, clanking, and the sounds of animals surrounded the wagon as they passed through what Nat thought must be the convoy. *How many of Mudug's men are out there?* she wondered. The wheels creaked to a halt.

"That way," a soldier said.

"I know which way, I'm not a fool," Mervin shot back as he cracked the short whip again. Minutes passed. The only sounds were those of the wheels rolling against the packed dirt road and the occasional grunt of encouragement Mervin sent toward the draft horses.

"We're clear," Mervin finally said.

Andris shifted from the back toward the front like a snake slithering over rocks. His body pressed against Nat as his hands worked a clip free. Light and fresh air poured through the small slit. He pushed a bag of rudit carefully to the side, creating a little opening.

"How many?" Andris asked.

"Fifteen soldiers. Ten or eleven wagons in the convoy," Mervin replied.

Andris let out a low whistle.

"Someone would have noticed something if we'd traveled with them," Mervin continued. "I've found you can push the regular guards into doing what you want them to do if you make a fuss. Easier for them to let a cranky old merchant through than to listen to him complain and stir up dissent among the other merchants. Mudug's inner guard are a whole different kettle of fish. They'd have had me in chains as soon as I said 'haruu.' We lucked out back there."

"That's an understatement." Annin's voice rose from the darkness. "Not that I wouldn't have enjoyed taking out a few guards, but that was cutting it close, Mervin."

Mervin chuckled. "My apologies, Annin. I'll consider your nerves next time."

"Let's hope that's the last of the guards until we reach Rustbrook. Make for the ruins of the Emissary House. We'll need to rest there before moving on. It's the safest place between here and Rustbrook, unless you have another idea." Andris leaned his elbows against Nat's ribs, crushing her. She let out a little gasp of pain, wishing he'd get off her.

"No, Emissary House is as good a place as any. No one goes near the ruins anymore. They're all afraid Mudug's guards will catch them, and the guards are afraid of the Nala, even this far north. I'll give you the signal if I see more wagons. But best you all stay under wraps until we reach the House," Mervin said.

"Agreed." Andris took a deep breath, pulled the rudit bag back into place, and refastened the clip. Little stars floated across Nat's vision when he finally slithered off her.

Fresh air flowed over Nat. The rank smell of five unwashed bodies combined with the odor of the rudit disappeared when she emerged from under the tarp.

Annin took a deep audible breath. "I've never been more thankful for fresh air," she said, sitting up. Half of the tarp flapped freely against the wagon bed. "I don't think I could've taken much more of being sandwiched between you two." She poked a finger at Andris and Soris. "You both smell like rotting mushrooms and rudit."

Soris stretched his arms above his head. Sweat stains marred his clothes. Nat peeled the drenched front of her tunic away from her chest. She sniffed and wrinkled her nose.

Andris slid out from under the secured portion of the tarp. "We'll be under here tomorrow, so get used to it," he said.

Benedict crawled out. "What are you complaining about?" His cheeks had a rosy hue. "That was an enjoyable ride. I slept most of the way."

"We know." Annin freed her face of her damp curls. "Your snoring was louder than a lumberman attacking a tree. It's a good thing we didn't encounter any more guards with all the noise you made."

The wagon creaked and groaned. Nat's feet landed on the soft grass. She looked around in wonder. Row after row of trellised arches created an overgrown, verdant covered walkway. Thin stalks formed columns that looked like four wooden ladders secured together. Tiny leaves sprouted from the stalks, forming a lacy pattern high above the walkway. Light shone through the holes in the leafy sky, making a pattern that moved on the ground.

"Beautiful, isn't it?" Soris placed his hands on Nat's shoulders and turned her gently. Long thin poles carved with every imaginable songbird were tucked between the columns. She took hesitant steps toward one pole and ran her fingers over the lifelike birds. "This is where our mother apprenticed," he said.

They walked past the green trellises. She paused each time she spotted a pole. The carvings of the birds were all unique. Some had wings extended, others had beaks thrust open in song or tiny feet clinging to delicate branches. Her father would love these carvings.

Mervin appeared at the end of the walkway, striding toward them on his long legs. "The ruins appear empty," he addressed Andris. "But it wouldn't hurt to do a proper search while I pull the wagon in."

"My thoughts exactly. Sister, go with Mervin and help him with the horses. Since you're so well rested, Benedict, help them set up camp." He fastened his sword to his wide belt.

"There's a well near the old stables. He can test the water." Mervin nodded in Benedict's direction. The Hermit bobbed his balding head in assent.

"Soris, Annin, come with me," Andris said. His eyes narrowed. "I believe the Sister can stand on her own, Soris."

Soris' hands dropped from Nat's shoulders. The three of them disappeared beyond the last leafy stretch of canopy. *Why is Andris always bent on sending Soris on some task without me?* she wondered. She climbed aboard the wagon and took a seat behind Mervin and Benedict. She understood that having Soris around the horses wasn't the wisest idea, but she could help Andris search the surroundings as well as Annin and Soris could.

"Heyah!" Mervin cracked his whip. The draft horses' massive hooves pressed against the ground, slowly easing the wagon around until it entered the walkway. Nat stretched her hand out as the wagon passed through the tight space. Her fingers brushed the leaves and the wooden poles.

"I see you're not taking my warning seriously, Sister." Benedict twisted around until he faced her. He bounced up and down as they passed over the overgrown path. Shadows and light scrolled across his face.

"What warning?" She loosened the clasp holding back her hair. She raked her fingers through her damp scalp.

"You're growing too attached to that duozi. Nothing good will come of it." He wagged his finger at her.

Nat twisted her lips to the side. She pulled her hair back into a tight bun and secured it with a metal clasp. "Soris. His name is Soris," she said, glaring at him.

The wagon passed under the last verdant curve. Mervin shifted his arms to the left, and the horses lumbered to the side. A single intact stone tower crowned the hill above them. Vines choked the scattered stone ruins of the Emissary House. They rode past an outdoor amphitheater with terraced rows of stone benches in the side of the hill. Chunks of rock and cracked slabs of granite covered the ground.

"He's no more Soris than I am," Benedict muttered.

Mervin turned the horses again, and the amphitheater disappeared behind them. The wheels caught in a rut in the overgrown road. Mervin's voice bellowed over the horses. The wagon lurched free, sending Benedict tumbling backward onto Nat. She pushed him off, and he rolled to the side behind Mervin.

"Sorry about that," Mervin said, but his lips curled into a little smile. *He did that on purpose,* she thought, wondering if he found the Hermit as grating as she did.

Charred logs lay in heaps by the road. She leaned over the side of the wagon and examined the burnt remains of a long rectangular building. Carvings of vines and birds curled around the blackened wood. A narrow door with a lock the size of her fist remained upright, bound to its burnt frame by wrought-iron hinges.

"What was that building?" Nat asked. Even in its current decayed state, she could tell it'd had no windows.

"Hmm? You mean the Discourse House? Nala stayed there on the rare occasions when the Emissary Sisters had to negotiate with the creatures outside the Rim or the forest. Each Emissary House had one, surely you've seen one before."

"She's a fringer," Benedict said with contempt.

"She's a Sister and deserves more respect than you've offered," Mervin corrected.

Nat gave Benedict a sidelong glance. Heat was rising to his face. She smiled. "I've never seen a Discourse House before," she admitted. Curiosity made her ignore Benedict's jibe. "Nala actually stayed in there?"

"Yes, with a contingent of your House on guard," Mervin said.

The wagon rumbled past the remains. The road sloped downward and the wagon picked up speed. A series of intact outbuildings dotted the side of the hill. Nat wondered if Mudug had left these alone because they were far away from the main buildings composing the Emissary House. Mervin pulled the wagon through the gate of an old corral. Grass covered the thick wooden poles of the decaying enclosure. She looked behind her. The hill obscured the Discourse House and the Emissary House, but the tower atop the hill was still visible. They had reached the other side.

Mervin pulled the reins taut. The horses slowed behind a narrow row of stables. They clopped a few more paces, then buried their heads into clumps of thick grass. Nat hopped down. The burnt remains of two barns flanked the stables. She ran her hand over the rounded river-rock walls of the stables. Benedict climbed down the wagon step. He limped around the horses and headed uphill toward the crumbling remains of a well.

Nat busied herself with buckles and harnesses, helping Mervin unhitch the horses. Their wide heads nudged her feet out of the way when she stepped on their next morsel of grass. She lifted a saddle off one horse and heard the sound of running water.

Water splashed down a wooden chute that led from the well to the stable. Thick wooden supports held the chute a few feet above ground before it entered a hole cut into the stone stable wall. Water coursed through the hole into a low trough near the corrals.

Benedict dipped a vial into the surging water and settled onto a stone slab at the base of the well. A dark shadow marred the vertical rise of the hill above him. Steps led from the shadow and disappeared in the grass.

"Is that a door in the hill behind Benedict?" she asked, following Mervin into the stable under the weight of one of the saddles. She dropped hers on top of a dusty sawhorse.

"You're full of questions." He removed a dirty cloth from his pocket and wiped his brow. He dipped the cloth into the trough and wiped his neck. Nat plunged her hands into the cool water and splashed her face.

"A little splash won't hurt, but don't drink it until Benedict tells us it's clean. Mudug's poisoned wells off the main travel routes. Keeps the merchants together and makes it easier for him to exploit their travels."

She cupped her hands and splashed the water on her face again. Streaks of dirt covered her hands as she rubbed her skin. She looked longingly at the water, then followed Mervin through the stable door.

Benedict waved his thin arm in the air. "It's good for the horses, but I have one more test to run before we can drink it," he called down to Mervin. Nat studied the shadowy opening again. A collapsed wooden frame poked out from the blades of grass in front of the door.

"The Sisters used that passage to get from the main House to the stables and those small buildings we passed," Mervin explained as he led one of the horses to the trough. Nat tugged on the lead of the other horse. She felt like she was pulling a bowling ball tied to a string. The horse lifted its massive head. Grass stuck out of its mouth.

"I wonder why they didn't build the stables closer. We're on the far side of the hill." Her horse nudged her to the side when it smelled the water. Bits of green grass swirled around the water trough as the horses drank.

"You can't always have formal negotiations. If a Sister needed to negotiate with a party discreetly, they would avoid the House and use the smaller buildings. With the stables so far away, not everyone would see who was coming or going. The Emissary Sisters understood the need for discretion. Maybe a little too well," he added. His hands knotted the horses' leads to a sturdy post. "I saw more than one rabbit off the road," he said, changing the subject. "I'm not settling for a slab of rudit tonight. There's a ball of wire in the wagon we can use for traps."

"Rabbit's better than rudit," she agreed. "Anything is better than rudit."

CHAPTER TWENTY-EIGHT

The soft rabbit fur slipped through Nat's hands. Mervin's pile of skinned rabbits lay in a pink heap next to him. He snapped the bones and sliced chunks of meat into the black pot. The fire hissed as droplets of water boiled over the rim. Andris had agreed to a fire, despite the danger that someone might spot them.

"If Mudug's guard passes through, they'll find Mervin, eating stew and resting after a long day of travel. He has a legitimate reason to be here, and the guards already know he's traveling this way," Andris explained tersely when Nat questioned the logic of starting a fire. "You worry about getting yourself out of sight and in position behind those boulders if someone approaches."

"The guards never come here," Mervin said as he stirred the pot.

Benedict crumbled bits of a dark-green herb into the stew. "It's not the guards we need to worry about." His face was dour and his eyes flickered toward Soris. Nat flinched. The Hermit was on a roll with his insults and innuendos.

"Soris or Annin will let us know if the Nala are around." Andris sliced his knife through Nat's skinned rabbits. He tossed a piece to Soris, who speared it on the tip of a pointed branch. Nat looked toward the tower. Andris had sent Annin there on watch before they'd started the fire and after she'd threatened to skewer Benedict when he'd called her a Nala spy.

"They didn't provide much warning back at the river, did they?" Benedict continued. Nat widened her eyes in disbelief at the words rolling off his tongue. "The creature almost had the Sister." Deep lines curved down the side of his mouth when he looked at her. "Luck kept her from getting bitten, not those duozi."

"I'm right here, Benedict. Hearing every word you're saying," Soris said. He eased his knife over a tip of a branch. Bits of bark flicked into the fire.

"Soris saved me." Nat lifted off her heels and pointed her knife at Benedict. "I didn't see you jumping up to help, and since when did you become so concerned about me?" Andris shot her a warning glare. She lowered her knife and wiped it on the overgrown grass.

"My concern is that we're trusting them to provide a warning." He thrust his finger at Soris. "The Nala never used to come this far north. How do we know it wasn't them that led that Nala to us? How do we know that—"

"I would've warned Nat if I'd sensed a Nala, but I didn't until it was too late." Soris kept his eyes fixed on the boiling pot. "That creature felt different than a normal Nala."

"Different?" Benedict scoffed. "You expect me to believe that? Your kind can sense the Nala miles away. Estos put this mission in danger by sending you. The best place for your kind is away from humans."

"Enough!" Andris barked, but Benedict paid no heed. It was as if he'd been storing hundreds of hateful thoughts and decided that tonight was the time for the world to hear every rant.

"Admit it, duozi follow the call of the Nala, they follow their ways. You don't belong among humans." He squared his shoulders and faced Soris.

Soris clenched his jaw. Clutching his knife and the pointed branch, he stood and took a step toward Benedict. Mervin laid a hand on his arm, restraining him.

"You're nothing but a danger to us all. You belong in Mudug's mines with all the other duozi!" Spittle flew from Benedict's mouth. His voice rose to a hysterical pitch.

"Duozi in mines?" Soris' expression changed from rage to confusion in a blink.

"Before Oberfisk left, he told me the guard had spilled that Mudug has all your like doing his dirty work in his mines." A look of malice clouded Benedict's face. "If I didn't despise Mudug, I'd congratulate him for keeping you mind-twisters away in a hole where you belong."

"One word of praise for Mudug, and I will bind and gag you and see you spend the rest of this mission in misery." Andris' voice cut through Benedict's labored breaths. "And my brother is not a mind-twister."

"Andris, you're letting emotion control your better judgment," Benedict said in a condescending tone. "He may have been your brother once, but now he's a vile, manipulative half-breed. Just look at how he's wheedling his way into the mind of a weak-willed Sister." Benedict gave Nat a contemptuous look.

Soris leapt on top of Benedict. His knife, bloodied from the rabbits, nicked Benedict's throat. Nat could feel his anger and saw a look of true fear in Benedict's eyes. Andris rushed forward and grasped Soris' hand.

"Soris, let him go." Mervin's low voice reverberated around them.

Soris looked at the cowering old man beneath him and dropped the blade. He stood and backed away, shaking off Andris' grasp. He glanced at Nat, breathing heavily through his flared nose, and stormed away into the stable.

"You will control your tongue," Andris said through clenched teeth as he lifted the Hermit to his feet.

The fear drained from Benedict's face. "I am only doing my duty in warning you. You saw how he attacked me." He looked white as the bleached rock underneath him.

"Spare me talk of your duty." Andris rose to his feet and stalked up the hill, disappearing behind the boulders.

"Go find more sage," Mervin said to Benedict as he stirred the pot. Benedict limped away, muttering to himself. Mervin retrieved the speared bits of rabbit smoldering in the fire. He dropped the charred pieces into the stew, broke the branches, and stoked the flame. The blackened pieces of meat looked like chunks of burnt wood bobbing in the boiling stew.

"Cohesive group, eh?"

Mervin's voice startled Nat. She'd sat frozen through the entire confrontation. She looked at him. Steam rose around his face.

"No," she replied. "Not in the least." Benedict's hatred and Soris' response were like a nightmare playing out in real life. "I'll check on Soris." She stood and brushed the bits of fur from her tunic. Mervin nodded and dug his long wooden spoon deep into the pot.

The sound of splashing water resonated through the stable. Nat paused near the nickering horses tied up near the stable entrance and watched Soris splash his face with water. He ripped off his soiled tunic and leaned his hands against the trough. A blue tint colored his neck and his right arm and formed bands across his upper chest and abdomen. Nat could see his pained expression and the tightness in his muscles as he clenched the side of the trough. Her heart ached for him. She wanted nothing more than to hold him and magically make everything he'd suffered since turning into a duozi disappear.

"Benedict's views are warped," she said softly as she approached him. His green eye met hers. "Don't let him get to you."

"Easier said. When you hear the same insults over and over, they're hard to ignore." He thrust his tunic into the water.

"Soris, consider the source. Do you really care what Benedict thinks?" She stepped closer, wondering what she could say to ease the look of pain on his face.

"No, but slighting you like he did put me over the edge. My brother didn't help, either." He faced her and leaned his hip against the trough. "Andris was angrier about Benedict praising Mudug than insulting me." She heard the hurt in his voice.

"Andris meant to defend you. He's your brother. He loves you and is looking out for you. Even I can see that. He just doesn't have the softest manner," she acknowledged, finding herself in the odd position of defending Andris.

"You think so?" His brow arched above his human eye. "Why am I just now learning that Mudug has duozi slaves in the mines? You'd think if my brother was looking out for me and my interests, he would have passed that bit of information on."

Maybe he's worried you'd do something stupid if he told you, Nat thought as she watched the anger ripple over his face. How angry would he be if he knew she'd had the same information and forgot to share it with him?

"He probably wanted to keep the focus on rescuing Emilia," she suggested, knowing the explanation was weak.

"Maybe." He crossed his arms over his bare chest and took a deep breath. Nat felt warmth in her cheeks as she watched him breathe. The urge to touch him, to comfort him, was overwhelming. His expression softened. "Why do you worry so much about me, Natalie?" His words surprised her.

"I . . . I care about what happens to you." She felt her eyes growing moist. *Do not cry,* she told herself.

"Maybe you shouldn't. There was some truth to what Benedict said, about me getting into your mind." She looked in his eyes and saw a glimmer of sadness. "You're strong." He moved closer to her. She could feel the heat radiating off his body. "Strong, intelligent, and beautiful. I've never met anyone like you." She tried to read his expression while controlling the fluttery feeling in her chest. "But even as strong as you are, the closer you are to me, the easier it is for me to enter your dreams and stay in your dream space, even if you don't want me to." He dropped his arms to his side. "That's what happened the other night when I saw your dream." He met her eyes. "I'd never try to twist your thoughts or dreams, but Annin can teach you how to shut me out. I'd understand." He pressed his arms rigidly to his side. Nat sensed there was something he wasn't telling her, but the look of resignation he wore concerned her more.

"Why would I want that?" She took a small step forward and placed her hand on the raised scar marring his shoulder. The blue welts felt hard under her fingers, like little stones implanted under his skin. "Why would I want to keep you out of my dreams or my dream space? Why would I want you anywhere except by my side?"

His neck muscles tensed under her touch. He backed away from her. He turned around with extended arms, giving her a full view of his blue skin and fused fingers. She examined every inch of his exposed skin, the tapering of his hand, and his faceted eye.

"Because I'm half Nala and an outcast." He dropped his arms.

Without hesitating, she rushed to him and entwined her arms around his back. His skin felt cool against her flushed cheeks. His arms hovered uncertainly around her waist, then pressed against her. "I don't care. Don't you know that?" she said softly. "You're why I came back to Fourline and why I'll stay," she vowed, not wanting to let him slip away from her ever again.

"You really believe there's a chance for us?" he asked, his voice filled with doubt.

"I do. I have to."

"I'm an outcast, Natalie. This won't be easy," he whispered into her hair, but his strong arms held her tightly.

"What's easy is never worth much of anything." She brushed her hand across his chest and took in his uncertain expression, as if he were waiting for rejection. She stood on tiptoe and kissed him lightly on the cheek before he could reply. He raised her off the ground, and she lost herself in the growing warmth of his embrace and the sensation of his lips on hers.

One of the draft horses pawed the floor. The animal flicked its head toward Andris as he stood in the shadow of the stable entrance. Andris took a deep breath, shook his head, and walked away, leaving Nat and Soris alone in the stable.

"Veer left," Annin said.

"Left?" Nat smacked into a broken beam. A jagged splinter of wood scratched her temple. She probed the tender spot and her fingers came away sticky with blood.

"How are you so clumsy?" Annin asked and let out an exasperated breath. She groped the deep pockets of her robe and removed a small linen bag. Nat's orb hovered between them, casting faint shadows against the dark dirt walls of the passage leading from the stables to the remains of the Emissary House.

"My orb was up with you because you were complaining about the dark, remember?" Nat winced as Annin inspected the cut under her orb's light. She looked past Annin toward the rotting wooden frame where she'd banged her head. The frame was like all the others she'd seen in the tunnel. The once-sturdy columns of capped wood wept with moisture. Long splits ran along its moldering surface. Dirt and ancient cobwebs covered the delicate birds carved into the column.

Annin rubbed her thumb across the gash, pushing ointment into the cut. Nat sucked in a quick breath. "Don't be such a baby," she said. Her fingers pressed against Nat's scalp, holding her hair away while she patted a thin strip of linen against the wound. Annin twisted Nat's hair to the side and wrapped a band around it.

"Thank you." She touched her hair just above the cut. The wound throbbed, but the ointment and bandage seemed to hold.

"You're welcome, but . . ." Annin jerked her chin upward. The light from the orb glinted off her Nala eye. "Don't move," she whispered. Nat's fingers twitched toward her dagger, but Annin shook her head. She felt a light pressure against her shoulder, like something was hanging off the side of her cloak. Without turning her head, she looked out the corner of her eye. Two furry legs as long as her fingers tapped against her collarbone. A golf ball–size body connected to eight legs crawled on top of her shoulder. Her heart pounded against her chest as she brought her hand slowly across to brush away the gigantic spider.

"Don't," Annin whispered, her voice so faint Nat could barely hear it. Annin's Nala eye contracted. The spider tumbled down Nat's arm, pausing in the crook of her elbow. The black body shone in the light. Its size dwarfed her hand, and the stiff bristly hair on its pointy legs brushed against her skin. Annin extended her arm toward Nat, and the spider crawled onto her cupped palm. She lifted her hand near the wall. The spider disappeared into a crevice by the broken beam. Nat brushed her hands over her arms. Her skin crawled.

"That's the only one, at least the only one in the immediate vicinity." Annin closed her eyes and took a deep breath. "Yes, that was the only one of her kind." She opened her eyes. "You were lucky. That's a tunnel eater. Not much even a Healing House Sister could do if one of those bit you, other than amputate a limb. They invade rodent and rabbit tunnels and wait for the animals to come in or go out. The animals never make it past a tunnel eater."

Annin walked around Nat, who stared at the crevice and shuddered. She ducked, keeping a wide space between her head and the broken beam. She skipped nervously over a clod of dirt that looked like a spider and followed quickly after Annin.

"How did you do that?" she asked, breathing quickly from nerves.

"Huh?" Annin darted around a corner and ran up a set of worn stone steps. "You mean the spider?"

"Yes, the spider. What did you do?" She stayed in the center of the stairs, as far from the bumpy dirt walls as she could get.

"I told it to go away." A faint light shone above them. "Haven't you seen Soris do that? He's pretty good for a new duozi. It took me a few years before I mastered the talent of controlling predators. But he's got more Nala in him than I do," she said as if explaining a basic ability.

Nat thought of the spider on Soris' tunic. *He had the same power?* She took the stairs two at a time to catch up. "You can control spiders?" The exit to the passage opened a few steps above them. Moonlight spilled over the cracked support beams and onto the pale stone steps.

"Not just spiders." A light wind coming from the tunnel exit lifted Annin's dark locks off her shoulders. "I can sense and control most predators, at least the ones weaker than the Nala." Nat wondered what predator could threaten a Nala. "I think it's like a silent lion roar letting any competition know to back off. I told you there were benefits to being a duozi." Annin paused and scratched her nose. "It's how we sense the Nala even without the remnant."

"So that spider thought I was your victim?"

"Kind of. It was more miffed at all the movement in the tunnel."

"The spider was miffed." Lines of disbelief wrinkled across Nat's brow.

"Yes, that and it sensed the blood from your wound." She grabbed Nat's hand and pulled her up the stairs. They emerged onto the overgrown grounds of the ruins. Wind cut over a jagged stone wall shielding the passage entrance from the remains of the Emissary House.

"I'm waiting here for him." Annin crossed her arms. The watchtower loomed in front of them. Andris' tiny figure waved from the balcony ringing the pointed top of the tower. "It's your fault we're late, let him bark at you first." She defiantly leaned against a wooden post.

The wind sent her curly hair lashing against a frieze of birds carved into the crookedly framed tunnel entrance.

"Do me a favor, Annin." Nat adjusted her cloak. "After my watch, fill me in on any other benefits of being a duozi."

"It's more fun to spring them on you." Annin ducked her head and disappeared into the passage to wait for Andris.

CHAPTER TWENTY-NINE

Nat shivered. Chilly wind whirled around the balcony of the watchtower. She stopped pacing in front of the ledge and secured the inner ties of her cloak to keep the wind from twisting the garment to the side. Her bright orb hovered by her head and curved through the air when she leaned over to check the dark grounds below.

She scanned the ruins of the Emissary House in the light of the half-moon. Two fluted columns made a monstrous skeletal shape directly in front of her. She imagined the vaulted ceiling or dome the columns once supported and felt a sense of loss for Sisters she'd never known. A thought tickled her mind, and she wondered about the discrepancy between the secluded meetinghouses near the stables and the wide public spaces of the House. *Why would Sisters keep private negotiations separate from the House?* she wondered. The building for the Nala made sense, if negotiating with them made any sense at all. But why so many other separate meeting places? Were there really that many secret negotiations? Was there that much need to be sequestered away from the main House? Even the passageway had nooks where someone could hide or watch unobserved as people passed.

She shivered again, thinking of what lurked in those dark places now. If the tunnel eater was any indication, she'd just as soon walk the long way around the hill than pass through the passage again, even with Annin as a guide.

A trembling in the leafy canopy caught Nat's attention. The movement of the vegetation unnerved her, and she found herself constantly glancing at the shaky limbs. *It's just the wind,* she thought. A strong gust ripped her hood off. Her cut throbbed. She pressed her hands against her skull, pushing loose strands of hair out of her eyes and away from the bandaged cut.

The doorway to the watchtower stairs offered a little protection from the wind. She retreated a few steps down the spiral staircase and pulled her hair tightly back at the nape of her neck. She glanced down the dark stairwell. It would be at least another hour before Soris would come through the passage cut in the hill and up the winding stairs to relieve her. She sighed and stepped back onto the windy balcony, knowing it provided the best view to spot anyone or anything approaching.

She glanced in the direction of the rundown barn and stables. From her perch, the boulders crowning the hill above the old well were visible. Andris and Soris were hidden somewhere among the rocks, but Nat couldn't tell where. A smile flickered over her face when she thought of Soris, then faded away. She'd felt at home in his arms, but she couldn't shake the thought that he was resigned to living as an outcast. Could the Healing Sisters do something more for him? If they could slow or stop the progression of venom, or whatever caused a person to change into a duozi, there must be a way to reverse the effect. She nibbled on her fingernail. She hadn't seen the laboratories in the Healing House, but wondered if they had the means of finding a cure or if they were even trying.

She heard a faint scratching over the rustling wind. She brushed her fingers against her orb and sent it around the curve of the balcony in search of the noise. The ball swayed in the air, buffeted by the wind, then disappeared from sight. She took a step closer to the ledge and peered over the crumbling bricks. Her boots ground against the bits of mortar scattered over the floor. *It must be the wind,* she thought again, trying to quell her nerves. Her orb rounded the other side of the balcony and hovered near the cut in her scalp, radiating warmth. She took a deep breath and relaxed, but her muscles tightened when she heard another sound, like a stick scraping against stone.

A pale figure scampered over the top of the pointed tower. Nat sucked in a breath as it launched itself off the roof, scattering corroded copper shingles that clattered onto the balcony. The wind caught the underside of the Nala. It sailed through the air and landed inches from her boots.

The Nala flung its daggerlike hand into the sky. Its skin was a sickly white and hung from its frame. Nat's eyes were drawn to the bulging ring protruding from its heaving chest. Her hands trembled as she tightened her grip on her sword and watched the strange-looking Nala. Its curved back undulated as it took a creeping step toward her. She inched back and caught a reflection in its eyes. Swinging her sword wide, she spun. Her blade cut into the legs of another Nala behind her. It flopped onto her back, screeching with pain. She grasped its slick arm and ripped it off her before it could sink its needlelike teeth into her skin.

The creature slammed headfirst into the other Nala, and the two rolled over each other. Nat's orb sped toward the creatures and cracked against their skulls, knocking them senseless. She ran to the creatures and plunged her sword into their pale flesh. The wind wailed around her as the writhing creatures slumped against the balcony floor. She jerked her sword free and kicked the bodies apart before slicing off their bulb-shaped heads.

"Soris." Her eyes widened, and she ran away from the bodies, realizing there could be more Nala. She flew down the crumbling tower steps. Her orb careened past her, zooming toward the passage and the stables to warn the others. A hissing sound raised the hair on the back of her neck. Another pale Nala landed in front of her. Nat stopped and teetered on the step before kicking the creature straight in the abdomen. It tumbled down the stairs and landed with a thud on the cold stone landing. She jumped the last few steps and quickly beheaded the Nala before taking off for the passage entrance. Her heart pounded as she ran across the ruins.

A Nala sprang over a crumbling wall in front of her. It landed with a crunch, scattering a loose pile of rubble. The creature knocked the broken bricks out of the way as it scurried toward her on all four limbs. It bowed its pale back, then shot into the air. Nat skipped to the side and jabbed at it with her sword, but missed her mark. The Nala wasted no time before it pounced again. She lashed out, keeping the creature away, but it jumped onto the edge of the wall and scrambled up the uneven stone.

The moonlight cast the Nala's long shadow over Nat. Her body shook and her hands trembled as she kept her sword ready, unsure what the creature planned next. She waited for it to spring, hoping she could move quickly enough to end it before it reached her. A deathly screech filled the air, and the Nala flung its head to the side and tumbled off the wall. Blood oozed from the arrow sticking from its back.

Soris stood between the wall and the tower with his crossbow stock tight against his face. He lowered his weapon and ran to Nat.

"Did it bite you?" He shoved her sleeves above her elbows and inspected her arms.

"No bites, they didn't bite me," she said, to calm them both. His tapered fingers pressed against her cheek. Nat heard more voices and looked up. Annin and Andris stood over the dead Nala.

"Check for more," Andris ordered.

Annin closed her eyes. The back of her robe clung to her body as the wind slammed her from behind. "Nothing!" she cried over the wind. "Soris?"

"No, I don't sense any more." Deep lines formed at the corners of his mouth.

"Pull it into the tower." Andris grasped the limp arm of the Nala. Its pointy feet flopped over the ground strewn with stones. Annin lifted the creature's head and frowned.

"In the tower!" Soris yelled over the wind. Nat followed him out of the wind into the macabre calm of the tower landing heaped with Nala bodies. She leaned forward to get a better look at the creatures and wiped sweat from her forehead, brushing the cut on her temple.

"You said you weren't hurt." Soris jumped over the pile of Nala and gently held her head between his hands.

"Don't get so excited." Annin knelt by one of the corpses. "She banged her head on a beam in the passage, it's nothing."

Nat gave him a tight smile and joined Annin. "What is that?" Her fingers traced the bulge embedded in the chest of each Nala. "The other Nala that attacked me by the river had the same ring in its chest." The tip of Andris' sword sliced through the skin. A pale tubelike circle burst, sending a fibrous liquid spilling down the open wound.

Annin looked up from the corpse and stared at Nat. "I think it's remnant," she said.

CHAPTER THIRTY

The pyre smoked before a blast of wind sent sparks scattering over the dry barn wood. Flames licked the broken boards and curled higher until they reached the pale bodies of the Nala. Nat stood close to the well, far away from the flames. Soris wrapped his arm around her waist. He pulled her close to his side, and they watched as the dawn light broke through the smoke rising in the sky. She leaned into him, trying to push away her sense of foreboding.

Annin strode from the pyre toward them, her hand clasped around the base of a stubby torch. Nat coughed as the wind shifted and sent the smell of the burning bodies in their direction. Her eyes watered.

"Mervin wants us," Soris said as Mervin waved, gesturing for them to join Benedict and Andris by the wagon. Benedict grasped the side of the wagon and pulled himself into the bed. His small figure disappeared under the tarp. The corner of the heavy cloth flapped in the wind. Andris tossed a bag of the rudit in the bed.

"I suppose he's in a hurry before that pyre attracts visitors." Annin's gaze lingered on the fire.

"Any ideas why the Nala had rings of remnant in their chests?" Nat asked as they made their way down the hill. The wind bent the blades of grass, slapping them against the hillside. She pulled her cloak around her and shoved her hands into the inner pockets.

"No," Annin replied. "We need Sister Ethes. She's done the most research into remnant. But none of it makes sense. The remnant in the Nala was not its own, it was from another Nala."

"Why would it have another Nala's remnant inside it?" Nat asked as she dug her fingers into her pockets, searching for her orb.

"I have no idea, but the Nala that attacked you last night weren't normal. They were like the one on the riverbank, withered and pale," Annin said. "What's wrong?"

"My orb." Nat stopped walking and flung her cloak open, searching her pockets. "Where's my orb?"

"It didn't come back to you? We saw it in the tunnel. It was waiting for us last night before we got to you." Annin glanced back toward the entrance cut into the hill.

"I sent it to warn you about the Nala." She ran her hands up and down the fabric of the robe. "I've got to go find it." She sprinted to the gaping mouth of the passage.

Quiet descended on Nat when she stepped through the opening. The dirt walls dampened the howl of the wind. She squinted in the dim light, hoping her eyes would quickly adjust. Soris ducked under the entrance and stepped by her side.

"You might want this." Annin appeared behind Soris and thrust the torch into Nat's hands.

They walked through the dark tunnel leading to the tower. Smoke from the pyre curled down the passage, sending everyone into fits of coughing.

"Somewhere up ahead, I think." Annin cleared her throat and moved quickly past Nat. "I remember seeing your orb right after we turned here." She pointed to the top of the concave wall. "There it is."

The orb hung motionless next to a split beam. Nat stretched her hand toward the floating sphere. It held fast. "Something's wrong." She approached the orb cautiously and curled her fingers around it. Intense blinding light shot out from the spaces between her fingers and filled a wide fissure beneath the beam. Nat gently pulled the orb to her chest. "Come look at this," she said in a hushed tone.

Soris and Annin moved closer into the cramped space next to Nat. She released the orb, and its light poured into the crevice. Darkened orbs were packed into the deep fissure. Annin reached in and pulled out a dead sphere. Dozens came toppling out of the crack and spilled onto the floor.

"All of you, out now!" Andris' voice boomed. His order echoed through the passage.

Soris grasped her hand. "We've got to go, Natalie. We don't have time . . ." He pulled her toward the entrance. Her eyes lingered on the crevice and the scattered orbs. Their darkened surfaces looked like giant black pearls.

Andris met them at the turn in the passage. "What are you doing? We'll be lucky to get through the forest now without running into any of Mudug's guards."

"We found something." Soris glanced over his shoulder at Nat, making sure she was still there.

"I don't care what you found, we are out of here *now*." Andris took two steps, then dropped to a crouch. The sound of shouting filtered into the passage. He crawled behind one of the loose beams and peered out the opening. He turned his head and mouthed the word "soldiers." The others joined him and watched the scene near the stable.

Their draft horses pawed the ground and twisted their heads. Mervin's long arm thrashed about, trying to control the animals. Three soldiers halted their horses in front of Mervin's wagon. The wind roared past the passage entrance, carrying snippets of angry voices. Mervin pointed to the pyre on the hill. Two of the soldiers twisted in their saddles.

"Where's Benedict?" Soris leaned next to Andris, keeping his body low to the ground.

"He's under the tarp," Nat whispered.

"Along with all our bags and my weapon," Andris added, shaking his head. He turned to Annin. "Do you have your crossbow?"

"No, it's strapped to my satchel," she said glumly.

"Sister, Soris?"

"I have my sword, that's it. Everything else is in the wagon," Nat said. Mervin shouted at the soldiers, gesturing again to the pyre.

Soris pulled a sharp knife from his boot and handed it to Andris. "I have another, but that's it." He unsheathed a second knife from his belt.

"They'll have us in seconds if we try an assault." Andris peered out again. "Annin, one of the tunnels leads to the private meetinghouses, correct?" Annin nodded and gestured to a dark split in the passage behind Nat. "Take Soris, get as close to their horses as you can under the cover of the grass. Try to spook them. That may give us the distraction we need. Go."

"Be careful," Soris whispered to Nat and then disappeared into the inky darkness after Annin.

"What's the plan?" Nat asked as she pressed low to the ground and watched the soldiers question Mervin.

"They'll see us if we try to sneak out. But if any of them make a move for the tarp, follow my lead."

One of the soldiers turned his great black gelding and rode toward the pyre. Its mane flipped about in the wind. The animal jerked to the side as the smoke from the pyre and the smell of burning Nala drifted toward him. The soldier dug in his heels, but the horse reared and bolted from the fire back down the hill past the stable. The soldiers called out as he disappeared around a bend in the road on his crazed horse.

The other horses stomped their hooves and twisted their heads in nervous agitation. Mervin frantically pointed to the boulders above the pyre as if he'd just spotted something. He snapped his reins. The draft horses lunged forward, followed in quick succession by the other soldiers' horses. The wagon bounced over the road. Rounds of rudit spilled from one of the bags and flopped on top of the loose tarp.

"Let's go," Andris ordered. He and Nat ran hunched over to the well and watched Mervin's wagon and the soldiers disappear into the forest. Annin and Soris pushed the overgrown grass aside from their hiding spots near the stable. Andris beckoned them forward with one quick wave.

"Nicely done," Andris said, but his eyes were on the empty stretch of road flanked by the forest.

"Those horses would have bolted without us once they smelled the burning bodies," Annin replied. "Now what? If they search the wagon, they'll find Benedict and all our bags and know Mervin and Benedict aren't alone."

"We'll make sure that doesn't happen." Andris sprinted toward the stable. "Into the forest. I want one of you on either side of the road. Stay far enough in the tree line so they can't see you." Annin and Soris split apart and flanked the road. "Sister, stay with me," Andris ordered. Nat nodded and followed him as he ran into the woods.

Thick pine boughs choked the forest, veiling Nat and Andris in a dense blanket of green. Wind twisted the treetops. Creaks and groans shuddered down the long trunks as they wove through narrow openings between the pines. The sand-colored road flashed through the trees. Andris and Nat increased their pace. She knew the horses would be impossible to catch if they continued to flee unchecked by their riders and Mervin. Their only hope was Mervin would try to calm his horses, slowing the procession of the riders.

The forest sloped downhill. Andris' foot caught on a root, sending him sprawling to the ground. Nat retraced her steps.

"Go," he whispered to her when she yanked him to his feet. She hesitated, then sprinted away. When she glanced back, he was running with a lopsided gait. She knew if she slowed, there would be no chance of catching Mervin. Glancing back one more time, she pointed ahead. Andris nodded vigorously, his face contorted in pain. She took off.

Gusts of wind, twisting into the woods from the road, hit her in the face and dried the beads of sweat trickling down her cheek. An ache formed in the back of her throat. She pressed on through the forest, slowing only when she heard a chorus of angry voices. She ducked behind a tree.

"My wagon will fall apart if we keep at that pace." Mervin stood next to one of the wagon wheels. "The rim is already coming off."

"Leave it on the side of the road, you fool." A soldier with a thick black beard brought his horse closer to the wagon. The other two soldiers glanced nervously into the woods.

"I will not abandon my wagon," Mervin said in a low voice.

"You'll do as I say, merchant. I don't know how you got this close to Rustbrook without an escort, but I will find out. Either keep up or leave your wagon behind."

Mervin crossed his arms.

"Rever"—he pointed at one soldier—"bind this man, and Willem, cut one of his horses free. We'll use the other to carry him to the city. The Nala can chase after his other horse. You'll answer our questions on the way to Rustbrook or—"

Mervin sprinted away into the woods as Willem and Rever dismounted.

"Stop!" the lead soldier yelled.

Mervin turned to face his pursuers and cracked his whip in the air. The beaded tip snapped inches from Willem's face. The soldier backed away, and Mervin unleashed the whip on Rever.

Nat jumped from behind a tree and kicked Willem in the back. The soldier fell face-first into the dry pine needles. She kicked his side, flipping him over onto his back before he could spring up. His poufy blue hat flew about in the wind.

"Behind you!" Mervin yelled.

The lead soldier hurtled toward her, knocking her to the ground. His hands encircled her throat in a chokehold. Sweat fell from his face onto hers, and the light in the forest grew dim in front of her eyes. She fumbled to clasp her hands together, then jerked her forearms down onto his before she blacked out. His face hit the ground next to her and he lost his grip. Nat gasped for breath and twisted her body. He suddenly arched his back and his face contorted. Andris' head appeared over his shoulder. His dagger was deep in the soldier's back.

"Andris!" Nat screamed as Willem, holding a sword, stepped behind him.

Soris flew across the road, scattering the soldiers' horses in all directions. He bowled into Willem. They rolled over one another and crashed into the base of a tree. Andris leapt over Nat and the dead soldier and slashed his dagger across Willem's arm. Willem cried out and clutched the slice in his uniform.

"Duozi, you're harboring duozi! You'll die for killing a soldier and hiding that scum," Rever said, pointing a shaky finger at Soris and Annin, who now stood next to Mervin. Mervin's whip snaked around Rever's arm. With one quick jerk, Mervin sent him into the trunk of a tree. His head thudded against the bark. Blood spurted from the gash in his temple, and he fell to the ground.

"Rope!" Andris cried. Soris twisted the soldier's arms behind him.

Annin sprinted for the wagon. The draft horses whinnied, but the wagon brake kept them in place. She jumped into the bed, looking for the rope. Her voice carried over the wind. "Get out of there, you coward," she said.

"Benedict," Nat mouthed to Andris. The soldiers had seen the five of them, but they hadn't seen Benedict. "Just grab the rope!" Nat called out.

"But—" Annin said over the tarp.

"Just grab the rope!" Nat called again, her voice tense. "Bring your bag, too," she added.

The wagon creaked. Annin carried the rope looped around her hand. She glared at Nat and dropped the rope at Andris' feet. The bag landed with a thud by Willem's legs.

Nat searched through Annin's bag and retrieved a cream-colored bandage. She started wrapping it around Willem's eyes when he suddenly dodged to the side and slipped out of Soris' grasp. He lunged for Andris, but Annin's arrow sliced into him before he even closed half the distance. He fell to his knees and landed face-first.

Soris and Andris dragged Willem's body and let him drop next to the other dead soldier. Nat felt sick as she watched the body flop lifelessly to the ground. She knew they were both dead because they'd tried to kill her and Andris, but her stomach roiled at the thought that they'd been alive just moments before. She ran behind the wagon and heaved.

"Is it safe?" The Hermit crawled from the back of the wagon bed. *Safe? Are you kidding me?* Nat thought as she watched him peer around nervously. He craned his neck to get a look into the forest. "Hmm, they're dead. Good." He limped toward the front of the wagon and clambered down the step.

Nat wiped her face with her soiled cloak. Benedict adjusted his tunic and took a breath of fresh air, as if dead bodies were the norm. The wind whistled around her. Soris and Andris joined her by the wagon.

"What do we do with Rever and the bodies?" Soris asked.

Andris leaned down and rubbed his knee. "Those are Mudug's personal guards. It wouldn't surprise me if they were searching for the guard we picked up at the abandoned farm." He pulled at his beard. A streak of blood covered his cheek.

Soris leaned back so he could see Mervin and Annin through the trees. "Then we should move quickly. Who knows when another guard will come down this road."

"The duozi can disrupt the memory of the one that's still alive, make him think they were ambushed by an angry convoy or bandits. Might be less risky than leaving the bodies to be found by Mudug's other guards. They'd be on the hunt for us for sure if we did that. Have her alter his memory," Benedict suggested.

Nat stared at the Hermit. "What do you mean?"

"She can modify his memory. She did it before to Rusrel. Made him think he'd married Emilia. If she was able to do that, she should be able to make the soldier forget who assaulted them," Benedict said with a hint of accusation in his voice.

"It might work." Andris nodded. "She was supposed to wipe your memory months ago." He pointed to Nat. "Before—"

"Before I realized how desperate you were," Nat jumped in, cutting off Andris before he could say anything else. She shuddered at the idea of Benedict knowing anything about her real life.

Andris' lips curled into a tight smile. "Exactly, Sister, because we were so desperate." He limped toward the forest. "We need to knock that one out again." He pointed to Rever, who groaned as his head rolled to the side.

Nat's orb hurtled through the air, passing Annin and Mervin, and clunked against Rever's head. He slumped forward, unconscious. It zipped back and landed in her palm. She tucked it into her pocket and looked up to find Andris staring at her.

"Not what I had in mind, but that worked just fine, Sister." His eyes flickered toward Soris, who stood by her side. "Mervin will take Soris, Benedict, and me down the road. Sister, you will stay with Annin to guard her while she messes with the soldier's memory."

"We should all stay," Soris said as he stepped closer to Nat.

"No." Andris leveled a look at his brother. "I want that wagon on the road and moving. You said it yourself, brother—who knows when another guard will come this way."

"I'll stay, then." Soris crossed his arms.

"Give me grace," Andris muttered through clenched teeth. "She's not a lily." He pointed at Nat. "I think she can handle watching the road while Annin works him over. We'll go slowly, I promise. The fewer of us around, the better, and I need at least one able-bodied fighter with me. No offense, Hermit."

Benedict shrugged and clambered back into the wagon.

"Then she can go and I'll stay." Soris didn't budge from Nat's side.

Andris grew a shade of red Nat had never seen before.

"I've got this." Nat placed her hand on Soris' arm. Soris opened his mouth. "I've got this," she repeated, wanting him to trust in her ability to keep both Annin and herself safe. Soris pressed his lips together.

"Thank you for shutting him up, Sister." Andris limped over the dirt road toward Annin and Mervin.

"Take a crossbow and another sword." Soris jumped aboard the wagon and began handing her weapon after weapon.

"Soris, I've only got two hands, and I have my sword. Give me the crossbow." She passed the extra sword back to him. Benedict made a sour face and ducked under the tarp, muttering something about bad influences.

Mervin walked up to the wagon. He ran his hand along the back of the bed and secured the clips. "Soris, Andris needs you to help him move the bodies farther away from the road."

Soris gave Nat a reassuring look. "I'll be right back," he said and jumped off the wagon. "Take more arrows!" he called out to Nat before heading into the tree line.

Mervin placed his large hand on Nat's shoulder. "There's a bend maybe twenty minutes' slow ride from here, Sister. Two roads join this one after it. We'll wait for you there. Be quick." He gave her a stern look. "You remember Wesdrono Street?"

"Yes," she answered and tied a quiver of arrows to her belt.

"Keep it in mind if you can't find us." The wagon tilted to the side when he placed his toe on the step. "This excursion isn't following the intended plan. Best be prepared for the worst."

"Thanks for the encouraging words." She stepped back when he released the long pole affixed to the wagon brake. The wagon rolled forward.

Soris and Andris ran out of the trees and sprinted for the wagon. Andris grabbed the edge and pulled himself onto the bed. Soris veered off and stopped in front of Nat.

"We moved them farther in so no one can see you from the road. She's already at work. You're certain you don't want me to stay?"

"Soris, get in now," Andris barked from atop the rolling wagon. Soris' eyes shifted from Nat to him.

"Go, I'll see you soon." She reached out and touched the rough fabric of his tunic.

"See you soon." His eyes lingered on hers, then he pulled away and ran for the wagon, leaving her standing alone in the middle of the road.

CHAPTER THIRTY-ONE

Annin knelt in front of Rever. The collar of his tunic was open, and she pressed her fingers against the pale skin above his collarbone. Her other hand dangled at her side. The outline of her closed Nala eye dwarfed that of her human eye.

Minutes passed. Nat eased away from Annin and edged between two trees. The spot didn't provide a view of the treetops, but she could easily see the forest, Annin, and the road. She took a long look at the dead bodies hidden under a cluster of bushes covered in red berries, and her stomach lurched again. She rocked on the balls of her feet, wanting to catch up with Soris and leave the bodies far behind. The forest felt lonely.

More time passed. Annin hadn't moved. Nat wondered if Mervin and the others had reached the bend, and she thought of Soris. He'd said it wouldn't be easy; none of this was easy.

Annin's hand twitched. Nat glanced through the branches, checking the road and the forest behind her again before moving closer to Annin. Her companion opened her eyes and sat back on her heels. A look of exhaustion settled over her face. Nat handed Annin a water gourd. She swallowed without taking her eyes off Rever. She took another drink and water trickled down her chin.

"How did it go?"

"How did it go?" Annin eyed Nat. "It was fantastic." Her words were laced with sarcasm. She slapped the cap on the gourd. "Imagine taking all the bits of color in a picture and rearranging each one so the picture looks totally different. Sound easy?"

"No." Nat blew out a sharp breath.

"Right answer, Natalie. Now go somewhere else, you're meddling with my focus. I'm not done." Annin waved her hand.

"You're planning on adding a few chapters?" Nat fidgeted with her crossbow. Her anxiousness was overtaking the nausea caused by being around the dead bodies. Annin's expression soured even more. "It's just taking you longer than I thought, and we may not catch up with Mervin."

"You try to do an implant on someone who's knocked out. It's ten times harder than when they're just dreaming." Annin glanced at the bodies near the berry-laden bush. "If you're in a rush, remove their uniforms now so we don't have to do it later."

"You want me to strip the dead soldiers?" Nat felt her stomach do another flip.

"No, I want you to remove their uniforms. Leave the undergarments." Annin closed her eyes. "Now be quiet so I can finish this."

Nat wrung her hands. She eyed the boots sticking out from beneath the bushes and walked as quietly as she could to the bodies. Removing the boots was simple, but when she ran her fingers over the thick blue vest buttoned around Willem's chest, her mouth filled with bile. She let her fingers do the work and tried not to look at their faces as each garment came off. Finally, she sat back on a bed of dried pine needles and stared at the pile of blue uniforms at her side.

"Two are plenty." Nat flinched, surprised by Annin's voice. Annin took a long drink of water and wiped the sweat rolling down the side of her face. "We don't need his." She gestured toward Rever. She grabbed a set of blue garments and stuffed it in her satchel. Nat did the same, her fingers poking through the bloodied cut on Willem's uniform. She tucked the fabric farther into her bag, then lifted the strap over her shoulder.

The soldiers' legs stuck out from the bush at crooked angles. Dirt and bits of dried leaves clung to their long undergarments. Rever, fully uniformed, looked out of place next to his stripped companions. Nat broke a few branches and dropped them over their bare feet, feeling they deserved something more than to lie naked in the forest.

"Feel nothing for them, Natalie," Annin said as if reading her mind. "They'd have tortured and killed any one of us without another thought." She shouldered her bag and ran into the woods.

Nat glanced at the bodies one last time and sprinted away.

"So what happened to them? What'd you implant in Rever's head?" Nat asked when she caught up to Annin.

"They found a merchant wagon filled with wine near the ruins of the Emissary House. The merchant bribed them with a few bottles, and they got drunk and started for a leisurely ride back to Rustbrook. A band of duozi working with the merchant ambushed them, killed the two soldiers, and beat Rever until they thought he was dead, then made off with two of their uniforms. They'll guess the duozi took off west toward the swamps. Don't look so skeptical. He'll believe it. There are enough elements of truth for it to stick. From what I garnered from his dreams, Rever hates duozi. I have no doubt the implant will work." She jumped over a log.

"You're the expert." Nat peered through the branches above them as they ran. The sun filtered through the still treetops. She felt uneasy. Too much time had passed since Soris and the others had left them behind. They moved swiftly through the forest. The worry that Annin had taken too long pushed Nat to run faster, and her feet flew over the ground. A flash of brown road showed through the trees. She slowed her pace as the bend in the road came into view. It was empty.

"The wagon's not here." A tight knot formed in her stomach.

"What a surprise." Annin plopped on the ground and shrugged off the bag.

"Get up, we need to go look." Nat grabbed her arm, ignoring the weary expression on Annin's face.

"They're gone, Natalie. Here, have a drink." She lifted the water gourd in Nat's direction. "Don't look so shocked. Andris wasn't going to wait for us. He just said he would so Soris wouldn't fly off and do something stupid. I imagine the conversation when Andris broke the news that they were heading on to complete the mission without us didn't go over so well. He'll probably win Soris over by telling him how much safer you'll be back at Gennes' camp, waiting." Annin rolled her eyes.

"What?" Nat felt every muscle in her body tense. "Why would he want to leave us behind? He needs us." She looked at the empty road, aghast.

"You don't mix emotions with a mission, Natalie. Andris is too seasoned a soldier not to recognize the risk in keeping you two together. Sit down." She patted the ground next to her. Nat slid down and stared at the empty road beyond the trees in front of her. "Soris is in love with you." Annin shifted her weight and leaned her head against the wide trunk.

"Love, no. He's not in love with me," she said, feeling her cheeks flush.

"All of us can see it, even that crazy Hermit. I'm not sure why you can't. Funny how the object of one's affection can be so blind, or distracted in your case. You've been so consumed with protecting him, saving him from being a duozi, you haven't noticed how he watches you and jumps to help you, listens intently to your every word. He sees your dreams, Natalie."

"What does his seeing my dreams have to do with anything?" she asked, feeling unnerved by the intense look on Annin's face.

"He didn't tell you?" Annin nodded in surprise. "Interesting. Well, he must have had his reasons, so it's not for me to explain." She shrugged.

Nat tossed her water gourd to the ground. "Would you stop toying—"

"I don't know exactly how you feel about him, but that doesn't matter." Annin cut her off. "It's obvious you like him. That's enough to worry Andris. He told me we needed to keep you two apart, that Soris might act rashly if you were in danger and could foul up the mission."

"Staying to guard you was a ruse then?" Nat narrowed her eyes.

"I can't say I really needed you, and you did not help my concentration," she added with emphasis. She stood and brushed the pine needles from the back of her tunic, then looked down at Nat. "The question now is what are you going to do?"

Nat took a deep breath, struggling to control her anger. She stood and faced Annin. "I didn't become a Sister, leave my home, and fight the Nala just so I could retreat to Gennes' camp." Her voice reverberated around them. "I didn't hold a dead duozi girl in my arms or watch Soris lose control in the Nala den to let the chance of hurting Mudug slip away. If Andris thinks so little of his brother and of me, that's his problem, and he can just suck it up. I am going to Rustbrook."

A smile crept over Annin's face. "I knew there was a reason I put up with you." She shouldered her bag and extended her hand to Nat. "Wesdrono Street it is then."

"Wesdrono Street?" She grasped Annin's hand and gave her a suspicious look, thinking of Mervin's comment before he left with the others.

"You didn't think I was actually going to obey Andris' order, did you?" Annin's Nala eye flashed in the filtered sunlight. She squeezed Nat's hand. "Mervin and Matilda have always had my back. Now all of us have yours."

CHAPTER THIRTY-TWO

The last wagon in the convoy rumbled onto the wooden slat bridge. The wheels made a slapping noise as they rolled over the planks. Nat and Annin dropped from behind the trunk on the back of the wagon into the thick grass. They ducked under the bridge supports and hid among the long reeds. The wagon pulled onto the road on the other side of the swollen creek. Nat let out a breath, finally relaxing.

"I thought we were done for back there with the wool merchant." She stretched her aching arms and looked through the slats above her. Crimson streaks crossed the darkening sky.

"So did I." Annin unwrapped the bandage that covered her Nala eye. "He kept looking at me." She leaned back against the sloping ground. "'Join the convoy, we'll blend in,'" Annin mimicked Nat's voice. "Insanity."

"It worked." Nat kicked off a boot. A large pebble rolled from its mouth. "Other than getting thrown off the wool merchant's wagon after he caught us hiding behind his bales, it worked perfectly. What did he call me? A ruff belly what?"

Annin laughed. "A ruff belly filer. It's this amphibian that clings to the side of fish or turtle shells. It wasn't meant as a compliment."

"I got that." Nat stuck her foot back into her boot and watched the water rush beneath the bridge. "Change now?" she asked. Annin nodded. She unhooked the filthy cloak she'd filched from a merchant's wagon and pulled Willem's uniform from her bag. She hitched the soldier's blue pants over her leggings and shoved her tunic into the gaping waist.

"This is huge." The uniform hung from Annin's shoulders and covered the tips of her fingers. "I look like I've been swallowed by a Nala."

Nat grabbed the shoulder seams and pulled the loose fabric behind Annin's neck. She untied her hair and twisted the hair tie around the ball of fabric. A blue notch stuck out between Annin's shoulder blades, but the uniform no longer sagged in the front.

"Throw the cape over your shoulders," Nat said as she shoved bandages in the soldier's boots to fill the empty space around her feet. The floppy guard's cap fell over her eyes. She tilted it back and tucked her hair under the wide band. Another carriage approached. "Ready?"

Annin nodded and slipped her bag under her soldier's cape. Nat considered the misshapen lumps bulging from Annin's disguise and hoped night would come soon to blur the lines of the ill-fitting uniforms.

The carriage rumbled over the bridge. They sneaked out from underneath the support beams, crawled onto the wooden planks of the bridge, then sprinted behind the wagon, using its bulky mass for cover. Nat felt like she was running in clown boots. Annin crossed the bridge with a splayed gait. Rows of towering trees greeted them when they reached the opposite bank. They ran silently under the moss-covered branches that twisted toward the darkening sky. Above them, crowning the top of the hill, was the geometric castle. Annin paused under the shadow of a tree.

"It's been a while," Annin said to herself as she gazed up at the castle. Nat joined her. She'd never seen Rustbrook from this view. Unlike the congested streets and crammed markets of the south side of the city, the north side of Rustbrook was an expanse of green. A hedge maze bordered by terraced parks spilled down the hill from the castle.

"That's how we'll get into the castle, but on the east side." Annin pointed to a wall above the maze. Her hand dropped. Shadows hid her expression from Nat.

"How do we get to Mervin's?" Nat asked, wondering what she'd say when she saw Andris. She wasn't sure which emotion was stronger: her anger toward Andris or her uncertainty about what Annin had said about Soris. She cared deeply for Soris and now knew he felt the same. But she questioned Annin's notion that Soris felt anything as powerful as love for her.

"Simple enough, unless we run into guards." Annin said, breaking into her thoughts. Annin took off, leaving Nat feeling uneasy as she chased after her.

The pair ran up the hill past the grand trees. Lights flickered on top of the white stone wall surrounding the city. They paused behind a thick trunk and observed the wall. Guards walked along the top of the barrier. Their figures passed by flickering torch flames. Annin sprinted to the next tree.

Nat followed Annin through the shadows of the trees until they reached the base of the great wall. Annin pressed her ear against the wall as if listening to its inner workings. Nat noticed worn House emblems set into the stone just as Annin placed her fingertips over the wing of an engraved bird. She pushed the wing, and a long slit, as tall as Nat, appeared in the stone wall.

"Give me a hand," Annin whispered.

Nat placed her palms against the cold stone and strained to move the massive slab. The crack widened into a narrow opening to a dusty passage. Annin removed her bag and tossed it into the dark. It landed with a thud. She squeezed through the opening and Nat followed, catching the loose fabric of the uniform on the edge of the entrance.

Annin shoved the stone back in place. The passage fell into darkness. Nat breathed in the stale, dusty air and sneezed.

"A little light," Annin whispered

Nat rummaged in her bag until her fingers latched onto her orb. Light spilled from the sphere and filled the narrow passage. The walls were covered in a frieze hidden by a thick layer of cobwebs and dust. Nat brushed her hand over it. Birds with long vines clamped in their beaks flew in the sun's rays. Engravings of crossed swords bordered the bottom of the wall. Her eyes followed the carvings as she brushed away more cobwebs.

"Where are we?"

"Shush!" Annin pressed her finger to her lips and motioned for Nat to follow. Little puffs of dust rose from the floor with each step they took. A few paces in, the passage narrowed, forcing them to turn sideways. Nat's nose brushed the wall, and long smears of dirt covered her uniform and face. When they reached a split in the passage, Annin knelt down and ran her finger over a loose stone. A fragment toppled into her hand, and an iron key clattered onto the floor. The echo rang down the passage. A satisfied look passed over Annin's face as she held the key. She rose and beckoned Nat to follow.

They passed under a low opening. Nat's orb spun ahead of them. Its light cut into the darkness and momentarily illuminated sun and bird carvings covering the walls. They walked silently through the dark passage until they arrived at an oval-shaped intersection. Nat leaned against the wall and took a long breath, trying to overcome her feeling of claustrophobia.

"It's safe to talk now. The first passage we came through is hidden behind the guards' quarters. We always keep quiet when we pass that way." Annin brushed dust and cobwebs off a door handle opposite Nat and inserted the key into a large lock.

"Who is 'we'?" Nat asked, thinking of the carvings.

"Mainly Sisters. Sometimes people who need to leave the castle without being seen. A whole network runs through the castle out to the Representatives' and Regent Buildings." She wiggled the key in the lock. "We'll use the passages to get Emilia out, if we find her."

Nat looked down the darkened hall and wondered if the woman who'd gone berserk in the Chemist's lab could remain quiet in such a confined space.

"Andris would never be able to find his way around here." Annin's face twisted as she cranked the key to one side. "At least not without me." She winked at Nat and the lock clicked. The door groaned and swung open.

They entered a small boxy room. Nat's knee bumped into a row of hinges set into the wall. She rubbed the bruise and wondered if Mervin's way into Rustbrook was easier than this.

"It's going to be tight," Annin said as she dropped to the floor. "Keep quiet and follow me." She lifted a rectangular hatch cut into the wall. The hinges creaked. Nat cringed, hoping no one could hear it. Annin shoved her bag through the opening and disappeared into the dark hole. Nat's orb spun in close circles, then zipped after Annin.

Nat got onto her hands and knees and peered into the tiny space. Her orb spun slowly in the dusty tunnel, casting light on the soles of Annin's boots. She tossed her bag in front of her and inched forward like a worm. Her orb floated slowly between her bag and Annin's feet. She heard a creak followed by a long scraping sound. Fresh air poured over Nat, and she took long gulping breaths. She watched Annin wiggle out of another opening and quickly followed.

Nat shoved her bag into the open and popped her head out of the passage. Her heartbeat settled as she looked around the odd room. Brass tubes ran up and down the wall and gleamed in the light of her orb. Shiny cups, shaped like half an orange, capped the end of each tube. She stood, brushed dust from her blue tunic, and examined the tubes. A thin brass disc covered each opening.

"It's a call station," Annin whispered. "The coachmen use it to call up to the rooms to let people know their rides are ready." She slid a disc to the side, revealing the open mouth of the half-orange shape. The disc swung back and forth when she let it go.

"Lucky for us no one's going anywhere tonight." Nat hid her bag under her cape and wiped the dust marks from the floor with the sole of her boot.

"Our luck will run out eventually." Annin cracked open the door. Cool night air flooded the room. "Let's hope we're not around when it does," she whispered as they slipped outside.

They sprinted down the side of a wide gravel drive and around a corner. Nat sniffed and smelled baking bread. *We must be near the kitchens,* she thought as they continued to run.

Soon the smell of bread was replaced by the reek of garbage. Nat glanced to her right and recognized the scullery entrance she and Soris had used months ago to gain entrance into the castle. The sound of voices and the clank of iron pots spilled out into the narrow alley.

"I've been here before," Nat whispered. Annin didn't have a chance to respond.

"Eh! What are you two skulking around here for?" A scullery maid dropped a wicker basket. Overcooked turnips fell from the basket and rolled toward Nat's feet. The maid took a step toward them and lifted her hand to shade her eyes. Light from the kitchen surrounded her, but Nat and Annin remained in the darkness. Annin hopped behind Nat.

"Just disposing of the Chemist's garbage." Nat ducked her head and lowered her voice. She stumbled back into Annin, trying to move away from the light.

"Why is His Chemistness sending guards to dispose of garbage?" The maid wiped her nose and took another step toward them.

"It's special garbage and if you're smart, you'll take that sodden face of yours back into the kitchen. Question the Chemist and you'll end up being questioned by the Chemist." Annin's fake baritone broke.

The girl's face blanched. She spluttered an apology and ran back into the scullery. Annin and Nat bolted down the garbage-strewn lane, jumping over rotten clumps of food and skirting the rats lurking along the crumbling brick walls. They burst around the side of the garbage bins at the end of the lane.

Annin fled into the night and Nat followed, recognizing a fountain, an alley, and a crumbling brick fence as they raced away from the castle into the heart of the city. They jogged down an alley behind a row of houses. Nat's foot hit a metal pail set near a fence. The pail tumbled down the alley, setting off a chorus of barks and howls. Annin cursed under her breath and snatched Nat's arm, yanking her to a stop behind a broken wagon.

Nat peered around the wagon and spotted a globe-shaped light at the end of the alley. A dark-robed figure held the globe aloft at the end of a thin pole. The figure was close enough that Nat could hear the swish of robes from their hiding spot. The light sputtered, casting broken shadows in a circle beneath the pole. The light bearer paused. The chorus of barking and howling slowly dwindled to a single wail.

The boots of the light bearer thudded softly against the cobblestone of the narrow backstreet. Nat fumbled for her sword, hidden inside the bulky fabric of the soldier's pants. Her elbow hit the broken wagon wheel. The figure stopped and lowered the pole.

"Your stealth has diminished." The woman's voice sounded amused.

"She banged her elbow, not me." Annin rose from behind the wheel. Nat dropped her sword on the cobblestone, startled by Annin's actions.

"Then you ought to choose a quieter companion." The light bearer lifted her pole higher and stepped toward the wheel. Piercing dark eyes and a sharp nose glowed in the light when she lowered her hood.

"Her strengths outweigh her many weaknesses, Matilda," Annin whispered and embraced the woman.

Matilda pushed the soldier's cap away from Annin's forehead and kissed her gently on the brow. "Mervin said I might find you lurking in the shadows, little Afferfly." She smiled down at Annin. "We must move away from here," she said, letting go of her. "A light bearer that lingers in an alley will alert more than just the dogs. Follow a few paces behind until I tell you it is safe to speak." She pulled the hood back over her face and turned toward Nat. "Do keep quiet," she said.

Nat picked up her sword and fell into step behind Matilda, feeling embarrassed and relieved.

CHAPTER THIRTY-THREE

"I've been a light bearer for three years," Matilda explained and set the pole in the corner of a long shed behind the bookshop. Wooden crates obscured one wall, creating a tight space for the three women. Nat sniffed and smelled the familiar unpleasant odor of rudit. She examined the crates, wondering if Matilda and Mervin used them to store food.

"I thought all the light bearers were Mudug's snitches," Annin said. She tugged the guard's tunic over her head.

"Which is precisely why I took the position." She gave Annin a wise look. "After people accused of aiding the rebels started disappearing, becoming a light bearer was the safest way for me to move around the city unnoticed. It provides Gennes' messengers an easier way to contact us, and I feed the castle guards a bit of information every now and then to avoid suspicion."

Nat lifted the guard's cap off her head, freeing her tightly bound hair. She shook her head in disgust.

"Why don't the people stand up to Mudug?" Nat asked.

"Fear and lies, Sister. Mudug's mastery of spreading both has bent most of the population to his will." Matilda folded her long black cloak over her arm. Her straight chin-length hair swung to the side. "I suspect your and Andris' appearance in Rustbrook is meant to straighten them out." Her lips curved into a smile.

"Andris is here?" Nat asked, feeling both relieved and agitated.

"Yes, they arrived late this afternoon. They're in the basement. I believe everyone will be surprised to see you. Except Mervin," she added.

Nat and Annin quickly removed their guard uniforms and followed Matilda through the yard choked with trees, past a small garden, and through a wide door in the back of the shop. Nat stumbled over a stack of boxes near the back entrance.

"Careful, Sister," Matilda scolded as she swiftly shut the door behind her.

Nat mumbled an apology and cautiously shuffled around in the dark away from the door. Her nerves were already on edge at the thought of confronting Andris and seeing Soris. She glanced at the beams of moonlight passing through a set of uncovered windows facing Wesdrono Street. The light cut through the half-empty bookshelves. Matilda's bookstore inventory hadn't improved since Nat had walked through their front door months before with Soris leaning against her shoulder. Annin tugged at her sleeve, pulling her away from her memories. She followed her down the circular stairs to the basement.

"Any news, Matilda?" Andris' voice floated up the stairs. Nat's foot lingered above the next step.

"No news, but I did find something." Matilda strode into the office with Annin trailing behind her.

"Annin? I thought you'd—" Soris' voice was followed by a crashing sound. "Where's Natalie?"

"I'm right here." Her boots clunked against the final few wooden steps. Nat ducked her head and when she looked up, Soris was in front of her. He had a puzzled look on his face. Nat accepted his extended hand and leaned close to his ear before alighting from the last step. "I didn't like Andris' plan," she whispered to him.

"Neither did I," he replied with a little smile that disappeared as he helped her off the last step and ushered her into the room.

The room was crowded with stacks of books and papers, a few worn chairs, a wide bench, and an overturned table Andris was setting upright.

"We had to get a little creative to make it here since your wagon was gone," Nat said, her voice strong despite her frayed nerves. She glanced at Mervin. He gave her a quick wink.

"You're just in time." Mervin stood, making room for Nat and Annin on the bench. Soris sat next to her before Mervin had a chance to reclaim his place.

Three triangle-shaped lights hung from the ceiling across from the bench. The green-colored panes cast a sickly hue on Andris and Benedict, who sat on narrow upholstered chairs.

"We were pondering how to get into the castle." Mervin poured a cup of tea. His large hands enveloped the delicate cup as he handed it to Nat.

She took a sip and glared at Andris over the rim. "Annin led us through the Sisters' tunnels in the castle to get here. I'm surprised you had any question about how we'd get in?" Her voice was calm, but she felt like flinging the tea at Andris' face. Andris leaned forward in his chair. His left eyelid twitched.

"And I have this now." Annin extracted the iron key from a deep pocket in the soldier's vest. "Makes getting in much easier." She tossed the key in the air, and Andris reached out to snatch it. He gave Annin a murderous look. "You have no idea where that key goes, so give it back," Annin said. She set her cup on the floor and uncurled her fingers in front of him.

Nat could tell she was enjoying poking at Andris and delighted in the scowl on his face. He rolled the key around in his hand, then slapped it into Annin's palm. His scowl faded and he nodded as if accepting the inevitability of their presence.

"Fine, Annin and Soris will rendezvous with Benedict, the Sister, and me at the Rewall. We'll use the tunnels once we get to the castle. Soris, explain the details of the plan to Annin and the Sister." He stood and banged into one of the lights. His hand shot out to steady the lamp.

"What is the Rewall?" Nat asked, not caring if she sounded ignorant.

"It's a slum west of the castle, Sister," Matilda answered.

Andris pulled at his beard, then looked at Mervin. "Mervin, can you arrange a boat big enough to take six people downriver? We'd want to depart from the west dock to avoid attention." He paced the tiny room.

"For six people?" Mervin asked. "I can do my best. You'll want it tomorrow, I'm guessing?"

Andris nodded. "Something that can get us as far from the city by midmorning. If a boat is impossible, horses would work."

"Horses might be easier. There's a stable west of the city I use when I need a good team for the mountain roads. The owner owes me a favor or two." Mervin set his own cup on the table. "I'll see to it. It will give me a chance to dispose of those bags of rudit I shoved into the crates in the storage shed. No use trying to hide something when the whole neighborhood can smell it, eh?" He turned toward the stairs.

"Mervin, before you go, finish telling me what you heard about Mudug's mines near the Keyen Mountains." Soris leaned forward and pressed his clenched fist to his chin. Nat glanced at the uncomfortable expressions on Andris' and Benedict's faces and wondered what conversation she and Annin had missed.

"You're asking about the duozi, I assume?" Matilda answered and cocked her head to the side. Andris cleared his throat and shifted from one foot to the other. Benedict hunched back when he heard the word "duozi."

"What have you heard?" Soris' voice bordered on demanding.

"We'll have plenty of time to talk about the mines after we accomplish what we set out to do." Andris moved next to Mervin. "Horses will work, Mervin. Let me help you with those rudit bags. Matilda, any chance you can scrounge up some food for the good Sister and Annin? I'm sure they're starving." He placed a hand on Matilda's back and ushered her up the stairs. "Mervin, after you," he said, nearly pushing him.

Mervin arched his brow and regarded him. "In a moment, Andris." He turned to Soris. "I sent word to Gennes of what we've heard about the mines, but it can't hurt to tell you, too. My information is that Mudug is sending people from the Rewall to work as slaves in his mines. I can't confirm any rumors that duozi are there as well." He glanced at Andris' hand still clasped on his arm. Andris let go. The towering man turned to Annin. "I don't know when I'll see you again, Annin, but the sight of you has been a blessing," he said in a perceptibly gentle voice. He leaned down and embraced her, then climbed the circular stairs. Andris clipped up the stairs after him. His face was the shade of a beet.

"I'll be right back." Nat shot toward the stairs, knowing this might be her only chance to confront Andris alone.

"You're not leaving me alone with them?" Benedict pointed to Annin and Soris.

"Would you shut up?" Annin growled.

At the top of the stairs, Nat grabbed Andris' arm just as Mervin's tall frame disappeared out the back entrance. "You had no right deciding to leave us," she said.

"This is my mission. I'll do what I think's best." He leaned forward and poked his finger at her chest. The store was too dark to make out his expression, but the tone of his voice told Nat plenty.

"What's best?" She slapped his hand away. "How were you going to get into the castle without Annin? What were you going to do? Barge in through the front gates?"

"I'm not going to risk messing up this mission. Keep your focus off Soris, Sister, or I will find a way to leave you behind."

"So abandoning us was about Soris." She leaned forward, feeling anger coil inside her. "You accuse me of losing focus because of my emotions? What about you? You left behind the one person who can safely get you into the castle just to get rid of me! Where was your focus? Where was your emotional check when you made that decision? I have proven to you that I can take care of myself over and over again. My focus was fine last night when I took down those Nala. My focus was fine when I helped capture Mudug's guard." She spat out the words. "Why can't you acknowledge that? Is it because I'm not from Fourline?" Andris shot her a dangerous look, but Nat didn't care. "Or is it because you don't think I'm good enough for your brother?"

"You have no future together. You will just hurt him more than you already have." Andris stepped so close his hot breath hit her face. Nat glanced at the floor, not wanting him to see the pained expression on her face. "When this is over, he won't be treated as a hero, he'll be treated as an outcast. He knows the reality of his future. Don't lead him down a path of thinking he has an alternative."

"Soris can step over to my world and live with Barba and Cairn. Have a life like Annin did. I'll work with Ethet and figure out some way to reverse the effects of his Nala bite so he can pass through the membrane. Maybe we can even find a cure for the duozi," she argued, voicing a hope she'd silently been fostering.

"If generations of Healing Sisters couldn't find a cure for the duozi, Sister, what makes you think you can?" He looked down his nose at her. "If you care for him, the best you can do is leave him to find his own way. Don't give him hope where there is none."

"There's always hope, Andris, always a chance of finding a cure. I'm not leaving him to live a life on the run," she said. Her jaw ached from clenching her teeth together.

"And that's why I left you in the forest. You can't think rationally when it comes to him. And I'm starting to think he may have the same problem with you." He looked through the empty shelves toward the grimy front window. "If we make it through the next few days, understand this, Natalie: you and my brother will never see each other again." He brushed past her and disappeared out the door.

CHAPTER THIRTY-FOUR

Nat uncurled her body from the tight confines of the wooden crate in Matilda's storage shed. Her orb rolled on the floor and spun before rising shakily into the air. *It looks like I feel,* Nat thought as she stretched her arms above her head. Her head ached and her eyes felt swollen.

The unpleasant smell of rudit wafted into her nose as she shook out her tunic and slipped it over her head. Why was she the lucky one who had to sleep in the same place Mervin had stored the bags of cheese? He'd removed them before she'd locked herself inside the crate with a hidden compartment, but the smell lingered. Now her hair and clothes reeked again.

The door to the storage shed creaked open. Nat reached for her dagger and her orb pulsated above her head, poised to strike.

"Put that down." Annin gestured toward the dagger in Nat's hand. She held a small tray. The smell of cinnamon filled the air. "Now would not be a good time to stab me. I'm being nice for once." She slid the tray on top of the crate. Nat's orb floated above the roll and mug.

"Is that what I think it is?" The aroma of coffee lingered with the cinnamon. She reached for the roll and grabbed the mug.

"Yes. You look like a bastle slept on your face," Annin observed.

"The nice just went out the window," Nat said with a full mouth. The coffee scalded her tongue, but she didn't care. She took another sip and pulled on her boots. "Where'd you sleep?" Even in the dim light of the orb, Nat could see a sheepish look on Annin's face. Nat buckled her belt and took another sip of the coffee.

"Upstairs, in my old room." Annin knelt and pulled Nat's bedding from the crate. Her nose twitched. "It smells like something died in here." Her face contorted as she balled up the bedding. She sniffed in Nat's direction. "Maybe it's you."

"Thanks, and I was just going to ask you if you wanted a bite." Nat shoved the remainder of the roll into her mouth.

"Hurry up. Soris and I are leaving with Mervin in a few minutes. Andris wants you in the shop. Washroom is behind the shed. Be quiet when you use it since Mervin and Matilda are risking their lives by having us here." She whisked the mug out of Nat's hand and disappeared out the door with it and the bedding.

Nat reduced her orb to a dim glow. It spun around the room while she pulled her hair back with sticky fingers. Other than the lingering smell of rudit, coffee, and roll, the shed looked untouched. She pocketed the orb and moved as quietly as she could through the dark yard to the washroom.

The wooden door creaked. She inched it closed and shuffled across the floor. Three galvanized tubs ranging in size occupied the top of a raised platform. She turned on the tap above the small tub and scrubbed the sticky residue from her hands. The cold water numbed her fingers. She cupped her hands under the stream, splashed her face, and looked at her dim reflection in the mirror hanging above the tub. A cold, blurry image stared back at her.

"Natalie?" Nat heard the door open and jumped at the sound of Soris' voice. He touched her arm reassuringly.

"What are you doing here?" Nat whispered. "Aren't you and Annin supposed to leave before we do?"

"Yes, so I'll make this quick. Don't be mad at Andris for what he did yesterday. It didn't take me long to figure out his motivation for not waiting for you and Annin. He swore to Estos that he'd make sure no harm came to you; he was just trying to protect you."

Nat kept quiet. She watched his shadowy reflection in the mirror, wondering what lies Andris had fed Soris to get him to believe he cared a shred about her safety.

"But he made a mistake and underestimated how important you are to seeing this mission through," he added quickly. "I may have my own reasons for wishing you weren't here, but none of them have anything to do with your abilities as a Sister."

She turned around, and he brought his hand to her cheek. His touch sent a wave of warmth through her.

"Promise me you won't do anything stupid today," he said as his gaze lingered on her face.

"As long as you don't, I won't." She looked him straight in the eye.

He laughed quietly, then dropped his chin. His expression grew serious as he brought his other hand up, cradling her face. She felt her heart quicken its pace. "One more thing, Natalie."

"What's that?" Her voice trembled as he leaned closer. Her words were lost as he pressed his lips to hers, kissing her gently at first, then pulling her tightly toward him as she curled her fingers through his hair. Her orb flared with light above them.

"I guess my orb knows I'm happy," she said when their lips parted. The orb dimmed, but she could see the smile stretch across Soris' face.

"See you at the Rewall, Sister." He brushed his hand over her hair. Still smiling, he slipped out the door.

"See you at the Rewall," she whispered, feeling a little weak in the knees. Her orb spun close to her heart, and she held it in her hands. *I will find a cure, Soris. After this mission is over I'll go back to the Healing House, talk to Ethet and Ethes, work through their treatments, find something . . .*

A sharp rapping sounded on the door. "Sister," Andris' said in a harsh whisper. Nat quickly splashed another handful of water on her face and bolted to the yard. "Nice of you to show up on time," he remarked when she appeared.

"You smell like rudit." Benedict's nasal voice rose behind her. He shuffled to her side. A long green robe trailed behind him. Nat squinted and noticed a brown wig covering his head. "Fringe Sisters. If I never meet another one, it will be too soon," he complained. She ignored the comment and inspected his costume. In the dark, he looked just like the Chemist.

"Are Annin and Soris gone?" She kept her eyes on the ground, knowing Andris would be able to read her emotions if she looked at him.

"Yes, and I'll thank you if we miss meeting up with them. Matilda is waiting." He thrust a heavy black cloak into her hands. The three of them moved silently down a stone path to a tall gate flanked by conifers. Andris pushed open the gate and peered into the dark alley. He motioned for Nat and Benedict to follow, then sprinted into the darkness.

They crossed a cobblestone intersection. Nat and Andris ran into the next lane with Benedict trailing behind them. Hearing the sound of running water, Nat glanced through the broken slats of a wooden fence while they waited for him. Water burbled out of a little fountain in the middle of a well-kept yard. The water flowed over the image of a sun. Nat smiled at the hidden symbol of the Healing House in the middle of Rustbrook.

Benedict caught up, and the trio walked hurriedly down a lane to a deserted market. A rickety buggy stood in front of a boarded-up stall. Matilda, dressed in a shoddy cloak, sat atop the two-wheeled cart. A brown donkey, hitched to the wagon, turned its enormous ears as they approached. Andris and Benedict climbed onto the back of the wagon and tucked their knees tight to their chests. Matilda arranged containers of garbage around them, obscuring them from view. Nat climbed onto the narrow bench after Matilda was done arranging the smelly baskets and burlap bags.

"Pull that hood farther around your face," Matilda advised as she snapped the reins. The donkey took a reluctant step forward. The cart didn't move. Matilda snapped the reins again and the donkey lurched forward, jerking the cart into motion.

The cart rolled along the bumpy cobblestones. Dim lights shone through a few windows as they rode through alleys. Matilda stopped to pick up a container of garbage even though the cart bed overflowed with refuse. A splash of water hit the donkey in the nose.

"Watch it!" Matilda cursed at a shopkeeper emptying a pail of sludgy-looking water into the alley. He scratched the dirty apron covering his massive belly, waved dismissively, and returned to the back entrance of his shop.

Little clusters of houses replaced the shops as they traveled on. The rhythmic clop of the donkey's hooves and the sound of the wheels hitting the cobblestones lulled Nat to sleep. She jerked her head up and blinked. The castle, under the light of the setting moon, appeared on the hill behind them. The cart passed underneath a high red-stone gate. Nat pulled her hood even lower when she noticed a slumbering guard on a chair next to the gate.

Despite being higher on the hill, the houses and shops they passed looked dilapidated. A dog bolted in front of the cart, chasing a creature with a long tail. Nat's skin crawled when she saw the rat clamber onto a rickety porch and scamper across the thin metal roof of a house. Potholes filled the street and the cart bounced dangerously.

"Where are we?" whispered Nat.

"It's the Rewall, the oldest part of the city, dear." Matilda's sharp nose stuck out from her hood. "Where the indentured ones live," she added.

"You mean slaves?"

"Yes." She nodded gravely. "Some are free to come and go and run their own businesses and lives if it serves Mudug's purposes, but they owe him debts and he takes his payment in many forms. So does the Chemist." She frowned and returned her stony stare to the road. "You'll find it easier to pass through the gates to the castle from here. I learned a few days ago that the Chemist has Mudug's guards bringing Rewall residents through a nearby entrance to his quarters in increasing numbers."

They turned onto a side lane. A square surrounded by crumbling open arches spread out in front of them. An earthy, putrid smell rose from the square.

"What for?" Nat scrunched her nose.

"Experimenting with riven." Matilda pulled the reins, and the donkey came to an abrupt stop. She hopped off the cart and lifted a burlap bag filled with rotten food and placed it in a trough that ran along one side of the square. "Get another bag," she urged Nat under her breath. "They'll topple the garbage if they try to climb out with that stack above them."

Nat obediently grabbed the uppermost basket and dumped the contents into the trough, wondering all the while about what Matilda had said. The garbage ran down a slide into a pit. A figure moved in the darkness below, mixing the garbage into a clump of brown dirt before carting it off. Matilda heaved another bag into the trough and dropped it loudly just as Nat heard a thud on the packed dirt behind her.

Benedict crouched next to the wagon. Andris, draped in a black cloak, ran across the square toward one of the columns supporting the curved beams. Benedict limped quickly after him. He grasped his long cloak, keeping the robe tight around him. Matilda gestured for Nat to follow them.

"Thank you," Nat whispered.

Matilda nodded once. "Take care, Sister." She climbed onto the cart.

Nat grabbed one more bag and spread its contents out along the trough, hiding Benedict's labored movements from the figures working in the pit. She let go of the burlap bag and it drifted down, landing on a clump of soil. Matilda's cart bounced over rubble strewn around the square and disappeared into the darkness.

The light of dawn colored the flags flying above the castle, but night still clung to the Rewall. Andris, Nat, and Benedict darted from the shadowy columns to the base of a watchtower. The curved cap crowning the tower stood empty. Andris reached into his pocket and produced a fake beard and mustache. He dropped them into her hands and disappeared around the base of the tower to find Annin and Soris.

Nat smoothed the fake beard over her chin, hoping Mervin had delivered Annin and Soris to their drop-off spot in the Rewall as easily as Matilda had the three of them. After her fight with Andris the night before, Annin had explained the danger in all five of them traveling together through the city. The plan made sense, but Nat's nerves were now on edge as she and Benedict hung back in the shadows waiting for Andris to return. She glanced at the old man as he fidgeted with the edge of his robe, thinking he looked as nervous as she felt.

Andris reappeared with them, and Nat let out a breath of relief. Annin and Soris pulled black cloth sacks over their heads, and Andris loosely bound their hands behind their backs. When he was done, he locked eyes with Nat and made a knocking motion with his hand.

Nat unsheathed her dagger and knocked on the narrow wooden door set into the old watchtower. The sound echoed in the quiet of the early morning. She waited, listening, but heard nothing. Andris made another knocking motion, his eyes wide with impatience. She rapped on the door again and heard a clanging come down the tower stairs. Andris pulled a loose black mask over his face. The door opened, and a bleary-eyed guard leaned against the frame. The smell of alcohol rolled off him. He swayed toward Nat.

"You smell like rudit," the soldier slurred and wiped his nose with his hand.

Nat sprang forward and held the dagger under his throat. "And you smell like death," she said in a low voice, pushing him back into the guard tower. He tripped over a stool and landed with a thud on his back. He scrambled up, balled his hands into fists, and was just about to spring on Nat when he froze.

Benedict coughed, lowered his hood, and raised his head. Andris, his face hidden by the mask, stepped behind him. "I wouldn't do that if I were you," the Hermit drawled. "Finding decent guards is almost impossible, and it would put me out if mine were injured. I don't like being put out," he said through clenched teeth.

"Your Chemistness?" The guard squinted in the dim light.

"Who do I look like, the city toymaker?" Benedict stepped forward and slapped the guard across the face.

"No, no, sir." The guard straightened. "I wasn't advised you'd be coming through the gate." Benedict glared at the guard. "Not that your activities are any of my business, sir."

Benedict nodded in approval. "No, they are not," he said sharply. He turned to Andris. "Bring them in," he ordered in an aloof voice.

Andris retreated through the door and pushed Annin and Soris, their heads and duozi features covered by the sacks, through the opening.

"Now, if any whining family comes looking for missing loved ones, you saw nothing." Benedict's voice held a steely edge. The guard looked at the hooded figures and nodded. "I'm glad we have an understanding. Now get back into that tower before I turn you in for being drunk on duty."

The guard stumbled up the stairs, glancing nervously back once to find Benedict still glaring at him.

CHAPTER THIRTY-FIVE

Andris guided the hooded figures with gentle shoves. They stumbled across a path set close to the castle walls, then ducked under the branches of a willow tree. Nat pulled Soris' and Annin's hoods off and dug her fingers into the loose knots around Soris' wrists.

Andris yanked the mask off his head. "Well done, Hermit." His praise sent a slight flush up Benedict's pale cheeks. Beads of perspiration clung to Andris' forehead. He stuffed his mask away and untied the rope binding Annin's wrists.

"Your beard," Benedict said to Nat as he leaned against a moss-covered tree trunk.

"Thanks," she replied and ripped it off her face. Benedict stretched over his withered limb, exposing the tall heel of one of his boots. Nat felt a pang of sympathy for him. He'd managed to walk with a straight gait since they'd encountered the guard. *His leg must be killing him,* she thought.

"No time to dawdle. Move," Andris ordered, directing them to a shed nestled in the willow grove. Nat passed through the decrepit shed's door. The interior smelled like stale dirt. Rows of old shovels and spades lined the walls.

"A little light, Sister." Annin's voice came from the darkness in front of her. Nat released her orb, and it illuminated piles of rusted, broken rakes that choked the back of the shed. Annin squinted in the sudden light, then disappeared behind an old wheelbarrow. The sound of splintering wood made Nat cringe. *Just get us into the tunnels before someone finds us.*

"Keep it down, Annin," Andris growled.

Annin emerged from behind the wheelbarrow, covered in dirt. "It's not my fault some Sister sealed over the hatch. Watch your head as you go down," she advised.

Soris peered into the dark stairwell in the floor of the shed. The orb spun around and descended into the hole, creating a patch of light in the darkness. He looked at Annin. "Snakes?"

She nodded and he jumped down the stairs, disappearing into the inky darkness. Nat moved to follow, but Annin stuck out her hand, pressing against Nat's chest.

"Give him a minute, he's clearing the unfriendlies from the path." She smiled crookedly. Nat shuddered, thinking of the tunnel eater.

Soris' face appeared below them. His Nala eye glinted in the light of Nat's orb. "It's clear." He stepped to the side. Benedict eased himself down the stairs, steadying himself against the packed dirt walls. Andris disappeared into the hole after Benedict.

"Your turn." Annin pointed to the opening. Nat took a deep breath and climbed down the crumbling steps. Roots wound their way through the dirt walls of the tunnel. She ducked under one that grew across the earthen ceiling. Its hairlike fibers clung to her hood and smeared her forehead with an earthy streak. She heard the sound of the hatch falling into place and Annin's soft footsteps. Annin sidled past and crouched on the dirt floor in front of Andris. Nat directed her orb to hover over Annin's head.

"This tunnel leads beneath the Representatives' Building." Annin drew a rectangle with a line running underneath it in the dirt floor. "The passage splits here." She marked a spot below the opposite side of the Representatives' Building with her finger. "We'll take the tunnel leading into the service quarters of the castle here and end at this spot, the old Sisters' accommodations." She leaned back on her heels. "Those rooms are adjacent to the courtyard where the Chemist has his quarters. This route should get us as close as we can go without walking the halls of the castle, I think," she added.

"You *think*? I thought you knew these tunnels like the back of your hand." Andris wiped a smudge of dirt from his brow.

"I do." Annin's lips curled down. "But so does Emilia. She may have divulged their location." Her words hung in the air. "Let me lead." She poked her finger at Andris. "I make the decisions on where and when to move forward. I can tell if something's askew."

His face twitched. *The notion that someone else would control the progress of this mission and decide its direction must be killing him,* Nat thought.

"Not advisable. You should lead, Andris. They can't be trusted," Benedict said nervously. Nat rubbed her forehead, wondering why he continually acted as if Soris and Annin weren't there or couldn't hear him. "There's a possibility they could lead us—"

"They could lead us where?" Annin thrust her face in front of Benedict. His eyes grew wide.

"Do you think this has all been a ruse to get you to a secret Nala lair?" Soris said to the Hermit. "If we'd wanted you dead—"

"Enough." Andris ushered Annin and Soris down the cramped tunnel.

Benedict huffed. "Did you hear? He's threatening me!" He waved his hands, casting snakelike shadows against the dirt walls.

"No one is threatening you," Andris said as if addressing a petulant child. "Annin, lead the way. Hermit, you're between the Sister and me. Perhaps that separation will calm your nerves. Soris—"

"I know, brother, bring up the rear." Soris exchanged a frustrated look with him.

The tunnel felt suffocating to Nat. The earthen walls curved in toward her head, forcing her to duck to avoid scraping her hair against the loose soil above her. Showers of dirt fell into her eyes and down the neck of her tunic, and she wondered if the tunnel would simply give way on them, burying them beneath the castle. The smell of rudit still lingered in her hair and clothes and mixed with the damp odor of the tunnel, causing Nat to breathe through her mouth.

Benedict grumbled until Andris told him he'd ride on Soris' back if he complained any more. The Hermit sniffed, but said nothing more. *Andris isn't helping Soris' case by using him as a threat,* Nat thought. Her orb zoomed by her head, lighting the path for those behind her. She shook the dirt out of her tunic and wished Andris would be more sensitive to Soris' plight.

"Keep your orb under control," Andris barked after it hit him in the head on its return run toward Annin. She shrugged, knowing she needed to be more careful. She'd noticed how sensitive her orb was to her thoughts. The orb smacking Andris on the head was likely not an accident.

A worn column appeared in the light of the orb. Its platelike crown held the earth in place where the path split in two directions. A thin line of birds, suns, vines, and swords decorated the border of the plate and curved around the front of the column. Nat ran her fingers over the designs, wondering how long the images had existed in this tomb-like tunnel.

Benedict emerged from the darkness, followed by Andris and Soris. The brothers wore a similar scowl on their faces. Soris gave her a reassuring smile, then his face creased back into the scowl. Annin wordlessly took the path to the left. Bits of flagstone lined the floor, providing a pocked path where the soil and roots had overtaken the stone.

But as they moved farther up the tunnel, the floor transformed into solid rock and the roots disappeared. Blocks of stone held the earthen walls back. Annin pressed her finger to her lips. Distant muffled voices cut through the silence of the passage. Nat imagined servants preparing for the day on the other side of the wall.

The group crept quietly through the dim tunnel. Nat could make out the faint outline of discs set into the walls. Her hands brushed over the discs, and she felt raised images under her fingertips. She bent down and examined one of them. A delicate vine wound around the rim and a bird, sun, and sword emblem occupied the center.

She was so absorbed with the markings that she jumped when Soris placed his hand on her shoulder. He led her around a bend. Under the light of her orb, she saw Annin press a disc set in the wall. A panel separated from the wall with a click. A moment of deathly stillness passed as they listened for voices and heard nothing. Annin dug her fingers into the panel, edging it open. Nat stood back and watched her vanish into the opening. Andris pulled at his beard and followed. Benedict wheezed and shuffled after him.

"Something's off," Soris whispered and gripped Nat's shoulder. His eyes were focused on the floor of the passage leading in the opposite direction from which they'd come.

"What?" She followed Soris' gaze and stared at the ground. Nat noticed a trail in the dust. She sent her orb up the tunnel. Its light revealed a single set of footprints next to thin lines in the dust that looked like the prints of a snake slithering over the ground.

"I sense . . ." He paused and closed his eyes. "I sense a Nala nearby."

"Are you sure?" she whispered. He nodded. Nat unsheathed her sword, hastened past the panel, and found herself inside a large closet. The doors of the closet were cracked open, and she could see a sliver of Benedict's back on the other side. A blue leg brushed past the opening as a Nala crept stealthily down from the top of the closet. Soris gave

Nat a quick look, then they thrust the doors open, whacking the Nala violently in the back.

"Its hand, its hand!" Soris warned as he leapt forward to pull Benedict out of the way of the flailing Nala. A spiked hand plunged into the floor inches from Benedict's leg. The creature compacted its lean body, balling itself up, and sprang off the floor, hitting the wall and then landing in an open doorway next to Nat. She raised her sword to kill it before it scurried into the other room. The Nala stopped short on its angular limbs. It lifted its bulb-shaped head, and its eyes expanded when it saw the markings on her arm.

"The Sister," it hissed and jumped at Nat.

Nat lunged, piercing the Nala's chest. The weight of the creature impaled on her sword brought her slamming down to the wooden floor. The Nala threw its head back and let out a hissing scream next to her. Andris sliced through its neck, ending the nightmarish sound. Blue blood pooled on the hard wooden floor and seeped into Nat's sleeve. Andris, Soris, and Annin raced through the doorway into the adjoining room to search for more Nala, leaving Nat alone with the corpse and Benedict.

"It had me." Benedict clutched his chest. His breathing came in labored gasps.

"It doesn't have you now," she said, more shaken than she sounded. The Nala had attacked her when it saw her markings. It had a clear escape route to the other room, but it had attacked her. She kicked the slack-mouthed head through the open closet doors. *Why didn't it run away when it was so outnumbered?* She slid her arms under the creature's armpits and hauled its body into the closet.

"Natalie, come look at this." Soris stood in the doorway of the adjoining room with a grave expression on his face. Nat shoved the closet doors shut and hastened to him.

Heavy moth-eaten drapes covered the windows of the old Sisters' accommodations. Closets and beds with tattered bedclothes lined two walls. Andris stood in the middle of the room, staring at the opposite wall. Even in the dim light, Nat could see the slash marks across the engravings covering the walls. She ran her fingers over the deep gouges that bisected the sun, bird, sword, and vine designs. Annin moved nervously around the room, checking behind the slashed bed drapes and glancing above to the beams that crisscrossed the ceiling.

"What is that?" Nat held her hand to her mouth. A pulpy mess of tissue, muscle, and bones filled a long shallow silver bowl set in the middle of the floor.

"Breakfast for the Nala." Andris sheathed his sword.

"The rest of the rooms are clear." Soris stood next to Nat. "I noticed marks in the passageway after you entered the closet, Andris. I think the Nala used it to get in here."

"Look at this." Annin held up a small silver basin of clear water resting on a wooden table. "The Nala wasn't here by accident." She wrinkled her face in disgust. "Someone invited it and is playing host."

Andris lifted an edge of the curtain covering the window. "There are the Chemist's quarters. Other than the passages, these rooms are completely sealed off from the rest of the castle?" He looked at Annin, and she nodded. He frowned.

"Is that . . . ?" Benedict limped through the doorway and stopped when he spotted the silver dish.

"It's mutton," Andris said unconvincingly. "Is there another nearby tunnel that's not connected to that one?" he asked Annin and jerked his thumb in the direction of the adjacent room.

"In a hallway on the other side of the courtyard." Annin edged away from the water basin.

"Soris, Natalie, secure the passage we came through and put that room back in order. I want no sign of how we entered these rooms. Benedict"—he beckoned to the Hermit—"keep watch and tell me the minute you see a guard or anything move in that courtyard."

Benedict limped toward the window and stood on tiptoe as he peered out the dirty panes.

Andris grabbed Annin. "Are there any more?" he asked with urgency.

"I think that was the only one . . ." Annin's voice trailed off as Nat and Soris walked into the next room.

"You knew it was in here, but she didn't?" Nat whispered to Soris.

He gave her a worried look and lifted an overturned table. "She probably wasn't focused on trying to sense them," he said quietly. "I mean, why would she? We're in the castle, not the middle of the forest. Nala should never be here." He righted a chair and opened the closet doors. A pointed limb fell to the floor. Nat jumped back, startled. Soris kicked the limb back into the closet. "Hold the door for me. I'll secure the passage."

"I think Annin's right, it wasn't here by accident." She kept her voice low as she eyed the headless body sprawled on the floor of the closet. In the dim light, the skin looked almost black. She felt her orb tugging in her pocket and released it. Waves of light fell over the body. *At least it's not pale white like the ones at the river and the ruins,* she thought and wondered why the creature's blue color brought her any sense of comfort. "Maybe Mudug is negotiating with the Nala again?" she suggested.

"He could be meeting with them about the trade routes or something else." The stone door clicked into place. Soris lifted the Nala's flaccid limbs and repositioned them before stepping back into the room. "Like children the Nala can turn into duozi." Soris' eyes held a steely look.

The thought of Mudug holding negotiations with the Nala to discuss terms under which he'd provide them children made Nat's stomach twist. "Maybe we'll find something in the Chemist's quarters that will tell us what it was doing here." Nat glanced at the creature. "It sure seemed surprised to see me," she said in hushed voice, realizing now that the Nala had looked as if it'd recognized her before it'd attacked.

"Doesn't matter. It's dead." Soris placed a reassuring hand on the small of Nat's back. "Remember, nothing foolish. Especially not now." His voice was light, but his face was creased with worry.

She glanced from him to the Nala's body. "Nothing foolish," she agreed and eased the closet doors shut with her foot before returning to the adjacent room.

Andris was listening intently to Annin as he fastened the silver buttons on the vest of one of the stolen guard uniforms. He lifted his head when Nat and Soris walked through the archway.

"Passage entry is sealed, and the room's cleaned up the best we could manage," Soris said.

"Good. Annin is certain there are no more Nala nearby." Andris gave him a questioning look, and Soris nodded in agreement. "We have to assume it was here either at Mudug's or the Chemist's request. Which means the most likely location for a meeting with them would be—"

"Somewhere in the castle but away from prying eyes." Nat looked out the window. The sight of the long stone building occupying the courtyard brought back a flood of memories. "Do you think they'd meet here or in the Chemist's quarters?" She turned to Andris.

"More likely the quarters." He eyed the gouges in the walls. "I can't see Mudug or the Chemist wanting to meet with a Nala in here. It's probable that the Chemist would relocate Emilia if his rooms were being used as a meeting place with that thing." He glanced in the direction of the adjoining room.

"He wouldn't risk moving her," Benedict piped up. "Too many chances that someone might see her."

"Let's hope you're right, Hermit. We stick to our original plan, except we'll depart through a different tunnel."

"And I'd like to know how that creature came to use a secret tunnel." Benedict's eyes narrowed. He turned and glared at Annin, then Soris.

"Do you really think we told a Nala about the passages?" Soris took two long steps and was in Benedict's face. "We saved you back there. You understand that? I could have easily let that Nala take you down before Natalie killed it."

Benedict dropped the curtain. "Makes no difference. This all smells like a trap to me." He gave Soris a stony look and walked to the far end of the room, away from Soris and Annin.

"Keep your focus," Andris growled at them. "Annin says there's access to another tunnel off the northeast entrance to the courtyard. She'll secure the opening. Soris, you provide watch and cover. The three of us"—he glanced at Nat and Benedict—"will make our way through each room of his quarters." His voice was heavy. "Everyone follows my lead. Even if we don't find Emilia, make your way to Annin and wait in the Sisters' passage until all of us arrive." He lifted the curtain. When he turned to Benedict, Nat saw a doubtful expression on Andris' face. "Ready, Hermit?"

Benedict adjusted his wig. "I will fulfill my oath to protect the queen regardless of the danger these duozi pose."

"Worry about the guards, not me, old man." Annin pulled her hood over her head. She cracked open the heavy carved door. Andris motioned from the window, and she slid into the courtyard behind a thick cluster of juniper bushes. She skirted the edge of the courtyard and disappeared behind the long building composing the Chemist's quarters.

"Stay out of sight until we've dealt with the guards," Andris whispered to Nat. Benedict pulled two packets of sleeping resin from his pocket and handed one to him. "If we can't knock them out with the resin, take them down," he ordered Soris.

Soris loaded an arrow into his crossbow. Andris and Benedict stepped out the door and strode toward the front of the building.

"Ready?" Soris whispered to her.

"Doesn't matter, does it?" She gave him a humorless smile.

"No," he admitted, "but it makes me feel better if I ask. Out you go." He nudged her with his boot and Nat crawled into the bushes. She pushed the fingerlike needles aside to get a better view. The morning light touched the opposite end of the courtyard, where the Chemist's garden spread out like a wave of green. She scanned the far wall, looking for Annin, but saw nothing. In the shadow of the building, Benedict straightened his robe. *It all rides on him,* Nat thought nervously. One slip, one misplaced word, and the mission, and likely their lives, would be over.

CHAPTER THIRTY-SIX

"Do you have any notion how long I've been standing here?" Benedict's voice rang through the courtyard. Two guards stepped out from under the wide overhang fronting the Chemist's quarters.

"Your Chemistness." The guards looked surprised. "We didn't expect you back so soon, sir."

Nat let out a sigh of relief. The Chemist was gone—hopefully for a long time. One guard gave Andris a sidelong glance. Andris kept his head low. The guards stood in uncomfortable silence while Benedict paced in front of them. *What is he waiting for?* Nat watched him with a growing sense of unease. She glanced at Soris' hiding spot. The tip of his crossbow was barely visible among the low branches of the flowering tree.

"Hands," Benedict ordered abruptly, his voice sharp and commanding. The guards looked at each other in confusion. "Put out your hands, you fools."

"Sir?" they said in unison.

"Do as I say!" Benedict lurched forward on his good leg and wobbled when his other foot hit the ground. He grasped one of the soldier's hands and wiped the sleeping resin across his palm. "Someone's raided my store of riven." His voice rose an octave. "Riven reacts to this chemical component." The soldier eyed the tan-colored smear marring his hand. "I'll know immediately if you've touched my supply." He dropped the stupefied man's hand. Nat watched in awe as the guards remained motionless and completely cowed by Benedict. The plan was working.

"Check that one," Benedict snarled and cast a suspicious look at the other ashen-faced guard. Andris stalked toward him.

"I promise you, sir, we . . ." His voice faltered and his eyes widened as the first guard swayed, then fell face-first onto the lush green grass. The guard's brows drew together as he looked at the unconscious soldier.

"I thought as much! An immediate reaction." Benedict glared menacingly at the second guard.

"Sir, I don't know anything about missing riven." He backed away from Andris and held his open hands in front of his chest. Andris feigned a stop, then lunged for his knees, knocking him down. They rolled on the ground, crushing a patch of ornamental grass and small boxwood bushes.

Nat saw a blur of motion out of the corner of her eye. Soris raced toward the center of the courtyard and lifted his crossbow to his shoulder. The arrow flew just as Andris rolled on top of the guard. The tip grazed Andris' hip and planted squarely in the guard's buttocks. Soris released another arrow, and it penetrated deep into the guard's side. His scream was low and gurgling. Andris clamped his hand over the guard's nose and mouth, smothering the writhing man. His cries died down.

"He shot at his own brother!" Benedict yelled. Nat looked about in confusion. He lifted his shaking hand toward Soris. "I told you! I told you they were not to be trusted." He stumbled away from Soris. His eyes held a look of crazed fear. He tripped over his long robe and landed on the ground.

"It was an accident," Nat said in a hushed voice, but Benedict took no notice. He scrambled to his feet and disappeared behind the Chemist's quarters. Nat hesitated, wondering if she should go after him, then heard Andris' low grunt of pain. She ran to where Soris was helping Andris to his feet. Soris pressed his hand against the bleeding gash in Andris' hip.

"Find Emilia," Andris said to Nat through gritted teeth.

Nat nodded quickly and raced toward the Chemist's quarters, leaving Soris with his brother.

The door of the Chemist's laboratory creaked open. The smell of death rolled over her before she even saw the bloodied cloth draped over a figure on the exam table where Soris had lain months before. A cloying, sickly smell hung heavy in the air. Nat stumbled into the room and clutched her hand over her nose. Her heart thudded inside her chest as she approached the draped form. Bottles and vials filled with cloudy liquids lay strewn across a table next to the body.

Nat inched closer to the table and pinched the folds of the stained cloth with her fingers. Slowly, she peeled away the drape. A gray-faced man with eyes frozen in terror lay under the cloth. Nat felt his cold neck under his pointed beard. *No pulse.* She steeled herself and rolled the cloth farther down his sunken chest, relieved she wasn't looking at Emilia's corpse but needing to know what had caused the man's death. A series of punctures dotted the skin above his heart. A pale blue tint covered his skin.

Nat dropped the cloth and directed her attention to the table and a single bottle containing a blue liquid. "Nala Venom" was written on the bottle's label in a flourished hand. She bolted from the room.

Soris glanced over his shoulder at Nat as he carried the dead guard toward the Sisters' accommodations. Nat shook her head to indicate she hadn't found anything. Soris quickened his pace. The soldier's arms bounced against his legs.

"Anything?" Nat jumped at the sound of Andris' voice. He steadied himself against the building's middle door and grimaced. Dried poisonous plants hung from the beams above his head.

"A body, but not the one we are looking for," she said and took a deep, shaky breath. *If she isn't in here . . .* Nat pushed the thought away and grasped the cold doorknob. It refused to turn.

Andris moved slightly to the side and drew his sword. "Kick it," he said in a hoarse whisper.

Nat stepped back and planted a front kick near the knob. The wood around the lock splintered, and the door crashed open.

Andris plunged into the room ahead of Nat. "She's not here." He scanned the cluttered room. "Check the last room, then we leave."

Nat didn't budge. The books, the table with the map, all the furniture, everything she'd seen before was still there, but no Emilia. "She was here before," she said, trying to reassure herself that she hadn't led them into this disaster for nothing.

Soris slid past Andris and skirted a pile of books to reach Nat. He placed a hand on her shoulder. "Come on, Natalie. She's not here," he said.

"Move to the next room," Andris ordered. "We're pushing our luck as it is." He turned to leave. Blood seeped through the makeshift bandage pressed against the wound in his hip.

Nat stared at the corner, where a window let in the weak morning light. *The window.* She squinted. *The window doesn't end at the corner.* She stepped over a broken chair and touched the edge of the window, feeling a crack where it met the wall. "Soris, help me," she said.

He was already next to her, prying his fused fingers above her hands into the small crack. A hidden door groaned open under the pressure.

Light from the window fell upon Emilia.

She sat upright on a high wooden pallet covered with a filthy gray blanket, her head tilted against the wall behind her. Her black hair hung in greasy tendrils around her head, and she wore a ragged brown shift that barely covered her legs. She opened her blue-gray eyes and looked at Soris. She jerked her legs protectively away from him. Bruises covered her bare calves.

"Blessed Rim." Andris drew in a breath and brushed past Nat. He dropped next to the pallet. "Emilia," he whispered. Her eyes darted between the brothers. Nat thought she looked as if she were a cornered animal deciding when to strike.

"What do you want?" Emilia's voice trembled and she clutched the soiled blanket.

"Emilia, it's me, Andris. Don't you recognize me?" He pulled off the guard's hat. He reached for the thin chain that bound her ankle to a metal ring on the floor.

"Don't touch my cord," she warned. Her eyes expressed only fear and not the slightest recognition.

"We're here to free you." Andris reached for his dagger to pry the chain apart. Soris took a step forward to help him.

"Stay away from me, creature." Her voice teetered on the edge of hysteria. Soris stepped back.

"Emilia, that's Soris, he won't hurt you." Andris calmly pleaded with her and inched forward.

She blinked and grasped a length of chain between her hands. "I said stay away!" The chain slashed through the air, striking Andris' forearm.

"Do you have any of Benedict's resin left?" Nat asked under her breath. Andris clutched his arm and looked utterly shaken as he stared at Emilia. "Resin, Andris," she said again in a hushed request. He pulled a crumpled packet from the folds of the uniform and placed it in her hand without taking his eyes off Emilia. Nat held the packet so it was out of Emilia's line of sight and slowly moved to the edge of the pallet.

"Not a lot of light comes through here," Nat said, trying to keep her voice even. Emilia's blue-gray eyes flashed with suspicion. Nat cautiously sat down and looked out the window, averting her gaze. Even with her back turned, she could feel tension radiating off the woman. Nat swallowed, thinking back to Sister Rory and her suspicions of what the Chemist might have done to her. If she didn't recognize Andris or

Soris, then maybe Rory was right, maybe memories of the people she loved were gone.

"It's cramped in here, too," Nat observed, still keeping her back to Emilia and the resin packet hidden from view. Soris lingered protectively in the doorway next to Andris, but Nat shot them a look of warning, and they both backed away.

"I suppose it is," Emilia said as if noticing her surroundings for the first time.

"What's your name?" Nat asked, wondering if she even remembered who she was. She edged a little closer.

"My name is . . ." Her voice died.

"It's okay if you don't remember," Nat said reassuringly as she faced Emilia. The chain drooped between her hands.

"He makes me forget," she said in a distant voice. She sniffed and her eyes came back into focus. "But you . . . You smell familiar." She reached for Nat's arm. Nat's sleeve fell back, revealing her vine and spear markings. Emilia paused and traced her fingers over the tiny spears. "No birds, I hate the birds," she said absently as she looked at Nat's markings. She buried her nose in the fabric of Nat's tunic. She clambered onto her bony knees and smelled Nat's hair. "You smell like rudit." A small light came into her eyes.

"Does that remind you of something?" Nat asked. Her heart pounded. She remembered the story about Andris hiding rudit in Gordon's kit before her coronation. She carefully moved the packet of resin close to Emilia's arm.

"It does!" she exclaimed. "It reminds me of . . ." She looked down at the tan smear on her forearm. "What have you done?"

"Nothing bad, I promise. Tell me what you remember about rudit." Nat looked into her eyes.

"The smell makes me . . . It makes me happy." Emilia sniffed Nat's hair again. After a few moments, her lids drooped and closed.

"Andris, Soris!" Nat called out and laid Emilia gently on the blanket. Andris limped across the floor and dropped to her side. He thrust his knife blade into a chain link near Emilia's ankle. Soris pulled the chain taut and the link broke, then he lifted her into his arms. Bruises and abrasions covered every inch of her exposed skin.

"Get her to the passage, we'll cover," Andris ordered with his eyes fixed on Emilia.

They crossed the room and paused briefly at the door. Nat poked her head outside. Nothing moved in the courtyard.

Soris closed his eyes a moment. "Annin's still near," he whispered reassuringly.

Andris took Soris' crossbow and they exited the room. Nat shut the broken door behind them the best she could. Bits of the dried plants suspended from the beams of the overhang showered onto their heads. Soris dashed past the third door set into the long building, Emilia's arm dangling near his thigh. They disappeared into the Chemist's garden.

Andris motioned for Nat to follow Soris. She sprinted toward the garden and crouched among the purplish vines winding up a trellis and waited for Andris to catch up. Soris vanished behind a boxy door set into the castle wall. *Annin better be there,* she thought. Andris grasped her shoulder and jerked her to the ground just as a drawling voice filled the air.

CHAPTER THIRTY-SEVEN

"Calm yourself. The Nala came alone with Sister Malorin. It gains nothing by attacking us. I warned the creature that my guards know nothing of its presence and would kill it the instant they see it. You have nothing to fear. Besides, my riven antidote will protect you from its bite," the Chemist added hastily as he strode into the courtyard near the garden. His dark-purple tunic swung around his knees.

"Your test subjects from the Rewall have done little to instill confidence that the riven antidote works." Lord Mudug reached out his meaty hand and clasped the Chemist's shoulder menacingly. His mustache drooped over his double chin. "Not one of them has survived the venom injection even after ingesting your riven concoction."

"What do you expect when you only allow me to test on children and broken adults?" The Chemist cleared his throat and waited for Mudug to remove his fingers. He lowered his voice. "If you'd give me permission to try the venom on a healthier specimen, then we'd have positive results."

"No!" roared Mudug. "I've enough unrest on my hands, and all the adults that can work are needed in my mines. You don't seem to grasp that I'm at the tipping point. I have less than a year before I can declare full regency, and I need metals from those mines for weapons to arm my men. The rebels could strike at any moment and will certainly do so after I claim regency." Mudug's face grew crimson. "There are still fools that believe Estos is alive, and I must be ready to cleanse the people of any thought he could return." His mustache twitched wildly.

"It was merely a suggestion." The Chemist backpedaled.

"My suggestion is that you perfect your antidote against the Nala as you promised you would years ago." Mudug loomed over the Chemist. "The day when we end our alliance with the Nala will come the moment I've quashed the rebellion. I'm wasting valuable time and bodies while you dither about with your antidote."

"Another reason to meet with the Nala. I can use the Rewall scum to continue my tests if the Nala provide you with more adult duozi to bolster your workforce in the mines. The Nala desire the duozi children over the adults. The children's minds are more malleable to the Nala's will."

Nat peered over a cluster of red-tipped bushes. Her ears burned as she listened to him talk about the duozi and the children. The Chemist's back was to her. His brown hair flapped above his head in the breeze. She inched closer and put her hand on the hilt of her sword.

A strong hand clamped against her leg. She looked over her shoulder. Andris had one hand on her leg and the other pointed in the direction of the door. He mouthed, "Emilia." Nat lowered herself into the grass and crawled forward, but froze when she heard Mudug's reply.

"If the Nala agrees to trade more adult duozi for children so I have the full workforce, I may be agreeable to what it asks. What does it want?"

"When the Nala arrived last night, it asked for our assistance in finding a Sister, a particular Warrior Sister. The creature was quite adamant that it discuss the matter with you. It believes a Warrior Sister invaded the Nalaide's nest. Malorin had no idea who it was talking about, but perhaps Emilia can help us determine which Sister it's seeking." The Chemist clasped his hands behind his long robe.

"It's mistaken." Mudug's jowls trembled. "There are no Warrior Sisters left in Fourline. I've met that end of our bargain with the Nala. It can go north and search among the fringe if it wants to find a Warrior Sister," he huffed. "Only a fool would attempt invading the Nalaide's nest, and Warrior Sisters are not fools."

"Possibly, but the creature was insistent. If we give it some scrap of information, a Sister's name perhaps, you may have a bargaining chip to get more duozi slaves for the mines. Emilia has extensive knowledge of the Sisters," the Chemist added in a wheedling voice.

"There are no Warrior Sisters in Fourline," Mudug repeated. His eyes narrowed. "And Emilia is worth too much to me at the moment to be tossed to the Nala for interrogation. I met my end of the bargain when I pushed the Sisters out of Nala territory and provided them with children and any young duozi we found," he sputtered, working himself into a rage. "If the Nala want more from me, my price will be very, very steep."

"Calm yourself," the Chemist said, placing his hands on Mudug's expansive chest. "Listening to its request is worth your time. It's better they believe we are still allies in this game. Think how useful they will be once we locate Gennes' hideout."

Mudug twisted his beard and regarded the Chemist. "Has Emilia been of any assistance to you in locating Gennes? If I knew the rebel hideout's location, the Nala might serve a purpose other than providing me with adult duozi."

The Chemist stroked his chin. "I believe she's past the point of usefulness in assisting us with locating the rebels."

"I told you not to permanently damage her until I tell you it's time." Mudug's voice rumbled like a small earthquake.

"Yes, yes, she is perfectly alive," the Chemist interrupted. He looked shrewdly at Mudug, whose belly strained against the enormous gold buttons securing his blue vest. "I will keep her until your coronation. But afterward, she is mine to dispose of as we agreed."

Andris dug his elbows into the loamy soil and pulled himself next to Nat. He gave her a frantic, demanding look. She wanted to stay and listen to more of the conversation, but she knew the information would make no difference if they were caught. Keeping her head down and her hips low, she covered the rest of the distance to the door and crawled through the narrow opening on her belly. Andris clamped a hand around her mouth the second he emerged from the garden behind her and pressed his finger against her lips.

The dim corridor extended the length of half the courtyard, then dipped down a set of stairs. The light from the cracked door extinguished when Andris inched it closed with his foot. Nat pulled her orb from her pocket. Annin peeked her head from behind a dusty tapestry and beckoned them to join her behind the heavy fabric. Andris and Nat ducked behind the dusty folds and passed through an opening in the wall.

"Where is she?" Andris placed one hand flat against the wall and clutched the wadded-up guard's hat to his hip with his other hand.

"Over there." Annin gestured down the passage as she slid a panel, sealing off the opening.

Emilia was propped against the wall. Soris dug his dagger into the lock on the manacle around her ankle. Andris limped over to her and dropped to his knees. He lifted Emilia's limp hand. Her bruises looked mottled in the light of the orb. "Emilia," he whispered in a pained voice.

"Where's Benedict?" Nat looked up and down the dark passage for a sign of the Hermit.

"He's gone," Annin said flatly. "He saw me when he fled from the courtyard. He knew where I was, but he chose to run the other direction. He disappeared into the castle right after Soris shot Andris. I'm sure his little mind figured Soris' next arrow would strike him."

"Soris made an impossible shot to hit the soldier," Nat said defensively. "How could Benedict even think he was trying to kill Andris?"

"Where have you been?" Annin tossed her head to the side and turned her attention to Andris. "Not that we've time, but do you need me to look at the wound to your hip?" she asked.

"No." Andris placed Emilia's hand in her lap. A look of misery flashed behind his eyes.

"Lift her up, Soris. We can work on the manacle later." Annin started down the passage.

"Give her to me." Andris addressed Soris, but his eyes remained locked on Emilia.

"She's light, but your hip . . ." Soris pointed to the smear of blood Andris' hand left on the floor.

"Give her to me," Andris demanded. He took a step toward Soris and curled his arms under Emilia's body. "I'll tell you when I can't carry her." He stroked her dark hair. "I'll tell you," he reassured Soris.

Nat watched bewildered. Was no one worried about Benedict? Her feelings toward him bordered on hate, but the idea of leaving him behind made her stomach flip. "We can't leave Benedict. What if someone catches him?" she protested.

"Since when did you become such a fan?" Annin stalked farther up the passage.

"I'm not a fan." She ran after her, Soris and Andris trailing behind. "I'm into self-preservation. If they catch him, he might tell them everything."

"I told you a long time ago he is a rat." Annin opened a small latch in the low ceiling. "Rats always find a way to escape." She grasped the edge of the opening and clambered through the hole. She kicked her legs wildly, then disappeared. She popped her head out like a jack-in-the-box with black curls springing around her. "Hand her up." She motioned toward Emilia.

Andris lifted her body toward the ceiling, and Annin wrapped her arms around Emilia's chest. Her thin legs bent at an odd angle as they passed through the opening.

"Careful," Andris barked.

"Keep up the yelling, and she'll be back in the Chemist's chambers when Mudug's guards find us." She extended her arms toward Andris. "You're next."

Soris encircled his brother's waist and hefted him up through the hole. Andris' face contorted in pain when his hip brushed the side of the hole.

Nat sent her orb after Andris and stepped into Soris' foothold. She gave him a worried look. "We can't leave Benedict."

"He made his choice. And don't even think about going back there. I'd have you out cold next to Emilia in a second," Soris threatened. His features seemed to sharpen in front of her eyes.

"I don't like it." She slapped her hand on his shoulder and slid her boot into his interlaced hands.

"I don't care." His voice followed her through the opening. Her orb spun ahead. The passage was little more than shoulder width, and her back scraped the ceiling even on her hands and knees. A thick layer of dust covered her hand when she lifted it off the floor. How were they going to get an unconscious woman through the dark space without causing more damage to her frail body?

"Give me your cloak." Andris yanked at Nat's garment. She unclipped the hook before he choked her. The fabric whipped off her shoulder. He rolled Emilia onto her side and arranged the folds of the cloak underneath her.

"I'll pull her." Soris lifted the access panel into place and eased past Nat.

"We're wasting time." Annin twisted around in the small confines. "They've found the guards, the Nala, or the broken door by now."

Andris dropped his hands and let Soris drag the makeshift sled through the passage after Annin. Emilia's limbs jostled against the uneven floor. Nat's orb spun close to Annin's head, and she swatted it away like it was some type of insect. They crawled down the passage and snaked past recessed panels and over sharp latches in the floor. Dust caked Nat's face and hands, and the inside of her nose.

Annin paused in front of a square opening cut into the side of the tunnel. The orb illuminated a tall stone ceiling below worn steps. Nat's hopes rose just thinking of walking upright again.

"How far?" Andris' voice sounded weak.

"We're on the opposite side of the castle. This way leads to the river beyond the Rewall. That's how far." Annin dropped down the stairs and set her fingers on the top step. "You can carry her down here," she said to Soris and walked backward a few steps, giving him space to climb down.

Soris grasped the edge of the cloak and slid Emilia toward him. Her knees and then waist bent, and her body descended into his arms. Andris lowered himself into the stairwell and landed at the bottom with a groan.

Nat jumped down the stairs, alighting next to Andris. She noticed the blood seeping through the guard uniform around his hip. She lifted the long slit of blue fabric and glanced up at him. "I need to bind this. It's bleeding too much," she said.

Andris shook his head. "I'm fine." He placed a hand on the step behind him and pushed himself into a standing position.

"Annin, do you have any bandages?" Nat asked, ignoring his refusal of help. A small pouch flew through the air toward her face. She grabbed it and untied the thick leather string that secured it.

"Use the ointment on the wound, then give it back," Annin said. Her fingers flew over Emilia's legs, checking her gashes and bruises, while Soris worked to break the manacle encircling her ankle.

"Pull down your leggings," Nat ordered Andris.

"What?"

"Do you want me to push dirt and fibers into the wound? Pull them down. When did you turn into such a prude?" she asked as he reluctantly lowered the leggings past his hip. Soris chuckled behind her. She wrapped a layer of clean bandage around her finger and dipped it into the ointment. Andris winced when she spread the thick substance over the deep gash running straight down his hip. She tossed the ointment to Annin.

"You done yet?" he asked as she pressed the bandage against the gouge and secured it under the tight wrapping.

"You can thank me later." She yanked up his leggings, enjoying the grimace on his face.

The thick metal manacle clanked onto the floor. Soris lifted Emilia into his arms.

"I don't know what the Chemist did to her," Annin said. She prodded a series of punctures on her exposed leg.

Emilia's eyes flew open and she leapt out of Soris' arms. She kicked Annin, who fell backward onto Soris, then took off down the passageway. Nat hurtled over them, chasing after the queen.

Nat's orb zipped past her down the rocky passage, bobbing beneath splintered wooden support beams and jutting rocks until it caught Emilia. It circled her head at blinding speed, creating a halo of light around her eyes. Emilia came to a crashing halt and crumpled to the floor, covering her eyes with her hands.

"Make it stop," she cried over and over. The orb slowed its spin until it simply hovered over Emilia's jet-black hair. Nat lurched to a halt. Dirt puffed into the air around her boots. She crouched near the queen. Emilia's breath came sharp and ragged through her sobs.

"Emilia?"

She lifted her face from her hands. Dirt streaked her hollow cheeks. Nat struggled to find any words to calm the woman.

"Sister?" She looked from the orb to Nat. Her eyes were full of confusion. "Where am I?"

"You're with friends," Nat responded, inching closer. Footfalls sounded behind her, and Emilia pressed her body against the sharp rock wall. "Stay back!" Nat called out. The footfalls ceased. "We're here to help you, to take you to your brother, Estos."

At the name of her brother, Emilia's body started to spasm. Her fingers clawed at the ground and she scrambled to her hands and feet. In two steps, Nat had her arms clenched around her, holding her in place. Emilia twisted against her grip, powerfully strong despite her wraithlike body.

The others ran up. Annin leapt onto Emilia, allowing Nat to wipe her arm with more resin. Emilia kneed Annin in the stomach, sending her to the dirt floor. "Get off me!" she screamed, then collapsed, unconscious, to the side next to Annin, who lay on her back with her feet splayed. Annin let out a relieved breath and pushed herself up. She retrieved the packet of resin with the fold of her cloak.

"Like I was saying." Annin brushed dirt from her knees and stomach. "I don't know what the Chemist did to her. But whatever it was, we need to keep her under until the Sisters have a chance to fully examine her. Is this all the resin we have left?" She held up the packet.

Nat and Andris nodded. "Benedict has the rest," Andris said.

"You keep it." Annin folded the packet over and pressed it into Nat's hands. Annin clutched her stomach and wandered down the passage, muttering angrily.

Soris lifted Emilia off the ground. "I'll carry her," he said adamantly before his brother could insist on it again. He pressed his forehead against Nat's. "That was a phenomenal hold," he whispered.

"Thank you." She smiled despite the pain running up her calf where Emilia had kicked her. She glanced back at Andris. His face was sullen and worried. "Go ahead," she said to Soris. "We'll be just a second behind you."

She leaned down to rub the muscle in her lower leg. Andris stepped forward and landed flat on his face.

CHAPTER THIRTY-EIGHT

"You tripped me," Andris snapped.

"My mistake," Nat lied and knelt next to him. "I need to talk to you about what we heard in the garden," she whispered.

He growled and clasped her shoulder to pull himself up. His fingers dug into her skin. "I'm fine!" he called out to Soris, who lingered near a turn in the dim passage. "Catch up with Annin, we'll be behind you."

Soris followed the light of Nat's orb as it zigzagged across the ceiling in Annin's direction.

"Make this quick. I don't enjoy our private chats," he snapped at Nat.

"You heard the Chemist and Mudug talking about the Nalaide and a Warrior Sister she's looking for?" Nat questioned him as he thrust his leg forward and hopped next to her. She slowed her pace to keep enough distance between them and Soris and Annin so they wouldn't overhear.

"Yes," he said. He clenched his jaw. "You think the Sister is you?" He readjusted his arm so he could grasp her shoulder for balance.

"Who else could they mean? I saw the Nalaide when we freed the duozi from the Nala cavern. It has to be me. Sister Rory said the remaining Warrior Sisters are north, away from Nala territory. There are no Warrior Sisters in the Healing House, unless Cassandra went off half-cocked and decided to invade the den—"

"No, Sister Rory's had her under control since we came back." Andris released his grasp. Tingling relief flooded her shoulder. "They mentioned another Sister, but I didn't catch what they said about her. Perhaps the Nala are after her," he suggested.

"I heard them talk about a Sister, too, but they couldn't have meant a real Sister. They spoke as if she were helping them. No Sister would help Mudug after he destroyed the Houses."

They walked a few paces in silence. "If the Nalaide is looking for you, it would explain why the Nala are this far north, and why they attacked you at the river and the ruins." Andris rubbed his chin. "Doesn't explain the Nala's withered state and the remnant Annin found inside them. But I'm not an expert on Nala."

"No, you're not, but Sisters Ethes and Ethet are," Nat said. Time at the Healing House would provide a chance to unravel what was happening with the Nala. It would also give her time to question the Healing Sisters about possible cures for Soris and the other duozi.

His eyes shifted toward her as he continued to stroke his beard. "The Healing House is not where we're headed."

"Maybe we need a change in the plan. What about Emilia? You heard Annin, she needs the Healing Sisters. Do you really intend to drag her back to the rebel camp now? Who can help her there? Not only doesn't she remember you, she's afraid—"

Andris pushed her roughly against the wall in a surge of rage. "Don't lecture me on what's best for Emilia." His forearm dug into her neck.

"You can't get through to her. How do you expect to help her? Keep her drugged up and unconscious like Annin wants? She needs the Sisters." Nat clawed at his arm and brought her heel down against his shin. He stumbled away from her. Anger flared in his eyes. His lips curled. Nat tensed herself for another attack, but it never came. Andris turned his head and limped down the passage. She rubbed her neck and jogged ahead to join him.

"You're a tricky little one," he spat. "Now that you know the Nala are on your trail, returning to the Healing House isn't about Emilia, it's about you and Soris." He glared at her. "You want him tucked away, safe from Mudug's mines and the Nala."

"Don't you?" she asked, thinking this might be the one point they agreed on.

"If I take Emilia and Soris to the Healing House, you can't come," he said and turned on her. "You'd only attract unwanted Nala attention. The best place for you is on the other side of the membrane."

"You wish." She laughed bitterly. Of course he'd use this as an excuse to push her out of Fourline and away from Soris.

"You find it funny, being the object of the Nalaide's attention?"

"No, just how fast you came up with a reason to get rid of me." She quickened her pace, forcing him to skip on his bad leg. The passage sloped downward, and the stone floor transformed into a packed path of dirt. The air felt cool against her sweaty face. She frowned, unhappy with the unexpected turn in the conversation.

"Do you think you'll help him, or any of us, by sticking around? If the Nala are after you, they'll attack anyone near you. Soris is at more risk if you stay with him." A satisfied smile crossed Andris' face. "And he'll want you back in that nasty little world of yours the minute he learns the Nala have you targeted."

Nat stifled an urge to trip him again. Her mind raced. Leaving Soris right now was not what she had planned. A hollow feeling formed inside her. She needed more time with him, and she needed a chance to work with the Healing Sisters on a cure.

"You know I'm right, Sister." Andris wore a smug expression. "You were responsible the first time Soris was bitten. Do you want to stick around and see it happen again?"

Nat stopped. "I never meant for anything bad to happen to Soris," she said in a strained voice.

"Of course not," Andris said, almost consoling her. "But you understand that the chance he'll be bitten again if you stay here with him is great. Duozi rarely survive multiple bites. Do you really want to take that risk, Sister?"

Nat knew he was purposely pouring on the guilt, but a tiny voice inside her head was screaming that he was right. She started walking again briskly. The truth of what Andris had said settled over her like a dark cloud. She clenched her fists, wanting to strike out at something. Andris shuffled behind her. She heard him slow his pace and wondered if he had any idea of the turmoil brewing inside her. They walked a few moments until Nat suddenly stopped and faced Andris.

"You have to promise to get him to the Healing House and make him stay," she said, knowing her words were a tacit agreement with Andris that she'd leave Fourline.

"I think you can come up with some lie to keep him there, Sister." Andris shot her a contemptuous look.

"If you haven't noticed, I don't control your brother, Andris. He's got a mind of his own. He'll go wherever he wants, regardless of what I say."

Andris laughed. "I never took you for a dimwit. An opportunist, yes, but not a dimwit. My brother would walk into a nest of Nala for you."

He already has, she thought. She dropped her head.

His expression softened. "I'll do what I can."

"Then I'll break off first chance I get," she said. An ache settled in her chest.

"Don't bolt quite yet, Natalie. I did make a promise to Estos to keep you safe. I can get you past the trade route south of Daub Town. The upper Meldon Plain isn't far from that route and leads back to the forest near the membrane. You can split off then."

She nodded in numb agreement.

"It's for the best," he added with a condescending tone.

"I know," she said, hating the words.

Andris called out and his voice echoed down the tunnel. Soris came into view. His strong arms cradled Emilia to his chest. Nat felt a pang of jealousy that melted away when he looked up and smiled at her.

"I'll carry her," Andris said. He bowed to Nat. "It's for the best," he whispered and then lifted Emilia from his brother's arms.

"I thought her eyes fluttered a moment ago." Soris arranged her ragged garment so it covered her thighs. Andris nodded solemnly and limped carefully forward with his burden as if he were carrying a precious treasure.

"You two were talkative." Soris fell in step with Nat. His fused fingers curled around her hand. The simple gesture took her by surprise and her throat grew thick with emotion.

"We were talking about Benedict." She coughed to hide the tremor in her voice.

"There's nothing to be done about it now. He swore an oath to protect Emilia, and I believe he'll die before breaking that oath again. We have nothing to worry about unless they catch him. And Annin's right, he's always been crafty. He'll find his own way out. Can't say I'll miss him."

"No, I won't miss him, either." She glanced at him, then quickly looked away as tears began to well in her eyes.

"I think I smell . . ."

"Please don't say rudit," Nat said with a groan.

"No." Soris laughed. "Fresh air."

They turned a corner. Annin stood in front of a vine-covered entrance with a thick slab of wood tilted against the passage wall. "Welcome to the end." She gestured to the vines. The stalks vibrated and glistened with tiny droplets of water. Nat dropped Soris' hand and listened to the sound of water raging beyond the curtain of vines.

CHAPTER THIRTY-NINE

Thin tendrils curled from the vine stalks and clung to the mossy wood of the passage door. When Nat pushed the green strands away, a coursing river came into view. Andris jerkily dropped to his knee and gently placed Emilia in the long damp grass choking the entrance of the hidden passage. Nat pocketed her orb and watched the river race by, but the rushing sound and swift movement brought her no sense of relief, even after the close confines of the passage.

Andris stood. He looked down at Emilia, then glanced at the three of them. "Annin, with me," he said with a note of resignation in his voice as he looked at Nat and Soris. "We'll rendezvous with Mervin. I'll send Annin back to let you know if we're in the clear. Don't let anything happen to the queen." He sounded threatening.

"We'll keep her safe. I won't make the same mistake twice," Soris reassured his brother. Nat looked down at Emilia and wondered how one woman could create such prolonged guilt in so many men. Andris and Annin disappeared into the vine-choked trees growing along the river.

Nat settled next to Soris in the grass and brushed away the leaf that had floated down upon Emilia's face. Soris' tapered finger touched the bruised welt where the manacle had dug into her skin.

"She needs the Healing Sisters. And she needs to be around those who can help her remember," Nat said softly. The more reasons she could plant in Soris' mind to go back to the Healing House, the more likely he would willingly go and stay. Nat placed her fingertips on Emilia's thin wrist.

"There's a problem with getting her to the Healing House. Several problems, actually." Soris wound his arm around Nat's waist, pulling her closer to him.

"I know." Nat bit her lip and crossed Emilia's arm over her chest. "Mudug, his guards, forests filled with Nala . . . Am I missing anything?" she added, hoping he hadn't overheard any of her conversation with Andris.

"Give me a minute and I'll come up with something else." He scratched his neck and examined the dirt covering his fingertips. "It would take us days, a week, to get there even under the best circumstances. Andris won't like it." He looked at Emilia's pale face. "But I agree with you. She needs the Healing Sisters, and we need to be there for her. I can't imagine what she's been through. She needs people around who won't manipulate her, people who love her, who she can trust and who speak the truth to her."

Nat felt shame twisting through her as she listened to Soris. She'd just tried to manipulate him so he'd do what she wanted and go to the Healing House. But if she had to leave, she needed to know he'd be safe. She drew closer to him and settled her head against his shoulder. He held her and they watched the river race by past the curtain of vines.

You have to tell him the truth about what's going on. You owe him the truth, she told herself as they sat in silence. Nat drew in a deep breath, preparing to disclose everything she'd heard in the Chemist's garden, when Annin burst through the wall of vines.

"We've got only three horses, and Mervin said Mudug's guards arrived at the stables just as he was leaving," Annin announced. "We need to move, now. The guards could be on us any minute."

Soris let go of Nat and lifted Emilia off the ground. Nat collected their weapons and followed Annin through the swaying vines. She heard the nicker of the horses before spying them behind an opening in the trees. They danced nervously, pulling against their tethers as Annin and Soris drew near. Nat checked the flickering leaves in the canopy above their heads. Nothing but green needles, leaves, and filtered sunlight. *Soris and Annin must be making the horses jumpy,* she thought.

Soris caught her eye. "Relax, Natalie, I don't sense any Nala." He placed Emilia in Andris' arms. Andris carefully lifted her onto the back of his horse, where she slumped over the horse's neck. Annin flung a cloak over Emilia, and Andris swung into his saddle. He grasped Emilia's waist, pressing her close.

Nat untied the reins of a caramel-colored horse with a white streak running down his nose. His brown eyes widened when Soris approached. She tightened her grip to keep him from bolting. Soris stepped back and Nat whispered to the horse, soothing the animal.

"I guess I'll ride with Annin." Soris backed away.

"May be best for now," Nat said, feeling a guilty relief that the chance to tell him the truth had slipped away. She slid her foot into the stirrup and mounted the horse. A bulging satchel hung from a loop behind the saddle. She silently thanked Mervin. They weren't in for a day trip and would need everything in their packs. She wanted nothing more than to feel the familiar weight of her Sister's cloak over her shoulders, but that would have to wait until nightfall at the earliest.

Soris loosened the third horse from his tether. Annin already sat astride the giant mud-colored beast. The horse shook his mane when Soris shoved his foot in the stirrup and settled in behind her.

"Stay close together to the forest." Andris spun his horse. Emilia's head rolled forward. "We're not returning to the camp. We'll make for the Healing House."

"The Healing House?" Soris turned his head toward Andris and gave him a surprised look.

"Yes, change in plans. Mervin thinks we can reach the middle Wisdom House ruins by late afternoon if we don't encounter any problems. We'll leave the ruins after nightfall and head for the trading route south of Daub Town, then to the lower Meldon Plain and the Healing House." He slammed his heels against his horse, which lunged away.

"Healing House by way of the Daub Town trading route?" Lines formed across Soris' forehead, and he looked utterly confused.

"Maybe that way's safer," Nat said, knowing Andris had selected the way specifically to get rid of her. She gave Soris a fleeting look. *I'll tell him about the Nalaide soon,* she promised herself, then urged her horse after Andris.

CHAPTER FORTY

Nat walked around a pile of rubble and watched Emilia. The queen was hunched over a tattered book in the remains of the middle Wisdom House library. A half dome made of glass and steel soared above her. Moonlight poured through the open expanse where the girders stuck out like metal fingers. Books that had once lined the complex web of the library's shelves were now piles of ash or disintegrating in moldy heaps on the marble floor.

Emilia gingerly set her book down and picked through a tower of intact volumes she'd collected from across the library. She brushed dust and rubble from each binding. Nat glanced at Soris, who sat on the massive marble reading table not far from Emilia. He flipped through a book, but his eyes weren't on the fragile pages—they were on Emilia. He would have her down in seconds if she tried to flee again like she had when they'd ridden up the crumbling steps of the ruins.

Nat rolled her orb in her hands, trying to figure out why Emilia had gone from placid to crazy and back so quickly. *She's calm around books, so let's see what she makes of this one,* she thought, retrieving the ancient leather-bound book Ethet had given her from her pocket. She approached Emilia head-on so she wouldn't startle her.

"I have a book," Nat said and held it out for Emilia to scrutinize. "A Sister gave it to me, but I can't understand the text."

Emilia accepted the book and studied the faded binding before opening the cover. "This is ancient script." She turned a page. "Written before the Rim Accord. I've never seen a book this old except in the westernmost Wisdom House. Where did you get it?" She regarded Nat as she carefully examined a page.

"A Sister lent it to me," Nat said, amazed at how lucid Emilia sounded. *Did the Chemist have her on some kind of drug that her body's purging?* she wondered as she studied her expression. The queen appeared curious and not the least bit paranoid.

"Does she read ancient script?" Emilia asked.

"I'm not certain."

"Find one that does. The ancient books often hold forgotten gems." A knowing smile broke across her face, and Nat was struck by her beauty. Emilia carefully closed the cover and held the book out for Nat.

"How are you, Emilia?" Andris brought over a small napkin filled with food. He placed it at the queen's side when she didn't respond. "I brought you some food." He shifted uncomfortably in front of her.

"I see that," Emilia said and retrieved the book she'd been reading before Nat's interruption. She ignored the food and scanned the open page. Nat glanced at Andris. He wore a distressed expression on his face.

"You really should eat something," Nat urged. Emilia reached for a biscuit without removing her eyes from the page and took a small bite. They watched as she chewed and swallowed.

"Sister, would you help me saddle the horses?" Andris said and spun around, not waiting for Nat.

"She was talkative with you," he said when they were out of earshot. Nat thought she detected a jealous note in his voice.

"She likes books." Nat shrugged.

"'She likes books,'" Andris mimicked. "Your conversation was the longest she's had with any of us, if you didn't notice. She wasn't the least bit aggravated when she spoke with you. She hardly acknowledged me."

"I noticed," Nat said, feeling as if he was blaming her for Emilia's cold shoulder. "Look, we don't know what the Chemist did to her, but I think it's safe to assume the memories she has or had of the people closest to her are altered. I think we're all strangers in her mind. Maybe she feels more at ease with me because I'm a Sister," Nat lied, knowing full well that Andris radiated a serious amount of nervous energy when he was around Emilia. *You'd put me on edge, too,* she thought. "I could try riding with her on the next leg. If she freaks out like she did before, I might be able to calm her down," she suggested.

"She does seem to tolerate you, not sure why." Andris tugged at his beard. "Fine, I'll let her ride with you. I'd rather not use the resin to keep her calm. She'll become addicted if we apply it all the way to the Healing House."

Nat nodded in agreement, wondering what form of opiate the resin contained. It had to be incredibly powerful if it could knock a human out in seconds.

"See if you can figure out what upsets her without distressing her further." He adjusted a blanket on Soris' huge horse. "I still don't know what set her off when we arrived at the ruins, but I want to avoid a repeat. You saw how she fell off my horse. She'll end up hurting herself if these outbursts continue," he said, lines deepening across his forehead.

"She lost it when your horse passed by the columns engraved with the emblems from each House," Nat replied and glanced at the distant columns flanking the crumbling House entrance.

"You think the emblems disturbed her?"

"I'm just guessing. She's seen my markings plenty of times and hasn't gone off the deep end." She handed him a halter and hefted a saddle onto Soris' horse.

After they finished saddling the remaining horses, Nat turned to Andris. "Do you want me to wake Annin?" she asked, thinking she could sneak a few moments with Soris on her way to rouse her. She wanted to tell him the truth, but still hadn't found the right time.

"No, stay where Emilia can see you. I'll wake Annin. If she reached Estos' dream space, she may have useful information about the safety of our new route." He tossed her satchel into the air and she grasped the strap. "Send your orb to watch the entrance, too."

"It's been quiet so far. No Nala," Nat said, thinking there could be a slim chance she and Andris had misunderstood the conversation they'd overheard between Mudug and the Chemist.

He brushed the horsehair off his hands and gave her a critical look. "Don't look so hopeful. A half a day without a Nala attack means nothing. You're still going home."

He left her brooding while she strapped her satchel to the back of her caramel-colored horse, preparing for another long ride that would bring her closer to home and farther away from Soris.

Nat stared at the top of the glen that rolled down to the river. A cool night breeze caressed her face, but did little to take the edge off her nerves. She turned and watched Soris rub his horse's tired legs. He glanced at Emilia every few seconds, keeping a watchful eye on the queen as she sat in a bed of blue wildflowers.

Nat's ride with Emilia had been uneventful and long. They had spoken of wildflowers and species of trees, but little more. Nothing she'd said had disturbed the queen or sent her into a fit. Emilia had watched the countryside in silence for most of their ride, which had suited Nat just fine. She was pleased Emilia hadn't had an outburst under her care, but even with all the time to think, Nat still couldn't come up with a way to fix the mess she was in so she could stay in Fourline.

I have to tell you sooner or later that I'm leaving, she thought as she watched Soris work his strong hands over his horse. He looked up and smiled. *Later,* Nat thought and joined the queen in the bed of flowers.

"Why don't the horses bolt from you?" Emilia's question startled Nat. She hadn't uttered a word since they'd tied the animals up at the top of the glen. Nat faced the woman. Her pale eyes focused on an object beyond Nat.

"Why would the horses bolt from me?" Nat asked.

Emilia twisted to the side so Nat could see her profile but not her full expression. "I was talking to them, Sister." She lifted her thin hand and gestured to Soris and Annin.

Annin, who had been lying flat in the grass at the crest of the hill, rose and brushed the dew from her tunic. She was waiting for Andris to signal that it was safe to ride down the open hill to the banks of the Rust River. Even in the feeble light of the moon, Nat could see Annin's face tense and knew Emilia's question had irritated her.

"This horse is too big to be frightened of much," Soris responded before Annin could say anything. He patted the horse's neck. The horse ripped another mouthful of grass from the ground and nudged his nose against Soris' hands. "I think the Sister's horse may have gotten used to us by now. Some eventually understand we won't harm them."

Emilia let out a harsh laugh. "Or you've lulled it into a false sense of security."

Nat shot Soris a warning look, hoping he wouldn't respond. Emilia's voice held an edge that Nat worried would lead to a full-blown outburst.

"No." Annin's voice cut through the twilight. "Horses are sensitive, but not stupid." She strode through the grass toward Nat's horse. She brushed her hand over his neck. The horse shifted nervously, but didn't bolt. "This one knows I won't hurt him." Annin dropped her hand, and the horse nudged her. "I assume you know I'd never hurt you," she said, looking up at Emilia through her dark lashes and Nala eye. "I helped you once, do you remember?"

Nat fumbled in her cloak pocket for the resin, wishing Annin would keep quiet. Pushing her to remember anything right now was tempting fate.

"Hmm," Emilia responded and tilted her head toward the sky. "I don't remember knowing a duozi woman, ever."

"I don't know if you did," Annin admitted. "But you knew a girl . . ." Her voice faded and she trailed her fingertips over the cream-colored streak on the horse's nose. Emilia's shoulders softened. She watched Annin with an intensity Nat hadn't seen from her.

"Emilia, would you mind riding with Annin on this horse?" Nat asked, glancing between them. Annin gave her a funny look, but Nat shrugged her off. If she had to leave them before they reached the Healing House, Emilia needed someone she could trust, or at least tolerate, to accompany her. Even after almost two days' journey, Emilia still seemed agitated around both Andris and Soris.

"I have a choice?" Emilia sounded surprised.

"Of course you do," Nat said a little testily, wishing she had a choice about going home and leaving Soris before she had time to work with the Sisters, before she had time to ensure he was safe, before they had time to figure out what was going on between them.

"A choice, a choice," Emilia repeated. She curled her fingers over her thumbs, making tight fists. She lifted her head. "The duozi may ride with me."

Nat breathed a sigh of relief and tucked the resin away.

"Call me Annin, not duozi." Annin brushed past Emilia. Nat thought she saw a flicker of a smile on the queen's lips before the expression faded away.

An owl hoot echoed up from the valley.

"Andris' signal," Annin announced and tucked her cloak to the side as she mounted Nat's horse. Nat discreetly passed her the resin packet, then laced her fingers together. Emilia stuck the sole of her boot into

Nat's hands and settled into the saddle in front of Annin. She sniffed the air.

"The Sister doesn't smell like rudit anymore," she confided in Annin. "I was getting a bit tired of the aroma."

"You put up a good show. I think she still smells like a barrel of rotten fish." Annin smiled down at Nat and kicked the side of their horse. He waded through the tall grass toward the crest of the hill.

Soris looked amused when Nat passed in front of his horse. She shoved her toe into the high stirrup. He leaned over to grasp her hand and pulled her up.

"Nice work, I've wanted to ride with you since we left Rustbrook, even if you do smell like a barrel of rotten fish." He kept his tone light as their horse lumbered forward. Nat wound her arms around his waist and squeezed tightly, pushing his breath out.

"If you're lucky a little of my smell will rub off on you."

"To be so lucky," he said wistfully.

The river looked like a black serpent snaking across the valley floor beneath them. Other than a few clumps of trees dotting the banks of the river, the hill and valley were naked of places the Nala could hide. Nat's shoulders slumped and she relaxed against Soris' back, letting her guard down.

"To be so lucky," she repeated his words.

"You alive back there? I think your spine went out." Soris looked over his shoulder as Nat tucked her head into his back and closed her eyes.

"I need to zone out for a minute," she said, not wanting to spoil the moment by telling him the Nalaide was looking for her.

"Sometimes I have no idea what you're saying to me."

"Just assume it's brilliant rambling," she said, burrowing her cheek closer to him. His back was so warm. She let herself drift a moment, never wanting to let go.

"I wonder what the Sisters can do to bring back Emilia's memory," Soris pondered aloud. His eyes followed Annin as she and Emilia drew closer to the river.

"Sister Rory had a theory about Emilia." Nat lifted her chin and set it against Soris' shoulder. She noticed Andris' figure appear from behind a copse of skeletal trees next to the riverbank. "Rory thought the Chemist forced Emilia to imbue orbs with her memories so he could track Estos and the others. Her memories may have been damaged in the process."

"Rory was right about the damage to her memories. The question is, can she get them back?" Soris added.

"I think there's a way. She responded when she smelled the rudit on me. It was as if the odor triggered a thought or a memory fragment in her. Maybe the memories the Chemist took from her were just visual. Maybe there's a way to reconstruct her memory from sounds, smells, and tastes from her past."

"How do you reconstruct a memory?" Soris asked.

"I don't know," she said. "But the Sisters will need help from people that knew her, like you and Andris."

"I don't know how much help I'd be. Andris knew her better than anyone else in our family other than Gordon."

Annin brought her horse to a halt by the trees. Andris held the horse's reins as she dismounted. Emilia remained in the saddle, observing the fast-moving river.

"How are we supposed to get across that?" Nat asked as the roar of the water grew louder.

"My guess, by those trees is a smugglers' bridge. Estos was right."

"Estos? Right about what?"

"Annin told me she got through to him in a dream-speak. Gennes and Estos have spies running the river. He informed Annin that there was a smugglers' bridge in this area. Looks like Andris found it."

"How does Annin reach Estos when he's so far away?" she asked, amazed by Annin's ability to stretch herself into Estos' dream space from such a distance.

"It's easy for her. She's known him for so long. She can find him even at great distances." He guided the horse through a rocky patch at the base of the hill.

"Do you think you could reach me, even if I was someplace else?" Nat asked, wondering if there was a chance she and Soris could enter each other's dream space after she crossed into her world.

"Maybe." Soris smiled. "But I'm not sure I'll get a chance to try. You keep telling me you're not going anywhere." He shifted in the saddle and kicked his horse.

Nat opened her mouth to tell him about the Nalaide but heard Emilia's agitated voice. She leaned to the side and saw the queen yank her arm away from Andris and run to the river.

"Not again," Soris muttered. He kicked their horse, spurring him into a gallop toward the commotion. By the time they reached the river, Emilia was sitting calmly on a rock, watching the water flow past her feet. Andris stood at her side with his head bowed.

"I am sorry." Nat could hear Andris' low voice as he apologized to Emilia. "I didn't mean to upset you." His arms hung at his side and he looked forlorn. "I only want to help you." He lifted his eyes. Deep lines creased his face. "Can you believe that?"

"I don't know." Emilia's gaze flickered over Andris, then she turned her back to the river. "I don't know what to believe."

"I'll help you, but you have to learn to trust me, please," Andris said. He bent down on his knees next to her.

Nat marveled at Andris' calm demeanor as she watched him quietly convince Emilia to take his hand. "What happened?" she asked Annin as she secured their horse to a low branch of a white tree. Soris dismounted and stepped next to Annin.

"Andris told her she would see her brother soon," Annin whispered and ran her fingers over a long ridge of the tree. "When she heard him say Estos' name, she got upset and screamed at Andris. I guess we know now not to mention her brother." She shrugged, then dug her fingers into the ridge of the tree. What looked like a long strip of bark fell away from the trunk into her hands. Its tip stretched to the top of the tree looming over them.

"Hand me the poles." Soris took the strip from Annin, and Nat realized it was a set of two very long poles rolled together. "I'd feel better if we were moving." He exchanged a look with Annin and Nat's stomach fell.

"Do you sense Nala?" Nat asked in a low voice. She surveyed the landscape behind them and saw nothing but dim moonlight falling on the lush hill.

"Yes, they feel far away, but I can still sense them."

Soris quickly dropped the poles into the river. The second pole rolled away until it was an arm's length from the first pole. A thin material spread out between the long pieces of wood. Nat knelt and touched the shiny fabriclike surface. It hardened under her fingers, and she jerked her hand back in surprise. The fabric solidified, forming a narrow bridge that spanned half the river.

Annin clutched the leather reins and stepped onto the bridge, easing the horse behind her. "Ready," she said to Soris.

He released a latch on the ends of each pole. A whooshing sound rose from the ground, and the ends of the poles extended to the other side of the river, creating a bridge across the entire waterway. Annin took a tentative step forward. Her feet dipped a few inches into the water, but the bridge held.

"It's made from the guard hairs of a bastle," Soris explained as Nat again ran her hand over the solid surface. "When it's wet, it stiffens until it's as solid as rock, but lightweight. Natalie, you can examine it some other time. Step on," he said with urgency and glanced at the hill behind them. He tossed her the reins to their horse and she stepped uneasily onto the bridge.

Water coursed over her ankles and the wide hooves of Soris' horse. She kept walking, not wanting to think what would happen if the horse stumbled or the unreal material snapped under her feet. She glanced up and saw Annin slosh across the end of the bridge onto the opposite bank. Nat looked behind her. Andris carried Emilia in his arms, and Soris led the last horse onto the bridge.

She could see Soris speaking to Andris and heard him say something about the Nala. Andris fixed his eyes on Nat and frowned before quickening his pace over the bridge. *He probably thinks the Nala are looking for me,* she thought as she tugged the nervous horse behind her. Her boots and feet were soaking wet when she stepped onto the dry ground of the bank. Her horse snorted when she pulled him away from the river's edge.

"Move out of the way!" Andris shouted behind her. He lowered Emilia to the ground just as Soris and the final horse stepped onto the bank. Annin dropped down and touched levers at the base of each pole. The bridge retracted with lightning speed. Soris grasped one pole and Andris the other. They raised the poles into the air. Water sluiced down the solid bridge toward them. The poles retracted farther into themselves until they were no taller than the tip of the tree next to Nat. More water poured from the surface as Soris and Andris rolled the flexible poles together. Soris leaned the rolled-up bridge against the tallest tree, where it blended with the bark.

"Emilia, you will ride with me," Andris said carefully, making it sound more like a request than an urgent command. Emilia let him lift her into the saddle without protest. Andris mounted the horse as soon as she had settled, and thundered off into the prairie.

"Two approaching from the south, Annin." Soris clasped Nat's arm and hauled her onto his horse.

Annin nodded in agreement and mounted her horse. "Nala in the far north, in the castle, and now out on the prairie." She turned her horse, holding the reins tightly. "Their movements are unheard of. Pretty soon, the Meldon Plains will be the only place the Nala aren't crawling through." She kicked her horse and galloped after Andris.

Nat clung to Soris as their horse lumbered forward, building a slow steam before breaking into a gallop. She tried to focus on the sound of the pounding hooves instead of the voice in her mind telling her she was the cause of the Nala crawling all over Fourline.

CHAPTER FORTY-ONE

Two nights' ride since the river and no Nala, Nat thought, thankful the most recent bit of forest was far behind them. She stretched in the saddle in front of Soris. Her body ached, and she had sores up and down the inside of her thighs and calves from the long rides. Soris gently rubbed her shoulders with one hand while she held the reins of their horse.

"You have no idea how good that feels," Nat said as he dug his thumb into her aching muscles.

"If my brother ever decides to take a break, you can show me," he whispered in her ear.

Nat smiled, but her smile faded away quickly. *I still need to tell him I have to leave.* Between guard duty, watching Emilia, and riding at a breakneck pace, she still hadn't found the right time to explain to Soris what she'd overheard in the Chemist's garden. She glanced over at Andris, wondering if he'd listen to her if she asked him to pause. She wanted to look at Soris' face when she told him she was leaving Fourline.

"Andris needs to stop," she said to Soris and tilted her chin toward Andris and Emilia. "Emilia's exhausted and he's about to fall off the horse himself."

"You know I already tried," Soris said. "He's determined to reach the merchant road south of Daub Town in two days." He rotated his neck, ushering in a series of cracking sounds. "I'll ask again once Annin returns from scouting," he said with a yawn.

"Figure out something that will convince him quickly, because there she is," Nat said and gestured toward Annin's familiar figure approaching on horseback. "She looks like she's in a hurry." Nat sat up straight in the saddle, suddenly alert as she watched Annin's horse crash down an incline blanketed with lichen-covered rocks. Sweat matted her horse's coat. *What now?* she wondered.

Annin brought her ride to a halt in front of Andris and Emilia. "Guards ahead, at the base of the hill." Her cheeks were flushed. "They have two children with them." Her mouth formed a hard line.

"Duozi?" Nat dropped from the saddle.

Annin nodded, looking grim. Soris turned toward the distant outline of the forest south of the prairie. "Nala are close as well," Annin said as she exchanged a look with Soris.

"The guards must be delivering the children to the Nala." Nat felt a tightness, like a ball of anger, building in her chest. Annin's expression mirrored her feelings.

"There's nothing to be done about it. We'll ride north and skirt around them," Andris said. He gently lifted Emilia's chin and poured water into her mouth. She swallowed lazily and her eyes closed from exhaustion. The three of them watched Andris without saying a word. He took a sip of water and lowered the flask slowly from his lips, eyeing each one in turn. "I know what you're thinking and absolutely not." He shoved the cap onto the flask.

"We can't leave them." Nat voiced what they were all thinking.

"I'm not risking Emilia's safety for duozi," Andris said, his jaw clenched.

"You don't have to risk anything for the duozi, brother." Soris sat rigidly in the saddle. His voice was low and almost cold. "The three of us will pick off the guard."

"No," Andris growled. Emilia's head snapped up at the angry sound of Andris' voice. He placed a soothing hand on her hair. "We are not engaging in a fight," he said, forcing a calm tone.

"We don't have to fight," Nat lied, knowing saving the children might be her last chance to strike against the Nala and Mudug before she returned home. There was no way she was letting the Nala take the children. "If they're meeting the Nala, we can spy on them and find out where they're taking the duozi. It's better to know where the Nala or the guard are going so we can avoid them." Let Andris believe they would just spy on the guards.

"You don't know the Nala are here for the children, Natalie." Andris' eyes narrowed into slits. "They could be after something else," he said pointedly.

"It doesn't matter why they're here, Andris," she shot back, knowing he was blaming her for their presence. "We have a better chance of avoiding them if we know where they're going."

"Leave the logistics of avoiding battles to me." He thrust his hand toward his chest. He turned his horse and Emilia's eyes fluttered open. Her face was ashen.

"The Nala won't sense Soris or me if we stick close to the duozi children," Annin said, joining in the argument. "If we move away from the children, there's a chance they'll know more duozi are in the area. That won't help your logistics, will it?"

"More reason to stay close to the children until the Nala approach," Nat agreed. Andris' features seemed to pinch together as he glared at Nat. "You and Emilia can hold back while we watch and see if there's an exchange. She could use the rest."

"Natalie's right," Annin said. "Emilia can't continue at this pace. There's good cover in the rocks, even a little rainwater pooled for the horses. There's more risk to Emilia if we continue on at the pace we've been going with no break."

"Excellent idea," Soris concurred, meeting his brother's grim expression with one of his own. "You can watch over Emilia and the horses while the three of us learn what we can."

"I don't trust any of you not to start something." Andris eyed them suspiciously. Annin stroked her horse and Soris untied his water gourd. No one looked at Andris.

"We won't do anything stupid," Nat lied, already thinking one child could ride with Annin and the other with Soris and her.

"What are these?" Nat whispered to Annin. She pushed the wild pup off her leg. Its pointed nose sniffed her hand, scrambled back onto her leg, and chewed on the lip of her leather boot.

"Gunnel kits," Annin replied, shooing away another ball of fuzz with her hand. "Something like your wolves or bears." She crawled to the edge of the overhanging rock above the guards. Soris brushed two kits off his legs and inched closer to Annin.

"Wolf or bear? There's a big difference." Nat eyed the sharp teeth of one of the kits as it sniffed and bit Annin's elbow. Annin hissed at the pup. It whined and scrambled toward the dark break in the rock behind them into what Nat assumed was their den.

"Doesn't matter," Annin said, rubbing her elbow. "Just be happy their parents hunt most of the night. The gunnel is one predator we can't control."

Nat glanced at the den one more time, then crept next to Soris. He pointed past the guards stoking a fire. Two small children huddled next to the rocks beyond the light of the building flames. Rope bound their wrists together.

"And there are the Nala." Annin narrowed her eyes and nodded in the direction of the long grass. One of the guards yelled. Two Nala heads rose like malformed bubbles. The creatures crawled on their angular arms and legs, then rolled their backs until both stood upright. Shadows danced over their skin as they approached the soldiers' fire. Nat breathed a sigh of relief when she saw their skin was blue and not white like the ones she believed were searching for her.

The guards drew their weapons and stood behind the fire. The Nala eyed the children cowering against the rocks.

One of the guards found his voice. "We were to meet tomorrow. Why are you here now?"

The Nala's hands clicked together and the guards shifted nervously.

"One of our own has not returned from a negotiation with your Lord Mudug," the Nala closest to the rocks hissed.

"I know of no meeting between Lord Mudug and your kind. We were told only to bring the duozi." The guard lifted his sword.

"Perhaps you speak truthfully." The Nala gnashed at the air, its sharp teeth striking against each other. The other Nala shifted its attention toward the duozi children and scampered across the trampled grass toward them. A girl, dressed in a thick woolen shift, shut her eyes and whimpered as the creature ran its hand over her shoulder. Nat felt Soris' body tense next to hers. "But perhaps not," the first Nala continued. "Tell your Lord Mudug that if the Nalaide's messenger does not return in three days, his trade routes will suffer. And," it added, "we await word of the capture of the Warrior Sister that invaded the Nalaide's nest. The Nalaide knows she passes freely among you. Her scouts have sighted the Sister we seek north of your city."

"I don't know what you're . . ." The soldier's voice faltered. He backed away toward the fire and his arm shot out toward the grass. "Gunnel," he yelped.

A growl arose from the darkness behind the Nala. An animal resembling a long-legged grizzly bear emerged from the grass. The firelight glinted off the gunnel's sharp teeth, bared and ready to snap. It lifted its plate-sized head, and another growl rumbled from deep within its broad chest.

The Nala closest to the gunnel pivoted, and its eyes bored into the animal as if trying to control its movements. The gunnel paused a flicker of a second, then launched toward the Nala with a deafening roar. It slammed into it and bit off its blue arm in one bite. Another gunnel roared out of the grass and rammed one of the guards against the rocks. The uninjured Nala leapt onto the gunnel's back and sank its fangs into the animal's shoulder. The gunnel reared up on its back legs and crashed onto the ground, crushing the Nala beneath it.

"Time to move." Soris grasped Nat's hand, and they slid down the side of the rock to an overhang above the children. Rocks skittered around them and tumbled down near the children. The girl glanced up just as Soris dropped his knife. The short blade landed near her feet. "Cut the ropes," he said to her in a loud whisper drowned out by the gunnels' roars.

She grasped it with her fingers and pressed the blade against the rope binding the boy. Free of the rope, he flexed his hands, grabbed the dagger, and sliced through the rope binding the girl's hands. The children crept into a split in the rocks and climbed with bare feet onto a narrow ledge to the left of Soris. They tossed him his knife. He gestured hurriedly for them to keep moving, and the children scrambled higher up the rocks.

Soris and Nat each lifted a child into their arms and carried them over the boulders. A hissing scream echoed behind them. *Two fewer Nala in the world to worry about,* Nat thought as she shifted the boy who clung to her with a fierce grip. Her foot caught in a narrow split in the rocks and she tumbled forward, slamming against her shoulder. Annin pulled her upright.

"You're a duozi," the boy said in wonder as Annin took him into her arms. Nat glanced behind her to make sure nothing was following them. Smoke and the tip of flames licked the far end of the rock formation they'd fled moments ago. Nat could still hear the enraged roars of the gunnels.

"Yes, and I prefer to be the living kind, so hold tight," Annin said, seeing the smoke and hearing the roars. She scaled another boulder with the boy clinging to her back. Nat clambered up after them and pulled her orb free from her cloak. The sphere skimmed over the plateau. She ran with it to the rock outcropping hiding Andris and Emilia. She heard Andris yelling and wondered if she was safer back with the gunnels.

"I knew this was going to happen!" Andris lifted Emilia into the saddle. Her pale eyes flashed as she looked nervously at Soris, who was already on his horse with the girl clutched to his chest. Andris' neck muscles bulged and his face looked dark red in the light of Nat's orb. "Sister, if something happens to Emilia because you disobeyed my order for them . . ." He pointed to the children.

"My oath supersedes your orders!" Nat yelled.

"It was my idea to bring the children, not hers," Soris interjected from atop his saddle. His horse high-stepped and snorted.

"I knew she'd addle you," Andris barked, keeping his eyes locked on Nat.

"Save the family fight for later," Annin said, boosting the boy into her saddle, "when we're far away from the gunnels."

"Gunnels?" Emilia lifted her head.

"We have gunnels on our tail," Nat answered. She took Soris' extended hand and climbed onto his horse, settling into the space behind the end of the saddle.

"The Nala and now gunnels are after you? You're quite the magnet, Sister!" Andris yelled. "What's coming next? A legion of Mudug's guards?"

"We don't want these children anywhere near a gunnel," Emilia remarked as if Andris had said nothing.

"Well said, Emilia. Don't you agree, Andris?" Annin asked with feigned politeness. She grasped her saddle horn and swung herself onto the skittish horse behind the boy.

"Two days' ride, Sister," Andris called out to Nat with fury in his eyes. He gripped his reins with one hand and clasped Emilia around the waist as he sat high on his horse. "Then you are back through that wretched hole to your world, if something, including me, doesn't kill you first!" He dug his heels into the animal's flanks. The horse shot up the rocky path.

Annin clutched the boy and kicked her horse into motion. The horses climbed out of the wide overhang and galloped into the night. Nat shifted her weight and clung to Soris while Andris' words rang in her ears.

"Something you want to share with me, Natalie?" Soris yelled over his shoulder.

Nat tucked her head next to him and swallowed. "Yes," she finally said, knowing it was past time to tell him the truth. The story of what she'd overheard in the Chemist's garden tumbled from her mouth as the wind whipped around them and the dark night descended.

The long night's ride seemed like a bad dream as Nat sat in the barn where they'd taken refuge after their ride. She smoothed the sleeping duozi girl's hair away from her thin face and thought of Soris' reaction to everything she and Andris had overheard after they'd rescued Emilia. He'd listened quietly, interrupting her only twice to clarify what the Chemist had said about the Warrior Sister the Nala were searching for and what Mudug had said about the duozi slaves in his mines. When they'd arrived at the deserted hay barn before morning, Soris told Andris he'd take first watch and disappeared without another word to Nat.

She glanced outside through the door. Annin and Soris were saddling the horses, readying them for the next ride. *I need more time,* she thought. She felt a small hand in hers and looked down at the girl. Her eyes were open; she stared at Nat's markings. The light filtering through the windows of the barn highlighted the light-blue skin on the girl's arm and neck.

"I've never met a Sister." The girl held the tip of her pointed hand to Nat's markings.

"You're going to meet plenty of them soon. They'll take good care of you." Nat looked up at the sound of creaking wood. Soris walked into the barn, kicking up dust that floated into the air.

"You won't be there?" the girl asked.

"No." Nat paused, thinking how much she wanted to stay with them and go to the Healing House. "I have to go back home." Her eyes strayed from the girl to Soris, who watched her intently.

He sat on the splintered floor next to Nat. "The man watering the horses has some breakfast. Go get something to eat before we leave," he said to the girl.

"Food?" she said urgently. Soris nodded. She raced through the barn door. He leaned against the broken panels. Nat watched him, waiting for an argument against her leaving on her own.

"Did you sleep?" he finally asked.

"No, you?"

The corners of his lips curved upward. "What do you think?"

"Soris, I . . ."

He moved swiftly toward her and pressed his lips against hers. His hand curled around the back of her neck. Dust swirled around them. Nat brushed her lips against his cheeks and tilted her head down, not wanting him to see the tears welling in her eyes.

"I will come back," she whispered against his chest.

"I'll be here."

CHAPTER FORTY-TWO

I will come back, Nat thought as she scanned the sun-beaten dirt road at the base of the hill. The merchant route was empty and safe for Andris and the others to cross before they turned south and she broke from them to travel her own path to the membrane. She wiped a trickle of sweat from her forehead and turned away from the road. Time was slipping away from her.

The duozi boy sat on her cloak a few meters away from where her horse grazed. Andris had demanded she take the boy with her when she'd offered to scout out the hills. She paused and watched him hold the loose reins tightly as the horse nibbled the grass around him. He brought his hand next to the horse's moist nose. Her horse didn't shy away and let the boy rub his stiff coat. A sad smile crept over Nat's face.

"He likes you," she said as she drew near.

The boy looked her way. "My dad has a horse that looks like him." His small voice broke, and he wiped his arm across his eyes. Nat could see a look of grief spread across his face. She retrieved her orb from her pocket, hoping to distract him. She was on the brink of tears herself.

The orb floated into the air above the boy's head, the bright light attracting his attention. The ball darted up and looped through the air, making the boy smile, but causing her horse to jerk to the side and pull on the reins.

"Will you help me send my orb to the others to let them know it's time to join us?" she asked.

The boy nodded. "What do I do?" he asked eagerly.

"It's easy. Just think of their faces with me, and it will find them." She lifted him to his feet. "You have to concentrate on their faces as hard as you can."

The boy bit his bottom lip and focused on the orb. Nat made it loop in the air twice, then sent it hurtling away. The orb skimmed over the top of the grass and dipped out of sight.

"Well done." Nat gave him a wink and a quick hug. She whisked her cloak off the ground and secured it over her shoulder. Her horse lifted his head and pulled the reins. "Hold on to him," she said to the boy as she unbuckled her satchel from the horse and slung the bag over her shoulder.

Either Soris or Annin would take her horse when they caught up. They had farther to travel to the Healing House and needed the animal now that they had the children. *I'm in for a long run,* she thought as she glanced over her shoulder at the hill. The Meldon Plain near Benedict's house wasn't far from the road by horse, but it would take time to reach it on foot.

She strapped her extra dagger to her leg and adjusted her sword and the crossbow. The boy watched her shift the weapons in studied silence. The light breeze pushed at his dirty hair.

"Annin will ride with you when she gets here," she said, sensing his unease.

He gazed past her toward the distant figures of their approaching companions. The boy's misshapen Nala eye suddenly widened, and he clutched at his ears.

"What's wrong?" Nat knelt next to the boy. Her horse stamped the grass and snorted.

A cry erupted from the direction of the road. Nat drew her sword and ran toward the crest of the hill. A merchant convoy burst onto the prairie below. Wagons, some devoid of drivers, streamed across the road. Draft horses ran wild, senseless to the whip blows raining down on their backs. Single horses without riders bolted past the wagons and spread out in every direction.

Nat ran back to the boy and grabbed the reins of her horse as a wild-eyed gelding galloped up the hill toward them. It reared and kicked the air, coming within an arm's length of Nat before galloping away. The boy tugged on Nat's sleeve. His hand trembled as he pointed down the hill.

Nala, both white and blue, flowed through the merchant convoy like water pouring from broken glass. A pack engulfed one of the wagons. Nat heard a fleeting cry amid the hissing and sounds of splintering wood. She saw another flash of movement as Nala flew over the heads of two blue-suited guards deserting the convoy. The guards closed ranks, protecting themselves and ignoring the cries for help from the merchants.

Nat's breath caught in her throat. White Nala scurried along the edge of the chaos. One arched its back and lifted its head above the tips of the grass, then darted toward the base of the hill beneath her.

Nat lifted the boy onto the horse. She barely had time to mount before the horse lunged away and galloped toward Andris and the others.

"A convoy's under attack by the Nala," she gasped when she pulled up next to Andris. Her orb returned to her and she tucked it away in her cloak.

"How many?" Andris held tightly to his reins. Annin and Soris dismounted in a singular movement and pulled their weapons free from satchels and ties.

"At least a dozen. They're attacking the merchants and Mudug's convoy guard. And I saw a group of white Nala split off and head this way."

"White ones? Like the ones with remnant?" Annin loaded an arrow into her crossbow.

Nat nodded. "Take Emilia and the children!" she yelled to Andris as she dismounted and tossed her reins his way. "They're after me. I'll distract them so you can get away."

Andris jumped from his horse and grabbed the reins.

"Don't be ridiculous, Sister." Emilia's voice rang above Andris' string of curses. "Andris, I'll ride with these children to the crest we just passed. You will aid the Sister." Her pale eyes shone with bright authority.

Andris' mouth parted as he tried to formulate a response. His sword clattered next to his feet where Emilia dropped it from the saddle. She reached down, yanked the reins from his hand, and turned her horse toward the girl sitting atop Soris' ride. "Stay close to me," Emilia said to her. The girl nodded. Emilia smacked her horse's rump and led the children and animals away.

Andris stood motionless, watching his queen gallop away with the two duozi children. He took a deep breath, then picked up his sword and strode toward Soris, Annin, and Nat.

"You may outlive this attack, Sister. But if Emilia is injured, I'll kill you," Andris growled. "Let's go even those merchants' odds."

Falling in line together, they sprinted toward the hill and down to the bloodbath raging below.

Nat paused halfway down the hill, horrified by the carnage playing out in front of her. The merchants were running from their wagons only to disappear into the long grass, pulled down by angular blue arms. Merchants without weapons flicked whips in the air and threw boxes and small crates in a futile attempt to keep the slinking creatures back. But the Nala pressed in, scuttling quickly to cut off the remaining merchants from each other and any possible escape.

Soris dropped to his knees next to Nat and brought his crossbow to his shoulder. The air hummed with the sound of his arrow as it flew past and struck the back of a Nala leaping onto an unarmed merchant. The Nala twisted in the air and landed on the ground.

Annin and Andris split off from Soris and Nat and ran straight for a merchant woman standing in a wagon bed with two children pressed against the broken panels. A lame draft horse caught up in a tangle of the harness writhed on his side in front of the wagon. The horse kicked the dirt and twisted his neck as the woman snapped a whip at a Nala grasping for the children with its long limbs. Andris swung his blade behind one of the creatures and its head flew into the air. Blood spurted from its neck, showering the wagon in a grisly wash of blue. Annin's arrow missed a second Nala as it darted under the wagon. Andris jumped over the writhing horse, chasing the creature. His sword flashed as he cut the Nala's head off its body.

Nat's feet felt like lead as she and Soris ran down the rest of the hill. Grass swayed in front of them. A white arm shot out from the grass and wrapped around Nat's ankle, sending her crashing down. She dug her hands into the ground, kicking the face of the creature clinging to her again and again until its head hung at a crooked angle. She scrambled to her knees and cut off its head before jumping to her feet.

"Soris!" she cried, spinning around, looking for him. *Please don't be hurt.* She caught sight of him a few paces away at the edge of the road, surrounded by four white Nala.

A fury rose in Nat. She dashed toward the ring, cutting one Nala down and stabbing another in the leg. Cries and hissing filled the air. A Nala leapt at Nat, and Soris shot it in the face, sending the arrow clean through the other side of its head. Nat skipped over its fallen body and chased the remaining white Nala down the dirt-packed road. The creature stumbled in front of her. Its head snapped back, sending flecks of venom to the ground. Annin stepped from the grass in front of the creature and reloaded her bow before sending another into its chest.

"Natalie, Annin!"

Nat whirled around at the sound of Soris' voice. He and Andris jumped from an overturned wagon, chasing two white Nala their way. Puffs of dust rose from the road as the creatures' pointed limbs slapped the dirt. The Nala caught sight of Nat and sprang off their back legs, shooting into the air toward her.

Two arrows whizzed past Nat and landed in the center of each Nala. The white creatures flopped onto the road and rolled over and over, crushing the shafts of the bows protruding from their chests.

"Estos! He's here!" Annin cried.

Estos, high on the hill, lowered his bow and ran with Rory and Cassandra toward the road. Oberfisk emerged from behind the Sisters and broke off in a run toward a group of merchants still battling a Nala at the edge of the fight. Nat backtracked over the road to the merchant train. Her heart pounded as she scanned the overturned wagons and piles of spilled cargo, looking for more white Nala. Dead Nala lay scattered over the road.

She caught a flash out of the corner of her eye just before a white Nala crashed into her side. She tumbled onto the hard-packed ground and her sword flew from her hand. The Nala leapt on top of her and wrapped its pointy hands around her neck. She slammed her fist into its eye and heard a crunching sound. The creature's grip on her throat loosened. She punched it again and then wrenched the Nala to the side, where it rolled into a grassy culvert.

Screams reverberated around her. She scrambled for her sword, clutching at her burning throat. When she looked up, Cassandra was running toward her. The Sister spun and sliced off the head of the Nala emerging from the culvert next to Nat. Cassandra's red dreadlocks flew about her head like serpents as she looked for more creatures.

"Thanks," Nat croaked, feeling her bruised neck.

"My pleasure," Cassandra said and yanked Nat to her feet. "Any day I kill a Nala is a good day."

Around them, the cries of fear were replaced by weeping as the merchants moved among the wounded and dead bodies strewn across the road. Nat passed Oberfisk leaning over Mudug's dead convoy guards, whose eyes were still wide open in terror.

Estos stood with Andris on the riding bench of a wagon, surveying the wreckage. Andris whispered in Estos' ear, then jumped from the wagon and freed the tangled reins of a horse. Nat watched him disappear up the hill in Emilia's direction.

"They're all gone, Lord Estos." Soris came running up the road with Sister Rory at his side. "Four Nala escaped into the woods. Three blue and one white." His eyes found Nat. She ran across the road into his arms.

A murmur rose from the merchants as they watched Estos hop off the wagon. The Sisters, Oberfisk, and a few of the merchants converged around him. Nat could hear him giving orders as she and Soris approached.

". . . any functioning wagons loaded with the dead and wounded back to Daub Town. And be quick about it. It's doubtful the Nala will return, but it's not worth the risk."

Nat let go of Soris. "They'll be back," she said as she pushed through the ring of people until she was in front of Estos. "If any of the ones that escaped saw me, they'll be back."

They were all looking for me, she thought as she looked at the grayish-white Nala corpses spread out on the road and draped over the side of wagons. The bulging remnant rings stuck out of their chests and the liquid oozed out their necks. "The merchants were in the wrong place at the wrong time. The Nala were out here looking for me."

"What are you talking about?" Estos asked.

"The Nalaide saw me after Soris, Annin, and I freed the duozi and killed the Nala in her den," she said with an edge to her voice. "She now wants me."

Estos stared at Nat, absorbing what she'd said. "Oberfisk, get these people moving," he ordered and ushered the Sisters, Soris, Annin, and Nat away from the merchants. "Andris is bringing Emilia to the ridge over there." He pointed beyond the hill. "Oberfisk can accompany the merchants to the next outpost to ensure their safety before they reach Daub Town. We have a rebel group a few miles from here he can link up with. The rest of us will move toward the eastern forest and the safety of the Healing House, like Annin told me you intended when she met me in my dream space," Estos said with certainty.

"You don't get it, Estos, they're looking for *me*," Nat argued. "The Nala are all over the eastern forest. I can't come with you. You and Emilia are too important to risk another fight, and we have duozi children with us. They'll come after you if I'm with you. It's better if I leave now and draw them away. I can return to the membrane on my own."

Rory leveled a look at Estos. "If what the Sister says is true, bringing her to the eastern forest with us will mean a certain fight with the Nala. A fight in the forest is far different than on an open plain."

"I'm not sending Natalie on her own," Estos replied.

"Estos, I know the way. I'll take one of the merchants' horses and stay ahead of them." The urgency in Nat was growing. The longer she was stuck arguing, the sooner the Nala would regroup and attack.

"She won't be alone. I'm going with her," Soris said and placed his hands solidly on her shoulders.

"No, Soris, you need to go with your brother and Estos," she said, pleading with him. "I can make it on my own."

"Natalie, I'm not going to the Healing House. I'm coming with you."

She felt as if she were being ripped apart when she looked into his eyes.

"I'll go with her. I can get her to the membrane." Annin stepped next to Nat.

"So can I. Stay out of this, Annin," Soris snapped.

"But I can get through the membrane if something goes wrong. You can't. Do you honestly think she'll go through that membrane and desert you if you're fighting Nala for her? You know as well as I do how stubborn she is. She's a Sister, Soris." Annin's voice grew louder. "She will stand next to you and fight. Do you want to risk that?" His expression wavered. "Think with your head, Soris, and you may see her again, alive. Think with your heart and you both may die. Is that what you want?"

Soris' face contorted with different emotions. "I'm depending on you, Annin," he said finally. He pulled Nat to his chest and buried his face in her hair.

"I made you a promise that I'll come back and I will," Nat said fiercely as she felt his heart pounding against his chest. "Let me go knowing you'll be safe. Stay at the Healing House." Her voice faltered. He brushed his hand across her cheek, wiping away her tears. He kissed her gently as the tears streamed down her face.

"Go, Natalie." He broke off the embrace and stepped away. "Go."

"Rory, get the two best horses you can find," Estos said as he watched Soris pull away from Nat. Rory turned on her heel and hurried toward the merchants' carts. "Annin, go through the membrane if there's any risk to you. Find me in my dreams if you can."

Annin nodded.

Estos looked at Nat. "I brought this on you, Natalie. I'm sorry."

"I made my own choices, Estos," she said as she looked at Soris one last time.

CHAPTER FORTY-THREE

After a day's hard ride and the thundering sound of horse hooves, Nat found the quiet of the forest unsettling. She glanced over her shoulder at the disappearing meadow by the crooked tree where she and Annin had set the horses free. *So close to the membrane,* she thought as she scanned the trees above her before sprinting over the faint path to catch up with Annin.

They ran silently over the path through the forest until Annin stopped abruptly. She placed a hand on Nat's shoulder, easing her behind a grove of aspens clustered among the thick pines. In the distance, the red boulder glowed in a shaft of sunlight penetrating the forest. A blue Nala, poised on the rock, stared into the woods. It blinked its faceted eyes before springing to the nearest tree and scrambling up to the top. The trees bent and swayed as it jumped from tip to tip, finally landing on the cliff face.

"Now," Annin whispered, pushing Nat toward the old path. They ran, skipping over the gnarled roots of dead trees upended by storms and decay. The red boulder grew in size as they drew near. Nat felt a tugging on her cloak and glanced over her shoulder.

Annin stood motionless, looking above her to the treetops. Three sets of shining concave eyes stared down at them. A chorus of hissing filled the air and little droplets of blue venom fell onto the muddy leaves on the forest floor. Nat glanced wide-eyed at Annin.

"The Nalaide, our queen, awaits you, Sister." The Nala's voice was a whisper above her, like a poisonous breeze.

Nat brought her sword close to her chest. She felt Annin's back press against hers, and the women stood locked in place next to each other. "How many do you see?" Nat asked through slightly parted lips.

"Three, maybe four."

Nat heard the string on Annin's crossbow tighten. The leaves rustled above them.

"What does the Nalaide want with me?" Nat asked, trying to buy some time. The membrane was several minutes' hard run from where they were, but she had no intention of leading them on a chase anywhere near the entrance even if Nala couldn't pass through. A barklike hiss echoed through the trees.

"Is that thing laughing?" Nat lifted onto the balls of her feet and dug into her cloak pocket, freeing her orb. The brilliant sphere rose into the air and cast sharp rays of light into the trees. A low hissing filled the air.

"Not anymore," Annin replied, her voice taut like her bow.

One of the creatures crawled headfirst, limb over limb, down the tree. It flicked away sodden leaves as it crept onto the forest floor and shifted into an upright position. Its emotionless eyes fixed on Nat's.

"You have taken what the queen treasures, Sister. You have taken our duozi from us. She wants them back, and she wants you." Its black mouth moved as if it were a separate creature.

"You'll never see those duozi children again." Nat tightened her grasp on her sword hilt. The orb pulsated above Nat, sending beams of light reflecting off her sword.

"We will find them and make more in time," the creature promised. "But she now has plans for you, Sister. She will make you her own."

Branches creaked as more Nala crawled from the trees to the forest floor and surrounded them.

"Two in front of me. Two more in the trees," Annin whispered.

"As I see it, Nala, you have two choices." Nat glared at the creature. "Die here, or leave with a message for your queen."

The creature cocked its head to the side. "What message is that, Sister?"

Nat took a deep breath. A tense silence filled the air. Her orb spun slowly above her, then rocketed into the Nala's face like a lightning bolt and smashed into its skull. She took two steps and severed the creature's head with one swipe of her blade.

"It's time for *all* of you to die."

"Behind you!" Annin called out as she shot an arrow into a springing Nala. A white Nala dropped into a bush next to Nat and leapt off its powerful legs toward her. She thrust her sword, but it jumped to a low limb above Annin. The branch broke, cracking under the creature's weight. It leapt from the toppling branch and the limb fell on Annin, pinning her to the ground. She cried out in pain, and her crossbow dropped from her hands onto the forest floor.

Nat hurtled over a dead Nala to reach Annin, but a creature landed between them, cutting her off. She slashed at it with her sword, connecting with its thigh. It screamed and toppled to its side. Annin struggled to push the limb off her arm while she kicked the injured Nala away from her. An arrow pierced the flailing Nala's chest, and it let out a wheezing breath. Startled by the arrow, Nat looked up to find two more Nala and Cassandra running down the path toward them.

Cassandra's screams scattered the Nala. The wild Warrior Sister cut the creatures down as they clambered up a tree, and their lower limbs fell onto the ground like dead branches. A wide smile broke over her face, and she hissed mockingly at another creature before impaling it with her sword.

Nat pivoted and stabbed a Nala that fell from a tree. She brought her sword over its neck, and the creature's mouth opened like a gaping pit as it let out a final sibilant breath. Dropping to her knees, she lifted the broken tree limb holding Annin in place. Annin cursed and clutched her arm. A splinter of bone stuck out from her ripped sleeve. Cassandra twirled around them, scanning the treetops as Nat examined the bone.

"The break's bad. I think you're coming with me," Nat said to her friend as she lifted her to her feet. Nat's heart was still pounding from the fight. She looked around at the dead Nala strewn over the forest floor.

"I'll dispose of them," Cassandra said as if reading her mind. "Estos said to return with the duozi if I could but you'd know where to take her to be safe." She nodded at Annin.

"I'm taking her, Sister. Thank you."

"So polite. It'll kill you if you're not careful. Now go!"

Nat stumbled back with Annin's arm draped around her shoulder. She pulled her friend down the path toward the rocks and the cliff looming above the forest. Annin let out a groan.

"Hang in there, Annin. Give me a second to find the opening." Nat searched the cliff wall looking for the way to the membrane.

"I have bone poking out of my arm," Annin said in a raspy voice. "I'm not waiting for your weak eyes to spot it." She stumbled in front of Nat and disappeared behind the rock.

Nat followed her and passed through a narrow split at the base of the cliff. She heard Annin groaning again as daylight disappeared in the dark crevice. Nat's orb spun next to her and filled the tight space with light.

Annin's head and one hand were through the membrane, but her legs strained against the ground. Nat shoved her knees against the rocks and pushed Annin's legs with her back, forcing her through the membrane an inch at a time. When Annin's heels disappeared, Nat pressed her hands against the vibrating membrane and slipped into her world.

She looked up and found Annin gasping for breath next to her. An orb not her own bobbed above her head then sped away from them.

"Barba!" Nat screamed, and her voice reverberated down the tunnel. She grasped Annin around the waist. Together they stumbled through the tunnel into Ethet's darkened laboratory. Nat's orb shot to the ceiling and filled the room with light. A red spotlight blinked on and off above the doors. Nat placed Annin on the exam table and grabbed the door handles, shaking them violently.

"They're barred." Annin's voice sounded like gravel. She shifted her legs off the table and tried to sit up. Nat turned, retraced her steps, and eased her back onto the table. Annin's face was ashen under the light. "The code box by the door." Annin pointed toward a small pad set into the wall. "Type in 'Sister'."

Nat fumbled with the keypad until she finally hit the correct buttons. Light flooded the room. Annin collapsed against the table. Nat grabbed a cloth from a neatly folded stack off the long counter and ran it under the faucet. She wiped Annin's brow.

"Seven, eight Nala, and what happens? A branch breaks my arm," Annin laughed as Nat wiped the sweat and dirt from her face before examining the splinter of bone. "I suppose it could have been worse."

Nat leaned over her and let out a hysterical giggle. "Could have been worse?"

Annin joined in, even as her face contorted in pain. Laughter spilled uncontrollably from both women. The two were still laughing when Barba burst through the door.

CHAPTER FORTY-FOUR

Five Weeks Later

An August thunderstorm rolled across the sky. The bay horse trotted inside the corral, snorting. Nat secured the gate and led her horse into a small covered enclosure next to the barn. Bits of hay, spiraling upward in the wind, stuck in her hair. She blinked, trying to get the grit and dirt out of her eyes. Lightning crackled in the distance.

"You're as nervous as if a Nala were around, Ob," Nat spoke soothingly to her horse. He nickered and shoved his nose gently against her shoulder. She patted his brown neck and let him go. He paced nervously in the enclosure. Nat wrapped the chain around the gate and slid it into the mouth of the lock. The high-pitched ring of the links banging against the gate followed her up the worn path to the weathered house. Rain droplets splattered against her hair.

The screen door leading to the mudroom slammed against the side of the house. *Need to fix that spring,* Nat thought as she pulled it shut and secured the latch and the inner door behind her. With her dad and Cal gone delivering and installing sets of custom carved doors to cabins in the northern part of the state, the list of to-do items to help her mom was lengthy. *From Warrior Sister to fixing toilets. At least we have an extra set of hands,* she thought. *Well, one extra hand.* Nat kicked off her dirty boots. A boom of thunder rattled the house.

"White milkwort." Marie Claire sounded unsure.

"Correct. Good or bad?" Annin asked.

"Good, for the cows at least."

Nat walked into the kitchen. Annin sat on a bench that ran the length of the kitchen table. Her broken arm, wrapped in a cast, was surrounded by an array of dried flowers. Marie Claire gently placed the dried white milkwort back on a piece of wax paper.

"Still at it?" she asked. Annin was helping MC identify wildflowers for her summer-camp project.

"Nonstop." Nat's mom gave Annin a grateful smile, and Nat felt relieved. Her mom had not been thrilled when she'd shown up at the house two weeks ago with her friend with a broken arm, eye patch, and hard-to-explain blue tattoo. Annin played the foreign-exchange-student-with-no-place-to-go card, and her mom seemed to buy it. But Nat knew Annin made her mom feel on edge—very on edge.

She'd caught her mom staring at her own markings since she and Annin had come home. Nat knew she was disappointed. She could read her expression so easily. *If you only knew what these markings meant, Mom. I think you'd be proud of me, after the heart attack,* she thought as she smiled at her.

"Horses secure?" she asked Nat.

"Boston's in the barn and Ob is in the enclosure."

"Good. MC, time to go. I want to get to town before this storm hits." Nat's mom lifted the box of repaired library books onto the table. The wax paper fluttered upward, shifting the flowers. Annin's good hand shot out, catching a small yellow flower floating toward the floor. Nat coughed, hoping to distract her mom from noticing Annin's extraordinarily fast reflexes.

"Just one more, Mom, and then we'll go," MC said.

"This one." Annin twisted the short stem between her fingers, and the bright-yellow flower with small petals spun slowly.

MC sucked on her bottom lip, a sure sign she was stumped, then her eyes lit up. "Tinker's penny!" she exclaimed. "I am so gooood," she bragged.

"Habitat, use, and alternative name?" Annin demanded, her voice serious.

MC stopped wiggling in her chair. "I don't remember." Her chin dropped to her chest.

"Grows selectively in wet places at the coast and high elevations. Unless you're in Four—"

"Annin," Nat said sharply.

The room grew quiet. Nat's mom cleared her throat and glanced at the young women.

Annin gave Nat a crooked smile. "Use?"

"I think you told me something weird." MC tapped her short fingernails against the table, then looked up at Annin. "Like it wards off evil?"

"Exactly." She leaned against the wall and winked at Nat.

"MC, we really need to go, now." Her mom hefted the box onto her hip and reached for MC's hand, all the while keeping her eyes glued on Annin.

Nat rubbed her forehead. *So much for getting over the weird hump with my mom,* she thought.

"I remember the alternative name," MC said as she grasped her mom's hand. "Meldon. You called it the meldon flower."

"Very good," Annin said slowly. "You might make a decent apprentice. Maybe even a Sis—"

"So, Mom, you and MC are going to town?" Nat asked quickly. "Annin and I can fix that leak in the basement bathroom sink. Anything else that you need from us?"

"No," her mom said, giving Annin one more quick, wary look.

"Watch out for the spiders in that downstairs bathroom. I found a big one down there last week." MC shivered and her ponytail shook.

Nat burst out laughing and Annin's smile grew wider.

"What's so funny?" MC asked, pulling on her green rain jacket. "They're nasty."

Nat wiped her hands on the rag and dropped the crescent wrench into the battered toolbox. Annin sat on the lip of the bathtub.

"I spoke with Barba."

"She called? Here?"

"Since when have I needed a phone?" Annin grabbed the toolbox with her good hand and stepped out of the narrow bathroom. "Ethet's lab is ready for us, and Cairn made arrangements for you to have extra privileges in the biology department this semester so we can work. He's telling everyone you're experimenting with a new latex for his theater creations."

Nat followed her up the worn carpeted stairs, thinking what effective liars Cairn and Barba were—and what an effective one she had become, for that matter. Annin dropped the toolbox on the floor and leaned against the pantry door. She extracted a small vial from the green work shirt Nat had lent her and downed its yellow contents.

"Are you sure you're up for this?" Nat asked. Using Annin as the test subject for what she had in mind was not risk-free. "Once that cast comes off, you can go back to Fourline. I know being here is hurting you. That's the second vial of meldon juice I've seen you take. You don't have to hang around here and keep me company. I'll figure something out without you."

Annin wiped her lip and rubbed her hands together. "Really? What are you going to do? Sneak into Fourline and find another duozi or ask a Nala if it will let you use it as a test subject? Maybe you can knock on the Nalaide's den door and get a blood sample. I heard she's looking for you."

"You should try being a little more sarcastic, Annin. I just meant that you don't have to do this. You don't have to help me with my experiments."

"Let's just say I have more to gain than just a boyfriend if we find something to counteract the venom."

Nat brushed past Annin and yanked the faucet handle at the kitchen sink. Warm water poured over her soiled hands as she scrubbed the grime away. She blinked, willing the tears away as she thought of Soris. She slammed the faucet shut and leaned over the sink.

"Do you know what I dream about each night, Annin?" Lightning flashed on the hill above the house, and the lights flickered in the kitchen. "I dream about all those duozi children dead in that Nala cavern. And I dream about Soris—but not some flowery-field reunion. I dream he's dead, too, crumpled at the base of a rock bed, in some Nala nest or in Mudug's mines with me standing over him, helpless to do anything." She turned. Annin's eye patch hung around her neck. The lights flickered again, then went out. The humming of the refrigerator ceased, and the kitchen was utterly silent as the two women stared at each other.

"I wondered," Annin said quietly.

"Wondered what?" Nat tossed the hand towel onto the counter.

"You do love him."

"Yes," Nat said haltingly, admitting it to herself for the first time. "I do."

"I'll help you willingly—not just for myself, and not just for Soris, but for you, Sister." She placed a small leather-bound book in Nat's hand, and Nat recognized it immediately as the book Ethet had given her before they'd left the Healing House. She looked up in surprise.

"I've been looking through it and working on a key to transcribe the script." Annin stood next to Nat and gingerly turned the pages to one that contained a series of pictures that looked familiar. A moment passed before she recognized the images from the tapestry in Gennes' camp.

"Notice anything interesting?" Annin pointed to the panel that depicted the bitten girl, her arm tinted blue, drinking from a dark yellow vial. Nat followed Annin's finger as she traced over the vivid drawing to the final scene, where the same girl, now a Warrior Sister, held a dagger to a Nala's throat.

"Her arm isn't blue," Nat whispered.

Annin nodded. The two looked up from the book and watched the lightning flash outside the kitchen window.

ACKNOWLEDGMENTS

I grew up watching my mom write her novels on an electric typewriter at a desk opposite our washing machine. The walls of her office / laundry room were covered with rejection letters that she affixed to the wall with brightly colored thumbtacks. I'm still not sure why she did that. Maybe staring rejection in the face, instead of letting it loom in the background, made plugging away each day to meet her self-imposed page quota easier. When she sold her first novel, we started a fire in the fireplace and fed those rejection letters, one by one, into the flames. I remember that day vividly, but what I remember even more is my mom's belief, persistence, and work ethic even when she was staring at a wall covered in rejection.

Mom, this book is dedicated to you. Thank you for your love and the many lessons I've learned from you over the years. You are all the Sisters wrapped into one.

Dad, thank you for your support and serving as my on-call scientist for this trilogy. I am blessed to have such wonderful parents.

To the editorial team at Skyscape, thank you for helping me shape these stories. Courtney Miller and Tegan Tigani, you have been inspiring and delightful to work with, and your insight has been a gift.

My agent, Valerie Noble, deserves more thanks and praise than I can offer.

I'd need another twenty pages to properly acknowledge my husband and children for everything they did for me and put up with while I was writing *On the Meldon Plain*. To sum it up, you are my deepest loves and I can't thank you enough.

ABOUT THE AUTHOR

Photo © 2015 Ally Klosterman

Pam Brondos grew up in Wyoming and watched her mom write novels on a manual typewriter. She graduated from St. Olaf College; worked in Shanghai, China; and received her juris doctor from the University of Wyoming College of Law. *Gateway to Fourline*, her debut novel, released in 2015. The Fourline Trilogy continues with book two, *On the Meldon Plain*. For more information about Pam, visit her online at www.pamalabrondos.com.